The Deadliest Players.
The Ultimate Game.

SIR KENNETH AUBREY—He was Britain's master spycatcher on a mission of vengeance: bring back East German defector, Kurt Winterbach.

KURT WINTERBACH—He was the son of Aubrey's life-long archenemy. The ultimate tool for the spycatcher's revenge, until Winterbach's death sparked a far more devastating game of high-tech disaster.

BRIGITTE WINTERBACH—She was the head of East German intelligence. A cold and ruthless opponent who would stop at nothing to avenge her son's death.

TIM GARDINER—He was the spycatcher's foster son. A Royal Army officer, he alone held top secret information about a possible Soviet takeover of Nepal. Now, he is the personal target of Brigitte Winterbach. . . .

And the ultimate East-West conflict is about to explode.

WILDCAT

"THOMAS [IS] IN THE FOREFRONT OF TODAY'S ADVENTURE/THRILLER WRITERS."
—*Publishers Weekly*

CRAIG THOMAS

WILDCAT

JOVE BOOKS, NEW YORK

This Jove book contains the complete
text of the original hardcover edition.
It has been completely reset in a typeface
designed for easy reading, and was printed
from new film.

WILDCAT

A Jove Book/published by arrangement with
Craig Thomas & Associates

PRINTING HISTORY
G. P. Putnam's Sons edition/January 1989
Jove edition/November 1989

ISBN: 0-515-10186-9

Jove Books are published by The Berkley Publishing Group,
200 Madison Avenue, New York, New York 10016.
The name "JOVE" and the "J" logo
are trademarks belonging to Jove Publications, Inc.

10 9 8 7 6 5 4 3 2 1

AUTHOR'S NOTE

My thanks, as always, to Jill for her habitually stern and invaluable editing of the narrative.

My one sincere regret regarding the book is that my father-in-law, Wilfred, who died on 22nd September, 1987, was unable to read it, having been one of my most enthusiastic supporters ever since my first typescript, *Rat Trap*, fourteen years ago. Thank you, Wilf. We miss you.

for
RAY BRADBURY
the joy of whose stories
first determined me to
become a writer

Vengeance I ask and cry,
By way of exclamation,
On the whole nation,
Of cattes wild and tame:
God send them sorrow and shame!

John Skelton: *Philip Sparrow*

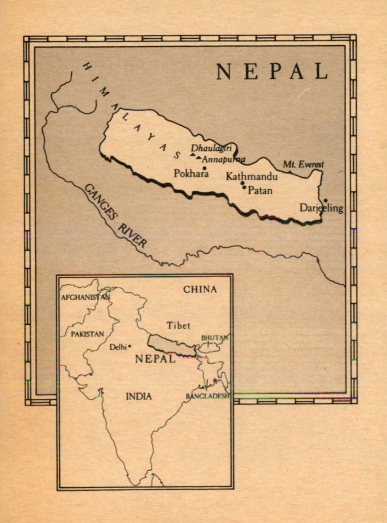

PRELUDE

"My way of life
Is fall'n into the sear, the yellow leaf:
And that which should accompany old
*   age,*
As honour, love, obedience, troops of
*   friends,*
I must not look to have . . ."

Shakespeare: *Macbeth*, V, iii.

The pale, chill light of the October afternoon fell sullenly across the garden, casting long, deep shadows from the apple trees and the tall hedge. Invisible to Kenneth Aubrey and his companion, a motorcycle buzzed like a huge, angry insect up the lane past the cottage. Aubrey's emotions seemed stirred to a thin, weary turmoil by the fading noise. Their *shoddy* offer! And after so many empty months! And to send Peter Shelley to make it . . .

He sensed his aged figure to be that of a prisoner or inmate of the garden. Pottering away time once so easily and otherwise occupied, while they made up their minds about him . . . And finally *this* was their decision, their scrap from the table! They needed his help, in this backhanded, slight way, but equally they had indicated that they did not trust him. He had returned like a species of plague-carrier, and only the newspapers had applauded. They could not bring themselves even to admire the man who had exposed and ruined Andrew Babbington, and had acted as if *he* was the traitor and Babbington his innocent victim! And now *this!*

He sighed loudly, angrily, stepping off the flagstones outside the French windows, onto the long lawn. The garden, already slipping into early evening, was daubed with splashes of late roses. Soon, he must prune them.

"Then, will you do it?" Peter Shelley asked, following him, his hands thrust into his pockets, chin almost on his chest; his face confused, even embarrassed, as Aubrey turned to him.

"I wonder they didn't send you with the poisoned chalice of some new security investigation in Ulster!" he snapped, his right hand waving dismissively. "I'm almost certain they have that gift in mind for me!"

"I—know nothing about that," Shelley replied, staring at the grass near his feet. Then he looked up, as if drawn by Aubrey's impatient, angry stare. "The Americans have asked them . . . they *agreed* I should approach you. You were in at the beginning, before he went cold. Now, he'll talk only to you. Come over only to you."

"It is a pleasant change to be trusted by somebody!" The anger was like a sudden and vicious indigestion, welling up into his chest. "For eight months I have been kept waiting like a suitor at a rich man's gate! Now, the CIA wants something done in a hurry, and they have to use *me!* I am sorry for their dilemma! I can imagine how vigorously they tried to persuade the Americans that I should not be employed!" He was shouting, and aware that he was beginning to rant like a bad actor. Yet he hardly paused in the tirade that came bullying into his thoughts. "They have kept me in their private wilderness . . . an old lion in their safari park!" Self-pity shaped the cold smile on his mouth. He brushed a hand quickly across his bald head. "They do not *trust* me!" His hands clenched into useless fists. He saw that Shelley's face was appalled. "Babbington was their prize, their flattering mirror—and I proved him, the Director of MI5 and their favorite son, to be a Russian agent. *Teardrop,* their operation to frame me, blew up in their faces. I was not ruined, Babbington was." He paused and smiled acidly, then added vehemently: "I will not be forgiven for that—ever."

At last it was over, like a recurring bout of malaria. He rubbed cold hands down his cold cheeks and walked away from Shelley, quivering and chilly, angry with himself for his display of childish temper. Shelley had offered him occupation, however menial, and he had found himself obsessed with his own grievances, real and half-imagined. Cottage and garden had become a hothouse, forcing the growth of strange, bitter weeds. And yet the anger was justified. Good God, he was right! They didn't trust him and had no intention of allowing him back. He should send their offer and their messenger packing.

"I realize the past months can't have been easy," Shelley offered, "not once you'd recuper—"

"Two months in a retired diplomat's beach bungalow in the *Bahamas?*" Aubrey snapped. "A prison with room service!"

"I—see . . ."

Aubrey stared into Shelley's face. "Perhaps you do," he admitted. The past months had shone a harsh light upon his character. He had discovered the lump of his ego like a tumor. He longed for the applause, the intimacy of powerful men. He hated and detested the idea that his career would end without their cheers. "Perhaps you understand a little," he added.

His career had shrunk to the little measure of his despicable need for their lasting approbation. Only then would he consent to go. But it would not be like that, not now, not ever again. Damn them!

Brusquely, he said: "So, Kurt Winterbach wants to come out, and now the Americans want him at the price!" Shelley nodded. Aubrey felt his bitterness subsumed in appetite. They walked past roses. Aubrey had laid out the new bed in April. He'd planted standard roses, too, beside the flagged path. Then, gardening had been his hobby, not his sole occupation. "First, he plays the reluctant bridegroom, then the Americans want to remain virgins . . . now, the affair is on again. Why?"

Shelley cleared his throat. His voice seemed easy with old intimacy, routine. "Some fault in Navy satellite surveillance on their seabed early warning system, so I understand. They're losing track of too many Soviet submarines."

"And young Winterbach knows their current whereabouts, their refueling points, details of their rendezvous with East German ELINT ships . . . mm. If they do have problems, I can see why he's suddenly so attractive." He paused for a moment, then said in greater earnest, "They realize what they might stir up, he being Brigitte's son? I did warn them when he first approached us. She is devoted to that son of hers. If he were to come over, she has the power to revenge herself very completely!"

"They think the game is worth the candle," Shelley replied, shrugging. "The Navy has the President's ear at the moment. What they want, they get."

"She won't forgive, or forget. Even if he's safe, and his wife and children come out with him, Brigitte will have a field day with networks, agents, contacts—theirs and ours. They do realize that, I suppose? That she could lay waste Western intelligence in East Germany—and anywhere else she has any influence!"

"I know. *They* know. Kurt is flavor of the month just now, however, and nothing else matters."

"Not that I would regret the blow to Brigitte personally—just the consequences for intelligence. I'm convinced that only she could have supplied much of the information Kapustin used in the preparation of *Teardrop.*" He shivered briefly, and grimaced. The memory of the weeks of his disgrace, his capture and arrival in Moscow still possessed the strength to inflict some slight physical reaction, a coldness. *Teardrop.* They had all but succeeded in ruining him and placing Babbington at the pinnacle of Intelligence. Brigitte Winterbach knew him better than anyone else on the other side of the Curtain. She must have supplied a great deal of the so-convincing detail about his past that had been used to frame him. He was utterly certain of it. "No, on a *personal* level, I would delight in wounding Brigitte. But, like all wounded animals, she will be dangerous if we and the Americans take away her beloved only son."

"You believe she was involved in—"

"Believe! I *know!*" Then he added mischievously, "I spoke to Babbington, alone, for just a few minutes. At Schwechat, when we were being exchanged."

"And?"

"He said very little. Boasted a great deal, of course. Bolstering his vanity as best he could. Giving off the distinct sense that he had been confounded by midgets. Gulliver trussed up by Lilliputians . . ." Aubrey knew his smile was vindictive. "Of course, he tried to tell me nothing, but vanity is a very efficient can-opener. London, he indicated, was where he had originally been recruited. Smiling, he could not help but show me it wasn't a Russian who recruited him—not at first. Anyway, he *volunteered . . .* dear me, quite a suitcase of vanities. At that moment, I was certain it was Brigitte who recruited him."

"Why?"

"She was at their London embassy in '56; she was recalled and promoted that same year. Somehow, she had set her foot on the ladder to the very top. And for a Jew and a woman in the MfS *Ausland,* her rise was remarkable. Even unique." He shook his head. "No, she had brought them a great prize. I'm certain she caught Babbington in her silken net. And that she was in on *Teardrop.*"

Shelley smiled. "I didn't realize you would find it so hard to refuse this job . . ." He broke off, realizing his insensitivity. Aubrey felt able to ignore the remark. Brigitte would be dangerous—but to hurt her by helping that weak, greedy, unattractive son of hers to defect . . . ? He felt hurried, tempted.

"They are *certain* Kurt wants to come over?"

"Yes. He resumed negotiations in April. The Americans became really interested only a few weeks ago. He must realize he won't get any higher over there, once his mother retires or dies. He's only where he is by the grace of her, anyway. So, both parties have agreed. And having agreed, it has to be done yesterday!"

"Where and when?"

"Next week—Venice."

"Venice?"

"He's attending a Conference of the Sea under his official cover in the Fisheries Ministry. And he's persuaded his mother, so he says, to get him and his family permits for a holiday in Italy after the conference finishes. Unsuspecting, doting Mama." Shelley tossed his head.

Aubrey rubbed his chin. "Poor Brigitte. She would kill him had she an inkling of what he intends." He looked up, his eyes glinting. "She'll probably kill me if we get him across!" He tapped Shelley's arm. "I'm joking, Peter—joking!"

"But if you feel there's any—"

Aubrey shook his head. "I am not going to throw this unimportant little task back in their faces, Peter. I am going to do it, and do it well. And I warn you I shall be taking all the credit!" A car passed along the lane. Aubrey smelled petrol in the cooling air. "I shall use this as a stick to beat them with, if I find I can't use it as a lever. It will at least ensure that I am no longer ignored."

Aubrey began vigorously rubbing his hands. Then he turned away from the hedge they had been patrolling, back toward the cottage. Impatiently, he said, "Come along, Peter. I'll light the fire. There's a lot to discuss, a lot of detail . . . come on, my boy, there's work to be done!"

PART ONE

The King
Must Die

"Thou art thy mother's glass, and she in
    thee
Calls back the lovely April of her prime"

Shakespeare: *Sonnets, 3*

1

La Serenissima

The gilt-framed mirror on the wall opposite her desk made an oval of the window behind her and its sliding rain. Beyond the reflection of her gray, frizzily-unkempt hair and heavy features, the Alexanderplatz glistened and was rubied with brakelights. The black spike of the Marienkirche was as vague as an image through oil. The view was chill and remote, and yet it did not have that effect on her. It was Berlin—*her* Berlin. She had never despised this ugly, gauche country cousin of the garish whore on the other side of the Wall.

She gazed at the rain for a while, abstractedly watching the city proprietarily, almost secretly, as if she had the square under surveillance. Then Brigitte Winterbach returned her attention to Kapustin's lengthy signal, received and decoded an hour earlier. *Condition Red.* Twenty-four-hour readiness. The operation was only days from implementation. She must reply to the peremptory signal that same afternoon, assuring Kapustin and his planning team that her people were ready, that the information he and the army demanded would be available . . . when? Today, tomorrow? She clicked her tongue against her teeth. Kapustin's pressure. Kapustin's demands! Her people had worked small miracles, and still Moscow Center wanted more—always more . . .

She must draft a signal to Lin Yu-Chiang as a matter of utmost priority. They had to be certain Beijing had not the slightest suspicion. Lin must also be forewarned they had reached

Condition Red. She lit another cigarette and leaned back in her chair. Its leather creaked. Two months ago, the operation was merely theoretical; a long-term objective. Two months ago, the King had not been incurably ill. The haste of the disease had been their haste. They would never be as well placed, the pro-Soviet faction never so powerful, again. It had to be now.

It had put her people under intolerable pressure. Even now, the intelligence gathering continued. Vital information was still lacking. Two months!

The room smelled of used ashtrays and stale smoke, like all the rooms she inhabited. Where had she acquired this fashionable sense of the unpleasantness of cigarettes—from Kurt's wife, from her grandchildren? She puffed gray smoke so that it rolled across the ceiling toward the mirror, masking the reflection of the wet, autumnal city. It became a scene from a child's book, wreathed in mists. Kurt had enjoyed fairy tales as a child. He still enjoyed dreams . . .

Looking through her half-lenses at Kapustin's signal once more, she felt a febrile, self-congratulatory excitement. The sense of pressure, of anger at Moscow Center, had evaporated. This was going to succeed—it really was. And her people had made it possible. *She* had made it possible. She could hear the beating of her heart, and her lips, as if savoring some exotic new flavor, moved as she read. She brushed ash from the page. Things were in place, other things were already in motion. The operation, which had appeared to her to be careering out of control down a steep slope, now had a defined and achievable objective. It seemed poised like some large wildcat about to spring on its prey. *Topi* was at *Condition Red;* ready to go. The King's illness had entered its final phase. No one expected them to move. Certainly not the British, who were leaving, nor the Americans, who were largely indifferent. And not the Chinese, who *would* be interested . . .

Lin *must* confirm that there was no possibility of a Chinese countermove.

She tidied the sheets on her desk, affirming the sudden neatness of her thoughts and of the operation. A certainty of success gilded the decoded signal. What they needed would be supplied. She continued reading, making occasional notes on a pad, ringing words and sometimes whole lines. In the mirror, the city receded. She heard the rain sliding coldly down the window behind her. Her wrist began to ache from her hurried scribblings.

Her heart leaped in what might have been alarm, as if some-one had attempted to snatch the pages from her desk. Her inter-com buzzed a second time. The room seemed almost dark out-side the pool of light spilled on her desk from the lamp. Then she remembered Kurt's appointment.

"Yes?"

"Your son, Comrade General."

"Send him in," she ordered with studied nonchalance, feeling already the irritation his appearance would provoke, together with her habitual helpless affection. His clothes, his manner—

The door opened. A moment later, Kurt had switched on more lights. She blinked, feeling the act was deliberate, to expose her age, her tired, aching eyes.

"—dark in here," he announced, as if he had found a scratch on a valuable table. His overcoat—she knew it was cashmere and bought on the other side of the Wall—was spotted with rain. He shook his umbrella, then leaned it against one of the filing cabinets. Almost at once, a small dark stain appeared and en-larged on the carpet.

As he approached her, she smelled brandy on his breath, saw the glint from his gold watch and the gold chain on his other wrist. His tie was askew, his hair blown awry. She moved her hands to tidy both, but his head flinched slightly and she merely smiled instead, offering her cheek. He bent his head, but she did not feel the brush of his lips. Indulgence and an innate Puritan-ism struggled against one another in her welcome. He brushed his fair, thick hair back from his forehead as if to please her.

"Mother," he announced, avoiding the affectionate diminu-tive.

She squeezed his arm and made him sit in one of the two easy chairs placed on opposite sides of a smoked-glass coffee table. She felt the slight of his not removing his overcoat, of his impa-tient glance around her office; his concentration on her desk. His mood was hurried and expectant. She quashed the rising feeling of disappointment, soft-focusing his presence in the room with memories. The small, lanky boy in short trousers, playing with a garden hose. Kurt looked at his watch, then at the rain smear-ing the window.

"Well?" he asked. "You've got them?" There was a casual eagerness. He did not anticipate disappointment; he never had.

Brigitte wanted to make him wait, puzzle him, even as she studied what was, to her, his physical beauty, avoiding the weakness, the clever lack of character displayed in his eyes. Bloodshot eyes. Kurt drank far too much.

"It was not easy, even for you, even *my* asking," she said. His expression was one of disbelief. She would not offer him a drink. "It was not easy—"

"But, clever little Mother, you managed it." The rain at the window insinuated a coldness into her thoughts. The game they played of mother and son was nothing but a cheap charade. She felt an acute physical pain in her chest at the admission.

Kurt's eager stare forced her to get up and cross to her desk, become the giver-of-gifts he expected her still to be. She had given him her whole life, but it was only the external part of it, her power, that interested him. Once more, she quashed the idea as another small treason, opening a drawer in her desk and bringing out a small folder of visas and tickets and passes.

"Here," she said, handing them to him. He offered a snatched kiss to her cheek before opening the folder and meticulously checking the contents. When he had finished, he looked up at her and smiled with a boyish satisfaction.

"Thank you—thank you. Anna-Lise will be . . . delighted. But, you're coming to dinner tonight. She can thank you herself!" A forced bonhomie, a small glance at the wall clock. Brigitte clenched her hands in her lap. He had pursued the visas for months. Now, he could not spend polite minutes in receipt of them. His soft leather shoes were spotted with mud.

"I hope you all enjoy Florence," Brigitte observed frostily.

Something furtive gleamed from the corners of his mouth and eyes for a moment, then he was smiling broadly. His thoughts had evidently already left the office, the city. For her, his happy face was shadowed by the thought of his future. He was disliked, he was casual in his work, he was weak, self-indulgent, insulting to more orthodox and less privileged colleagues. When she retired, he would go no further. Possibly, he would begin to decline. He did not possess the tenacity—the *character,* she forced herself to admit—to hang on, to fight his own battles. His face darkened as he registered her preoccupation.

"Another black mark in their little ledgers?" he sneered. "A well-earned, *short* holiday outside this damned country, and they act as if you'd given me a million dollars! Pathetic bunch of—"

"Kurt—please!" she interrupted. "You have visas for Anna-

Lise and the children . . . be *satisfied!*" She had wanted to say, "*Be careful,*" but could not.

He waved a dismissive hand. And stood up.

"I'll bring you a cameo, something nice," he offered in mollification. She felt the ease with which she forgave him as pleasure, not weakness. She tilted her head. He kissed her cheek, held her upper arms for a moment, then released her. She felt flushed; delighted. "We'll be expecting you at seven." Now, the role of dutiful and affectionate son was something he wore more easily, as if there was no other persona.

"Enjoy your Conference of the Sea as well as your holiday."

He tossed his head. "I'll try to stay awake." His easy smile was at its most winning.

"Try not to upset the Russian delegation too much."

"The barbarians?" He was irritated once more. "I'll try, Mother . . . we, we'll talk tonight. You can lecture me then!"

The door closed behind him. Brigitte wrapped her arms across her chest and hunched her shoulders. The darkening square of the window again drew her. The wet city was lumpy and shadowy out there. The rain was, at last, stopping. The whore on the other side of the Wall already bellowed with light. The Alexanderplatz looked dingy. What made her think like this? A cashmere coat, a conference in Venice, a holiday in Florence? Or because she could find no commonality between her son and the city? No place for him here after her retirement? She sighed aloud: a pained, troubled noise. Then she returned to her desk. She could do little for him if he would not listen to her.

She sat down heavily, closing a door on all but the immediate future. There was time enough, perhaps . . . She accepted the convenient fiction.

Two weeks . . . it was unlikely to be longer than that. In two weeks, the King would be dead. The pro-Soviet faction would take over. She put on her glasses, and checked her notes. Nodding, she began to draft the signal she must send to Lin. She became intent upon its wording.

He awoke from dreaming of his mother and an untroubled, satisfied sleep. He moved his hand. The place in the bed beside him was smooth and cold. He turned his head. Beyond the empty pillow beside his, the alarm clock showed him it was three in the morning. Anna-Lise had got up. Immediately, he understood her worry and its cause, and his momentary irritation was absorbed by concern. Kurt sat up, pushing the bedclothes away from him. He thrust his feet into leather slippers and drew on his thin dressing gown. He picked up his cigarettes and lighter from the bedside table. She had been upset by the strain of pretense even before she had need of lies and evasions. She would be looking at the children. Already, he felt sympathy rather than concern. The contempt even of his dreams for Brigitte allowed him no sense of doubt. Anna-Lise would be all right; eventually.

The children's bedroom door was open, but Anna-Lise was not in the room. Nor in the kitchen. The French windows to the garden were open in the lounge. The night was cool, fresh after the rain. He all but turned back for his shoes, then clicked his tongue. Leather slippers were the least of his worries, where he was intending to go. Kurt smiled and patted his pockets as if they contained the tickets and the visas and permits. His feet squeaked across the wet lawn toward the shore of the Langer See. The hump of the Müggelberg was dark against the stars. Lights dotted the surrounding woods, revealing the presence of other wooden bungalows and dachas. A privileged suburb he could now, if not despise, certainly hold of no value.

He bent, trying to see her form in silhouette against the lake's moonlit water. Romanticizing their encounter. He would have to reassure, comfort. Anna-Lise was helpless, really. Needed his guidance, protection, as always. Coming as soon, and with such pleasure, as Brigitte left them after dinner. He had blurted it out like a schoolboy, and that had been silly of him. Anna-Lise had tried to hide her head like a pet tortoise. It was as if Brigitte had been back in the room with them; uniformed and powerful as far as Anna-Lise was concerned, and suffocating both of them. His reassurances had seemed to soothe; evidently, they had not had a lasting effect.

He caught sight of her silky negligee. She crossed the perspective of the wrinkled water like a glossy advertisement for the lifestyle he had promised her and himself. In America. She turned as she heard his footsteps across the wet, sloping lawn. "Lise, what is it—you'll catch cold . . ." He took hold of her. She moved into his embrace with the lack of hesitation of a well-rehearsed actress, though he knew there was no element of pretense. She was shivering. "There, you're already cold." He rubbed her arms, her shoulders, chafing them gently. "What is it . . . mm?" He kissed her hair, her forehead. It was like kissing a child woken from a bad dream.

"I'm frightened," she murmured at last. She had already ceased shivering. Her voice was almost calm. "It will be—six days, Kurt, *six!*" The breathing became once again that of a small animal, her teeth chattered. He luxuriated in her dependence, her helplessness. He would look after her. She would realize nothing bad could happen. She was frightened of Brigitte, of course. Who wasn't except himself?

"There, there, sweetie, there," he soothed. "Nothing will happen, nothing can go wrong. Don't be frightened of my mother—she suspects nothing." It was true. Brigitte was oblivious to any plans her son had. "There, now—" He held her away from him. She sniffed. He smiled indulgently, encouragingly. "That's *better!*"

"But—six days here, without you, before we can come—"

"They'll pass in no time." He lit a cigarette. They began walking side by side along the edge of the water. Waterfowl rustled and creaked in their disturbance. He felt a deep satisfaction. "You're coming on a holiday to Florence. Don't think of anyone or anything else."

"But if something happened?" She was aghast at her own idea.

He put his arm around her shoulders. "*Nothing* will happen! The English—it is arranged. It will be simple. They will collect you from the airport . . . like a taxi!" He laughed with childlike pleasure. Squeezed her shoulders. "You'll see. Think of it as a holiday. You won't *mind* leaving, will you?"

She shook her head on his shoulder. "No. We'll be together . . . can't I come *now?*"

"No. We talked about that. Best you come later. For a holiday." He was soothing her again. Like rubbing away one of her headaches. "Headache?" She shook her head. "Good." He talked just to use the confident tone that would calm her. "The Americans are now very anxious to acquire my knowledge. Not of fishing or fisheries." He laughed. "All the things I know about the barbarians and their submarines." He sighed. "All that *boring* stuff!" He squeezed her against his side jovially. He breathed in deeply, his gaze taking in the lake, the hill. He did not envisage anything more isolated or larger in scale than this for his weekend place in New England. This place was fine, except that there was always that sense of the invisible, ever-present fence around it, imprisoning him. No, his dreams focused on the apartment overlooking Central Park.

His feet were cold and wet in his slippers. There was a careless satisfaction in ruining their soft leather.

"We won't tell the children anything . . . they're so excited at the idea of a holiday."

"No, not a word. One long holiday . . ." He sighed. He clearly recognized that it was her dependence which had attracted and held him. He had had other women, too much like his mother for comfort. They had needed nothing from him; there had been disappointment in their eyes and voices, away from the bed. They had all been too—too competent to require what he offered. Except Anna-Lise . . . and the two children. He felt suddenly cold, as if her fears had lain latently in his muscles and only now affected them. If something should go wrong, if they should not get out—

"We'll go in now, Lise," he announced. He could sense the invisible fence beyond the trees and the lake and the dotted lights.

"Yes," she agreed at once.

Nothing will go wrong, he instructed himself. It's all too well organized, it's all arranged. Nothing will go wrong . . .

Kenneth Aubrey could never decide his real opinion of Venice. At times, it was little more than a gaudy cruise liner berthed off the Adriatic coast. At others, it became a symbol of power, arrogance and greed that had justly declined into a tourist haunt. Finally, it was probably—despite the jostling crowds whenever he came—that golden place countless writers and artists had found.

But he was intensely irritated now. The pigeons moved in stiff, gray waves across St. Mark's Square and the crowds jostled in the pale, full October sunlight. Kurt Winterbach had *staged* his defection, his moment of coming over. It could have taken place in an hotel, in some quiet *calle* or *campo*—but no, he wanted it to take place upon this crowded and gaudy stage. The security problems were appalling, even with Italian help. So many windows, so many arcades—so many *people!* And he had merely pouted at their objections and confirmed his theatrical plans. Aubrey shifted his position on the sloping terrace of the main façade of the basilica. The Roman numerals of the Clock Tower, below the scowling golden lion, showed ten minutes to five. The two huge bronze statues with their hammers seemed as expectant as himself, poised on either side of the great bell. Below in the square, the crowds moved and changed like shifting sand-dunes. He had wanted the rendezvous to take place on the Zet-tere, where it faced the island of La Giudecca. There were no crowds there and Winterbach could have been taken off at once by motor launch, direct to the airport or the main railway sta-tion. There, there would have been no risk that he had been un-obtrusively tailed. But *here!* Really, it was too much!

"Have you spotted him yet?" he snapped at Shelley, who was leaning on the marble balustrade, field glasses pressed against his eyes. Pigeons rested below them on the waterspouts. Pigeons lifted away like a breaker, as if to dash against the windowed cliffs of the buildings surrounding the piazza. All these offices, museum rooms. Impossible to check a fraction of them.

There were three dozen men in the square awaiting Kurt Win-terbach's arrival. If there were three dozen and one, his family would be prevented from leaving. Even that had not impressed the handsome, weak, stupid son of Brigitte! Aubrey felt hot and loosened his cravat. Removed his straw hat and wiped his fore-head.

"No sign of him yet," Shelley murmured.

He would enter the square from beneath the arches at its southwestern corner, as if he had been shopping in the Calle dell' Ascension. They had told him which shops, which bags to be carrying, what to wear—how to watch for a tail. And he'd smiled through it all with the arrogant confidence of a doted-upon son who had always deceived his mother with ease!

Did he resent the German's bland belief that nothing but good could happen to him . . . or resent the scant lack of respect he demonstrated toward Brigitte—clever, powerful, ruthless Bri-gitte? A pigeon landed near Shelley, pecked at the marble of the balustrade, then eyed Aubrey inquisitively. Like Kurt Winter-bach, it seemed totally unafraid. Did he resent the added com-plexities the German had brought to the easy coup he had envis-aged in the garden of his cottage? Was that it?

Winterbach had claimed to feel safer in the crowds of the square.

"Yet?" Shelley merely shook his head, the glasses sweeping slowly, with an uninterrupted rhythm, across the expanses of marble and concrete and brick and people and birds.

Aubrey glanced up at the clock. 4:55. He was minutes late already. It struck Aubrey with the force of a shadow on an X-ray plate. "Damn . . ." he breathed.

On the Zettere, in 1939, he remembered suddenly, Brigitte had been ten years old, dark-featured and desperate in her fear that they would catch up with her father—as Aubrey had handed her into the boat to take her and her father to the railway station. He shook his head, realizing that he had known Brigitte for almost fifty years, from the very beginning of his career; almost from his own youth. And been her enemy for forty of those years . . .

"Anything?"

Impatience in Shelley's whisper. "Not yet." Then: "Wait a minute . . . in the shadows, walking forward now . . ." He adjusted the fine-focus of the glasses, his temples creasing into lines as he concentrated. "Ye–es—yes, it's him, just coming into the square. Let's hope he remembers the sequence of maneuvers." Shelley straightened, and waved down into the square, sighing.

Aubrey raised his own glasses to his eyes, as if to bring an opera stage into closer focus. He moved them in fussy little jerks until he scanned past the expected face, then found it again above the bright summer shirt, open-necked. Kurt Winterbach—her son. Recognition brought a strange silence around him. His attention narrowed upon the enlarged features. There was a sense almost of gloating which he found distasteful but which he could not quell. *Her* son, the son of one of his unholy Trinity—Babbington, Kapustin, and Brigitte. The information she must have supplied to the other two—the whole of the *Teardrop* file as it touched on Berlin. Aubrey had no shred of proof and yet he knew with certainty that Brigitte had been involved in the scheme to disgrace and ruin him . . .

. . . and now he would turn her beloved only child into a defector, a traitor. He sensed his ragged, quick breathing, was aware of Shelley watching him rather than the square. But he continued looking at Kurt's face.

He was unlike her. He looked like the father, very German rather than a Jew. He was what she had tried to make him, almost as if he had received plastic surgery. She had removed part of her own Jewishness in this Aryan young man. Her face now, or in 1939 or any of the years between, was as clear to Aubrey as that of Kurt. Brigitte stood beside him like a shadow.

First move—diagonally across the square, heading northeast, thirty paces. Kurt moved. Aubrey scanned the movements of others. There were perhaps twenty more pairs of glasses and camera lenses moving behind various windows, sweeping the scene. Kurt halted. Used the camera he wore. The anticipation of success, of revenge—yes, Aubrey had admitted that to himself days earlier and concentrated upon it ever more fiercely since— coursed through his frame like a crude sexual desire. Kurt *must* not have been followed, there must not have been a tail. Surely, the man realized his wife and children would never get out if he was followed and seen coming over?

Someone down in the square waved an all-clear. He heard Shelley grunt with satisfaction. At one window of the Procuratie Vecchie along the northern flank of the piazza, a blind was lowered, then raised halfway once more to confirm the signal. Clear . . . His breath sighed out. In the strange silence that seemed to surround him, he heard the clack as the minute plaque changed in the right-hand window of the Clock Tower. The first of the two statues beside the great bell raised its greened-bronze hammer. Aubrey flinched as before violence.

On the first flat, hard stroke of five, he returned his attention to Kurt, and immediately became rapt again. Remembering, too, the ten-year-old Brigitte as he handed her into the boat, the scene possessing a curious monochrome quality, robbed of color by fog and memory. He sensed that it was more of a childish adventure for him than it was for the small, dark, intense girl holding her father's thin hand. Their breaths had smoked and mingled. He could almost taste the droplets of breath and fog on the woolen scarf he had worn, despite the present heat. He squinted down at Kurt, the sun very low over the buildings at the other end of the square.

Second move, another diagonal which would take him to the ranks of chairs and tables outside Florian's. He could faintly hear the café's small orchestra before his attention narrowed even further. Scarves, large, dark eyes, worried and relieved faces, his voice thin in the fog, his hearing alert for footsteps, the slap of almost-unseen water, the creaks of the boat, heavy coats, cheap suitcases. The freight of impressions from almost fifty years before remained vividly with him, then faded as Kurt once more came to a halt, as if contemplating an overpriced coffee. He took more photographs of the square. Pigeons lapped against a shore of sightseers.

A second wave from the middle of the square. Shelley signaled back. The windowblind went down, then up again. Clear—so far.

Aubrey glanced along the balcony to where a young, dark Venetian armed with a camera and wearing the headset of a Walkman merely nodded. The cassette player was rigged to receive radio messages from watchers at the windows around the square. Clear . . .

Third move, to the exact middle of the square, then Kurt paused to look at watercolors on a stand, to talk to the girl who was the purported painter and who was Italian Intelligence. The girl was smiling, displaying her wares. Kurt seemed unhurried, unworried. Aubrey stared at his clear features. He looked younger than thirty-five.

Fourth and final move . . . Kurt walked more swiftly, almost jogging directly toward the main façade of the basilica. Now the other watchers would be seeking someone else hurrying, the tail that might be there exposing itself in surprise. Aubrey followed Kurt's hasty movements until he could see the small balding spot at the crown of the man's thick, fair hair, see only head and shoulders before he passed beneath the balcony, into the basilica's porch and under the arch and the dome depicting the Creation in goldwork and mosaic.

His mosaic had come together. Wave from the square, nod from the young man with the Walkman, the blind being lowered and raised again. Clear! He realized as he lowered the glasses that his hands were trembling and his eyes ached. He felt weak.

He cleared his throat. "Let's collect our prize, Peter," he announced with a casual joviality that was badly acted. Shelley studied him keenly for a few moments, his cheek reddened by the low sun, before he nodded in agreement.

They moved along the balcony, disturbing a waddling pigeon that had just settled. It rose into a pale, cloudless sky over the basilica. Then Aubrey moved behind the replicas of the four bronze horses and through the doors of the upper archway into the suddenly dim, musty, close interior of St. Mark's Basilica. The sense of fog and winter returned, and Brigitte's face seemed to stare at him in baffled hurt in the gloom. He enjoyed the sensation as he waited on the marble gallery looking down the length of the nave, beyond the crowds to the rood beam and its apostles and saints, as his breathing gradually returned to normal. Goldwork shone, mosaics glowed everywhere. Shelley nudged his arm.

He turned his head with a clutch of expectancy at his chest, and Kurt came along the gallery toward them, his face a bright mask of relief and certainty in the striped sunlight coming through the windows and slanting across him. Aubrey hurried a few steps to meet him like a new possession. He extended his hands, shook Kurt's suddenly hesitant hand vigorously, almost smirking. Kurt's face was older, with a sense of danger now that there was no scenario for this moment of his defection.

"Welcome—welcome!" Aubrey offered, already gripping the younger man's elbow, turning him back toward the narrow staircase. "We must hurry now—"

Kurt observed the young man with the Walkman, another agent who now pressed closer, and seemed satisfied. His body and face relaxed. Already, Aubrey saw, he had regained the casual, arrogant confidence of the boy who had successfully tricked his mother; as if he had stolen money from her purse and lied to her effectively.

"Yes, of course," he said in a confident English he was evidently proud of. "But, first, before our journey, I must call my wife."

"Later!" Aubrey snapped.

Kurt's face darkened to that of the spoiled son. A group of Italians towed behind a guide with a wand held above his head squeezed and nudged past them. "I must do it at once. I said that I would call as soon as we made our rendez—"

"Tonight!" Aubrey barked impatiently. "Our task now is to get you safely away—"

"I must call my wife! She expects a call!"

Aubrey wiped moisture from his lips. "Do you realize the danger of your situation? We—*you* must follow my instructions to the letter."

"As soon as I have telephoned my wife!" There was a peculiar mixture of defiance, relief and concern in his tone which disconcerted Aubrey. He felt suddenly as if he had never dealt with the man before, had no insight into his motivations. He turned to Shelley. Kurt had not moved, merely become more bricklike, solid. "Can we—" he suggested.

"There's a secure line in the Procuratie Vecchie—we could—"

"Good!" Kurt interjected. "It will not take much time." He seemed more malleable now, but Aubrey sensed the child who had resisted Brigitte beneath the surface. The sunlight's stripes seemed to dip further down into the nave, and the rood beam and the altar beyond it were shadowy and colorless. "Shall we go?" Kurt added peremptorily.

"Of course—please." Aubrey indicated that Kurt should fall in behind the young Venetian with the headset. Shelley pressed behind Aubrey, his face creased with doubt.

Aubrey attempted a smile of certainty. Shelley merely shrugged and looked at his watch. 5:15. Aubrey, caught in a slab of sunlight, felt himself assailed by dust motes.

Brigitte snatched up the receiver more in instinct than premeditation. She had arrived early to dine with Anna-Lise and her grandchildren. She had anticipated relaxation. But Anna-Lise was worried and uncommunicative; almost furtive. Brigitte hardly felt the warmth of the afternoon, even though midges clouded about her head near the water. There was something—she was alert to it like an animal to a strange yet recognizable scent.

Her grandson teased her granddaughter in a red plastic pool, showering her with water from an inverted bucket. The smoke from her cigarette curled under the awning over the patio. Mallards waddled across the vivid green grass. The extension beside her on the table rang, making her jump, and she snatched it up. "Yes?"

"Anna-Lise." Over the phone Kurt sounded almost breathless, as if he was excited, had brought her a good school report, and then in surprise and disappointment: "Mother!"

Anna-Lise appeared, wiping her hands on the bathroom towel. Her face crumpled into anticipatory shock.

"Didn't you expect me?" Brigitte asked with mock joviality. "It's Thursday! Just because *you're* not here!" She again blew smoke toward the striped awning. Her eyes narrowed, watching his wife. "And how was the conference?"

"The conference?" Why did she have the sense of a lack of privacy at his end of the connection? A roomful of people? Was he in a bar? "Oh, fine . . . yes, that was fine."

"And you've begun your vacation?" What was the matter with Anna-Lise? It was as if she saw either the whole of her past or all of her future passing before her. "But—yes, I'll hand you over, you don't want to talk to me—" She held out the receiver to his wife, consciously avoiding a study of her expression. Anna-Lise snatched the telephone with trembling, curled fingers.

"Kurt!" she exclaimed.

Her grandson's shout of pleasure pierced Brigitte. She got out of the wicker chair and went indoors. She felt as if the two sides of her brain were no longer connected. In the cognitive half, she was puzzled, worried, a mother. In the instinctive half, which had guided the left hand of her life for so many years, she already knew. Venice—holiday—wife and children—a room occupied by others—pestering her for visas . . . it had the logic of a mathematical formula, though entirely below the conscious level. Her head ached in its dichotomy. She pressed a gnarled hand to it and walked slowly, as if blind and in unfamiliar territory . . .

. . . directly toward the bedroom and its extension.

Carefully, guilt and terror in equal proportions, she lifted the receiver, hesitated and then leaned it against her cheek. His voice betrayed him as much as Anna-Lise's face. She had been frightened—frightened of *her!* She needed reassurance, she couldn't keep up the pretense, what if *she* asked questions, how could she keep their secret, oh, why did he have *to ever begin this?* Brigitte felt breathless, as if suffering some asthmatic onslaught. She leaned against the wall. She was a stranger to them, an object of contempt to her son.

She suspects nothing, don't worry . . . His words. He was confident of it, nothing to worry about, *tell her you have one of your migraines, she'll believe it* . . .

She stifled a gasp, as if in physical pain. She could not help but listen to his easy dismissal of her . . . while the instinctive, professional part of her brain had already begun to envisage the means of recovering him . . . knew why; recollected and dissected the dreamy contempt in which he had held the State. Remembered the laughter, his dislike of the Russians, his anti-Semitism, his extravagance and his drinking.

"The day after tomorrow, you'll be here—at least, not here but where we'll be together. Don't worry now . . ." Love, kisses, promises, love, kisses—laughter at her fears of his mother, kisses, kisses . . .

The connection hummed. Brigitte put down the extension and hurried in obedience to instinct out of the bedroom and into the bathroom. Even as she sat heavily down on the edge of the colored bath, she had begun to know how she could get him back.

She heard her grandchildren screaming with laughter in the garden, and the squawk of a duck. As if they had already begun a new life.

● ● ●

Aubrey felt dubious, angry, cheated in some way; or as if Kurt's affection for his wife and children had been visited upon the group of people in the room like an illness. He was impatient to get his prize away, and in the same moment deeply unnerved by the proximity he had felt to Brigitte. Disturbed most by the evident carelessness with which the son regarded his doting mother. The putting down of the receiver, the sense of somehow having abandoned the wife to Brigitte's intelligence and curiosity, stayed with him like a nagging toothache. And yet Kurt kept smiling at him as at some senile relative!

"We must—" His concern burst through. "Are you *sure* your wife can—*deceive* your mother?" he demanded. Aubrey felt Shelley tense, watched the dark, clever faces of the Italian surveillance team near the window where long shadows fell, studied Kurt; who shrugged.

"There's no problem . . ." He hesitated for a moment, then he said: "Brigitte thinks Anna-Lise is stupid—weak. A toy . . ." He smiled. "She will think she is fretting because I'm away, or fussing because she has to pack, to organize. It will be OK, Mr. —*Sir Kenneth* Aubrey. I am sure of it." And there really was no flicker of doubt in Kurt's eyes, amazing as that seemed to Aubrey. It was Brigitte who was even now in the same room as the wife. The wife was frightened—how on earth could Brigitte not notice? "Sure," Kurt repeated, palms outward. Then he looked at his watch. "Is it time to go?"

Aubrey sighed theatrically. Calvino, sitting on the edge of the office's one large desk, shrugged. His part of the operation had been successful. He might share Aubrey's evident doubts, but regarded them as of no consequence to himself.

"Thank you, Giovanni," Aubrey said. Calvino nodded, smiling.

"We owed you at least one good operation, my friend," he said. "And now, I think we really should go . . ." He stood up, straightening his creased jacket. The low sun was cooler now, almost vanished behind the buildings of the Ala Napoleonica at the piazza's western end. Aubrey clenched his hands into fists in his pockets and stared at the telephone on the desk. Brigitte was there *now,* in Kurt's home. Her suspicions *must* be aroused!

The safe house was in Fiesole, overlooking Florence. Someone would book into Kurt's hotel in the city. He and the CIA would carry out an initial debriefing in the safe house, Kurt's family would join him there; later, they would all be flown to the States.

The simple arrangements seemed threadbare now, like an old, dull carpet.

Aubrey realized that the success of Kurt's defection was vital, uniquely important to him. Anything less would be regarded as a complete failure, and laid at his door. He would never again be given an opportunity to re-establish his reputation, his . . . *gravitas,* in the intelligence community. He would be put out to grass. Damn Kurt Winterbach!

Shelley's voice intruded. "Sir, the piazza has been swept—it's clean. We should—" Impatience mingled with a residual respect.

"Yes, Peter, yes!" Aubrey snapped. He turned his straw hat in his hands like an unregarded steering wheel. He stared at the telephone, and then once more at Kurt. His sense of failure mounted. He sighed, slapping the hat against his thigh. "Very well—very well. Let us go!" He gestured Kurt toward the door. He got up with a careless ease and eagerness. He really did look, Aubrey thought, like a man without a care in the world. A man on holiday.

Brigitte . . .

He saw once again, in fogbound monochrome, the sharp, clear, dark eyes of the child he had handed into that boat almost fifty years before. Now, her expression was accusing, even malevolent. Aubrey knew, with a nauseous certainty, that she would never let Kurt's family out of East Berlin, not now. He felt unnerved and very old, as he followed the eager Kurt into the uncarpeted corridor where their footsteps seemed to clatter on the polished floor. The noise provided an echo behind them like the sounds of pursuit.

2

Another Aspect of Shiva

"You will leave early in the morning? I understand. It is the ninth day of Dasain. As a very English Buddhist, the sight of so much goats' blood . . ."

Timothy Gardiner looked down toward the tranquil evening surface of Phewa Lake, smiling. He felt the moment of bitterness cross his features like a cloud, and then it was gone once more. The huge mountain of Macchapucchare glowed redly with the sunset and reflected like the tail of a submerging whale in the water. A faint mist was rising from the lake. The air was fresh and cool. The lush greenness of the vegetation was losing its color, as if dyed.

He sighed involuntarily, empty of anger, frustration, disappointment for the moment. He sighed for the place, for what had ended, for friendship; sighed most of all for the old man who had been a sergeant when Timothy had first joined the Brigade of Gurkhas ten years earlier—his experience limited and his Nepali little more than rudimentary.

"Perhaps it's better to leave the day after the soldiers' festival," he murmured. "It was Armed Forces Day in Kathmandu today." He fell silent for a moment, then added more sharply: "Best leave it at that, mm?" It was difficult to express the bitterness he felt. The scene and the evening worked against his feelings, calming him.

"It is a sad time for you—for us," the old man murmured.

"It's a bloody crying shame! What the hell will your young men *do?*" The anger came now, loosened like a small landslide.

"Be rich. Your government has paid them handsomely for no longer wanting their services." His English had hardly rusted, and his mind was as sharp as ever. He wore his medal ribbons on his jerkin still, and did not appear ridiculous. "They will farm . . . at least, they will be wealthier than those Nepalis who are not ethnic Gurung who have also been dismissed." He paused, then cleared his throat. "And what will you do, Captain Timothy?"

"Go back." Gardiner shrugged.

"You will remain in the British Army?" Already to the old man it was an alien institution, nothing to do with his hill village.

"I shouldn't think so."

"What else do you know? Forgive me for . . ."

"It's true." He sighed once more. He was staring at the darkening lake, where canoes slipped through the mist, half-formed and shadowy. The lights from tourist chalets and hotels were dim globes or yellow splashes.

He looked up from the lake, picking out the straggling but numerous lights of Pokhara. Then it seemed, as it always did here, as if all there was to see were the peaks of the Annapurna, with Macchapucchare the closest and largest. The mountains filled the whole of the northern and western skyline; their massive flanks now ghostly.

"It's a bastard—it really is!" he suddenly exclaimed, as if shouting at the skyline or the new hotels dotted by the lake and the main highway to Kathmandu. He saw the old man nodding, with understanding and not without mockery of a gentle kind. There was a trace of amusement on his flat, pronouncedly Mongoloid features.

"Some of our men will join the Indian Army, of course," the old man announced. "A choice you cannot—" He broke off.

"Then they can continue to sacrifice goats to Durga as soldiers—"

"Where will you belong, Captain Timothy?"

Gardiner shrugged. "Who knows. I'm thirty-three. I shouldn't have any trouble . . . know anyone offhand who wants a redundant Queen's Gurkha officer?" His face began to smile even before he completed the question.

"Come back here?"

"I would have no place here . . . besides, I have to report to

London, then to Church Crookham. After that, who knows? I have a long leave coming."

"Then come back here . . ."

Gardiner looked grim, staring down at the rolling white surface of Phewatal and the dotted, glowing eyes of lamps along the shore.

"I want to put all this—behind me. Try to start again." Impulsively, he patted the old man's shoulder. "*You* understand, old friend." The old man nodded.

You were always a romantic, Gardiner told himself, not looking up. His thoughts were filled with an intense, childlike bitterness, so that he wanted to shout, indulge in temper. You became *involved.* The Gurkha officer and his little brown or yellow men, loyal to each other unto death . . . what a *hoot!* Kipling's lines came into his mind like the muffled noises from the shoreline. *You're droppin' the pick o' the Army because you don't 'elp 'em remain . . .*

Kipling. The romantic view—tosh. Gunga Din had been turned off by the Ministry of Defence like an old horse . . . Gunga Din and all his like.

Scrap the Gurkhas . . . rationalization, old boy . . . won't need 'em once Hong Kong goes . . . won't be anywhere to base all those Gurkhas after '97 . . . the army won't have much use for them after we give Hong Kong back to China . . . morale's gone . . . served their purpose . . . best days behind 'em . . . He'd heard all the excuses dressed as reasons. It's a real bastard, he fumed inwardly.

The Himalayas seemed almost on the brink of movement like huge ghosts. He could hear the noises of meals being prepared for tourists and villagers. Singing and the pulse of a single drum. He had no wish to feel orphaned, but he could find no other mood. He stared at the lake and the lights and suddenly wanted other company than that of the old man. Strangers; tourists who would not remind him of Nepal, but of the places he would have to rediscover.

"Plenty of tourists after the monsoon," he remarked. "The country will have to survive on them now." He thought for a moment, then added: "Some of them are in time for the King's death and the state funeral. Make a nice climax to their holiday!"

"Indeed," the old man said softly.

"When the avatar of Vishnu dies . . . oh, don't worry, they'll send a Royal out for the ceremony! What a bloody irony!" He turned to the old man, his hands thrust into his trouser pockets. "In Kathmandu, the thousands of goats they kill tomorrow won't help . . . they say the King has only days . . ."

"I understand. The Prince is returned from Harvard?"

Gardiner nodded. "So I heard."

"You will eat with us this evening?"

"Of course. First, though—"

"I understand. I shall return." Three men, presumably tourists, drifted along the track just below them, talking quietly. Their short-sleeved shirts moved like flags in the gloom. They were speaking in German? Gardiner listened more attentively. Yes, German. There seemed an unrelaxed discipline between them, as if two of them were subordinate to the other. Businessmen, presumably.

They moved out of his hearing toward one of the low hotel bungalows along the shore, passing into the mist, which was now dispersing gently. The reflection of the mountain again shimmered in the lake.

"Many Germans here?" he asked idly, knowing that the old man would recognize the language from exercises with BAOR.

"Yes, many. Recently."

"Tourists?"

"I—think so . . . is it not difficult for them to come?"

"From Germany? I shouldn't think so."

"Ah. I understood it was, but that was years ago."

"You mean they're from *East* Germany?"

"I do not know. Many think so."

"What are they doing?"

"Behaving like other tourists. Walking, riding in buses and cars, taking photographs."

"They must be from the embassy in Kat."

"So many?" The old man shrugged. "I must return. Please do not hurry, Sahib Captain Timothy. You are our honored guest."

"I shan't be long . . ." he murmured abstractedly. The old man left his side like his shadow detaching itself. It was a silly idea, but he turned to watch him fade into the dusk, and could not rid himself of the constricted feeling in his throat. The old man vanished. Above and only hundreds of yards away, Gardiner could see the lights of the village and hear its noises. "Shan't be long," he repeated with affected lightness, moving off toward the lake, almost at once forgetting about the East Germans.

He heard the plop of fish still feeding on the evening's last insects. A fisherman's canoe slid through the still water, and he heard the rustle as its nets were stowed. Noises from a restaurant, laughter from a bar. He passed quickly from ancient to modern, as if walking out of his own past into an uncertain future. He turned into the first bar, climbing its three wooden steps and walking across its veranda.

The place was like a tidied-up, hippieless bar on Kat's Freak Street. Psychedelic decoration, but clean tablecloths. No sweet smell in the smoke. He crossed to the bar and to the middle-aged ex-hippie, still earringed and long-haired but shaven and brisk in his service, who ran the place. He ordered an imported beer, then took it to an empty table in one corner. The bar was almost empty, quiet except for the three young Gurungs, evidently ex-soldiers, laughing and swaying at their table on the other side of the room. They had watched him enter. He thought perhaps he recognized one of them. But they were no longer acquainted and they ignored him. Most of the younger ones had done so in the village. Another small, bitter capsule to swallow.

There were three hikers, early for the season immediately after the monsoon, at another table, their rolled-up sleeping bags and backpacks on frames beside them on the floor. Their beards were new and sparse. And two of the Germans who had passed him, he guessed, at another table. Gardiner studied them with an idle curiosity—which sharpened not at their German or their accents, but at their bearing, their manner. Soldiers. Men temporarily out of uniform, like himself.

The rock music from speakers high on the bar's walls was out-of-date, its volume turned down. He smiled. His twin brother Simon, dead from heroin addiction, would have been able to tell him which band, which year. It wasn't Simon's own band, from any of their incarnations. He had been reminded of Simon often in Kat. Simon had come in the seventies, too young and too late to catch the Chapati Express, only to inhale the last fumes from its departure. Poor Simon. A wrecked hotel suite in Frankfurt, his body twisted and yet somehow at peace on the unmade bed, splashed on the front page of every national newspaper. *Rock star dies of drug overdose* . . .

He dismissed Simon's memory and continued watching the two Germans. Soldiers, or intelligence officers. Uniformed men,

relaxing as intently as if they had recently completed an inten-
sive training course. Their conversation, when he could catch
at it, was innocuous, dull. His attention wandered once more,
skating like a water-boatman across the two weeks since his return from Hong Kong as if memory was a placid pool. It wasn't,
but he felt himself temporarily removed from the emotions beneath its surface.

The farewell parades and ceremonies and sacrifices . . . the
last flight home on Royal Nepalese Airlines, the disbandment
at the Depot in Kat, the paying-off of the men . . . the farewells,
the presents . . . the mooching around the Mess or the streets
of the capital, the drinking . . .

He knew he was again indulging the maudlin mood that had
accompanied him for most of the last fortnight, yet he had no
desire or need to shake it off. The Germans were an insufficient
distraction. His brother had been dead for more than eight years,
his youth and money wasted. He did *not* want to think about
Simon. Or about the disbanding of the Brigade . . . but there
was nothing else to exercise his mind.

A second beer. He was hungry now, and more than ever
maudlin; self-pity seeped with the rock music. Dully, he
watched a Chinese enter, order a whiskey, sit with the two Germans. The Chinese were everywhere in Nepal, supervising road-
building, mostly. Minutes later, the third German came into the
bar. He greeted the Chinese. The Gurkhas left in a swaying
group, clinging together like seaweed in a rough tide. The hikers
were directed to the nearest, cheapest hotel. Gardiner finished
his beer, still idly watching the Chinese and the Germans in ani-
mated conversation. He could not hear what they said.
Strangely, the Chinese seemed to speak some German. Cosmo-
politan Nepal, he reflected with a slight toss of his head. The
beer was affecting him more than it ought. But then, he hadn't
eaten since breakfast and he'd walked in the hills most of the
day, as if driven out of the village rather than being its honored
guest. It was time for dinner.

He made to stand, looking across the room at the group of
Germans and the Chinese. It was as if he saw the man's face
at night. In the well-lit bar—and the Chinese was not in
shadow—it seemed as if he were further away, standing in deep
shade. Night, and hard white lights on gantries and watchtow-
ers. Wire. Fences and barriers. The face of the Chinese suggested

such images as a context for his features, a means of recognition. And yet he couldn't know the man . . .

The night persisted. Chinese faces were not all the same to him, not after three Hong Kong postings . . . Hong Kong. Night, lights, a border. Dull, hopeless faces, guns and uniforms . . . Without considering, he had sat down again, to study the Chinese without drawing attention to himself. He had seen the Chinese—hadn't he?—in Hong Kong, at the border crossing between the New Territories and the People's Republic. He had seen that face through his binoculars as he superintended the handing back of illegal immigrants. A hundred poor devils to be returned, signed for and forgotten. The Gurkha patrols caught them, processed them, sent them back. But *this* Chinese—not one of those being shipped home . . . one of those waiting, superintending the exchange like himself. That scar on his right cheek, almost touching the corner of his mouth, coming down as far as the jut of the chin. Surely he'd seen it, however unlikely it was, at the crossing point? Perhaps three times?

A man of fifty, maybe forty-five. In the uniform of . . . People's Liberation Army Intelligence Corps!

He stared at the face. Slowly, its familiarity waxed and then waned like a moon. It had been the scar, nothing more, that was reminiscent of the intelligence officer on the far side of the Hong Kong wire. No, it was not the same man. How could it be, here in central Nepal? A ridiculous coincidence, and the effects of beer at altitude . . . he smiled at himself. The similarity had all but disappeared.

He left then, satisfied. No one seemed the least interested in his departure. Outside, struck by chill air and the clarity of the stars, he felt no more than hungry. He dismissed his mistake with a rueful shake of his head.

And yet there was a niggling curiosity, as he looked up at the thick, cold stars. Not about the Chinese, of course—no, the Germans. Men who evidently were men who habitually wore uniform. They were the object of a more sensible curiosity altogether. They occupied his thoughts as he walked quickly back toward the village. *East* Germans. What did they want in Pokhara? Nepal was an intelligence backwater. What were they up to here?

Perhaps he should try to find out . . .

•   •   •

The reluctant mist, gray and thick for most of the morning, had at last moved off the lake, revealing the solitary fisherman in his rowing-boat, his rod like an aerial, his line trailing away aft. Occasionally, he used field glasses surreptitiously. Evidently, he worked for the British or the Americans and had Kurt's family and bungalow under surveillance. By now, he would be only too well aware of Brigitte's presence.

The boat and its occupant were an object of clear, virulent hatred. Anger surged again and again in her body. She had control of her features, her voice, her emotions—just. Most of the previous evening and night she had been barely rational. The fisherman-observer evoked the night's mood each time she looked at him. She had scrabbled after the means of getting Kurt back home without alerting the suspicions of her own service. Clung to it like someone about to fall from a high place grabbing any handhold, any purchase. Just as she had struggled to achieve a belief in his essential innocence. He *would* come back, he had been persuaded, bribed, seduced . . . she did not dare contemplate the awful, emptying idea of *choice* on his part.

She had not been able to screen the house and detain Anna-Lise and the children alone, so she had to bring in a small team who believed they were using Kurt's house to keep a neighboring bungalow under surveillance. So that Anna-Lise and the children could not leave. She glanced at her watch, then out once more at the fisherman in his still boat on the cold lake. It was already almost too late to get to the airport to catch the flight they had been booked on to Frankfurt—then to Florence . . .

She turned from the bedroom window, her eyes lighting on the telephone that had betrayed her son. Then on the stupid wife, propped tearful and plain against the bedhead like a large rag doll. A doll, a plaything . . . but he would come back for her sake. She ignored her rage at having to use this, this *toy*.

"Stop sniveling!" she snapped, and Anna-Lise flinched like a beaten child. The children, disappointed and puzzled, were being driven around in her limousine. Ice-cream and the zoo, perhaps . . . it would need little more to pacify *this* one! The woman on the bed suddenly represented all Kurt's weaknesses, his aimlessness, his suitability as a target for them. "Oh, here!" She thrust her handkerchief into his wife's curled hand.

Brigitte stood at the window, smoking. It pleased her to be filling this chintzy, *pretty* room with acrid smoke. The fisherman was using his glasses again. She stood perfectly still, knowing she was observed. Then she said, "Come over here, Anna-Lise." When she heard no movement, she snapped more loudly, "Come here at once!" The bed obediently creaked, silk slithered.

Anna-Lise shivered as Brigitte put her arm around the taller woman's shoulders. The boat remained still for perhaps a minute or more, just as they did. Then the fisherman swiftly reeled in his line and stowed the rod. Took up his oars and began rowing toward the far side of the lake.

"You can sit down now," Brigitte announced dismissively, walking away from her.

By this afternoon, Kurt would know. And he would ring here and she would talk to him. And—they would return him because he was a devalued currency. They would return him . . . ? He would come . . . ? She rubbed her forehead where the headache was beginning again. They would understand that they would gain little or nothing from a reluctant defector, realize that he might even begin to claim he had been kidnapped . . . they would return him quietly, quickly.

She moved through the living room, then the kitchen, her attention distracted by her once-more welling anger and fear, yet itemizing the fittings, the furniture, and their Western origins. Oak cupboards and a dishwasher from West Germany, curtains from France or England, a thick woolen carpet. Things were scattered like coins. She could not help but see his price in them. All he would have to do to ensure an endless, readier supply of *things* would be to tell the Americans or the British the secrets he dealt with, the secrets of the Russians he so despised. He had only ever valued things . . . like that toy in the bedroom.

Standing in the cold air outside the kitchen door, she thought of Kapustin. One of her team crossed the lawn in overalls, carrying what purported to be a box of plumber's tools. He might have been an accuser. Brigitte shivered. Kapustin, if he ever so much as suspected . . .

She breathed deeply and regularly, calming her churning stomach and beating heart. Kurt would ring this afternoon. She must ensure that he return at once. He must come back!

Shelley watched Aubrey hurrying toward him, urgency making him seem bent and struggling against a great wind. In the full, soft sunlight along the terrace, his face seemed empty of decision. Shelley reluctantly confronted his mentor's age and his loosened grip on the situation of Winterbach's defection. Aubrey halted anxiously beside him, like someone who had hurried for a bus only to find himself queueing impatiently in the rain.

Shelley looked down the cypress-darkened slopes toward Florence, avoiding the angry frustration that was vividly in possession of Aubrey's features. The city seemed like a frozen, red-tiled sea breaking against the hill on which Fiesole and the safe house stood. He listened to Aubrey's breathing with the attention of a doctor.

"How—was he? Did you persuade him?"

"No, I did not!" Aubrey snapped back angrily. Shelley saw him moving in his peripheral vision. "I've tried every argument, every trick—he knows as well as we do that the situation's in his mother's hands now. Damn it! We have to find out, like supplicants, what she has in store for us . . . he *must* make that call!"

"But he refuses," Shelley said softly. The afternoon sun was warm on his head and neck. Florence was insubstantial in its haze. The knowledge that Winterbach's wife and family would not be coming out to join him was like a small, chill breeze.

"I have promised him that we will try to get them out, if he cooperates."

"Not much chance we'll achieve that."

"I realize that, Peter!"

"Sorry . . ." The Arno glittered like twisted silver braid; the hills enclosing the valley and the city were dark blue with trees, speckled with villas.

"I lost my temper with him," Aubrey admitted. "Of course it's something of a farce, his pretending to his mother. She has sent us a clear signal she knows he's trying to come over . . . but he must play for time!" Aubrey's fury swarmed around Shelley's head like a cloud of midges.

"Is he greedy enough to stay out without them?"

Aubrey was silent for some moments, leaning on the balustrade of the terrace, his knuckles white, his shrunken form seeming tired at the same moment it threatened activity. Then he said: "He's greedy, yes. For toys. Like many of them . . . but no, I don't think he will stay."

"But we have enough time to—make it worth our while. He can have the Swiss account, the gewgaws on any future trips abroad—"

"What does Brigitte intend doing?" Aubrey demanded fiercely. He banged his clenched hand on the balustrade. "Does the woman even know what she intends?" He sighed. "What

I know is that our American friends arrive tomorrow and they will find themselves with a very reluctant defector indeed!"

"Then what do we do with him?"

"He must make that call—put her off-balance. *Use* his power over her." He squinted up into Shelley's face. Shelley thought he looked very old, at a loss. His only answer seemed to be to shrug.

Shelley stared down at the amphitheater of the Teatro Romano as at a palpable irony. The Monastery of St. Francis beyond it seemed suddenly appropriate to the small, ascetic, monklike features of the old man beside him. Florence in its haze was unreal, and yet at the same time it suggested the unimportance of Winterbach's fate. He was small-scale. Aubrey had enlarged him with personal significance; the key to open the doors people were intent upon closing against him. The American interrogators would gut Winterbach quite efficiently, however reluctant he was to talk. In that sense, he was worth the candle. He'd eventually be handed back to Mummy. Aubrey was making too much of it. Things got out of proportion for the elderly. Sacrilegiously, he thought Aubrey might be better occupied with the rising price of groceries in his local supermarket. His features, however, remained carefully neutral.

Inwardly, he sighed as he said, "I'll talk to him. Perhaps by now he's had time to arrive at a more sensible attitude." It all depended, he thought, on whether his mother pressured him to return immediately. Would she threaten the wife and children in some way? If Kurt Winterbach could delay his return—if they could make him do so—then the CIA team would have time to make the whole operation at least a qualified success . . . and save themselves a great deal of money. That was really the only problem—to prevent his mother dragging Winterbach home immediately. The other problems were only in Aubrey's imagination. "Shall we try?"

"Yes. I think he might have had time to realize he must exploit his power over Brigitte . . . as long as he will play out the hand!"

"Let's find out."

The villa was light and cool, marbled, tiled, pillared. Pleasantly indistinguishable from as many as fifty others dotting the slopes around Fiesole. Winterbach was on the second floor, guarded in an unlocked large-windowed room filled with dark blue shadows, a single bed, two easy chairs. Rugs were sprawled

on a polished wooden floor. The window looked east toward Set-
tignano and the river.

Kurt Winterbach was hunched on the edge of the bed. It was,
undoubtedly, the position into which he had declined as soon
as Aubrey had confirmed that there could be no doubt; Brigitte
appearing at the bedroom window, arm around the wife's shoulders, had been an unmistakable signal. The contact had been
allowed to see it, then get away to make his report.

As soon as Kurt recognized them, his eyes flickered toward
the telephone on a small, delicate table near the window. Ellis,
who had been guarding him, shook his head silently, stood up
and went out, leaving his newspaper, open at a crossword, folded
on the upright chair he had occupied. A sparrow watched all
three of them for a moment from the windowsill, where paint
flaked and the shutter creaked in a puff of breeze. The startled
sparrow disappeared. Shelley, aware of Aubrey's uncertainty,
became at once the figure of authority.

"Do you—feel up to calling your family, old man?" Shelley
asked. At once, Kurt's features creased in an exaggerated terror.
"She will be expecting you to call, you see," he explained patiently. "You told us your wife would call from the airport, before she changed flights. Your mother will be expecting you to
call." Kurt seemed to be retreating along the bed, toward the
wall. Shaking his head slightly, repetitively. "We need to gauge
her—attitude. It would really be for the best if you called." Aubrey had moved unhelpfully to the window. Kurt's lips began
moving. Then he spoke.

"I'll have to go back now!" Kurt wailed, the words bursting
like an intruder into the room's warm silence.

"No!" Aubrey began.

"Sir Kenneth!" Shelley interposed immediately. He kept his
features blank but his hands became clenched in the pockets of
his cream slacks. He spoke soothingly to Kurt: "We—we shall
have to bargain them out."

"She won't let them out!" Kurt wailed once more in a voice
that made Aubrey turn from the window. It was the shallow,
all-encompassing despair of a child. "She'll keep Anna-Lise and
the children there until I go back—I know she will!" He might
have been ten years old, speaking of a wicked stepmother. Kurt
was evidently contemptuous and distraught in the same moment. "She will, she's like that—" He broke off, as if confronted
by implacable, parental indifference in the two Englishmen. He

swallowed with a dry, sobbing noise. A fly buzzed around the still fan suspended from the ceiling.

"You—once you have talked to her, we'll have a better idea of how to take the next step," Shelley persisted like a children's nanny; firm but understanding. "Are you ready to make the call, old chap?" Shelley asked. Kurt stared at the telephone. Jerkily, he sat down with the receiver on his lap and dialed the number slowly and with desperate concentration. His legs fidgeted. Shelley looked at Aubrey. Kurt finished dialing.

"Well?" Aubrey whispered, watching Kurt for any sign of attention. The German was concentrating his entire awareness on the rug by his feet, his body having slumped into the rag-doll untidiness of an utter absence of hope.

"I don't know." Shelley whispered back, gently picking up a second receiver on the table. He heard the distant ringing. Imagined Brigitte. Watched Kurt. Considered Aubrey. "I'm not sure . . . she's a lot of power over him, though he thought she had none." His hand was over the mouthpiece of the telephone as he spoke softly. Aubrey nodded in agreement.

It was unimportant, Shelley thought. Fuss about very little . . . he'd be opened like a tin, then sent back, no harm done. The mother would hardly *hurt* his wife and kids, surely? And it wouldn't be worth the hassle of getting them out now—not for what Winterbach had to offer. Diminishing returns . . .

Nevertheless, he tensed as he heard the receiver at the other end picked up and a voice announce the number Winterbach had rung.

He offered the receiver to Aubrey as the woman spoke.

"Is that her?" Aubrey merely nodded. Shelley pressed the receiver against his cheek as Kurt blurted out:

"Mother, has anything happened? Why hasn't Lise telephoned me? I've been worried about her—why are *you* there? Mother . . . what's wrong?" Shelley felt his whole frame relax. Kurt did not even seem to be play-acting. Perhaps he wanted desperately to believe in the fiction. "What is the matter there? Put Lise on—can she come to the phone? Have they left? Are they going to call from Frankfurt?"

Kurt looked up at Shelley. His eyes were bright, either with cunning or concern. It was a closed-room situation where only bluff might buy time. If it failed, then the Americans must come in today. Use drugs to accelerate the debriefing . . . if they had to put Kurt on a flight back to East Berlin at once. He nodded encouragement to Kurt.

"Is it one of the children? Is someone *ill?* Mother!"

His hand tugged the telephone with convulsive little jerks. He seemed absorbed by the role he was playing. Perhaps he really believed he could, just once more, trick his doting mother.

"Kurt," Shelley heard Brigitte announce heavily, "Lise and the children will not be able to join you."

They were intent upon photographing the two luggage trolleys as they were towed away from the Avro 748 twin-prop aircraft sitting in splendid isolation on the tarmac. The flanks of the mountains were golden. The evening flight from Kathmandu had landed ten minutes earlier at Pokhara's airport. The tourists had wandered, dazed by their sudden impact with the scenery surrounding them, toward the small, almost ramshackle terminal building, and now their luggage followed. All day, the behavior of the three Germans—the Chinese had left on the morning flight to the capital and Gardiner had not thought of him since— had puzzled, even infuriated him. He felt like a child on whom adults had played an incomprehensible joke. Curiosity had dulled to boredom through the warm idle day, and how he was angry with himself for the waste of time involved in this foolish attempt at surveillance.

Just to fill another twenty-four hours? Just because he did not want to return to the Depot, collect his few belongings and travel warrants, fly to Delhi—then home. MoD, then Church Crookham—then what? That tiny, anonymous flat in South Ken—was that home? Even so, farting about watching three Germans was no bloody job for a grown man!

He could hear, in the sweet, cooling air, the click of the shutter, the winding of the motor. The camera was mounted on a tripod for steadiness, huge-lensed and with, no doubt, fast film to cope with the lessening light. They might have been photographing for some glamour calendar, so careful had they been with light and shade, focus and number of shots of precisely identical scenes. The morning flight out, the noon flight in, the afternoon flight out, the evening flight in . . .

. . . using an expensive portable camera-recorder, the tripod camera, a dozen different lenses. Then there was the surveying equipment, the graphs and notebooks, the maps and charts, the bundles of sketches, the tables of figures. They had moved posi-

tion a number of times, eaten in strict order, remained sober—
and watched the town's small airport all day, concentrating on
their work like men under pressure of time or results. Yet he
was no clearer as to their object than he had been in the morning.

His field glasses were making his eye sockets ache. He was
seated with his back against a rock, beneath the thick shade of
a spreading tree, sixty yards from their position, beneath a similar dark tree. The noise of their camera ceased and he could hear
their muffled voices in the evening stillness. Mustard fields lay
between the outcrop they occupied and the single runway and
low, huddled buildings of the airport. The River Seti was invisible in its gorge behind him, marked only by the three spans of
white concrete that were new bridges. He could see the dam on
the far side of the airport.

He turned back to the Germans, unable to distinguish their
words. The scrape of the tripod being closed. The camera, theod-
olite and the heavy binoculars went into bags or gleaming metal
boxes. He heard a zip drawn sharply closed. The very clarity
of the sounds added to the unreality of the day.

They knew the exact length of the runway, the stopping distances of the aircraft, the weight and size of their cargoes and
the number of their passengers. They knew the volume of air
around the airport before the mountains rose up on every side.
He yawned. They knew *everything* about the bloody airport at
Pokhara! He rubbed his stubbled face, sliding further back into
the tree's shadow, pressing against the rock. The track they
would take headed away from him. There was no danger of discovery.

At the exact moment each aircraft had landed, there was an
almost frenzied use of cameras, camera-recorder, charts and tables, binoculars; so much so that he had watched with bated
breath in anticipation of some drama; an overshoot or even a
crash. He obtained no insight, only frustration, feeling he had
witnessed an event of great significance to its participants while
remaining himself utterly ignorant.

They had completed their packing-up. In single file, they
walked away from him down toward the airport and the road
running beside it. It was darker now, and he gratefully lowered
the glasses as their silhouettes became indistinct. Unreality
pressed like an ache at his neck and the back of his head.

"Damn," he breathed softly, stretching his arms and legs
without troubling to stand. "You're a stupid bugger, Gardiner."

At least, he continued silently, you've avoided the sacrifices and the smell of all that blood. Dasain's ninth day was almost over. By darkness, when he returned to the village, he would not see the spilled animal blood nor smell it above the scents of cooking. "Damn," he repeated, climbing slowly, luxuriously to his feet.

He placed his glasses in his small backpack, where they rustled against the wrappings of the food he had eaten around midday. Spicy meat and goat's cheese. Spiced bread.

Perhaps the old man was right. Perhaps he should come back.

He shook his head. No way. Definitely not. It would be like living in a place that was becoming a ghost town. Rather London than losing the past entirely. He'd always have memories of Nepal, the Brigade . . .

To avoid painful reflections, his mind returned to the Germans. The intensity of their activities as the evening flight came in to land . . . it was almost as if they reached out hands to *weigh* the bloody aircraft! What a bloody stupid idea and what a bloody waste of time! He could see no sense to it, no reason for what they were doing so furtively. It was secret, that was obvious—they were up to no good . . . but what the hell kind of naughties were they engaged in?

He shook his head. It had passed the time emptily enough, and perhaps he should be grateful for that.

He hefted the small pack onto his shoulders. He began to whistle as he climbed the slope, leaning forward, striding easily. Bloody daft . . .

And yet they had been so *intent* . . . So preoccupied with their measurements, their calculations and observations . . .

Curiosity nagged, refreshed by the coolness of the evening. What the hell were they up to?

It was difficult to concentrate. She could hear his childish self in his voice, and the appeal of that was direct and unsettling. Also, to her rage, she clearly sensed others listening, could almost hear their breathing—

"What do you mean, Mother?" she heard him ask, and the bluff departed from his manner for an instant. Then, once again, he was the smiling child denying he had stolen from her purse, had thrown stones at the neighbor's cat. "What is *wrong?*"

"You know what the matter is," she snapped. "Where are you—exactly where? Who is with you?" She listened intently for an intake of breath that might not be his. She heard him swallow.

"I'm—the place . . . Florence, of course! But that's not important . . ."

Still he persisted in lying to her. She began to shout, all instinct and skill lost. "You know that I know, Kurt! It's just—*stupid* to pretend like this! I know what you're trying to do. I won't let you!"

Instinct and cunning returned. She heard someone else breathing on the line, slower than Kurt's stung, angry inhalations, but nevertheless quickened by disappointment. Then that momentary coolness disappeared once more.

"Come home now—at once!" The fear seeped like fog off the lake. Her peremptory demand was a plea; he had to come home, and at once, so that she could cover his tracks. His life, her authority, hung by a thread, by the telephone line between them. She both loathed him and feared for him. In her lap, the message from MfS *Ausland* to contact Kapustin at once. Her report from Lin was late. Kapustin . . . if he so much as—

"Who is there with you?" she demanded.

"No one!" he cried like an accused child.

"Don't lie to me! Is it the Americans or the English? *Tell me!*" Her body was shaking, her forehead burned. Didn't he realize what would happen to him? Had she protected him that well from reality? Kurt, Kurt!

"There's no one here," he persisted.

She spoke to the voiceless listener. "The game is over. Whoever you are, send my son home at once. He will tell you nothing now. Do you hear me, Kurt, you will tell them nothing!"

"She'll get back everything!" She heard his muffled whispering. He *was* frightened now, of her . . .

Another voice whispered back words she could not hear. The dialogue, kept from her, enraged her further. Her son was talking about her, was afraid of her in front of them!

"Kurt!" she shouted. "Who is *there?*" As if locked out of her own apartment by strangers.

"I'm not coming back," she heard in a pouting tone. "There's no future for me now, is there? *You'll* see to that!"

She could hardly believe it, hardly swallow. "Kurt!"

"It will be just like being in prison for the rest of my life! Let Lise and the children *go!*" He was breathing quickly, heavily. Her ears rang as if some kind of helmet enclosed her head. "*You* tell her," she heard him say. "If you want my help, Sir Kenneth Aubrey, tell her to let them go, tell her!"

She sensed him holding the phone toward Aubrey, even before the enormity of it being *him,* of all people in the world, struck her. She rubbed her forehead, listening, her mind hurrying into panic. And becoming cold. Kapustin—Kurt—*Aubrey*—no time, immediately . . .

"Ask your new friend," she announced after half a minute of humming, crackled silence, "whether you should believe me or not, Kurt, when I tell you that you must come back at once." She paused, but she heard nothing but his breathing. "Unless you do, you will be compromised. And your wife and children will be compromised. I can do it with one telephone call, one set of instructions. It will not be difficult. Your friend knows me well, perhaps better, in this instance, than you do, my son. Ask him whether I will carry out my threat or not!" She was half-afraid of her own coldness, afraid, too, of his outburst, his lack of rationality in speaking to her as he had done.

She continued with the same icy calm: "He will make you understand, for your sake, for Anna-Lise and the children, perhaps for his own sake, too, that you must come home. Tonight." She sighed. Kurt was still vividly in her thoughts as a shifting, multiple image of past and present selves—but there was something like a cold, small, empty room in which the situation could be examined in a hard white light. "You will be here in your own house," her voice continued, "by this time tomorrow."

She knew she was powerless to protect him. They could use drugs, even physical violence, and Kurt would be unable to resist either. She could begin no search for him, she could alert no one without breaking open a wasps' nest. Yet they would understand that his cooperation was lost to them now. *He* was worthless!

She accepted that she would settle for his secret return, unharmed. Whatever they learned from him . . . there must be no fragment of proof that he was ever in their company for a single moment. Anna-Lise was ill, Kurt had returned home immediately. There was nothing suspicious in that. She cleared her throat.

"*You* understand," she said, addressing Aubrey or whoever else was listening, "that my son is now worthless to you. He must be returned home without being compromised. As if he had returned for personal reasons. Do you understand me?"

Kurt's breathing had a sobbing quality in the ensuing silence. It was as if she talked to other adults over his childish head. "You will, if you consider the matter, realize that this is the only sensible course of action. The matter will be forgotten—no one else will be involved . . ." She paused, sensing the listener's realization that she was threatening an intelligence war unless they capitulated, then she concluded: " . . . as long as my son is returned unharmed and at once. In an hour's time, you will call again. There are details to be arranged." She removed the receiver from her cheek, and her nerve almost failed her as she attempted to break the connection; as if she was abandoning Kurt. "Goodbye, my son," she added finally, and forced down the receiver and the hand that held it until the instrument rattled onto its rest. That small noise seemed both clumsy and fragile, the breaking of crystal. It triggered an appalling weakness, and sudden tears. She had not suspected they would be lurking in ambush for her.

It was the same lakeside bar, the same muted rock music and aging ex-hippie but no drunken ex-Gurkhas tonight, and only two of the Germans. He paused for a moment, and then went up the three wooden steps into the smoky atmosphere. He ordered a beer, exchanged empty pleasantries with the owner, then sat down on the opposite side of the room from the Germans. They possessed the same aura of satisfaction, of relaxation earned by effort, that had surrounded them the previous evening.

He had not intended to seek them out until the following morning. Yet this idea of keeping them under surveillance had sprung on him. He felt boyish, even happy. It was a temporary escape from himself, and therefore to be welcomed. Little more than a game, but played with a child's intensity, he admitted.

He drank his beer quickly, but tonight it seemed to have no effect on him. The scene as he walked across the bar, as he ordered a portion of curried chicken warming on a hot-plate, and as he returned, cutlery stuck into a pocket of his bush shirt, was without danger or risk of any kind. It *was* a game in that sense. A holiday occupation, divorced from the other fifty weeks of living in any year. He sat down and began eating. The Germans paid him not the slightest attention. They were talking of soccer, women and shared memories. Their conversation was innocent—what he could understand of it.

Gradually, his excitement disappeared with his hunger. He felt foolish, like a man who has rushed to dress, being late for an appointment, and forgotten his socks. The Germans were drinking quickly and enjoyably. It became increasingly silly to sit there, watching them. Hands waved, voices laughed, became louder, and the Germans slowly became tipsy, then drunk. An hour passed. Gardiner drank a third beer. He was feeling stiff and weary after his day's occupation. He wanted to sleep.

The third German joined his companions a little after ten. Fierce whispering, but Gardiner had lost interest long before their voices again became raised and the old round of topics became their subject once more. He stood up. The older German, to whom the other two seemed subordinate, watched him do so, but with only a vague interest.

"Good night," he announced, and went out into the cool of the evening, their laughter pursuing him, almost pointing him out for ridicule. What a bloody silly idea!

He strolled slowly back to where he had parked the Land-Rover, with its military license plates, under the trees near the gates of the Royal Palace, fiddling in his pocket for the keys. Laughter from a bar, the smell of bread already from the Shanti Bakery. The smells of other cooking, warmth glowing from open doors and windows. The hum of insects. The noise of footsteps behind him in the empty street, which had halted suddenly as he paused. The water glittered to his right, a raft puttered across the lake from the Fishtail Lodge, its group of passengers clear in silhouette against the moonlit water. The wake of the craft cut across and dissolved the huge, calm reflection of Machapucchare. Gardiner shivered, as if the lake's surface was distressed by a chill breeze. How could he have heard footsteps?

He looked behind him. For a moment, it seemed as if a shadow moved to conceal itself within the deeper shade cast by the trees, thirty yards away. He tugged the keys of the Land-Rover from his pocket. The shadow did not detach itself from the gloom. The smell of newly baked bread was sharper in his nostrils. He felt the evening turn more chill. The mountain's huge reflection slowly became still once more. Silly—

He no longer believed in the shadow. A trick of the light.

The Land-Rover was another fifty yards away. He looked up at the stars, large and unwinking as pebbles in the soft sky. He sighed. His sensations were muddy and confused. Pokhara seemed ruffled, disturbed like the mountain's reflection by the passage of the raft. It was not the same place as it had been only moments earlier—

He had turned swiftly, twenty yards from the Land-Rover. The shadow had detached itself from the trees and was now stranded in light from a restaurant. Laughter from its veranda seemed to point out the figure. It was one of the Germans.

The realization made a dull, solid impact like that of a blow. He felt winded; stranded in this lakeshore street in a known-now-unknown place. Why were they following him?

The figure hesitated, glancing toward the restaurant. They had seen him, then . . . they had known, all the time, that he had been watching them. He represented a danger—or was he merely an object of curiosity to be observed and judged?

He thrust his hands into his pockets. His throat was dry. The German lit a cigarette, occupying the interval as innocuously as he could. Gardiner turned away, tried to whistle and failed, and walked on toward the Land-Rover. How could the German follow him once he started the engine? He was angry with himself for the way in which they had so easily—

A second shadow, beside the vehicle.

He felt his breathing become difficult. He halted irresolutely, turning on his heel. The German behind him was strolling casually toward him. The gates of the Royal Palace seemed very tall, the building behind it as dark as if the King had already died. He shivered almost uncontrollably. He was ten yards from his transport.

The second German lifted the hood, reached into the engine compartment, and his hand came out holding something small. The distributor cap? It didn't matter. The man held up the object like a jewel. The German behind him had stopped once more. The disabling of his vehicle was quick, professional, certain. What would they do now? The street was darker here, the moonlight somehow thinner. There were trees everywhere, no lit or occupied buildings to either side of the King's winter residence. The place expressed their intention vividly.

Footsteps behind him, the German at the Land-Rover slamming down the hood and beginning to move . . . Gardiner froze. Seven yards away. He glanced behind him. Six yards. Both men were smiling, confident. Laughter from somewhere, the banging of the raft against the jetty fifty yards away, the noises of passengers eager to disembark. The smell of the bread and the cigarette the first German threw down as they closed on him.

3

A Window Onto Winter

Shock and terror lent him insight but not volition. A blade gleamed in the left hand of the German near the Land-Rover. The noises of the disembarking passengers were louder, as if they had become an amused audience. The smell of bread. The blade was a *kukri,* and Gardiner understood the deception they intended. There were many disgruntled dark faces in Pokhara and the surrounding villages, many ex-Gurkhas drinking heavily. A killing out of resentment; even robbery. A local matter.

The blade was hypnotic, strange in a pale hand. An image of an identical *kukri,* interposing itself between his stomach and the thrust of a Kalashnikov's bayonet, as he stood similarly rooted with shock; the body of the guerrilla skidding alongside and past him on the churned mud of the monsoon season. The image prickled his body like a cattle prod.

The blade hesitated. A small crowd closing on them from the direction of the jetty. Something muffled and angry from the closer of the two Germans. Pale hands and faces—

Gardiner blundered like an animal against the man who had spoken, hearing the breath expelled in surprise. He half-turned, his legs stiff and weak. The *kukri* continued to fascinate, to close more slowly. The empty hand fumbled inside a linen jacket. Hands reached for him from behind, but the man was still off-balance and Gardiner again heaved clumsily against him, throwing him onto the ground. Then Gardiner seemed to take only two or three awkward steps before he was embroiled in the crowd of passengers making their way to the restaurants and bars. Hands grabbed for him, there were angry voices. He elbowed and pushed his way through them, soft stomachs yielding, shoulders moving aside, protests beginning. He looked back at the recovering, already-moving Germans as if at an accident from which he had dazedly staggered away.

His breathing was ragged and loud, his legs still weak; the passengers from the raft were more ready to contest the street with the Germans. The raft puttered out across the moonlit lake, already too far away to provide an escape. Gardiner began running. The blade of the *kukri* moved again and again in his imagination and in memory, too; the senior NCO who had saved his life in Brunei, killing as instinctively as the Germans were prepared to do. There was ineffectual shouting behind him, anger in English and Nepali. The Germans were free of entanglement, walking quickly until the crowd ignored them and they could begin to run. He was whole seconds ahead of them. They meant to kill him; just because he had seen them watching a backwater airport?

He ran along the lakeshore, the smooth water like a mirror, a bright backcloth against which they could not lose sight of him. The lights of tourist lodges and cheap hotels seemed like images from a night train. The tents of hikers, mud huts with the glow of oil lamps leaking through their inadequate walls. The noise of rock music. The landscape, his immediate surroundings, seemed unreal, fantastical. His body was hot and his heart pumped in his too-small chest. He looked behind him. They were running now. Already, they were closer.

He recollected that there had been three of them in the bar, in what seemed the same moment as he saw a European emerge from the huge, spreading shadow of a banyan tree. Emerge and move with definite purpose: interception. Two behind, one coming from his left. The two behind him seemed spurred as he was slowed by the arrival of the third man. The *kukri* was vivid and somehow hopeful in his mind. *They had to be within arms' length!* They wanted to deceive any investigation. *Arms' length . . .*

He blundered between tents, stumbling over and wrenching free a guyrope. Someone bellowed distantly. Moving his hands in front of him like a child playing blindman's buff, he pushed through the small encampment that had sprung up like mushrooms after the monsoon. The lake narrowed. The lights of the

Fishtail Lodge across the neck of water that remained. Moonlight after the tents. Noises behind him. The shadow of the dam ahead like a penciled horizon, mountains ghostly behind.

He paused for a moment, catching his breath. Fifty yards away. He was beneath two banyans marrying their branches above him. The shadow was inky, yet he felt exposed. The three of them had converged; halted and become uncertain. He was in deep shade, they were outlined against the moon on the water. He could hear occasional, distant traffic on the new roads around the airport and the dam. He was shaky with exertion and shock. Purpose deserted him. He tried to quieten his breathing, holding his hand over his mouth to stifle the noise he was making.

Any café, bar, hotel, lodge?

He knew they would not be dissuaded by company. They would simply surround him, pretend acquaintance, take him out between them, mocking his protests. The village? He would be safe there, surely? If you get there, he answered himself, on foot, in darkness.

They were gesturing toward the small grove of banyan and peepal trees. Thick hedges of thorny spurge marched away from the grove toward the dam. Their voices were urgent, still confident. Two of them moved toward the trees, the third looked up and down the lakeshore.

Then spoke. The heavily accented English made his fear and isolation more oppressive. He began to shiver. The chain of cause and effect. *Karma.* The casual curiosity of lifting a stone only to find a cobra. That was all he had done, he had not been *serious* about it, just curious—now, they were determined to kill him.

"Englishman, where are you?" the voice called. "Where are you?" Almost seductive. They seemed to *know* him. "You can't get away." With each two or three words, the speaker's head turned robotically, alert for intruders on the shore. "We only want to talk to you."

Gardiner moved further back into darkness, clumsily feeling his way between the huge, twisted trunks. The two searching for him were now themselves in shadow. Immediately, he could hear the tread of shoes, the rub of fingers against bark, almost hear their breathing. He continued to retreat, aware that he could do nothing else, that no idea could be extracted from the jumble of oily fears at the back of his mind. He thought of his aloof, strange father and his desperate skills, knowing how much he needed those same talents for survival, and how certainly he lacked them. His father would have already reduced the odds against him by simply killing at least one of the Germans. He would have retreated only to attack. Gardiner shivered at the memory of his father as much as at his own helplessness.

The bark was rough against his cheek, cold-seeming. His fingers tapped shiveringly against the tree as if transmitting a Morse signal . . .

He remembered the guerrilla had emerged from the trees, Kalashnikov and bayonet held stiffly out in front of him as he ran. He seemed to skim the pools of water, the churned mud, his hair slicked by the downpour, his black, loose trousers sticking to his thin legs. Gardiner had watched him in the same frozen, appalled mood as now, unable to move . . . until the Gurkha NCO—the old man from the village in the pride of his middle years—had simply stepped into the guerrilla's path and opened his stomach to the breastbone with the *kukri.* Menace had become a slithering, shapeless lump on the mud of the clearing.

One of them was close, and making more noise. He stared beyond the shadows toward the glitter of the lake. The third German was no longer silhouetted against it. More noise, as if one of them was beating the bushes for a game bird. Moving away to Gardiner's left—he was safe . . . noise, a grunted curse—

You bloody fool!

A crooked arm wrapped across his throat, a body pressed against him, the outline of a gun thrust into the man's belt sharp in the small of his back. Decoy! The noises had been intentional. His assailant grunted with what could only be delight, his breath was hot on Gardiner's cheek and neck. Gardiner could not breathe, could hardly squirm. His right hand was pressed numbingly against the trunk of the banyan, his left was twisted behind his back. He was pulled backward, off-balance, while the man's bent arm tightened on his windpipe. He gasped, fought for breath.

"Hier!" He did not understand the grunted German, translation had gone, consciousness was next. *"Gerd—Dietrich—hier!"*

Gardiner's left hand was open, feebly grasping the stuff of the German's jacket, his trousers, his shirt, tugging like the grip of a curious baby. Then he squeezed on something. His back burned and he gasped in pain . . . the German was shouting, he drew in lungfuls of air, the German slid against and down a tree, holding his genitals where the trousers were stained. His face was very white in the shadow, against the trunk.

"Was ist?" was all he heard shouted, then: *"Paul?"* His throat was still constricting within the remembered arm, he still could not breathe. He staggered away from the wounded man sitting beneath the tree, howling in pain, his pale hands dark now. He blundered against a trunk, a low knurled branch. Staggered on, coughing, wanting to retch, dragging in inadequate little gulps of night air. Behind him, the anger, curses and yelled agony.

He stumbled out of the grove, following the slope of the land and the line of the spurge hedge, its closed blossoms like flecks of blood in the white moonlight. He did not look behind, not once. Air filled his lungs, his legs seemed stronger, but the pain in his back was fiery. The line of the dam became a gray, pale sheet hanging against the low, gleaming stars. Headlights washed the stars away for a moment, then their lamps reasserted themselves. He blundered up one slope, scrabbling on all fours when he slipped, down another sharp slope, leaning backward against earth and jutting rocks. Brushed through ordered lines of citrus and banana trees, broad leaves like dark scimitars.

Headlights, haloing him. Concrete or tarmac beneath his feet. He fell to his knees, waving his arms absurdly in a semaphore to halt the oncoming vehicle. The truck swerved, then slowed to a halt. A Gurung looked down from the truck's cab. A fruit merchant's name and address on the canvas hood.

"Are you—can you take me to Kathmandu?" he stuttered in Nepali, still on his knees, looking up into the small, dark face that seemed amused as much as surprised. Gardiner saw the Brigade-issue woolen pullover, bereft of insignia, and felt a huge, nauseous relief spreading outward and downward from his chest. "The Depot," he said, coughing. "Can you take me to the Depot?"

"Yes, sir. Get in, sir. Sahib."

Gardiner groaned at the imminence of safety and climbed shakily to his feet. There was no sign of the Germans.

The American's contempt for Aubrey was casual and evident. Shelley bridled at it, even as he was forced to admit its likeness to his own ambiguous feelings. Aubrey seemed hunched into his chair in an attitude of defeat—and inadequacy, Shelley was forced to admit. The recognition possessed all the vigor of a previously unexperienced passion.

"This is all just shit, man," the CIA's Head of Rome Station announced to the room, pouring himself a large bourbon. He had brought the bottle with him, just as he had brought the two interrogators and the three heavies in a second car. The hairs on Shelley's neck and wrists prickled, as if the American wore a charge of static electricity around him. Even pouring and swallowing his drink there was the untutored energy of a hyperactive child. "I mean," he continued, jabbing his glass in Shelley's direction, "this kind of thing went out of style a long time back."

Shelley cleared his throat. Aubrey, who had seemed inattentive, glowered. His retreat from responsibility was all too evident to Shelley. "Perhaps . . ." Shelley demurred softly.

"Perhaps? Maybe?" Roth snorted. "The guy upstairs should have been turned, or just dumped. He isn't worth the trouble. In two weeks, maybe less, the Soviets will change the codes, the RDVs, the channels—the whole ball game!" He raised his arms. "It isn't worth the hassle." He walked toward Shelley, deliberately and obviously ignoring Aubrey and lowering his voice slightly. "I mean, the guy's mother just calls Langley and says send him home! It can't be *real!* Threatening maybe fifty arrests, assassinations, terrorist activity *inside* the US, here in Italy . . . she even threatened to frame the Company with her son's kidnapping, can you believe?" Shelley made as if to speak, and Roth's face hardened and his hand waved dismissively. "I'm here to tell you that your boss has screwed up. A genuine made-in-Britain screw-up! Anders doesn't like having the Director on his back and I don't like having Anders on mine. Most of all, I don't like pissing into the wind over this guy just to make the investment look better!"

"It's a small operation that unfortunately went rather wrong," Shelley murmured. Roth's eyes gleamed and he sat down lightly on an armchair, so that both of them faced across the large-shadowed room toward Aubrey, whose hands plucked at the pages of a book.

Roth leaned toward Shelley. "Small? You call it small—I call it shit, man! We should never have gotten involved. We're really wasting the Company's time here with these penny-ante games!"

"You have revolutions to foment, I suppose?" Shelley remarked acidly.

The American's eyes glinted. "Policy to decide and effect," he replied. "We leave it to you British to play the kids' games in the world—"

"While you make it safe for democracy?"

Roth laughed. One of the new breed, barely forty, brash, un-polished, unmindful. Trekking the world with an evangelical mission to civilize it, Shelley thought. The CIA were becoming much more difficult to interest in Europe, in tradecraft, in the *secrecy* of espionage. They played on the world stage now and enjoyed the fame.

Roth said: "Your day's over, Shelley . . . you people. Just like his surely is." He gestured with his empty glass toward Aubrey; professorial in his attention to the book.

"Perhaps . . ."

"There's no perhaps in this case, Shelley. This is the best you people can do, uh, this screw-up? Time your team got off the football field." Roth was grinning with complete assurance, knowing the two experts were drugging and filleting Kurt Win-terbach in an upstairs room.

Shelley felt angry with Aubrey because in some obscure sense this was his doing. He was angry with his masters who had given Aubrey *this little job, to keep him out of our hair . . . you under-stand, Peter?* Aubrey had pestered them for employment. Now, the old man's cavalier attempt to thrust himself back on to the stage had resulted in this, this *fiasco!* It was a real, bona fide fuck-up! SIS looked worse than bad to an unwavering American gaze.

He looked at Aubrey as if willing him to occupy the room instead of shrinking from its shadows and proportions. Aubrey seemed willful in his deliberation over the book on his lap, his gray features and his silence like that of a casualty patient wait-ing in an interminable queue for treatment. He heard Aubrey's dentures click, and his features registered an involuntary dis-taste.

Roth crossed the room to the bottles on the sideboard. Shelley glanced at his watch. Almost twelve. The interrogation had lasted three hours already. In another eight or nine hours, Kurt was supposed to present himself at the East German Consulate in Florence . . . summoned home because of his wife's sudden illness. It was all arranged. And it was a bloody mess, a trivial, awkward, unimportant little fuck-up that would provide Au-brey's service epitaph. He became just too old to cope . . .

Roth stood at the sideboard, crystal tumbler glinting in his hand, watching Aubrey like an amoral, predatory cat.

Aubrey suddenly lifted his head and addressed Shelley, disregarding the existence of the American. His face was hollow with what could only be guilt, as he removed his half-glasses.

"I should have left Brigitte well alone," he announced. He plucked a handkerchief from his breast pocket and began cleaning the spectacles, carefully, almost obsessively, then continued without once looking up: "I saved her life a very long time ago— and she has hated me for forty years. I knew she was mixed up in *Teardrop,* she had to be. But, instead of regarding that as merely the nature of the beast, I wanted revenge. Petty, wasn't it?" He looked up, sighing. Roth's features displayed a bemusement that clarified as easily as heated butter into amused contempt. "Very petty." He paused, then added: "I wonder what Brigitte will do now?" Worry invested his tired features.

Shelley felt a pluck of pity, evoked as much by Roth's total abstinence from feeling as by Aubrey's words. Then Roth announced loudly:

"Jesus—what a screw-up!" He tossed back what remained of his second bourbon.

Brigitte Winterbach felt outrage surge in her the moment Andrew Babbington stepped through the door of her office. His appearance seemed to provoke the completion of some electrical circuit within her—herself, him, Kapustin, Kurt, Aubrey—so much so that he seemed to notice the feelings displayed on her features. She felt he was reading her thoughts, knew about Kurt and Aubrey. Andrew Babbington was part of the chain of cause and effect that had been forged by *Teardrop* and which now, more than ever, bound her and Aubrey in enmity. She knew she should have left Aubrey alone, kept out of the whole affair—just as he should have *left her son alone.*

"Comrade General Winterbach," Babbington murmured, coming toward her desk, free hand outheld.

"Comrade General-Lieutenant Babbington," she replied, taking the proffered hand. Momentarily, the grip and the eyes flinched at the recent rank. Then Babbington's bearded lips parted in a chilly, formal smile. He placed his flat briefcase on the desk, his eyes glancing across the files, the copies of signals received, the envelopes of photographs, the small, neat heap of video and audio cassettes. Proprietarially. Brigitte was angered by a returning sense of the pressure this man had put her and her people under for two months. "Please sit down," she offered stiffly. A clutch of fear just under her heart as she met his gaze and struggled with muscular betrayals around her mouth and eyes.

"I have just two hours before my flight leaves," he announced. He threw his overcoat over the back of a chair, then seated himself, plucking spectacles from a leather case.

Bearded, she thought, he looked younger. Or perhaps it was the open-necked check shirt and the sweater, the assumption of an Englishman's weekend casualness. His shoulders had lost that stoop of enraged defeat that they had worn when he had first arrived in Moscow . . . traded for Aubrey.

"You have everything I requested?"

Brigitte nodded. She coughed into a clenched fist, unable to trust her voice without first clearing her throat. It was as if a dangerous animal had entered her office. Her stomach was watery, the nerves all over her body as tender as bruised muscles.

"Everything the Center requested—except for the final reports on the feasibility of the two airports—"

"Those reports are crucial!" he snapped.

"I realize that."

"Without those calculations, the rest of this material is—wastepaper."

Her fear became anger. "The preliminary findings are here. I expect transmission of the full reports this evening."

"They were required two days ago," he persisted. He removed his glasses and glared at her. Kurt retreated in her awareness, left the room. Only she and Babbington occupied its shadows, antagonists over nothing more than *Topi.* "Your people have slipped well behind schedule—"

"For two months they have been achieving the impossible!"

"The King could be dead in two days!" His voice rose slightly, and she realized the greed with which he approached the culmination of the operation, its significance to him. She no longer feared betraying the truth about Kurt. He would not notice sufficiently to become suspicious. "Our friends in Kathmandu have told us as much. Your people must be ready—ours must have the necessary information."

"We will be ready. The sabotage campaign can begin the moment the King's death is announced. That is well in hand."

"It must look spontaneous—right-wing elements, the disaffected, the beginnings of a coup—"

"It will. We have been over these details many times. My people understand what to do, how and when to do it. You worry too much . . ." She lit a cigarette, smiling coldly to discomfort him.

She exhaled, concentrating on earliest memories of him. Suez and its aftermath, the young high-flyer in the British security service who volunteered; greedy for eminence, for secret power. There was still about him that overweening vanity that had first trapped him . . . and which had probably led to his underestimating Aubrey. She watched him as he riffled through the heap of files he had drawn to his side of the large desk. He was as intent as a child. His features became heavier, a miser counting gold. He flicked through sheets of conclusions, qualifications, running his finger down pages as if adding columns of figures. She smoked noisily, and prevented Kurt from reasserting his presence in her mind and the corners of the shadowy room. Babbington's scheme, *Topi.* Part of his embracing and complex revenge on the country that had exposed and reviled him. She thought of Aubrey, but dismissed him at once as her stomach churned and she felt her face lose its neutrality.

Eventually, Babbington looked up. His eyes were satisfied but his tone refused compliment. "We *must* have the feasibility figures, for the computer."

"Tonight."

"Transmit them on immediately to the Center."

"Very well."

"Is there something else?" he asked suddenly.

After a long moment, she shook her head. "Nothing."

His gaze seemed to become cruelly attentive. She stubbed out her cigarette vigorously to disguise the shaking of her hand. "No, there's nothing wrong. Nothing can go wrong."

He shrugged. He picked up the video cassettes one by one, inspecting their labels. Now with his glasses donned, he looked like a schoolmaster. He began tapping at the edge of her desk with neat fingernails as he read. Tension tightened around Brigitte's forehead and temples until she felt she must scream. The wind prowled across the Alexanderplatz and around the building's corners; smacked the rain hard against the glass. Babbington eventually looked up, flicking his spectacles aside.

"Good," he announced. He seemed as satisfied as he might have done after a rich meal; only slightly discomforted by the operation's ingredients and mass. "So much for detail. Now, what about our friend the Chinaman?" He smirked as he saw Brigitte bridle at the insult.

"Colonel Lin is confident that his disinformation exercise continues to succeed."

"He realizes, of course, that it has to?"

Brigitte nodded frostily. "He is to be trusted."

"I said nothing about trust—only competence."

"Agreed," she sighed.

He sat back on his chair and smiled. He seemed to be luxuriating in confidence.

"You're certain of the British?" she asked.

"Yes . . . they've been meaning to give the country up for years. Expecting it to become another Chinese colony, like Hong Kong after '97." He yawned, as if the subject bored him, but his eyes glittered. "They'll accept a—change of government— just as the Chinese will be forestalled by events. Once our friends are in control, any move on their part will alienate most of the world. *They* aren't strong enough to go through years in the wilderness again. And the Indians would rather our friends than the Chinese . . ." He shrugged. "Neatly packaged. A rather better Christmas present than Afghanistan, wouldn't you say?" He smiled, but she saw dissatisfaction break through like a fracture.

She understood. It *was* wearing away at him. There *were* times when he thought of himself only as Kapustin's errand-boy. She felt an identity of rage with him against Aubrey. She glanced at the large map of Nepal she had had tacked to one wall that afternoon. Was that what this was, all *Topi* consisted of? A means of gratifying childish, frustrated rage? The thought discomforted her. Kurt began to turn back the edges of her awareness.

It *was* true of Babbington, she decided, as his gaze followed hers to the map. Red circles, black lines, flags and pins, explosive little stars . . . and the whiteness of the countless peaks of the Kingdom behind that graffiti. Babbington was smiling as if recollecting carefree youth. Yes, it was his revenge on his country. Everything he had done since the beginning of the year, everything he would go on to do, would be another stab of the knife, another round of ammunition. Kapustin was right to regard him as almost as valuable in Moscow as he might have been in London. Babbington was goaded by a pure, lasting hatred. A hatred of Aubrey, of former colleagues and masters, of the very country he had betrayed and which he now regarded as having betrayed and rejected him. His self-esteem had been mortally wounded by people he considered his inferiors. They could never be forgiven.

His face closed as he turned from the map and saw Brigitte's intent gaze.

"Your people have done well," he remarked patronizingly, patting files and tapes. Then he looked around her office. "This could belong to a social security clerk," he observed, smiling at her heightened color. "I thought you'd have had better. Still spoiling that dim son of yours?"

Her blush, her nervous hands, would be regarded as a reaction to his sarcasm. She gripped the arms of her chair, her face narrowed and careful. Kurt's image faded.

"A drink?" she suggested in a husky voice.

"You really ought to cut down your smoking, Brigitte," he laughed. Good. His cleverness was always at the mercy of his arrogance.

"Are you too superstitious to drink to success this early?"

He shook his head. "No, by no means. A drink, certainly. Scotch, please. No ice or water." She bridled. He must have been born with that casual superiority of voice and manner. Not even Kapustin, let alone herself, managed it with as much ease and conviction.

"Of course." She crossed to the bottles arranged on their tray.

"He's out to grass, I hear. Finished for good, so the story goes . . ."

"Who?" she asked too quickly, the bottle clinking loudly against the tumbler.

"Who? Our mutual bogeyman, of course!" The epithet could not keep the anger from his voice.

"Good," she murmured as she turned with the drinks.

"Good," he said, evidently disappointed by the label on the bottle near her elbow.

He awoke, thick-headed, the empty bottle rolling onto the floor and away from his cot as he stirred and dislodged it from the crook of his arm. His nostrils seemed filled with the once-encountered and now-imagined smell of blood from the previous day, when the thousands of goats and buffalo were sacrificed in the Kot courtyard behind Durbar Square. It was as if the air of his room and the air outside it were both still heavy with the scent, and the buzz of insects he could hear was that of feeding flies. His stomach heaved, and he sat up. Loose ballast seemed to move heavily behind his forehead. His eyes fixed at once on the empty bottle where it had come to rest under a wicker chair. He rubbed his unkempt, damp hair slowly, as if massaging his hangover away.

His eyes slipped unfocused toward the brown envelope on the bedside table. He blinked. In the address panel, his name and the Depot's address. His rank. Gardiner groaned. His recall to the Ministry of Defence. Disciplinary action. No wonder those stupid buggers in the Mess last night had been smirking like cats . . . they'd all known. *Gardiner's in the shit, right up to his eyebrows* . . . The handful of Gurkha officers not yet placed or reassigned or prematurely pensioned—the hangers-on rather than the stayers-on, as he'd called them to their faces—now believed he was worse off than any of them. They expected MoD to simply—let him go . . .

He swung his legs out of bed, waited until his head stopped lurching, then gingerly stood up. Savagely, he aimed a kick at the bottle and missed, then picked up the envelope and flung it across the room. It fluttered like a tired bird and settled near the window. He crossed the room and raised the rattan blind, almost flinching, but the air outside was sweet. Nine in the morning. Kathmandu lay in a jumble of tiled roofs and temple spikes whose pattern was an immediate, sharp pain to sight and memory. He looked down at the buildings and parade ground and courtyards of the Depot.

Two Nepali army officers getting out of a Land-Rover. *Of course, there'll now be the additional charge of mislaying one of Her Majesty's vehicles, Gardiner* . . . And laughter at that, from all of them. He'd stormed out of the Mess, his face white with anger, fists clenched at his side. *Court-martial to follow* . . . He had been reported by the Brigadier for insulting and then striking a superior officer. He'd always known he would be—even though he'd not been charged immediately. MoD would have to deal with it . . . no one really cared, only enough to file a bloody report!

He'd not bothered to tell them about why he'd lost the Land-Rover, about the attempt on his life. They would only have laughed even more loudly. His army career was up the creek without a paddle. The army would be rid of him. What's more, he didn't really care. The bloody army had already evicted him from the only real home he'd ever known, so stuff the lot of them!

He remained leaning on the windowsill, his head hanging listlessly, his thoughts churning over old ground, turning everything into mud as if a regiment had exercised there. The regiment of old anger, old self-pity. The two Nepalese officers passed
out of sight. They, like the occasional remaining Gurkha who
wandered into view wore the *tika,* the rice immersed in red liquid on their foreheads, in symbol of the tenth day of the festival,
Bijaya Dashami.

Christ, he thought, he was in a real bloody mess!

Aubrey slipped into his thoughts, wearing a reproving frown.
Shaking his birdlike head slightly. Gardiner grinned despite
himself. His former legal guardian would not approve, would
be as disappointed as any Puritanical Victorian parent at his behavior, the close of his army career. He remembered vividly the
devastation, the uncomprehending, enveloping grief on the old
man's face at Simon's funeral. Could almost feel Aubrey's half-
fainting weight against his arm and side now. He felt keenly
ashamed of the news he must bring the old man. And it all
seemed so undeserved—his own fate, Aubrey's pain, the fate of
the Brigade.

He felt the envelope's edge under his bare toes and scuffed
the thing away from him across the floorboards. He stared out
over the parade ground, seeing it weeks earlier, during a monsoon downpour. Lines of small, dark men in sodden uniforms,
made gray by the thick curtain of rain, the whole scene back-
grounded by black-green vegetation. Men checking in equipment, checking in lives. Being paid off. Men *steaming* in the
warm rain as they waited. A sodden, weary end to the last of
the Brigade.

The scene slowly faded, as if the impression of the downpour
finally erased it. He stared unseeingly over the town, hardly
hearing its myriad noises: gongs, cries, traffic, and the silence
behind the noise that seemed to emanate from the direction of
the Royal Palace to the north of the Depot. Eventually, the smell
of cooking reawoke him, making him aware of his empty stomach. He could not remember whether or not he had been sick
during the night, or if he had eaten the previous evening. He
shook his head as if to loosen stubborn memories, and blinked
his vision into focus. He looked out over the Depot, squinting
in the clear morning light.

His arm began to quiver as his grip tightened on the edge of
the windowsill. He shook his head repeatedly, as if in denial.

The Land-Rover, however, remained in his sight, parked perhaps a hundred yards from the Depot's boundary wall. He had no idea when it had arrived. There was no one near it. He could not read the license plate, of course, but he knew it was the one he had been forced to abandon in Pokhara. *Knew* it!

He heard his own hard breathing. Both his arms were quivering now as his weight slumped on them and fear grew. The vehicle was a message, a signal. They were waiting for him.

He heard the door close softly, but the noise echoed in a magnified, disturbing way, as if his head was a long, dark corridor. He turned onto his back. The stars through the open window remained on his retinae like torches in the distance. The noise of the door slurred then faded, and his head seemed to coalesce again, narrowing from the width of the pillow, sharpening its focus. Ellis had left the room, he did not have long. He must do something . . .

He tried to dampen his mouth and throat by sucking at his cheeks. The awful stale, poisonous taste remained. He struggled to sit up in bed. His head seemed to spill forward, as if his body had tripped over something. His vision of the darkened room came and went. He groaned, then stifled the betraying noise. Nausea lurched and threatened. He gagged, clamping his hand over his mouth. His arm was sore, and he rubbed it, perfectly aware of the way his sleeve was neatly rolled back, of the tiny pinpricks that were as evident as the gooseflesh and hairs on his forearm. His thoughts were no longer split. He knew they had used drugs and that he must have answered many of their questions. People always did. The questions rumbled along the horizon of his mind even now, like a distant storm that had all but spent itself. *How many ELINT vessels . . . where . . . when was that? How many of them not fully armed . . . operational at one time . . . why not Cuba?* Endless questions . . .

They rumbled on, growing more distant, convincing him he had all but recovered from the effects of the drugs. He should have slept . . . what had kept him awake, made him sit up? His own questions hurt, like lightning flashing from the distant storm of the interrogation. There was a pain behind his eyes.

Sitting up in bed, just breathing in the cool, pine-scented air, just listening for Ellis's return, seemed a vast and wearying effort. He rubbed his face. That seemed to tire him, too, to drag at the flesh like putty and remold it to uncomfortable shapes.

He held his head, keeping his thoughts together. What conviction had wakened him and kept him secretly awake for the last— hour? What was his conviction? Slowly, it grew in brightness.

He would never see Anna-Lise and the children again.

He nodded in time to its rhythm, utterly convinced. He didn't understand how he knew, but he did know. That was what was important, the fact that he had been granted the knowledge in time to do something about it. Gratitude was a sweat breaking out all over his torso, his forehead and throat, and instantly cooling, so that it refreshed and wearied in the same moment. He would never see them again. The British and the Americans would not give him back? There seemed a flaw in that. They would kill him, then? He shivered, but dismissed that idea, too. They *would* give him back for his mother to punish him? He nodded vigorously, ignoring the flashing pain the movement caused. *That* was what they intended. Aubrey had spoken with his mother, his mother had spoken to the Americans in Washington . . . it was all arranged. When he was returned, his mother would keep them away from him . . .

He bit his hand to stifle the cry. Fear had wakened him, rushing through him like yet another drug. In an instant, he had seen the window and the stars, the guard, the outlines of the room contoured and shadowed by the single table lamp—and understood that he was to be punished. Understood that Brigitte had already locked Anna-Lise and the children away from him and would keep them apart from him.

His thoughts were cloudier now, though. Under the door, the clean strip of light. At the window, the stars, as big as if daubed by a painter. The cool air flowing into the room. The fear gripping him icily, making his whole body shiver, making his eyes and nose leak. They would send him back to his mother . . . they *would* . . .

Kurt began to snivel, wiping furiously at his nose and eyes, wiping the tears and mucus savagely on the bedclothes. Nausea lurched again in his stomach, his bowels felt loose. The window yawned like a mouth, enlarging and diminishing as if speaking. Yawning . . . he yawned, then sniffed loudly. Then listened. No footsteps, not yet. There would be more questions from his mother, she would look at the pinpricks on his arm just as she used to inspect his shirts, his underwear to see if he had been with girls. Then she would know he had blabbed, answered the questions still rumbling on his horizon. Anna-Lise and the children would be confiscated like pocket money, as if he had wet the bed.

The window gaped wide. The big stars. They would send him back to her.

He had given away the barbarians' secrets. To the Americans. He *must* get away. The gaping window . . .

He shuffled out of bed, rocking to and fro like a drunk when he stood up. Cramps gripped his stomach and he doubled over, clutching his belly and groin. He shuffled to the window, still bent double, and leaned out. The air caressed him like a hand smoothing his hot, damp forehead. His mind lurched through the window, but he caught his scattered thoughts and drew them back behind his temples. Yes, get away . . . somewhere, anywhere . . . prevent them sending him back to *her!* Groggily, he stepped over the sill onto the narrow stone balcony, gripping its wrought iron to prevent himself toppling outward. His head reeled, his thoughts flying away from him like water violently shaken from a dog's coat.

He looked to his left. A thick, dark drainpipe, clamped to the wall. Dizzily, he looked down. His room was on the second floor. He could see the cobbles of the villa's courtyard. He looked down at his feet. Socks, but no shoes. Shoes might hamper him . . . mightn't they? A fever of indecision shook him. *Should he put on his shoes, for God's sake?*

Anna-Lise and the children . . . there was no time to waste, he must get away, gain time to think, to decide, to make things turn out as he wanted . . .

His head was clear now. The conviction burned in the center of his mind. He reached for the drainpipe and gripped its cool iron. Tugged at it. Firm. Fifteen feet, twenty? He swung his legs over the balcony, sitting on the railing for a moment so that there was a cold strip arching across his buttocks, then he reached out once more, breathing in deeply, gripping the drainpipe with both hands, shuffling his bottom ready to swing outward—

—light in the room, a yell like one of pain, a shouted profanity . . . someone crossing the room . . .

Kurt clung to the drainpipe and began to descend as Ellis's bulk reached over the balcony to grab at him. The man was shouting at him, yelling like a madman, his face distorted.

Aubrey sat upright in his chair, blinking, the shouts from the room along the corridor urgent, fraught with panic. He rubbed

his eyes, stood up to stumble against the book he had dropped
when he fell asleep, clutched his dressing gown around him,
shuffled his feet into the loosened slippers, and hurried . . . Ellis's
voice—*Kurt!*

He opened the door. It was like turning up the volume of a
radio. Ellis's shouts were louder, more desperate. *Come back,
you little fucker!*

He blundered against Shelley in pajamas, Roth still dressed,
in the suddenly narrow corridor full of dazed and struggling
people, but he was first through the door of the room in which
Ellis was guarding—

—window. Ellis's bulk leaning—no, stepping over the balcony, arms grabbing at something. The bed was empty. He staggered forward, thrust to the window by Roth or someone else
trying to get past him. He heard himself cry out, but had no
idea of his words, simply that they were urgent and desperate.

Then he heard someone screaming, over and over, a single
word.

"No, no, no, no, no, no, no!" He recognized Kurt's voice as
he stumbled over the windowsill and leaned heavily on the iron
railing of the balcony. "No, no, no, no!" Then: "Leave me alone,
leave me alone!"

Aubrey heard himself cry out: "No!" Just once.

People moved with undersea slowness in the courtyard.
Lights glared out from windows and flung-open doors. Kurt
stared at him like a baffled, trapped animal. He was screaming
at the top of his voice. He loosened his grip, as if to beat at a
cloud of insects around his face, and fell gradually, almost balle-
tically outward, turning over slowly like a high-diver.

"No!"

Kurt struck the cobbles of the courtyard headfirst. His body
assumed a stiff, unreal pose, his neck askew, his head broken
and leaking. He twitched once.

Someone reached the body, knelt, looked up and confirmed
that it was a body.

"No . . ."

Aubrey was icily cold.

"Dear Christ Almighty, what a screw-up!" Roth, at his side
and leaning out like a cheering spectator whose team has scored.

Aubrey felt sick, staring down at Kurt's unmoving form on
the cobbles. Surrounded by four or five people. He felt Brigitte's

shock and grief as a physical pain, a stitch in his side as if he had run a long way without pause. Felt her rage, and power. "No . . ." he breathed slowly. "No . . ."

He felt it welling up inside him, inflating like an obscene balloon, the unreasoning, hot anger, this violence he so detested and which belonged to his father. Kenneth had always described Richard Gardiner as the *most dangerous man I have ever known* . . . He loathed it in himself, even as its growth excited him: a puberty of rage. But Timothy Gardiner did not feel foolish or mocked any longer, despite the sarcasm of the Mess at breakfast, despite the evocations of the Disbandment Dinner and its aftermath his fellow officers had encouraged.

The camera was slippery with anxious, angry perspiration in his hands as he sat at the café table, his features in the shadow of the bright umbrella. The East German Embassy was across the slow, crowded street. Everywhere, the bloodlike badges of the *tika* on every forehead, even those pale ones of some of Kathmandu's Western residents. The river Bagmati's scent was muted by the lack of heat in the day. Occasionally, an almost-fresh breeze blew off the brick-brown water. The dying King in his Palace to the north settled on the street like heavy clouds.

The town climbed and slid and humped like colored, frozen waves. Across the river, Patan of the Golden Roofs gleamed like untidily piled precious metal in the sun. His anger isolated him, robbing the scene of the affection in which he habitually held it. He felt cold.

Eventually, one of the two surviving Germans would emerge from the Embassy. Of that, he was convinced. He had arranged his lenses on the white tablecloth beside him like a black condiment set. When he saw either or both of them, he would photograph, follow . . . and prove they were not diplomats but intelligence agents; killers, protecting something important. Kenneth would know what to do . . . their faces must be on file somewhere in SIS.

Tension jumped like pinpricks in his arms.

Left the bloody Land-Rover outside and forgot all about it? Must have been bloody pissed, Gardiner . . . ha, ha, ha . . . Wouldn't you be, getting a letter from MoD like his?

Their mockery hardly impinged. Even the letter seemed in abeyance, in a sort of limbo, just like the horrors of the Disbandment Dinner, amid the handing over of the Colours to the Nepalese army's C-in-C, witnessed by Embassy types and MoD visitors. His drunken outburst, the attempt to remove him, his shouted insults, his striking that pompous fart of a Major . . .

Little of it seemed real, none of it important, not as—

—one of them, the older of the two, came down the Embassy's steps into Tripureswar Marg, lighting a cigarette, putting on dark glasses. Gardiner raised his camera, pretending to wave it at buildings and passing saris, then refining the focus of the telephoto lens on the German's profile, moving the stiffly held camera as the German began walking away from him. This was the one who had called out mockingly to distract him while the other had slipped behind him . . . this was the one who had *ordered* him killed!

He was gripping the camera and lens too tightly. He squeezed off exposure after exposure, the motor winding on loudly. Brunei, Belize, Goose Green . . . He'd glimpsed this other self in all those places, but never so fully before.

He slapped money quickly on the table and stood up, gathering the other lenses into his zippered bag, slinging that by its strap from his shoulder. The camera dangled from his neck. He began to follow the East German, on the opposite side of Tripureswar Marg, weaving through slow crowds, smelling old blood occasionally from recent sacrifices. The German strolled unconcernedly fifty yards ahead.

He bent his head to attend fastidiously to the zipping of the camera bag. When he looked up again, a venerable truck loaded with vegetables spurted rolling blue smoke across the wide street, and when it cleared, the German's safari jacket had vanished.

Panic. He crossed the street in a ragged, dodging run. Café tables and chairs seemed to litter the pavement like flotsam. Bullocks and trucks and buses choked the thoroughfare. He jostled saris and black coats, white shirts, pushing through their restraint. One corner, then another, shop windows, the sudden steps of temple or ministry. He was only fifty yards ahead, he must have turned, must have entered . . . must—

—safari jacket, pushing through a crowded sidestreet. Gardiner turned into the narrow street, the German ahead of him, taller than the crowds moving as slowly as lava, still unaware of him. Relief was chilly and breathless in his chest.

As he pushed as gently through the crowds as he could, he felt aggression isolate him. Only he and the German were real.

Garuda in stone devoured a snake at the door of a narrow temple. A stone Buddha in a niche in a wall, pressing itself glumly on his awareness. A mural of Bhairav, many-armed, a stone carving of Shiva with a huge phallus.

The German turned into a wider street. Gardiner, still keeping fifty yards behind him, moved more easily. Faces and eyes stared out at him from shrines and reliefs and murals. Shiva and Parvati engaged in sexual congress, the god wearing his necklace of snakes, the goddess arousing him. Ganesh the elephant god. Vishnu the preserver; stone lions and goldwork. The place became phantasmagorical as his urgency thrust him on. The smell of blood and incense heavy in the air, mingling with petrol fumes and the smells from fast-food stalls.

Suddenly, he was no more than twenty yards from the German, his attention distracted by a saffron-robed priest, splashed against the street's garish light and color like a mark of disapprobation. He stepped into the shadow of a shop's awning, ignoring the shopkeeper's attempts to interest him in trinkets. The priest passed him, shaven-headed, intently distracted, the *tika* daubed on his forehead. Gardiner felt breathing difficult, the street hot at midmorning. *A very English Buddhist, perhaps only a part-timer . . .* Aubrey had said that of him in gentle, affectionate mockery. *Something to go in for, like stamp collecting or modeling, on rainy days and Sundays . . .*

A small, rather ugly stone image of the Gautama Buddha in a niche beside the shop's cluttered window. He felt disorientated. The saffron robes crossed in front of an old Mercedes. What was he doing, pursuing this German who had wanted him killed, somehow intent upon aggression rather than self-preservation? He had a vision of himself which he wished to reject. He rubbed his forehead. The German had seated himself at a café table with a Chinese . . . the Chinese from Pokhara. He pressed back under the awning's inky shadow, though neither man was looking in his direction. He felt cold, shivery. The priest passed out of his thoughts, the reliefs and paintings and statues along the street, the spikes of temples and shrines seemed to lose a dimension, become no more than a backcloth. He *did* recognize the Chinese, even out of uniform. It was the officer on the far side of the New Territories' wire in Hong Kong, receiving back the illegal immigrants. It *was* him!

He saw now they were seated at adjacent tables, not at the same one. The Chinese was reading, the German looking about him. He raised the camera to his eye, and the faces jumped into close-up. Lips moved. They were talking to each other while pretending no connection existed between them. Automatically, he began taking picture after picture. The priest vanished, the place was no more than a tourists' backcloth, the smells diminished. He felt himself narrowed and determined. Each depression of the button, each whir of the motor was aggressive, like a series of aimed blows. Both men together . . .

The shopkeeper ignored him now. He leaned against the curves of a small stone Buddha beside the shop window. His elbow rested for steadiness in one of the Buddha's open hands, his weight against the statue's crossed legs and lap. The statue's face stared with the essential abstraction and concern out into the sunlight. An old Mercedes drew alongside him at the pavement's edge. The camera continued to click and whir. The German seated at the table turned his head toward the camera—and smiled. The doors of the Mercedes slammed. The enlarged, close-up head nodded in the viewfinder.

He glanced to his left, toward the Mercedes, and recognized the three men as white, European, and one of them as the other German from Pokhara. Each face was alert with purpose. Gardiner looked wildly back toward the café tables, and realized he had become an actor in a drama, the two seated men watching him intently. The stone of the Buddha was hard against his arm and side as if it, too, wished to restrain him.

It was a trap. They'd led him here, now they'd surround him and simply remove him like a package collected from the shop. The three white, intent, competent faces were very real against the muted, distant backcloth of the street.

4

One Bound for Awakening

As they came for him across the dusty, light-filled gap between the shop and the Mercedes, he vividly remembered the one he had wounded the previous night. He heard the muffled noise of the pistol in the German's waistband, felt the burning of the detonation against his back and buttocks, heard the high scream from the man strangling him. His whole frame began to shake as he glanced around wildly. A garish parrot screamed in a wicker cage hanging from the shop's awning. He could hear its claws shuffling on its perch. Pale eyes and intent white faces closed on him.

He staggered slightly, off-balance. The nearest German grabbed for him, making as if to encircle his shoulders in recognition of an acquaintance, grinning. He stumbled back into the quickly inky shadows of the shop, blundering against one, then a second customer. The parrot continued screaming as if attacked. The Germans thrust through the open doorway. Gardiner held the camera against his chest like a talisman. The shop's contours were heaped and folded like a landscape with customers, staff, bales of silk, fruit, gewgaws. He moved behind a row of freestanding shelving ranked with tins. Curries, vegetables, canned fruit, meat. His eyes and his whirling brain could not avoid the ceaseless inventory. He was still facing the doorway and the glaring light. The East German he had followed into this trap appeared as a dark shadow, seeming to shoo away the Chinese beside him. The Chinese nodded once and vanished.

Then he followed the others into the shop, amused at the darting of Gardiner's eyes, the indecision that squirmed in his frame.

Panic grew, pushing him like a crowd toward the Germans, who seemed lulled by their numbers and the dimensions of the narrow shop. One fingered colorful silk, another bent to look at finches in a cage. The senior German folded his arms across the breast of his safari jacket, comfortably satisfied. Two of them closed the gap between himself and them slowly, casually. Canned tomatoes, curry powder—panic. He blundered against a customer and saw the small, slim woman wince with pain. Moved behind an assistant with a check overall over her sari, and pink rubber gloves holding a dull-eyed fish, its scales decorating the gloves. Inventory . . . his mind was uncontrolled. He was unable to decide, to *think.* The counter of the shop jabbed against the skin on his back, sensitive from the pistol's explosion.

Slight alarm, a gesture from the German in the doorway. Quicker movement . . . he could not do anything but watch them. He slid along the counter, slid through its opening, heard the shopkeeper begin to protest in a puzzled tone . . . heard the German closing on him call his name.

"Timothy! Fancy seeing you here, old boy!" Grinning again, reaching for him. His name, they *knew his name!*

"It's Timothy!" another of them called out, as if repeating the charm that would hold him until they could lay hands on him.

He swung the camera, catching the German across the face with the telephoto lens, opening the skin over his cheek. It released him, and he turned and bolted down the narrow corridor, pursued by the shopkeeper's yell and the pounding feet of one of the Germans.

He passed through a jumbled back room where two old women sat wrapped in gaudy cloth, then there was a smell of urine and the blinding light in a cramped courtyard. A severed goat's head in a fly-covered, dried red stain revolted him, thrust him across the dusty, glaring yard and into a narrow, twisting alleyway that smelt of ordure and rubbish and sacrifice. There was shouting behind him.

Both ends of the alleyway were blind to him. A thin dog was snuffling rubbish, there was the muted noise of traffic from somewhere. Yet he seemed cut off, aware only of the dog dragging a bone, the muffled cursing of the injured German and the quick, decisive orders of their leader. He looked wildly about him, saw the first of them emerge from the courtyard, and began running.

The dog skittered away like something kicked aside as it saw him coming.

The alley's first sinuous twist took him out of sight of them. Glimpses of courtyards, rubbish stacked or tumbled, narrow dark doorways, glazed, drugged eyes. He slipped into a slitlike passageway between two rows of tall, narrow, grubby dwellings. It was barely wider than his shoulders. His arms scraped and banged as he hurried. He felt trapped, but not afraid. Then another alley, slightly wider, instinct as much as knowledge guiding him.

The glimpse of young girls at a window. Heavy makeup on the experienced, smirking faces of almost-children. Loud, coarse cries, as if they were cheering on his pursuers, expecting blood. The sweet smell of incense and heavy perfumes and bedlinen.

Another alleyway. He moved quickly, hardly out of breath. He was heading north with the vigorous twists of a flying insect. He sensed they had fallen behind, were beginning to have to ask for sightings.

They could have killed him many times . . .

He was halted by the thought, as if he had turned into a blind alley. His breathing at once became harsh, as he leaned against a flaking wall. Windows above, a narrow corridor where a bullock roamed, the noise of singing and bells. He realized he was where he had intended, near Freak Street—Simon's street, where he and the other hippies and addicts and seekers-after-something had hung out. It seemed that Simon had brought him here again. They could have killed him, he was an easy target . . .

Then they wanted answers . . .

He looked back down the alley, where upper stories seemed to lean toward each other to form an avenue, dim and odorous. The Germans were not in sight. The street was empty except for the bullock and three pecking automatons that were dusty chickens. He had to get to the Embassy, and get whoever was Intelligence there to talk to London and to Aubrey . . . who would understand, would know what to do.

Aubrey. He banged the flaking wall of the noisomely smelling house with his fist, grinning as if he had won a race. His head filled with images of Venice, of quiet *campos* and *calles,* he a smaller and younger self walking beside Simon, the two of them tugged along by Aubrey's dry, arid little sermons on architecture and Venetian history. His imagination filled with recollection and satisfaction. Still no one in the street. He turned and jogged easily along its narrow, winding length until it opened into the Basantapur Square.

Rickshaws, trinket sellers, small groups of loiterers. Somber sobriety after all the other images of the town. He remembered the imminence of the King's death. It seemed the whole square contemplated it. Swords, knives, bangles, necklaces, and tourists to buy them.

The portraits of the King were everywhere, many of them wreathed with the various colored ribbons of illness, death and the warding-off of misfortune. No sign of the Germans. He crossed Basantapur Square toward Ganga Path and then Durbar Square. A saffron-robed priest, a statue of the Buddha, garish, silently screaming faces on temple walls. The British Embassy was more than a mile away, on Lainchaur with the other embassies and consulates.

And they knew that as well as he did! He had to hurry. A rickshaw passed him, empty. He all but hailed it in his new urgency, then lowered his arm. Where New Road met Kanti Path, the main bus routes coincided. He would catch the bus.

He felt vulnerable now, a man with urgent news who might be waylaid. He looked back across Basantapur Square from the shadow of an awning. Birds trilled and protested in the shop's interior. A dog snuffled near him. One of the Germans emerged from the alleyway into the sunlit square. His features were urgent, alert. Gardiner slipped across the shop's window and doorway, then into a narrow, crowded street of shops. As he turned the corner, he began to hurry. There had been only one of them. Where were the others? Already at the Embassy?

She was aware of herself in the morning crowds as a dull, plain, old woman whose fur coat was somehow too expensive for her face and frizzy hair beneath her fur hat. She was too short, too dumpy for the coat. The morning sun behind her had lit the Brandenburg Gate, revealing the blankness of the Wall through its Doric columns. Her driver had eased the official limousine along the crowded pavements. The evident identification of the black Mercedes with herself was what made people turn, or pause, then walk on.

The Bebelplatz was crowded with students and traffic. The eighteenth century seemed to threaten from the massiveness of the university, the library, and, ahead of her, the Cathedral of St. Hedwig. West German television trucks stood outside its main doors like a line of taxis. With Porsches and BMWs and Audis and foreign cars. The cold made her head ache cleanly, emptily. *Topi* was mere stray wisps, like her hair beneath the hat. The remainder of what Moscow Center needed had been transmitted late in the night. Kurt had then come rushing back into her head like air filling a sudden vacuum, implosively. Kurt and the report from Gerd Brandis, in Kathmandu, concerning the British officer who had had Gerd's people under surveillance—had even seen Lin. Photographs, the wounding and death of one of her people, elusiveness . . . how dangerous was this man Gardiner? *Who* was he . . . and why did she feel a tinge of familiarity about his name, his Gurkha connection? She had ordered the man discreetly taken, quickly interrogated, then disposed of. Rogue, Gerd said. Unpopular, about to return to face disciplinary action in London . . .

. . . she could not afford to consider Gardiner's aroused interest as accidental. She must be certain.

The cheapness of her son's betrayal pricked at her, as if the looming, domed cathedral provoked his image and that of a sobbing, weak, pathetic Anna-Lise—in Brigitte's flat, and discreetly guarded—dribbling out the whole story.

A long West Berlin bus arrived, followed by a moving van. At once, like street peddlers, people and their wares debouched. The cased bases and cellos seemed magical in their surprise. Overcoated musicians . . .

She was almost on the point of asking a technician unloading silver metal boxes from a station wagon when she remembered. The maestro from the other side of the Wall and his tame orchestra! A television program recording in the cathedral, some cultural gesture. She could not recall what it was they were to record. Beethoven? She moved closer, drawn like a child to a shopwindow.

Anna-Lise sobbing, her son *planning* his defection, dazzled by the toys of the West . . . and perhaps the *importance* his defection would grant him, the *independence* . . . ?

The admission seemed wrenched from somewhere at the back of her mind, and it chilled her more than the morning. Three Mercedes limousines drew up twenty yards from her. She recognized people from the Ministry of Culture. Then she recognized the maestro. White-haired, sleek still with wealth but moving slowly, awkwardly, out of the car. Fuss, greetings, respect amounting to awe. She felt it herself even as she began to mock.

Karajan. He laboriously climbed the steps to the great west doors. Brigitte seemed drawn after him and his entourage. Security men recognized her immediately and saluted. Older men nodded, she smiled at one of them. She felt as if she were sneaking into a cinema as a girl, without paying for admission. And realized she was trying to escape images of her son in the anticipation of watching Karajan rehearse.

Rehearsal, yes . . . someone informed her when she asked. *Recording this afternoon . . . of course, Comrade General, I'll tell your driver to park.*

She thrust her gloved hands deeper into the coat's pockets and climbed the steps. The crowd which had gathered was now slowly dispersing. Mostly young, mostly students. The security people on the doors saluted crisply. Mostly young . . . *Kurt!* She paused at an almost coronary pain, stumbling on the top step, angrily waving away proffered support. *Kurt,* deserting her.

She held the rough, worn edge of one of the west doors. She felt an unusual reluctance. Memories of passing the place many times as a very young girl, with her father. Uniformed officers, jackbootedly glamorous, with gilded wives and more-gilded whores, ascending these same steps. The sounds of music from within. When Berlin was divided not by politics but race. She tossed her head. Her breathing had calmed.

She sat down on a straight-backed, hard chair, far back down the aisle. Karajan had removed his overcoat but not his flamboyant white scarf. Orchestra and chorus hurried. Soloists in denim and sweaters. She remembered now it was Beethoven's final symphony, and sighed with anticipation. She briefly recollected the young, narrow, dark features of the English army officer who concerned Gerd Brandis—then dismissed them.

A final settling. The gruff bark of Karajan's instructions. *Last movement . . . we begin at bar nine, Presto, baritone's recitative . . . this was poor yesterday . . .* Brigitte settled herself, wrapping her coat about her legs. The cathedral seemed colder than the square outside. Coughing, tuning, silence. She rubbed her forehead, then the gesture became a gentler stroking movement. In tempo.

No, no, no . . . dolce—it reads dolce in my score . . . and once more, with greater impact . . . ma divoto, ma divoto! You are not singing the school song!

The choir floated their voices in the great nave. Brigitte allowed herself to be immersed in the sound . . . she opened her eyes angrily, as if startled from a magical dream, at the deferential yet urgent touch on the sleeve of her coat.

It was her driver.

"Yes?" she snapped.

He bent to her ear and whispered. Then retreated as if from a burst gas main. She felt her cheeks draw in, and her heart seemed hollow. It was as if her whole frame collapsed inward, unable to support its own mass now that there was only emptiness. Her grief shuddered through her like a malarial fever. She could not believe the truth of it, yet there seemed no energy, no voice, to protest its falseness. Kurt was dead—a car accident . . . his body, *body*—now in the consulate in Florence. Kurt . . . It was an accident that seemed to have happened to her, as if she had somehow been traveling forward with the music's energy and was now halted by collision with *this* . . .

She knew her body, lolling in the hard seat, must look as doll-like and snapped as his must . . . She was in physical agony. *More joy, this is a hymn to* joy!

"No!" she cried out, just once, before she felt her driver dragging at her sleeve again, clutching her against his side, making her walk. She saw only her own uncertain feet on the flagstones, and then the descending steps. The music had vanished.

"You're little more—and I'm sorry to say this to you, Gardiner—little more than a troublemaker." The Third Secretary smiled like a cat. "Most of the trouble you make is for yourself, I admit . . . but now you want to involve me, Aubrey—HMG. No go, I'm afraid." He continually looked at his watch, as if it were a polished mirror of his evident lack of interest.

"For Christ's sake, will you listen to what I'm saying!" Gardiner shouted, angry with himself for his loss of temper. He felt unreasonably out of control. People like Middleton had always angered him, but now he seemed goaded into damaging his own arguments. "They tried—very seriously—to kill me, Middleton . . ." Middleton's raised eyebrow was a cattle prod. "For Christ's sake!" Gardiner exploded, banging the desk between them with his fist, his angry movement making the legs of his chair scrape on the polished wooden floor.

"Calm down, Gardiner—you're like a bloody madman." Middleton rubbed his hands through his thick, dark hair. He might even have suppressed the beginnings of a yawn. Then he tapped the buff file in front of him with a pedagogue's insistent forefinger. "Your travel warrants are in here. I was going to ask you to call by for them. Your movement order, your *appointment* at MoD—all here." Middleton smiled at his returned authority. "You don't seem to have calmed down one little bit since that fiasco at the Disbandment Dinner. Do you think you're doing yourself any good?" It was a parental tone, despite the meager years between them in age.

"So, you're not interested, then?" he snapped in a surly tone, staring at the file on the desk.

Middleton shrugged, the irritation plain for a moment on his smooth, suntanned face. Then he said, "Look, I have no idea—neither do you—what those East Germans are up to . . . but it doesn't matter, does it?"

"What doesn't? That they tried to *kill* me?"

The disbelief was evident on Middleton's full lips, in the line of his jaw.

"I don't know what they did or didn't try to do. And I suspect you're not too clear, either—"

"I was there!"

"Sober?" Again, the raised left eyebrow, the small contemptuous smile. As if Gardiner had forged a parent's signature acknowledging receipt of a bad school report. Gardiner ground his teeth and pressed his fists into his thighs.

"Fuck off," he growled.

"I was wishing you the same, old man." Middleton sighed. "Look, I know it must be hard for you—"

"Bollocks," Gardiner interrupted sulkily.

"—but you have to wake up to reality. HMG is severing its long connection with the Kingdom of Nepal—Gurkhas and all. We *all* know that. Everyone's going to be moving in here from now on, *including* the East Germans. They want a few of the construction jobs, the plums, before the whole place becomes a Chinese colony." Middleton smiled. "Just think of it as another Hong Kong, without a treaty. That's what's on the cards. The Chinks will be controlling things here in five years' time, and the Russians and the East Germans won't matter a toss then . . . oh yes, the Chinks will keep a friendly eye on the place for us." Again, Middleton smiled. "And *that* will suit HMG very nicely indeed!"

"Christ," Gardiner breathed through clenched teeth, tossing his head cynically but not in surprise.

Middleton looked at his watch. The flags above the Palace

were limp in the windless noon, but not yet at half-mast. The haze hung like a new sobriety over the buildings, the whole city. Even the Himalayas.

"I—have to be in attendance at a cocktail—some kind of reception, old man. Will you excuse me?"

"What—?" Now his tone was one of disbelief. "You think I had a brawl with some Krauts because I was pissed in a bar? Is that *it?*"

Middleton stood up, undeterred. "I'm sorry, Gardiner, I can't help, I'm afraid—"

"Then let me talk to Aubrey!"

Middleton shook his head. "You're not authorized to use Signals—I'm sorry. Talk to him in London . . . though from what I hear your former guardian is a busted flush." A faint, indulgent smirk.

"What?"

"Not in favor, I'm afraid. Definitely on the substitutes' bench these days."

"Let me talk to him!"

"Do it in your own time!" Middleton snapped back, his features darkening. He picked up the file and thrust it toward Gardiner. "You're to take *this* back with you. Our report on the Disbandment fiasco. Your tickets are in there, too. Now, if you'll excuse me?"

Gardiner stared through the window, as if the scene were no longer hazy. Then he said, sheepishly, looking down at the file he had accepted: "Can you—can I leave by the rear entrance?"

Middleton burst into a braying laugh. "Dear God, Gardiner, you're in a worse way than I thought! I thought *we* were the cloak-and-dagger people, not the army!" He continued laughing at Gardiner as he ushered him to the door. Then, mockingly, he put a finger to his lips as he eased open the door. "Quietly, then, old man . . . if you're certain they're really out there, waiting to give you a good hiding." And laughed once more.

Gardiner flinched at the noise, clutching the file and his camera to his chest, preceding Middleton down the corridor.

"When—when's my flight out?" he asked.

"Tomorrow afternoon."

He had to survive for twenty-four hours . . .

There was a predominant sense of running away from something which was evident to Aubrey but, it appeared, to no one else.

It was in everything around him—even the oil-painted, unreal light and landscape. The safe house was being tidied by a team from Drycleaning before being deserted. He was surprised at the strength and persistence of the guilt he felt concerning Kurt's death.

He stared down at the red-tiled, domed and spired city. His arms were folded across his chest, Shelley was beside him drinking coffee in a leisurely fashion; no more than a businessman about to leave his chosen hotel to catch an early flight home. Kurt's death was more than an accident, it was a nuisance, and one which had stirred up Langley's hornets. Signals from the CIA had become gibes, mockery.

And it was his responsibility.

"My petty vengeance wasn't worth *this!*" he suddenly burst out.

"I just don't understand you!" Shelley snapped back in the tone of a son-in-law dealing with an elderly relative forced by circumstances into his home. Aubrey looked up at the younger man in surprise and disappointment. "You should be worrying about the effect this fiasco will have at home," he continued, his tone now that of the concerned wife. "Langley is making things as difficult as possible for you."

"There have been very few people in my life, very few I have ever felt close to . . . she was one of them," Aubrey murmured. Shelley's impatient snorts punctuated his phrases, but they were ignored. "I have been close to her, despite our forty years of enmity." Then Aubrey turned his gaze back to the city floating in its pellucid morning light. The distant past invested the moment. Brigitte was a teenage girl, it was 1943, she was in her school uniform and the autumn leaves were heavily scattered across the school's paths and lawns. Washington. The vivacity of the memory made Aubrey wince, then past clashed and lost with present as Roth appeared on the terrace, dictating into a tiny recorder held against his cheek. Roth. To him, the consequences would be in how many agents they lost to Brigitte's anger and on whom they could succinctly and completely lay the blame.

Himself . . .

" . . . whole business wrongly handled by London . . ." Roth paused in front of them, grinning, then continued pacing the terrace like a guard. " . . . what was learned may be valuable, but we're going to have to deal with all the shit that could now come our way just because . . ." Aubrey heard before Roth's voice became no more than a murmur. Shelley seethed silently beside him, his whole body stiff and crouched. Aubrey felt a sudden and unexpected distance between them.

He was finished now. Roth's words and Shelley's slight movement away confirmed that. Roth turned at the end of the terrace and began to trawl his condemnations back toward them.

" . . . something we should never have gotten into—small potatoes, they can't even handle this kind of thing any longer . . . there should never have been London control."

Roth made his bid for a more important posting, Shelley had begun to calculate his own version of events. Aubrey felt himself left with the truth. Drycleaning—a team of four—emerged from the French windows behind them, to report to Shelley.

" . . . the accident was staged on the lower slopes, down toward the city . . . sharp left-hand turn, the car out of control, a steep incline, car came to rest where it would be seen in daylight . . . broken neck and other injuries consistent . . . body discovered by a motorist soon after dawn, reported . . . police, then East German consulate official . . . body taken away . . ."

Roth's glowing report, Aubrey thought evilly, of the CIA's cleanup operation which had put Kurt's body into a hired car before involving car and body in a faked accident. Papers, details, cover story, all arranged.

"A telephone call—for Sir Kenneth," Ellis announced, looking shamefaced, still distressed that he had gone for a sandwich, believing Kurt to be in a drugged sleep.

Ellis held a cordless telephone receiver in his hand, jerking it in Aubrey's direction like an explosive device a trickster had left him holding.

Reluctantly, Aubrey took the receiver. "Who is it, Ellis?"

"Sir Geoffrey, sir." Ellis looked appropriately gloomy.

"Very well." His nod dismissed Ellis—and Shelley, who drifted away along the terrace like an aimless houseguest, hands in his pockets. Peter had . . . hard to admit, but Peter had his own and different priorities. Aubrey moved the switch to Talk and extended the receiver's aerial. The crackle, then strange inertness of a secure line. "Good morning, Geoffrey."

"Kenneth, is that you?" It *was* Geoffrey Longmead, GCMG, the Cabinet Secretary. No secretary, no aide, no message to be passed on. At once: "Kenneth, how the devil did this farce ever occur?"

"Geoffrey, I'm afraid it simply—"

"Simply nothing, Kenneth. The PM is furious . . . she's had the two DGs—*both* of them—in already this morning. Damage assessment and containment. She wants to know what to do, Kenneth, and I'm afraid I had to tell her we must ride out whatever consequences there might be. The Americans are *furious!*" There was little of Geoffrey's careful, mandarin drawl, his unshakable equilibrium. He was angry, prepared to blame.

"Geoffrey, I'm sorry things have turned out—"

"Kenneth! This is no longer a little hole-in-the-corner defection, it's rapidly becoming a full-blown crisis of confidence. Orrell at SIS is very cross . . . even Bill at the DS felt the PM's wrath, and he had nothing to do with it! What can you have been thinking of? Do you realize that the President called the PM on *behalf* of the CIA? Halfway through the night in Washington? The word the President used—quoting his Director, I believe—was assholes. They're calling our intelligence service *assholes,* Kenneth!"

Aubrey found himself patrolling the terrace. Shelley had gone indoors with Ellis. He and Roth were alone, both with machines clutched to their cheeks, both moving slowly as if in some intricate dance. Aubrey felt his cheeks heat because of Roth's presence. He looked away, blindly down at Florence afloat in its own light.

"Is that what really matters?" he snapped. "The opinion of a newly appointed, somewhat gung-ho Director of the CIA?"

"No. What matters is that his President is prepared to be his mouthpiece on this occasion. The defector doesn't matter. His death is unimportant. Except that the CIA firmly believes it will start what they call a shooting war—and they are blaming *you* for that!"

"Brigitte's not a fool . . ."

"Who? Oh, yes, of course . . . well, even that doesn't matter. How much cooperation can we expect from the Americans over the next months, if this is their immediate reaction? We did not need this, Kenneth, we really did not need it!"

Aubrey remained silent. Tiny smears of interference slid across the ether as he changed position. Roth was now standing watching him, hands on his hips. It was very easy to despise—and fear—the man. He represented a breed which was becoming more familiar in SIS, even the DS. Aping the CIA. He shook his head in Roth's direction. The man merely grinned, and returned a thumbs-down signal. His arrogance took the breath away! Aubrey turned his back on him.

Eventually, Longmead said: "Look, Kenneth, you're coming back this afternoon. I think we'd better talk at once. I'll be here. Try not to delay." And the connection was immediately cut.

Roth seemed to sense that the call was over even before Aubrey pressed down the aerial. He turned away and entered the villa through the French windows.

In the sunlight, Aubrey felt suddenly chilled. In memory, he clearly saw the dark, already-plain features of the girl Brigitte had been. The wooden bench, the leaves scattered on the school lawns. Her uniform, her improved English. Their shared sense of her father engaged on secret work: an atomic bomb. What came to him as strongly as the memory was the sense of personal threat Brigitte represented in the present. Her beloved only son was dead. She would hold him responsible. He had wakened a dragon.

She was surprised that her body no longer appeared stunned and numbed by her grief. Instead, she felt a rage for movement and activity. Her thoughts could settle on nothing. She had not been able to return to her flat, announce his death to Anna-Lise, give his murder form. Almost, she resented her daughter-in-law having to be told at all, resented the portion of grief she would take.

But her office constricted her. She had refused all calls, had seen no one except her secretary. Coffee heated in a pot. The room was filled with cigarette smoke. The one action she had taken, as if in anticipation of a time when her thoughts would be her own once more, was to remove Aubrey's file from her cabinet and open it on her desk. It was like a diary waiting for appointments. Aubrey . . .

Looking down from her high window, it was almost as if she could see Kurt crossing the square, dodging the traffic. A squeal of brakes, the flash of brakelights, buffeted her. She was forced away from the view. Aubrey's file was thick, almost fifty years of information. Open like an insult. She swept at it, grabbed for what remained scattered on her desk and flung it at the offending window. She cried out, wanting to trample on the sheets and photographs. Her son was the innocent victim—undoubtedly innocent—of *that man's* kidnapping, that man's scheming, his desire to hit back at her, wound her unhealably!

She cried out once more, her breathing violent. She stood over the images in monochrome, the separated sheets. And dropped onto her knees painfully, immediately gathering the papers into an untidy heap. It was as if Aubrey were escaping her, scattered like this. Pictures, pictures of him, of others, so many others and years . . .

. . . a young, dark face, an army uniform. A recent photograph, a series of photographs . . . Kathmandu. Mountains in the unfocused background. Yesterday's photographs. She stared with the attention she might have given to an image of Kurt. They had been in Aubrey's file. Had she placed them there? Why had she? No, they had been on her desk, disturbed and jumbled in her rage. Gardiner . . . Timothy Gardiner.

He *did* belong in the file! She found it difficult to breathe. The cigarette she had dropped was burning a small black hole in the carpet beside her. She ignored the smell of the smoldering nylon. Gardiner . . .

She shuffled through the file, scattering sheets impatiently. It was here, the answer to the young man's familiarity was here somewhere. Sheets rustled and creased, were thrown aside. Years and dates and operations, so many years . . . Early? The young man was *too* young! She discarded 1946, the whole of the 1950s, the '70s, too recent . . .

Where, where, *where?*

1948. Her father's death. Aubrey's responsibility—she threw the report from her, so that it sailed across the room like a wounded bird before falling. Gardiner.

Richard, not Timothy. Constant, the double. Gardiner, the rogue agent, had killed Constant, and Aubrey had helped him escape, settle in South Africa. She read the report with a feverish haste and interest. *Wolfsbane.* Aubrey had—twins, Gardiner's sons . . . Aubrey had become their legal guardian! Gardiner's wife had been callous of her sons, *Aubrey had become responsible for them!*

She raised herself from the floor, gripping the edge of her desk, her old joints creaking, snapping in the hot, dense silence of the room like stepped-on twigs. The report on the operation that had become known as *Wolfsbane* was clutched to creasing in her other hand. She was dizzy with the impossibly good fortune. *Timothy* Gardiner. She felt her feet had crossed a threshold. A loose sheet of Aubrey's file dangled on the edge of her desk like the fold of a tablecloth. On it she saw her own name, and her father's Jewish surname. 1939. She remembered looking down onto the platform at the border station at Aubrey, already balding as a young man, arguing in fluent German with a Nazi officer and Italian police. The Nazi officer still wore the detachment of a future enemy.

She wished, devoutly, that they had exposed and killed Aubrey, then.

A real son for a legal ward . . .

She picked up the telephone, then slapped it back onto its rest. Pressed her intercom switch. A swishing silence. Her secretary was waiting for her to speak. Aubrey had saved her life, become her friend, killed her father—killed her son. Of the last, there was no doubt. She would have his pretend-son killed. *Lex talionis*—an eye for an eye. Its patterned simplicity satisfied.

"Gerd Brandis in Kathmandu—at once. I want the signals routed to me here. Arrange it. *My* priority identification." She did not wait for an acknowledgment but snapped up the switch. Seek and destroy. Gerd could be relied upon to carry it out quickly and efficiently.

She drifted reluctantly to the window, after clamping her telephone to the amplifier. She lit another cigarette and stared down into the Alexanderplatz at noon. Crowds, traffic, normality. It had an anesthetizing effect. She felt a contemptible little gratitude for the respite. And as Brandis came on the line, she was aware of how high her office was above the square, how distant she was from the moving dots below.

"Gerd—the officer, Gardiner—" she began. She felt little or no time passed while their messages were scrambled, transmitted, unscrambled. Brandis interrupted her, it seemed.

" . . . embassy cocktail affair . . . Middleton, the Third Secretary, was expansive after a few drinks . . . the boy is completely on his own—"

"Gerd, listen to me! I want him eliminated. At once. Do you understand?"

Almost immediately: "Brigitte—General—did you hear what I said? There's no danger, he isn't official, not even—"

"I want him eliminated, Gerd. Do you *understand* me?"

"I think any action of that kind might prejudice—"

"Gerd, kill that man Gardiner!" she screamed at the ceiling, fists clenched.

"Very well, Comrade General—if those are your direct orders . . ."

"They are!" she snapped. Then: "Transmission ends."

"Acknowledged."

It was as if a wildcat had crept out of her mind and now stretched on the carpet. A secret, cunning, dangerous cat. He had described things in that way, once. *We must be secret like cats,* while the Italians and the Germans searched for her and her father and Aubrey struggled to save them, two German Jews . . .

Now, the cat was hers, and it would kill Aubrey by killing the only person who had ever been like a son to him.

"Kurt!" she cried, shivering.

The guest house was in Pie Alley, and its best room had cost him fifteen rupees; less than a dollar. The odor from the toilet in the noisome courtyard permeated the whole place. Om Lodge was owned by an ex-Gurkha and his wife, a Gurung from his own regiment. Gardiner had been welcomed, then had asked for secrecy and become merely accepted. The burden of an aged relative, lodged from a sense of duty.

Gardiner squatted cross-legged on the rush matting, staring at the slowly waving, hypnotic flame of a butter lamp in its small bowl. He sought calm and experienced no more than exhaustion, a restless, twitchy weariness. They had been watching the British Embassy by the time he left, they had been outside the Depot waiting for him. He knew they were looking for him now and that they would be waiting for him at the airport the following day.

He had disappeared in the unpaved, untidy street that hid itself behind the Temple of Ganesh in Durbar Square before it straggled and slouched down toward the river. Its smell was even more foul than that of the river, its noise constant and bellowing, its dogs thin. Then he had remembered the Gurkha and his shabby, two-story guest house whose clientele consisted entirely of hikers and students and dropouts, and he had gone to earth, knowing as he did so that it was nothing more than a temporary refuge. He was trapped in Kathmandu. They would be waiting at the airport for him. *And no one would listen to him—!*

He had attempted meditation, but the mantras would not come. He needed *samatha,* the necessary calm, bodily and mental, but he could not purify his thoughts of distractions and hindrances. The faces of the East Germans intruded, enlarging and diminishing in the room's shadows like images on a blowing curtain. Aubrey, too, intruded, a somehow more plausible destina-

tion than Buddhist meditation. Mice or rats scratched behind
the walls and in the overhanging eaves, the room smelled, *he*
smelled—of fear and exertion and anger. His Buddhism seemed
more than ever a flirtation with the irrational, not a search for
inner peace or a deeper self; an escape from the fixed and ordered
framework in which he had spent most of his adult years. But
the world surrounding him now was itself irrational . . .

Groaning, he stood up. The small flame of the lamp flickered,
throwing his form hugely and diffusely on the walls of the
cramped, dirty room. He rubbed at the stubble on his chin. The
camera bag lay on the bed, the sum of his possessions. The noises
of Kathmandu seemed distant. He felt more than ever divorced
from the town's familiar context.

Aubrey intruded again.

*. . . tried women, drink, even Buddhism . . . Timothy, what
is it you're looking for? I can't help you, my dear, unless you know
what you're looking for . . .*

A gentle, logical inexorability, Aubrey smiling kindly as he
spoke. A dinner somewhere with the old man who had been his
guardian, a man who had never seemed puzzled or lost. Gardiner waved his arms loosely, as if feebly grappling the room's air.
He *had* to talk to Aubrey. He looked wildly at the camera bag.
Their faces were all there. He must show them to Aubrey—

—must get out. He rubbed his arms, shivering. They knew
he was alone, without help.

The smell of cooking insinuated, making his stomach ache
with hunger. He must eat, then telephone . . . telephone, then
eat. Swiftly, he crossed to the door, snatching up the camera bag
as he passed the bed. He belched with tension, tasting the chang
beer and yak cheese he had eaten during the afternoon. His hand
closed on the door handle.

A rat scrabbled behind the cracking plaster. Someone moved
furtively in the corridor outside, slowly giving voice to a loose
floorboard. It was the slowness of the creak, the sense of carefully distributed weight, that alerted him. He released the door
handle and stepped back, staring at the door, waiting for it to
open.

Then something moved on the roof, too heavy for a bird or
even an animal. Too careful, too slow. The door handle tensed,
then moved very, very slowly, like the minute hand of a clock.

5

The Fire Sermon

Late evening, ornately decorated corridors, tall windows. Behind most of these doors were only dingy, unlit, dusty spaces, vaultlike, filled with alien bric-à-brac. There was nothing for him beyond the carved and gilded doors.

Kapustin strode with his typical rolling peasant's stride, large square hands waving, head tossing as he rehearsed his anger once again. Beside him, Babbington thought of his wife and son . . . the woman who could not disguise her hatred and contempt for him whenever he called, and the young man who was ex-Eton, ex-Guards, ex-City, *ex* . . . The Hooray Henry adopting that last grotesque mask of patriotism and denying him effusively to every Fleet Street rag that cared to listen. His wife's impotent rage at her inability to free herself from him, and his son's petty vindictiveness seemed sent to plague him now, just when he required a clear head, a certainty of optimism and direction.

"We could have initiated *Topi* any time in the next two years! Now, it's nothing but hurry, hurry!" Kapustin ranted.

Babbington looked out from the windows, as from the lower deck of some vast ocean liner that was gliding past the elaborate, alien towers of the Kremlin's cathedrals. Lamps were haloed with an early frost in the black air. Red stars glowed on pinnacles. And, across the river, where he could pick them out with painful clarity, the lights were on in the British Embassy.

Almost automatically, he murmured in reproof of Kapustin: "We'll never have a clearer field than with the King dead."

Kapustin paused in his stride. "I *know* your opinion, Andrew," he said heavily. "I'm not even disputing it." He placed a hand on Babbington's shoulder, reaching up to do so. Babbington kept the flinch from his muscles. "It doesn't make the operation any easier, or guarantee us any greater degree of success, though, does it?"

Kapustin's broad features were both angry and wryly amused. His eyes glittered with their habitual cunning. Babbington could not grant the man intelligence or vision. Animal cunning, that was it.

"It *will* work," he assured. At the same moment feeling that worm of disappointment twist in his intestine. It possessed the physical pain of an ulcer. He kept his face clear of reaction. *Son, wife, friends* . . . exchanged for . . . ? Barbarians like Kapustin.

For a long time, perhaps four or five months, he had refused the women they offered. It seemed a means of preserving the old distance between himself and the barbarians—between himself and Kapustin, most of all. But that was gone now. He accepted the whores—*clean and classy* as Kapustin described them!—just as he had accepted the flat on the Kutuzovsky Prospekt, after the hotel suite, even though the decorators were still in. Accepted the medal, too . . . *Hero of the Soviet Union.* Accepted the rank, finally . . . *Comrade General* Babbington! He had become Kapustin's deputy, his creature.

"It will work," he reiterated, staring through a tall window across the river. The Embassy seemed like a doll's house, pale-featured, a small oil-painting in the too-heavy frame of the Tainitsky and Blagoveshchenskaya Towers. The red-flagged towers and the stretch of high wall between them were indeed like those of some prison. The worm twisted once more in his stomach, making him feel nauseous.

Aubrey! Aubrey was responsible . . . Aubrey was finished. He clung to the thought as to a cherished emotion.

"Maybe," Kapustin admitted. "It would help, of course, if your friends on the Council there were a little stronger. In a year's time, they would be!"

"They'll cope," he said levelly. "They have all but a majority on the King's Council. If we include the greedy with the committed, then they are strong enough."

"They have to make the arrests *stick!*"

Kapustin was walking again, down the endless corridor lined with busts and ornaments, sofas and tables, windows and doors. Mocking Babbington with its likeness and unlikeness to country houses, the Paris Embassy, ministerial buildings in Whitehall. Marble, bronze, gold.

Babbington sighed theatrically and halted, hands on his hips, looking down at Kapustin's squatter figure, his broad-yet-closed features.

"The documents have been delivered, the accusations framed, the signatures forged, the bank accounts massaged . . . it *will* work, Dmitri, it will." He smiled in a precisely calculated way, and stroked his beard. His back was to the windows, and awareness of the wall and the river which cut him off from the Embassy diminished. "Our targets on the Council will be implicated in the civil unrest following the King's death—they will be exposed as its instigators. I give you my assurance. What more do you want, Dmitri?"

The doors opposite him were open. Into the St. George Hall. A line of columns, each supporting a statue of Victory crowned with laurel. Rich ornamentation and stuccowork. All of it dedicated to the Russian armies since the Middle Ages . . . victory . . .

Bronze chandeliers.

Babbington felt more relaxed; not at home, but at his ease. The place lost its alien patina and no longer resisted him or marked his difference.

Kapustin shrugged and slapped his shoulder once again. He tossed his head.

"An old man's caution, like a child's really. Checking countless times that the light is switched off, not walking on the border of the carpet . . ." He grinned. "I know it is going to work. But, when I've been with Nikitin, I sometimes wonder. I get too much the smell of consequences, of the stakes involved . . . come on, Andrew—a drink?"

Babbington merely nodded. He did not look at the doors or the windows as they continued along the corridor, but directly in front, as if he saw clearly ahead of him a precise goal, a destination. *Topi,* his scheme, would be successful. It possessed pattern, symmetry. It balanced massiveness with grace, planning of the most meticulous kind with the bluntness of easy and complete success. And, within it, like the essential life or vision of a painting or sculpture, it possessed the delight of damaging England. That was its beauty.

They entered narrower corridors, dimly lit, and the doubts returned and the worm twisted vaguely, as if half-asleep in his stomach. They climbed stairs. The rooms of the Terem Palace, musty with old and lost power. The Tsarina's Golden Chamber. Low vaulted roofs, like those of damp English churches, and as empty. Cold. He had disliked that part of the Kremlin where Kapustin had occupied a suite of offices ever since refusing to move out to First Directorate's plate-glass headquarters beyond the ring road. His own office he disliked, too, adjacent to Lenin's old rooms in the Senate building.

Once more, doors were open, gilding glowed in dim light, gold was everywhere; he felt calmed. Kapustin's secretaries and aides stood to attention as they entered the outer office. Gray filing cabinets, functional office furniture, a gilded, vaulted ceiling; portraits of Soviet leaders, a bust of Lenin, ikons staring gloomily across the room. Kapustin, gathering a sheaf of papers and files, gestured Babbington ahead of him into the inner office, then slammed the door. He threw the files and papers onto his desk. Lamps glowed outside. Babbington lowered himself easily into an armchair.

Kapustin fussed with an ornate cabinet modernized and lit from within. Bottles clinked. "Scotch—straight?"

"Please."

"Nikitin's really worried about the Chinks—"

"We've been over that with him."

"I suggest you don't let him hear your peculiarly English exasperation," Kapustin chuckled, pouring the whiskey, measuring the amount in the tumbler. "He's always worried about the Chinks."

"You allayed his fears, I take it?" Babbington accepted his meager Scotch with a slight nod. Sipped. "You *did?*"

"I did. I told him Deng's successors are engaged in one of their interminable power struggles, that the last thing they want right now is a foreign adventure. They'll accept the *fait accompli* we present."

"And did he believe you?"

"He did."

"Good." Babbington sighed. He would have liked to have the heavy curtains pulled across the window of lamps and stars and towers, but did not wish to ask. "They'll be cautious about foreign involvement for at least the next couple of years . . . which is why you're wrong to regret our haste in this thing. Now *is* the right time."

Kapustin sat down heavily, his age revealed. He puffed out air, as after effort. Swallowed vodka liberally. Smacked his lips, then said: "I agree. The Chinks can't be seen to be invading the country. We'll be in by invitation to restore order, a different matter altogether. I told Nikitin that."

"Good. The British, too, will ignore the existence of the secret accord they reached with the Chinese—'New Territories.' " He grinned and sipped more Scotch, grimacing at its blended acridness. "Colonel Lin, Brigitte's chum, has been *most* invaluable . . ."

"You've wanted to hurry ever since you came over. Wanted to hit back." Kapustin was smiling. "Bugger up that agreement between the Chinks and your people. I sometimes wonder whether we really want or need that place."

"We don't want the Chinese in there, at any rate. Even Gandhi doesn't want them on his northern border. And by comparison with your Afghan adventure, it's a rather cheap operation. A sound investment." Babbington finished his drink and held out his tumbler. Kapustin scowled, as if he had been begged from in the street. But reluctantly stood up, took the glass and refreshed it with a small splash of whiskey.

"Very well. You can begin the bombings tomorrow—no, make it the following day." He was at his desk again, reading a signal report. *"Field Trial* is airborne. I don't think we want a bomb at the airport while that's going on, do you?"

"Very well. Two days' time. And if the King's already dead, another three or four days should wrap up the opposition and our invitation to the party will have been issued." Babbington smacked his lips and stretched in his chair. "That sounds all right—fine, in fact."

"You think this car crash was just an accident?" Kapustin asked abruptly.

"What?"

"Brigitte's son."

"Probably. What else?"

Kapustin shrugged. "Nothing, I suppose . . . poor old girl, I wonder what it will do to her? As for the son, I never liked or trusted him. Dim and greedy. A little shit, in fact. Still, he's dead now. We'd better watch the old girl, Andrew—she needs to be up to the mark over the next two weeks."

"Agreed."

Babbington watched Kapustin studying the papers through his reading glasses, holding the pages toward the light of the desk lamp. He got up and walked to the window. Drew the heavy brocade of the curtains across the red stars, the spires and domes and the wall and the river. He felt it was like a child shutting its eyes against a threat.

I despise everything my father has done to my country . . . a traitor, pure and simple. Babbington rocked on his heels, as if a large bird had flown against the now-hidden window. *His* son . . . a pity *he* hadn't killed himself in a car accident!

He breathed quietly, deeply, calming himself once more. He would keep the newest, latest whore on for a few more days. He would go back to the flat tonight. It was all arranged. *Topi* would work. There was nothing that could be done to prevent it succeeding.

Especially Aubrey, who was in decline . . .

He ground his teeth because he wanted to be the cause of Aubrey's downfall.

The handle of the door continued to move, slowly. Gardiner stared at it, his limbs paralyzed. He experienced the slow, swelling rise of panic from his stomach to his chest, then into his head, which seemed to inflate almost to bursting. He held his hand pressed to his temples as if to constrict the swelling sensation. He moved a step toward the door, even as it began hesitantly to open. Then he turned to the window as someone scrabbled on the roof's loose tiles, pausing on the eaves before his feet came slowly into view, dangling outside the window, seeking the sill.

Only a shout would suffice to relieve the pressure of panic; only a scream. Movement, action, violent haste—*direction?* The door moved silently, almost quivering with the effort of control required to enter the room undetected. The man's torso was in the frame of the window now, some light from the street throwing his shadow hugely on one wall, then wiping it like a dark cloth over the other walls, over himself. The door was open three, four, five inches now . . .

When the man was able to hunch on the windowsill, Gardiner would be seen, standing stupidly, sacrificially, in the center of the room. The German would call out, the door would fling open wide, there would be two of them—there was a curved *kukri* in the waistband of the torso in the windowframe. They had come to kill. There were no questions he could usefully answer, he was simply to be removed.

A hand on the edge of the door, the other one's feet firmly planted on the windowsill, the torso using its arms to climb down into a squatting position, bringing the face down. He clutched the camera bag against his chest like a shield. *His legs would not move!*

Move!

He walked stiffly, unfreezing, his body shaking and breaking out wetly across chest and back. He stumbled, then banged his seemingly inadequate weight against the door. A cry, the fingers flexing and wide in a shriek of pain as they released the edge of the door. He slammed the door shut and turned to the window. One of the faces from Pokhara, gleaming in the light of the lamp—which he kicked over as he rushed at the hunched man on the windowsill who was holding on with his left hand, drawing the *kukri* from his belt with his right. Its blade flashed with familiar menace. He held the camera bag in front of him as the knife moved through the leather of the belt, almost drawn—

—and bundled as if playing rugby into the man now precariously balanced, hearing the explosion of his breath, swinging the clutched camera bag at the twisted features, at the hand drawing out the curved knife. Pushing because he was aware of the man behind him in the doorway, cursing and beginning to cross the room. There was no other way. The German was simply an obstacle, and he was pushing open a door that had something lodged behind it—heaving at it, brute strength—

—and falling. A cry from the German, his breath close to Gardiner's cheek, his arms flailing and his eyes very white and frightened. Impact and dust. Gardiner was breathless, jarred, his hand numbed by the blow of his elbow on the ground, his knee bellowing with pain, the German's face directly against his own, eyes open, whites exposed, mouth and throat desperately crying for air.

Gardiner rolled over, groaning. The bag lay beside the muddle of their bodies. His leg was twisted under him, his arm looked broken. Gardiner crawled to the gleam of the *kukri*, the dust they had raised settling on him. He coughed, scrabbling up the knife and the bag, tottering to his feet, staggering a few steps and leaning against the wall of the guest house, hearing the German at the window above cursing and beginning to climb down. He staggered into a weaving, drunken trot, then ran. Shadows enlarged and diminished around him, as if belonging to four or five pursuers. He stuck the knife awkwardly into his waistband, cutting his finger.

Narrow alleyways, twisting streets, all unfamiliar but somehow recognized, he moving as confidently and desperately as a rat in a half-known maze. He slid against an unlit, moon-paled wall, the smell of rotting vegetables and scarcely dry blood thick in his nostrils. The nosing of dogs somewhere ahead in the deepest shadow, making him flinch. His mouth was loose and wet, his chest heaved, his legs seemed determined to buckle. The smell of urine and ordure. The noise of traffic in the distance. The sound of people from open, unlit windows. A bed creaking.

He must be somewhere near the river. He could smell its sluggishly rich odor. He had a map. He must use it—find a light and look at the map. He listened. Nothing hurried in the night. He had shaken them off. Anger began to intrude. The violence of his escape did not seem amateurish, merely effective. He scuffed his boots in the dust.

His breathing had settled, and he moved away from the wall, out of the moonlight. He must talk to Aubrey. The river, and Patan of the Golden Roofs on the other bank. The valley widening once he emerged from the narrow street, so that he saw slopes, crops, trees marching away down shallow slopes. Patan heaped quietly like something unrequired until daylight. He breathed in the river's scent. Aubrey had become a reassuring presence.

He was at the confluence of the Bagmati with its tributary, the Bisnumati. Cars and trucks crossed the bridge, heading down the southbound highway the Chinese had helped build. He heard an incongruous bicycle bell somewhere. The air was cool. Villages straggled away to the west, toward Pokhara, dotted with lights. Electricity pylons marched as huge shadows against the stars. Chickens clucked amid the low cottages and shacks that had gathered like penitents near the confluence of the two rivers. He began walking, bag slung from his shoulder, *kukri* now concealed inside it, his mood one of brittle, clever confidence. With hindsight, the Germans had become incompetent, to be underrated. Aubrey was no further away than the nearest telephone.

He remembered coming to this straggling, dirty, poor part of

Kathmandu before. A dozen Gurkhas, dismissed for smuggling heroin. Three or four of them, related to one another, had settled here, unable through their disgrace to return to their villages in western Nepal. He shook aside the memory as distasteful; the men had become smugglers, petty criminals, pimps—anything crooked they could find to do. Good soldiers, they had made effective villains, eventually boasting of their forfeited pensions as feed for chickens. He admitted he had idealized them, perhaps like all his soldiers. But they had gone to the bad . . .

He found a dingy café, still open but deserted, after ten minutes' walking through the shabby, shadowy district of low huts, lean-tos and shacks. He went in. The woman came forward from the passage behind the counter. The man glanced up, his eyes admitting recognition of an officer if not of his identity, then returned his attention to his newspaper and cigarette and barley beer.

Gardiner ordered a chang beer, then smelled food; its scent wafted out of the kitchen somewhere at the rear of the café. The man watched him as he spoke Nepali, and nodded, grunting at his newspaper. He was certain Gardiner was a Queen's Gurkha Officer now, and identified him in some vague way as an opponent.

He ordered *gundruk,* vegetable soup, and buffalo steak and boiled rice. The woman agreed it was available. He asked if they had a telephone. The woman pointed to a cluster of shadows at the far end of the room, near the sign for the toilet. He made out the loop of a telephone cord, and thanked her.

He wiped the greasy receiver on his sleeve, then began dialing. Glanced at his watch. It would be—what? Six-thirty, a little later, in London. He'd try the flat first. At least Mrs. Grey would be there. His breath caught at the familiarity of the housekeeper's image. The night enlarged and became more dangerous around the dim, dusty light of the café. His eyes prickled. Mrs. Grey, thousands of miles away, Aubrey thousands of miles away . . . come on, come on. His mind began to chant the little ritual of urgency, over and over. Come on. The man watched him now with a veiled curiosity and bright, sharp eyes. A Limbu from the east of Nepal, by the cast of his features. His study of Gardiner seemed deeply suspicious. The telephone continued ringing in Aubrey's flat overlooking Regent's Park, and he felt himself hopelessly distant from the place.

To his intense disappointment Mrs. Grey answered, giving the number.

"Mrs. Grey!" he blurted. "Mrs. Grey—it's Tim! I must speak to Kenneth, urgently!"

"Mr. Timothy—where are—Sir Kenneth's not here, Timothy."

"Where is he, Mrs. Grey?" His urgency was frantic, unsettling him, as if he had just had diagnosed the real nature of an innocent-looking sore on his skin. "I *must* talk to him!"

" . . . Florence . . . back in London now. I believe he is with the Cabinet Secretary still. He called to tell me so."

"Can you—can you get a message to him—now?" His forehead felt hot, his body feverish. He was alone, alone . . .

"I—don't think I can interrupt—"

"Mrs. Grey!" he shouted. "You have to get hold of him for me! I *have* to talk to him now!" He felt just as if he were ringing from school. Mrs. Grey had answered his plaintive, cowardly little calls, even that long ago!

"Is there something wrong, Timothy?"

"Yes, yes, there is," he confirmed, taking the shortest route to her sympathies. "Yes, it's very important that I talk to him immediately. *Very* important."

There was doubt in her voice, the doubt she had often displayed to his former self, as she said: "Well, I don't think I can interrupt Sir Kenneth in the *Cabinet Office* . . ."

"Please, Mrs. Grey—you have to get a message to him now!"

He glanced across the café. The woman had placed a knife and fork at one of the small tables, and now put down the soup and a spoon. Its smell forced his hunger into the center of his awareness, into his salivating mouth. The man was intent upon his newspaper, even as he lit another cigarette. He seemed carefully unconscious of the scraps of conversation he must be able to hear.

"I—I'll try. You'd better give me your number, Timothy."

"I'm in Kathmandu . . . it's . . ." He gave the number that was almost obscured by dirt and grime. Relief seemed overgenerous, exaggerated. "Please hurry!" he added, now almost acting his earlier anxiety.

"I'll try."

"Bless you, Mrs. Grey." He put down the receiver with a clatter. Hunger obscured almost everything except the ridiculous sense of relief, of all-rightness. He crossed to the table, murmuring to the man that he was expecting a call—OK? The man merely nodded.

Gardiner ate ravenously, his appetite enlarged by tension and danger and the relief of both. He hardly raised his eyes from the soup bowl, then from the buffalo steak and the rice. Gradually, he became calmer, recovering the shallow, impervious confidence he had felt after he had escaped from the guest house.

He glanced at the telephone, to find the man using it. Irrationally, he was angry. Aubrey could not possibly telephone yet, not for some time . . . but he felt enraged by the sight of the man using his own telephone! Arguing about money, from what he could gather. A sense of excitement in the man's voice, repeated assertions of his certainty, the haggling over more money. One hand waving in emphasis, the voice little more than an intense whisper. Drugs, whores, it might be anything . . .

He returned his attention to the overcooked meat on his greasy plate, washing it down with the last of his beer.

He was relieved when the man put down the receiver and returned to his newspaper, leaning on the counter, paying him no attention. Gardiner glanced at his watch. He would wait for the call. He was safe here.

She had returned to her smoke-staled office for the same reason as she had allowed Kurt's body to remain at the undertakers until the following day . . . she could not bear to be near the painted, tidied mockery of what had once been her vain, greedy, beloved son. Anna-Lise and the children were being looked after by doctors, nurses, relatives from her side of the family. She had no wish to be anywhere near her daughter-in-law, despising her stupidity and her grief and her complicity in what Kurt had attempted.

Almost immediately, the grief came back in a wave of physical pain, unremitting. She knew she had forestalled it only with a huge effort—partly by thinking contemptuously of her son, thinking of him with a professional cynicism. She pressed her hands into her stomach, gasping for each breath; drowning. Her eyes streamed with tears, her mouth moved loosely, as if to call for help.

Eventually, it receded, slipping away like a tide down shingle, rasping like her sobs. She was able to light another cigarette, her legs were strong enough to allow her to patrol her office, and the window's evening darkness was not foreboding. It was nothing but an opening on a windy night, filled with stars. Some thin cloud was being dragged hurriedly across the moon. Traffic filled the Alexanderplatz.

Flowers had been delivered to her office and lay across the carpet in a corner of the room. Eventually, even they seemed to lessen in color and profusion, like lights no longer hurting her eyes. She began inspecting her desk, avoiding Aubrey's file where it lay half-masked by other papers. There was no message from Kathmandu.

"Who's out there?" she snapped into her intercom. She had not noticed the secretary on duty as she entered the outer office. Or the guard in the corridor as he saluted.

"Pieter, Comrade General."

"Any word from Brandis?"

"Since—which report did you last receive, Comrade—?"

"Is there a report which announces the English officer is dead?" she snapped.

She heard the papers on Pieter's desk being shuffled, then his apologetic: "There's nothing here, Comrade Gener—"

"Then tell Signals I want full voice contact with Kathmandu at once—now, whatever their priorities. Do it, Pieter!"

She flicked the switch up. Gerd Brandis had better have the answer she wanted. *Timothy Gardiner is dead, Brigitte.* That was all she wished to hear. She walked away from the desk, agitated. She drew repeatedly on her cigarette, blew the smoke out loudly, could not remain still. She had to know . . . she *must have him dead, tonight!* It made her hot, jumpy, like a nervous disorder rather than revenge. It was less than grief, but she desired it. It would not equate with what she had lost, but she would settle for it, nevertheless. *Anything* to wound him! Anything to cause *him* grief!

The intercom coughed apologetically, then Pieter said: "Comrade General, they're ready for you in Signals now."

"Thank you, Pieter."

She crossed the room and slumped heavily into her chair. The leather creaked. Her quivering hand brushed signals and papers as if smoothing a cat's fur. Reports from Washington. The deal beginning to be made. CIA counterthreats against the embassy there, the East German staff at the UN, names and addresses supplied. You hit us, we hit back. Aubrey, by implication, being offered up as a sacrificial goat. Her hand closed into a fist. She was not ready for compromise. Gardiner, at the very least, had to be eliminated before that.

She switched on the encryption unit attached to the green telephone. Picked up the receiver. Signals acknowledged her ID. It was as if she heard the wind outside knocking against the aerials on the building's roof. Within seconds, Brandis was on the satellite link, his voice flattened and unmusical after emerging from the decoding circuits of the encryption unit.

"Gerd—you haven't reported—" she snapped unreasonably, swiveling in her chair so that she clearly saw the tired, strained features of a very old woman reflected in the window; scarred and pocked with lights from the square.

"General, there is nothing to report . . . not as regards—"

"Why not?"

His voice was more distant as he replied, slightly closed, as if he were leaning over his desk, sifting through reports. Then Brandis said, almost in irritation: "Brigitte, I've got as many people as I can spare—more, even—on this wild-goose chase—"

"It is not!" She was shocked at the half-hysterical, childish outburst.

"—people who should be doing other things . . . the bombings, the marches. I'm using natives here I can't spare from the first phase of the operation!"

"Nevertheless—"

"He—gave two of my people the slip. The skill of desperation—"

"You *lost* him?"

She thrust aside an image of Gardiner, his photograph sticking out from beneath a heap of files, squinting into the sun, young and dark.

"We'll get him, General. But I can't spare any more *people!*" Strangely, it was as if Brandis were disobeying her, that the operation's priorities were those of strangers. "I *need* the locals. They can't be spared for this. Not yet, at least."

For her, she admitted, there was only the personal. Aubrey and herself. Two powerful and anonymous people acting out their spites and revenges and affections. That was the sum total of her thirty years of service, his forty and more. He had caused her son's death; she would kill the nearest thing he had ever had to a son. She saw Kurt's prettified, waxy features resting on a silk pillow in a polished box and saw the horror on the old woman's face reflected in the window.

"You must spare them," she announced. "You must find him."

"But, the operation?"

"You must find him and kill him." Implacability was easy, chiming with the rage and grief inside her. She swiveled viciously from the window, adding: "I realize what is at stake, Gerd. I do not need reminding. But this business *will* be taken care of."

There was a lengthy, crackling silence, and then she heard a strange whistling noise; a decoded sigh.

"Very well, Brigitte. I understand."

"Good. That's all, then. Find him, Gerd, find—"

"Just a second, General!"

"What is it?"

"—a report . . . what does it say, Müller? God, your handwriting! When was this?" Then he addressed her a few seconds later. "There's a report from one of our locals. We know where he is, right this minute!" Relief rather than excitement, even through the distortion of the decoding. "He's in a café, eating a meal. Down in the—"

"Go and get him," she replied, suddenly weary. "Quickly, before he vanishes again!"

She flicked off the unit and put down the receiver with a heavy, laborious use of her hands and arms. Slumped back in her chair. The business was all but over, Gardiner almost eliminated. She felt empty, but not simply because her revenge had been short-lived. There was that indifference to the operation, to *Topi*. It did not matter to her! She had been prepared, was still ready, to ruin it for the sake of the personal enmity between herself and Aubrey. She rubbed her eyes. The office was distant and unfamiliar. She was no different from Babbington, whose only motive was revenge—his on a country, hers on one man; her father's murderer, her son's murderer.

In the vacuum that occupied mind and body, she began to sense the first stirrings of a dissatisfaction. Even with the young man dead in Kathmandu, Aubrey was still alive. Gardiner did not begin to equate, begin to pay for Kurt's death.

She groaned aloud, rocked by the loss of all the unquestioned certainties, the loss of what had always seemed so important: her professional self. Thirty years . . . and she had lost her hold on it as easily as on some viscous substance. It simply wasn't *there* any longer. She rubbed her face quickly, repeatedly. A patina of age had been cleaned from a painting, revealing an empty canvas. The portrait had disappeared along with the smoke and dirt and varnish. And Aubrey was still alive, still whole . . .

"So, Geoffrey, we have, as they say, reached the bottom line. It seems appropriate, don't you think, to use an American expression? The bottom line. A life peerage, if I go quickly and quietly!" It was said of the Cabinet Secretary that asking him a direct question was the equivalent of poking a stick at a sleeping cobra. His eyes glinted behind his heavily framed spectacles. His hands seemed to take a firmer hold on the edge of his desk. "I am neither landed nor senile. I own no newspapers, manage no trade union. I simply do not qualify for the honor you wish to bestow on me, Geoffrey!" Irony was never lost on the Cabinet Secretary; broad sarcasm was tantamount to an avowed hostility.

Aubrey thrust his hands into his pockets and walked away from Longmead's desk. His anger unsettled his stomach and affected his breathing. *A life peerage*—good God in Heaven, what did they think he was?

"I'm—sorry you feel that way, Kenneth," Sir Geoffrey murmured, his voice pinched with an effort of control. "It was not the PM's intention to insult you by making the suggestion."

"Was it not?" Aubrey remarked to the wood-veneered filing cabinet in front of which he stood.

"It was not."

Aubrey remained with his back to the desk. *Who's Who* on the shelf in front of his eyes; *Debrett,* too, as if in temptation or mockery. Other international directories of the famous, Pepys and Bagehot. The usual literary furniture of the Cabinet Office. He stared up at the ceiling, oblivious of Sir Geoffrey. Ornate coving. He gazed at his feet. The edge of a faded, valuable Persian carpet. English watercolors on the walls, high bookcases, deep furniture. The mockery of the room was its very familiarity. For most of the recent past, he had inhabited rooms like this one. He had expected to continue to do so. Perhaps even in the Cabinet Office, as Chairman of JIC or some such courtier's appointment with which to end his career. But *not* a life peerage!

"Why are you all so damnably eager to be rid of me, Geoffrey?" he asked meditatively, no trace of feeling in his voice. He felt somehow cleansed by outrage. Fear and lost eminence had churned in him ever since he had left Florence. Now, there was little or nothing of either. He turned. "Why is that?"

"As you know, Kenneth, our transatlantic cousins are rather steamed up about this whole messy affair . . ."

"A sacrificial goat?"

Sir Geoffrey's eyes gleamed. "Just so."

"There's still useful work I can do!" Aubrey burst out, immediately regretting his candor.

Sir Geoffrey shrugged, then adjusted his spectacles. He leaned back in his chair, hands in his pockets now, paunch creasing his waistcoat.

"I don't know, Kenneth. Your service is settling down rather well under its new DG, as is the DS." There was a veiled malice, an evident enjoyment. "You've rendered invaluable, loyal service, of course . . . but there's your age. You couldn't expect—surely . . . ?"

Aubrey felt belittled. Breathing deeply and carefully, he confronted the harsh light thrown upon himself, upon the past months. It was without shadows. He realized, perhaps fully for the first time, with what bitterness he had always contemplated the close of his career. Amputation might be a better word for the sensations that had passed through his mind on many evenings during recent months. The light shone mercilessly, so that no corner of him seemed unilluminated.

There was a glimpse of the quizzical in Sir Geoffrey's eyes, and Aubrey once more turned his back, effecting a flourish of indifference as he did so. He thrust his hands deeper in his pockets. He *had* desired JIC, even a KCMG to supersede his KCVO, and the continuation of his uninterrupted journey, the one he had long ago set out upon.

He turned to Longmead. Sir Geoffrey was losing patience—losing it always a virtue with him—and his gaze was more than ever quizzical, even irritated. Aubrey saw, detested and then dismissed, the stick propped against his chair. He felt a sense of the old, impatient energy that had accompanied his career like a wife. In the street outside, a pair of headlights passed and swelled as the car drew to a halt.

" . . . threatening all kinds of withdrawal of intelligence sharing unless . . ." Sir Geoffrey seemed as if broadcasting the current news from Washington. And luxuriating in doing so. Aubrey recalled with a faint amusement his bullying in the witness box of a Canadian court, attempting to prevent publication of a book about the Babbington affair. His humiliation had been complete and temporary. *Twice the man now,* they said of him, intending no compliment.

"No, Geoffrey," he announced.

Longmead appeared nonplussed. And at once snapped: "Then I am empowered to request your immediate resignation." His eyes gleamed, catching the light of the lamps. If it had all been some elaborate pitfall, Aubrey had no interest.

"No," he repeated. Then: "I'm sorry. Of course, my resignation. Naturally."

"Oh—I see . . . in that case—"

The telephone rang, startling them both like a recent invention. A second pair of headlights flashed off the ceiling, causing the Cabinet Secretary to glance upward and become aggravated. His objective had, apparently, been achieved. He picked up the receiver, glaring at Aubrey as he did so. It was like a station waiting room of Victorian times, ornate and plush; he merely a passenger delayed there.

"What?" Sir Geoffrey's irritation was amusing. "This is *ridiculous!"* He was holding the telephone toward Aubrey, his face purpled. "Your *housekeeper!"* he growled in disbelief. Aubrey smiled to complete his discomfiture. Took the receiver. Mrs. Grey . . . the room diminished, as if someone had turned out the lights on a stage set. "I have no *idea* why they put her through to *me!"*

"Yes, Mrs. Grey?"

"Simply because you were with me, they thought it sufficient that you be allowed your *private* calls!"

"What?"

"Master Timothy seemed very agitated, Sir Kenneth . . ." And so was Mrs. Grey, to recollect Timothy as a boy and refer to him as such. "I wondered—I'm sorry if . . . but he insisted, I felt I had to . . ."

"Mrs. Grey—just calm down and tell me what he said," Aubrey soothed. He felt Mrs. Grey's tension and sensed his whole frame quicken. He perched himself on the edge of Geoffrey's desk, while the Cabinet Secretary fidgeted and began to gather papers together, pointedly ignoring Aubrey except to evidently wish him gone. "No—tell me *exactly* what he said!"

" . . . I didn't like to interrupt . . . and you know Master Timothy has a very vivid imagination, especially as a—" Mrs. Grey persisted in her explanation.

"Then he rang you *twice.* "

"I'm sorry, Sir Kenneth, I really didn't—"

"No, I'm sorry, Mrs. Grey. Now, please tell me what he said the second time." His fingers drummed on Longmead's desk like the supple digits of a younger man. He felt quite breathless, but with a tense, eager excitement. "What did Timothy say?"

Longmead paused sufficiently in his preparations for the Cabinet meeting to murmur acidly: "That young man is in rather a deal of trouble, Kenneth. He hasn't been behaving himself at all well, according to Giles Pyott."

"Be quiet, Geoffrey!" Aubrey snapped. "Yes, go on, Mrs. Grey . . . he said what? He was in danger? How in danger?"

Longmead shuffled papers, pressed them beneath his crooked arm, stood almost to attention, then wiped his spectacles with a florid handkerchief. When he had put them on again, he announced: "I'll send someone to lock up, once you have finished with my telephone."

He closed the door dismissively behind him. Aubrey barely glanced up from staring at the carpet in his concentration. His free leg swinging insistently.

"East Germans . . . wanting to *kill* him?"

"It's the only reason I agreed to call you, Sir Kenneth. Master Timothy—he did sound frightened. Perhaps desperate." Guilt occupied her voice, then anxiety. She spoke as though thrusting a suspicious, dangerous package toward him.

"How long ago did he call?"

"The first time was—"

"The *second* time, Mrs. Grey."

"Fifteen minutes ago. It took me all that time, even using the numbers you gave—"

"Yes, all right." The situation was strange and familiar. He registered not a single one of his body's habitual, daily aches and protests. *East* Germans. "Have you arranged for him to call again?"

"I didn't know what—"

"How long between the calls?"

"Thirty minutes, a little more."

"Then he'll call again. Don't leave the telephone. Stay near it. I'm coming home at once. If he calls, tell Tim to ring in . . ." He glanced at his watch. 7:10. "Each hour, on the hour—have you got that . . . take his number, but tell him not to stay where he is unless he's *certain* he is secure! Have you got all that?" Mrs.

Grey repeated his instructions, her voice filled with little fears. "Tried to kill him—you're certain of that?"

"It's what Timothy said, Sir Kenneth." Then her voice broke completely. "He will be all right, won't he?"

"I don't understand why the Depot—why he isn't secure there. What do they want with him?"

He could not, *would* not, believe it was Brigitte. It had to be coincidence. East Germans in Kathmandu?

"Did he say *why?*"

"Er . . . he said something about photographs, airports. He couldn't understand what he'd stumbled on, Sir Kenneth. Yes, I'm certain that's how he put it."

Aubrey snapped his fingers. "We're wasting time, Mrs. Grey. If he calls before I get back, try to get some details from him. Who these people are, how close they are to him . . . tell him to keep *moving!*"

"Yes, Sir Kenneth—"

"I'm on my way!" He snapped down the receiver. He had the sensation of a gulf crossed. Kurt's body lay on the other side of it, but so did Longmead and JIC and his old service. His task was to save Timothy from whatever danger confronted him. For that, he would need help from Peter Shelley, from Giles Pyott at MoD, perhaps. But it was a personal matter. It was— unselfish, and he felt the better for that. Much the better.

He picked up his walking stick and twirled it, sensing the old blitheness that urgency and danger had always brought. He knew he was *capable* of saving Timothy, even if Longmead had closed his door, and a great many others. The past months were an illness from which he had now recovered. He felt well again.

Something to do!

He slammed Longmead's door behind him and scuttled with renewed vigor down the corridor.

"Come on, come on . . ." His breathing clouded each section of the window through which he kept a constant, panicky sur- veillance while the telephone line hummed and clicked, then the distant number in London—he could see the telephone, the hall- way, the room from which Aubrey should be coming now— began to ring. "Aaaah . . ." He sighed aloud. The small panes of glass nearest his peering face clouded again. The telephone box, antiquated and British, was in a dark, narrow, silent street. A few dim globes of light, floating apparently in the night, and the round, glowing stars. The occasional dog, occasional human noises and footsteps. The telephone in Aubrey's flat continued to ring.

He had left the café perhaps only two minutes before they had arrived. It was the owner's increasing interest in him, as if he had him under surveillance. Then the offer of another drink, on the house, as he rose to leave, scattering notes on the table in payment, confirmed his instinct. He had intended to wait outside in the shadows until he heard the telephone ringing. He had waited, but only to confirm what he knew would happen. A car screeching down the next street, swerving wildly around the corner. The East Germans rushing into the empty café. He had hurried away, quivering with relief and self-congratulation. Now, he was near Durbar Square, moving back into the center of the warren of the Old City's streets. The midnight was chilly, the city's fetid smells almost sweetened by the drop in temperature.

Someone picked up the receiver.

"Kenneth!" Clouded panes, obscuring the street. He wiped at them with his free hand. Now he *needed* to see. "Kenneth, it's Tim!"

"Mr. Timothy . . ." Mrs. Grey again! He clenched his fist, banging it down on the coin box. "Sir Kenneth's on his way. He's not here just at present, he shouldn't be very long. I rang as you asked. He asked me to find out—"

"Mrs. Grey! They are trying to kill me. I don't know why. They are East German intelligence agents, I'm certain of it . . ." Gradually, the tramping irony of his tone lessened, his voice becoming merely a vehicle of explanation. "I have photographs of them, and I'm sure Kenneth can identify them, or have them—"

A car slid past the lighted telephone box, moving slowly like a gray fish through dark water. It disappeared around a bend in the unpaved street, but he saw the splash of its brakelights on a house wall the moment after it vanished. His hand begun quivering.

"Mrs. Grey—quickly . . . did he say anything? What—can I do?"

"Sir Kenneth said you are to call in every hour, on the hour."

"Mrs. Grey, I think I have to be going . . ." The white paint of reversing lights glowing brighter on the same wall. Then the rear of the car came into view, and the brakelights went on once more. A door opened. "Every hour!" he shouted into the receiver, then slammed it down, thrusting open the stiffly sprung door with his other hand—

—which reddened and prickled as it was cut by the exploding glass from the shattered pane. Redness spread, pain intensified as he ran, hearing more glass shatter, then the pluck of a bullet against plaster.

"Peter—there's a list of things I need. This is a Curtain close-down operation in all but location. I have to get the boy out tonight . . ." Aubrey paused for Shelley's response, and heard only his breathing from the telephone, and the not-quite silence of a dinner party beyond.

Eventually, Shelley murmured: "I—sir, you've resigned . . . at least, so I've heard." Shelley and his wife were entertaining the new Director General of SIS and his pushy, snobbish wife. News had not traveled that fast, it was old news, something decided long before he saw Longmead. Aubrey felt anger rise into his throat. "I—dinner's on the table . . ." Shelley added awkwardly.

"Getting cold, is it, Peter?" Aubrey heard himself sneer. Then concern for Timothy burst out. "Someone is trying to kill the boy—some *organization* is trying to kill him. Do you understand, Peter? He needs *help!*"

"I—had Middleton on the line earlier today . . ." Shelley paused, as if anticipating further scorn or anger, then continued: "He called it tipping me the wink. He thinks"—Shelley cleared his throat—"he thinks your young man is imagining it. Off his rocker, was how he put it. And he gave me a rather graphic description of—"

"Peter, *I* am telling you the danger is real. I presume my word carries a little more weight than the Third Secretary in Kathmandu!" The level of laughter rose around the dining table.

"There's nothing I can do tonight, Sir Kenneth."

"You must, Peter. He can't get out alone. He's not *trained* . . ."

"I *promise* I will look into it tomorrow. Unofficially, Sir Kenneth. I'll talk to Middleton." Again laughter. Someone called Shelley's name. The voice sounded like that of the former ambassador to Washington who now headed SIS. A strident female voice—the wife—was audible, and the consenting murmurs of others. The ordinariness of the business going on behind Shelley was mocking, indifferent. "Tomorrow—"

"Tomorrow will be too late, unless I miss my guess!" Aubrey snapped, clicking off the Talk switch and closing the aerial. Impatiently and in fear, he threw the telephone onto the sofa beside him. *Damn Peter Shelley!* Shining new Deputy Director's armor waited in the corner of his little castle, and it was in his size, it would fit, if the new DG liked him. The dinner party was important, and Tim's danger unbelievable. "Oh, Peter . . ." he murmured, staring at the carpet.

He looked up at the mantel clock. Ten minutes to nine. It was dark outside, the Park cloaked, the lights beyond it shining out like lamps beneath shallow, dark water. Tim would not call for ten minutes, it would give him the chance to assess the situation. While in Cheam or wherever it was Shelley now lived, the respectability of a former ambassador assessed the respectability of a potential Deputy. Peter Shelley would have, Pilate-like, to wash his hands publicly of—what? Former associations, former regimes?

The intelligence community had acquired an erstwhile ambassador and a Permanent Secretary to the Treasury as its overlords. Men of unimpeachable background, service and morality. Longmead's recommendations. Stainless steel, Teflon-coated. Aubrey realized how casually he had thrown away his forty and more years of service—because the boy had panicked and come to him, because he was in danger.

The telephone chirruped, startling him. Five to nine. He snatched it up, tugged out the aerial, flicked the switch from Receive. "Yes, Tim—yes?" he blurted.

"Uh, Kenneth? Giles Pyott here. Sorry if you were expecting a call. Look, I just wanted to talk to you about that young man of yours, Gardiner."

"Yes?" There was a sudden, deep hollow in Aubrey. He was certain Tim was dead. "What is it, Giles?" he demanded breathlessly.

"Look, Kenneth, I only rang to say that this mess he's in— the Disbandment Dinner fiasco . . ."

"Oh? I—I hadn't heard . . ."

Three minutes to nine. Perspiration prickled on his forehead and he rubbed at it impatiently. Mrs. Grey entered the drawing room, carrying a silver coffeepot and a cup on a tray. He waved her to put it down, shook his head at her worried expression.

"Well, get him to tell you. I just wanted to assure you that I'd—try to ameliorate the problem when he faces his disciplinary hearing next week. I've arranged to be a member of the panel . . ." Two minutes to nine. "I think we can be fairly confident it won't be the end of his army career." When Aubrey made no reply, Pyott added: "I just thought you'd like your mind set at rest. Do you want the details of what he's alleged to—"

"Giles, I'm—I'm grateful. Look, I'm expecting an urgent call, now. Can we—I'll talk to you later!" He could not keep the anxiety from his voice.

"I'll get off the line, then. Goodbye, Kenneth. Sorry to hear about your own—"

Aubrey flicked the switch. Mrs. Grey proffered his cup, but he waved it aside. One minute to nine. The mantel clock had a tendency to run a minute or so behind. It was already nine, even past the hour. He fidgeted on the sofa. Simon and Timothy. He had lost Simon . . . Timothy, too?

The telephone, slippery in his clenched hands, blurted and he flicked the switch, pressing the receiver to his ear.

"Yes, yes—" Mrs. Grey stood before the closed drapery, her hands wringing and entwining. "Yes, I'll accept the charges!" The sense of distance, powerlessness. "Tim?" he all but shouted.

"Kenneth!" Gardiner's relief was as vivid as his own, rushing through him like a chill breeze. Making saliva in his throat. "Thank God!"

"Tim, are you all right?"

" . . . just a scratch. I'm OK. Think I've given them the slip . . . haven't got long, though. It's organized, Kenneth! They really want to find me badly. Guns, now . . ." He seemed to run down like a battery-operated transmitter.

Aubrey shivered. "Tim, who are they?"

"Didn't Mrs. Grey—" A child's huge disappointment and irritation.

"She did. Now tell me. Where are you?"

"Telephone box. Durbar Square. There's no one about."

"Keep looking—three hundred and sixty degrees. Look at everything! Now, who are they?"

"East Germans."

An image of Kurt's leaking head against lamplit cobblestones made Aubrey shudder. It couldn't be anything more than coincidence, not yet, not this quickly.

"You know that?"

"I followed their leader when he came out of the Embassy.

I *know!* I've got pictures, you'll be able to identify them, won't you? You'll know them?"

"Perhaps. And they want to kill you?" He was surprised at his professional detachment, as if he floated at some distance from this incident as from so much else.

"They do. And they've got locals working for them. What's going on, Kenneth?"

"I don't know, Tim . . . Tim, are you keeping a good lookout?"

"What? Oh, yes—forgot . . . sorry." He sounded like the schoolboy, like the young man bereft of his twin brother, stunned into sober conformity at the funeral and afterward. "OK at the moment."

"Are you armed in any way?"

"Knife. Haven't got a gun. Can you get me out, Kenneth? The fucking Embassy is hopeless. They've got it cut off, anyway. And the Depot, and the airport. I've got a flight booked, but I can't use that now—"

"I understand." He was no longer talking to a man in his thirties, or in the present at all. There was a little lost boy at the other end of the connection. He was tightly fitted into the role of guardian, surrogate father.

"How will you get me out? The streets are empty—it's two in the morning. I'm becoming an easier and easier target. They'll find me soon, I should think—"

"Keep looking!"

"How will you get me out?"

"I—I'll think of something . . ."

"You mean you don't have a plan?"

"Not yet, Tim . . . look, I'll get you out, I promise you that. Meanwhile—"

"Meanwhile, I could be killed!"

"Tim, listen to me. Keep on the move, don't book into a hotel, don't go to friends. Don't trust anyone! Call me every hour, on the hour. Don't go through the operator again. Get hold of plenty of change. I'll get on with—"

"Every half-hour."

"I need time, Tim!"

"I'm alone!" Gardiner cried out as if in retaliation. Aubrey felt himself thrust into the young man's fears, and the warmth and comfort of the drawing room seemed illusory.

"I know, my boy. I understand, believe me. Very well, in half an hour. Keep to the shadows. Be careful and be quick. God bless—"

Gardiner had gone, the lost connection humming. Aubrey listened to its emptiness for some moments before switching the telephone to Receive once more. He dropped it onto the sofa and rubbed his cheeks with both hands. They felt clammy.

Mrs. Grey cleared her throat with a small, polite, desperate noise. "Is he—all right?"

Aubrey nodded. "At the moment, Mrs. Grey." His eyes were focused on the door, and he said: "It's a pity one of us can't simply go next door to his old room and switch on a light—eh, Mrs. Grey? This isn't one of his nightmares. More is the pity."

"What will you do, Sir Kenneth?"

He glowered at her, and spread his hands. "What can I do, Mrs. Grey? I am no longer a member of my country's intelligence service. No one will listen to me—at least, not in time. What can I do?"

6

A Declared Emergency

"OK, so all these places marked in red are staked out?"

"Yes."

"He'd be a bigger fool than he appears to be if he went within a mile of any of them." Gerd Brandis rubbed his smooth chin, then plucked at it as if regretting a lost beard. The large-scale map of the city lay opened like a starched tablecloth. "And the latest count is fifty people on the strength . . ." He sighed. "I hope Brigitte realizes the risk all this activity is to the operation! What the hell she's so obsessed with this Gardiner for, I really don't know. However, if the General wants him dead, then dead he must be. Tonight."

He held the files against his chest, as if to protect their contents from the unimportance of the search for Gardiner. The files contained *Topi*—first phase. The bombing campaign, the disinformation, the demonstrations and riots. The fake right-wing coup which would let Moscow in. Why the devil Brigitte was bothering with this one unofficial Englishman . . . her son's death, he supposed. She sounded distraught, in need of a long rest. And revenge, lashing out. Would a man have reacted in the same way?

The secure room beneath the embassy carpark contained twenty people; his *Topi* team. The room was divided into cubicles, like the innards of a radio. The strips of carpet were connecting wires and cables. One section was responsible for those generals and senior police officers who were committed or bought. Another dealt with the pro-Soviet faction on the Council of Ministers. Another with the radio and TV stations, and the telephone exchange. It was organized, efficient, ready. This obsession of Brigitte's with Gardiner was like dropping all this complex machinery into a bucket of water.

He had to report to the leader of the pro-Soviet faction early that same morning. Flattering the man into believing his importance to them was equivalent to his self-importance. The latest bulletin on the King's health would be delivered to Brandis in another hour's time.

Gardiner was a bloody distraction! As if they didn't have enough to do already!

He glared at the map. Somewhere there. They didn't think he was badly hurt. Traces of blood like an animal's spoor in two telephone boxes . . . all the boxes were marked on the map. Who was he trying to call? Every hour, it appeared, on the hour. From the change he'd abandoned in the one callbox, it must have been long-distance, international? Was he professional? Brandis shook his head. He wasn't—for certain he was an amateur. But he had to keep on calling, apparently.

He clicked his fingers. "The telephone exchange!" he snapped. "Get on to our most senior man inside. I want to know who he's been calling, and why. I want this business wrapped up quickly. We'll—" He grinned, ignoring the small part of his awareness that pointed an accusing finger at the time lag before the idea occurred to him. He should have thought of it at once! *Topi* had got in the way. "We'll find out who he's calling, then get—yes, we can rig it so that he stays on the phone long enough for us to trace the callbox he's using!" He slapped the closest of his aides on the back, heartily. "Let's get on with it! Next time he calls, we'll have him!"

He had rung Giles Pyott at home. Aubrey's description of Gardiner's predicament seemed exaggerated, all but absurd, even as he related it. His words had the sound of loose pebbles being dropped into a well. Major-General Sir Giles Pyott had listened politely, even sympathetically . . . and had gone to the lengths of promising that he would look into the matter in the morning. *Tell your young man to get back to the Depot and have a good night's sleep . . .*

9:24. Tim would call in another six minutes. Aubrey stared at the battered guidebook he had found on the bookshelves in

Gardiner's old room. A city he had never visited, strange names he could not pronounce. A young man running and hiding in those unknown streets. A profusion of alien temples. A city and a country Timothy had come to love; in which he had found a kind of unreality which satisfied him. Now, the real had intruded. What the devil had he stirred up? He could not, despite momentary fears to the contrary, bring himself to believe that Brigitte was behind it. It had a symmetry he instinctively rejected. *He,* surely, not Tim would be Brigitte's target?

Mrs. Grey fussed at the corners of his distraction, clearing trays and cups, drawing curtains in other rooms, washing dishes in the kitchen, preparing supper. Her presence in the flat was like a growing charge of electricity. Traffic passed, and voices. Walked dogs barked occasionally. Aubrey felt trapped, confined. He was powerless, and it was a new and unnerving experience. He flicked at the pages of the guidebook. Statuary and mountains glared richly up at him. Buddhist monks, and landscapes of enormous beauty. Tim's country.

He looked at the telephone beside him once more, then at the clock. 9:27.

I gave him too much Kipling to read as a boy, he remembered saying once—who was it to? Tim's headmaster, or perhaps Giles Pyott when Tim first became a Queen's Gurkha Officer. His thoughts turned morbidly on the sourness of that casual remark. He could well have killed his . . . not son, but something like— killed him with Kipling. Tolkien and Buddhism from his brother, Kipling from his guardian, their amalgam with loneliness, his father's forced disappearance from England and his mother's libidinous pursuit of wealthy South Americans and Arabs and Italians, had produced . . . what had his headmaster said? *Too rich a fantasy life, Mr. Aubrey. Far too rich, I'm afraid, for his own good.*

Simon had lived, and died, his fantasy of wealth and fame. Tim had been straitjacketed, and had even become contented, in the Brigade of Gurkhas.

9:30. He stared at the telephone, which remained silent. He heard a small alarm clock sound from the kitchen. A moment later, Mrs. Grey appeared in the doorway, a worried frown on her features, wiping her hands on a small green towel. He motioned her to sit opposite him. The telephone refused to ring. He forced himself to think. What could he do? There must be something, someone? The Kathmandu police? Surely the boy could go to them? The telephone seemed larger. Hard and gray like a stone. He checked the switch was on Receive, tugged the aerial in case it was not fully extended. Kept the instrument in his hand, loosely. Why not the police?

The place is alien, he reminded himself. It is better to trust no one.

The room seemed taut with the telephone's continuing silence. He could not look at Mrs. Grey. 9:32. He fidgeted, shuffled his feet. The helplessness that filled his awareness was an agony. To be so *helpless* when Tim was in danger, when he was relying on him!

He stared at the open guidebook on his lap. The street map of Kathmandu. Where was he, where was he *now?* The telephone chirruped, he flicked the switch with clumsy, almost numbed fingers.

"Yes?" he asked breathlessly.

Timothy Gardiner, too, seemed out of breath. Noises in the background, a subdued murmur of voices—

"Kenneth! Christ, I just missed them that time."

"Where are you?"

"One of the hotels—the telephone in the foyer. Can't register though. Wouldn't feel safe. Well, what's the plan, Kenneth?" There was something boyishly excited about Timothy, as if he were outwitting ponderous, rather dim adults. Dangerously confident now—

"Who else is there?"

"Party of Japs, by the look of it . . . come back from a night out, hundreds of cameras!" It was as if he had been drinking, or taking drugs. He was careless, half in love with the dangers surrounding him. "What's the plan?"

After a lengthy pause, Aubrey said carefully: "Are you certain they're watching the Depot and the Embassy, Tim?"

"What? You don't believe me, is that it? It's all a *joke?"* His anger was childish, too, bitter and outraged.

"No, Tim . . . it's just that—look, could you trust the police?"

"What do I tell them? That some East German *diplomats* are trying to kill me?" Clicks and splutters of distance on the line. "Are they likely to believe me?"

"Then break a shop window and get yourself arrested!" Aubrey looked at Mrs. Grey, whose features were angry. "I'm sorry, Tim. I—just don't know what to do."

"Can't your people get me out?" Gardiner cried plaintively.

"They're not my people anymore, Tim. They won't help us . . ." He felt his own anger at Longmead and the rest of them transmuted into outrage on Tim's behalf. *They* were leaving him to the mercy of whoever wanted him dead. They would not take his word that the boy needed help!

He flicked the guidebook. The connection was cut, the line clicked, purred, clicked. He felt helpless. Gardiner had vanished. He continued to stare at the telephone until Mrs. Grey took it from him and switched it back to Receive.

Aubrey stood up wearily, feeling the aches and nudges of age. "Come on, Tim, come on . . ."

He walked to the window and dragged the curtains apart. The glass was cool, almost chill as he touched it. The lights north of Regent's Park climbed laboriously up an invisible slope. He was still clutching the guidebook. He automatically flicked its pages. Faces, scenes, temples, mountains. The street map. Which hotel was it? Come on, come on—

Brown pages of tourist advice and information—where to eat, what to eat, hotels . . . why was he reading this? The telephone remained silent. Mrs. Grey shuffled on her chair's edge and he could hear her suppressed, anxious breathing. Hiking routes, rafting holidays, mountaineering, day trips, airlines. He couldn't use the airport, couldn't . . . sightseeing flights, see the beauty of Everest from the air?

. . . air?

The telephone blurted. He snatched it from Mrs. Grey, dropping the guidebook as he did so.

"Tim!"

"Kenneth—we were cut off."

Clicks and splutters on the line. Yet the connection was good . . .

"Was it you, Tim? Did you cut us off?"

"No."

"Neither did I . . . look, give me another half-hour, I think I could—I'm *sure* I can get something arranged. In case we're cut off, give me the number there . . ." Hotels, *hotels!* "Use hotel telephones, Tim, only hotels. I'll try each one in turn, the first-class, in turn—get them to page, page 'Mr. Richardson,' got that?" He stared at the guidebook Mrs. Grey was retrieving from the carpet. "Tim, you remember that guidebook on Nepal in your old room?"

"What?"

"The one with—" Mrs. Grey held it up. "With the girl's face on the cover, paperback?"

"I think . . . yes, I remember."

"There must be a copy in the hotel bookshop! Get one. That list of places to stay!"

"Why? What's the matter?"

He could not say. The isolation of Tim, his own lack of backup or authority, everything seemed to conspire to unsettle his nerves. The interruption of the call must have been accidental, and yet it delayed Tim, kept him just where—

"Tim—listen to me. Get out of there now!" He looked down the list of hotels in Kathmandu in desperation. "A first-class hotel, Tim—remember the number sixty-eight. *Sixty-eight.* Half an hour! Now, get away from there!"

He cut the connection viciously and flung the telephone into the nearest chair. It bounced onto the carpet. Mrs. Grey clucked as she retrieved it. He stared at the guidebook and its list of Kathmandu hotels. There were sixty-eight double rooms in the Annapurna Hotel. Would Tim realize when he saw that same list—would he?

"Was the telephone tapped, Sir Kenneth?" Mrs. Grey asked nervously.

Aubrey shrugged. "I don't know, Mrs. Grey—I don't know. That interruption could have been accidental, but I can't risk it. I only hope he understands the significance of sixty-eight. He mustn't call here again."

"He will be all right?"

"I have to save him, Mrs. Grey. Now, quickly, give me the telephone." A quarter to ten. "I must get something organized!"

"He's gone—"

"Then you were too slow getting there! The call was held long enough after it was traced!"

"Sorry, Colonel . . . we did our best—"

"Not good enough! The call was to Aubrey in London—was it taped by our friend at the exchange?"

"We instructed him to do so—"

"Then find out! We need to know the arrangements." He snorted. "Stupid bloody kids—how the hell did they miss him?" He waved his hands in the air, as if the room's occupants were an orchestra he was about to conduct. "There'd better be a bloody tape of that call!" he threatened in his loudest voice.

● ● ●

"Yes, I'm so sorry, Mrs.—er, Grahame . . . it is a matter of some importance—of course, I understand . . ." The woman was shouting through her sniffs and the saliva in her mouth, dragging in air like an old bellows and exhaling rage, jealousy, even a kind of narrow, unlit despair. The nakedness of her emotions agitated Aubrey. Tim's safety lay beyond them as on the other side of a high, solid fence. "Please, I'm sorry to distress you, but have you a number where I can reach him?" He looked down at his right hand clenched on his thigh, at the foot that fidgeted on the carpet, at Mrs. Grey's sensible low-heeled shoes and support stockings passing to and fro at the periphery of his vision, and felt himself becoming hot and impatient. "Yes, Mrs. Grahame . . . but you do understand, surely? I am—his managing director, this is a matter of business, whatever the time . . . I see . . . of course, no, please don't distress yourself—" Her emotions were frightening. "Please, Mrs. Grahame!"

The air was sucked in, the expletives, the four-letter words, the labels, came out. Then she screamed: "She works at the travel agency! Her name's Emma—*Emma Bliss!*" Then the sobbing continued, racking and uninterrupted.

"Thank you, Mrs. Grahame." He put down the telephone and looked up at Mrs. Grey. "The directory, Mrs. Grey!" he snapped. "Let us pray the libidinous Grahame prefers his bed to his board!" Mrs. Grey hurried into the hallway, returning with the directory, already thumbing over the pages, running her finger down columns of names. "Well?"

"You should have asked for the address."

"Would she have known it?" He shook his head. "Well?"

"Quite a few Blisses . . . more than one E. Bliss—look."

He placed the directory on his lap, and began dialing without pause. Once . . . no reply. Twice . . . a man, no his wife and daughter were neither of them named Emma—*and who are you, may I ask?* Flats, flats, he thought, scanning the list . . . there? He dialed, his leg pumping up and down in his agitation.

Five to ten.

"Miss Emma Bliss?" he demanded.

"Who's this?" A young woman's voice, irritated.

"Miss Emma Bliss who works at the Grahame Travel Agency?"

"Yes—who are you?"

"Please let me talk to Mr. Grahame."

"What makes you think—listen, whoever you are . . ." A man's voice, muttering in the background. Aubrey felt a chill of success, and shivered.

"Listen to me, young woman. I am the managing director of the company that *owns* the travel agency. Put Grahame on. Tell him it's Aubrey!"

He heard her repeat the name and the information, and the man's soft curse, then her upbraiding tone begin. The man silenced her with a whispered snarl. Then:

"Yes, sir—sorry about that, sir. Just—going over some difficult business . . . bookings . . ." The girl had mocked his servility at first, now she laughed. Grahame silenced her with another snarl, his hand evidently over the mouthpiece. Presumably SIS knew who the girl was, she'd been vetted. "Sorry, sir—what can I do for you?" The breezy, professional voice.

"I want transport immediately. Send that girl out of the room, Grahame—get her to make coffee, or something."

"Sir." He listened to the tiny squabble muffled by Grahame's hand, and felt his own anxiety grow. It was a matter of prayer that Grahame had not heard he had been forced to resign. Travel should not have heard, not yet . . . please.

Grahame announced with the tone of a victor: "That's settled. Now, sir, what's the matter? Don't often get you yourself calling in—"

"Grahame—just shut up and listen!"

Ten o'clock. Where was Tim now? He had fifteen minutes to begin to get something arranged. Grahame was within a mile of SIS's travel agency.

"Sorry, sir. All ears."

Grahame had not heard of his resignation. He was simply relieved that Aubrey seemed to accept the transparent fiction of his explanation.

"I want a safe journey arranged, out of Kathmandu, for tomorrow morning, early."

"Kathmandu—Nepal, sir?"

"I don't care how you do it, but it has to be quick, and secure. One man. He's in a closedown situation, can't use the airport, railway, possibly not the main roads. I want him out within six hours."

"Christ, sir, you don't want much, do you?"

"Grahame, are you reliable? Your wife doesn't seem to think so!"

He heard the indrawn breath quite clearly, then: "I have to have more time—"

"There isn't more time. You're responsible for our travel arrangements, emergency or otherwise. I don't want visas, currency, passports—I want a man *safe!*" His anger was hot and frightened. "Listen to me, Grahame. This man is not a professional, he can't survive long enough for you to complete your fornication! He must be out within the next six hours, at daylight or earlier in Kathmandu. A quick exit. He is dealing with professionals, East Germans. Now, get into your trousers, then into your car and down to the agency!" He could not prevent himself imitating the distraught, irrational Mrs. Grahame. "He needs no cover, no papers—just *transport.* Everything booked in the name of *Richardson*—understand? Get on with it, man!"

He threw aside the telephone in what he observed had become something of an habitual gesture. He stared at it, clasping his hands together to still their quivering. Kurt and Brigitte . . . his situation was a mirror image. He understood now, through the anticipation of loss and grief. He was appalled by its potential symmetry.

He looked up at Mrs. Grey.

"I—I'm sorry I lost my temper," he sighed. She merely nodded.

Five minutes past ten. After three in the morning in Kathmandu. He shivered.

"Can he do something?" Mrs. Grey asked.

"Who? Grahame? He *must!*"

Empty streets, awareness of them seeping like an icy chill into Tim. He shivered again. Would he understand what the number sixty-eight signified? Could he get hold of a copy of that damned guidebook? Was he already lost?

"Run that bit again!" Brandis rubbed his head as if toweling himself dry. "The number again! And where's that bloody guidebook?"

Maps littered the floor near him. Photographs, including one of Gardiner that had been distributed to everyone. Sheafs of reports scattered, too. Brandis listened to Aubrey's voice. *Sixty-eight.* What the hell did it mean?

He glanced at the wall clock, angry that the whole of the operations room had become focused upon the tight group of people around his desk. Damn Brigitte and her bloody son! The boy had probably wanted to go over, anyway, hadn't been kidnapped at all. *My son is dead!* she had bellowed down the line at him. *Aubrey killed my son, I want Gardiner dead!* She hadn't even been able to keep her motives secret, make it merely a matter of security.

He sighed. Ten past three. Half an hour, Aubrey had said. That meant a quarter past three, they had five minutes.

Five people around his desk, all of them poring over photocopied sheets duplicating the list of hotels from that bloody guidebook. He clenched his hands against the sense of Aubrey's cleverness. 3:11 showing on the clock's broad, plain face, the second hand moving in quick little jerks.

"Sixty-eight!" he exploded. "Sixty-bloody-eight! What does it mean, Müller?"

Someone else answered him, eagerly, with the shock of discovery and the fear of appearing wrong mingling in his words.

"The Annapurna! Look. Sixty-eight double rooms!" He pointed, jabbing at the figure on the duplicated sheet in his hand. "Look!"

"Any others the same?"

People scanned. "No . . . no, sixty-five . . . no!"

"It can't be that easy," Brandis offered, cautious now. His hands closing and unclosing, staring at the sheet that lay between them. Sixty-eight . . .

He snatched up the map of the city center from the floor near his foot, spreading it like a crackling cloth over his desk.

"It's up on Durbar Marg, near the American Express office. Who's nearest?" He looked up at the clock, fearful now.

"Two men at the British Council offices!"

"Send them!" 3:15. "Are they armed?"

Someone consulted a list.

"No, two locals, on foot, maybe bikes . . ." It sounded ridiculous now, the odds even in favor of Gardiner.

"Christ!" He rubbed his hair in frustration. "Send them on lookout. Get a car up there now! Armed men. Christ—do it, don't just stand there!"

"God, Kenneth, it took some working out!" Gardiner announced, almost gay with tension. "I had to pinch the hotel desk's copy of the *Insight Guide!* Then sixty-eight . . . almost too bloody clever, Kenneth!"

Aubrey looked at the clock. 10:16. One minute of increased danger, a minute when Tim wasn't moving, wasn't concealed.

"Not clever at all, Tim," Aubrey replied, the relief still unsettling his stomach, the glimpses of Mrs. Grey's drawn features distressing him further, "not if they're listening in, not if they have the guide, too."

"God, do you think . . ." Like a manic-depressive swing into melancholy, fear edged back into Gardiner's voice. "What—what can we do, Kenneth?"

"I don't know!" Then, more calmly, he said: "I'm making arrangements, Tim, don't worry about that. But you have to hang on there, you have to stay—free, for a little time yet. Do you understand?"

"You are doing something, aren't you?" It was like an accusation.

"Tim, I promise you!"

"Sorry."

"It's bound to take time," he soothed, afraid that Gardiner would suddenly, with the insight lent by fear, question how he would pass on any information securely. If they *were* listening, he daren't tell Tim over the telephone how he was to get out of Kathmandu. If Grahame came up with a route, a means of transport, if, if . . .

And if they were listening, and had the guide, he couldn't use the double-room signal again! He snapped his fingers at Mrs. Grey, pointing at the guide lying on the carpet some feet away. She retrieved it, handed it to him, feverishly opened at the list of hotels.

"Map, map!" he whispered intently. The map crackled as Mrs. Grey opened it. She held it before him—like his mother, he suddenly and irrelevantly remembered, holding a newspaper before a reluctant fire, trying to draw it. He looked at the map, at the list of hotels, at the telephone numbers, the number of rooms, the star ratings, the facilities, the addresses, the map again, one finger tracing points in the city . . . the alien, unknown city. He listened to Gardiner's quickening breathing. "Do you know the exits from that hotel, front and back?" he asked.

"What? Oh, yes, I did look . . ."

"Clear?"

"So far. Hurry up, Kenneth . . . there's no one about except the cleaners. I'm getting some queer looks from the desk wallah."

Telephone numbers . . . furiously, he began adding the sums they made, each one different . . . ? An exhilarated fear. That one . . . no, another the same sum . . . that one? The map trembled in Mrs. Grey's hands. He glanced around its edge at the clock. 10:19. Too long, too long!

"Listen carefully, Tim. Half an hour. The British snake makes ten. Understand? Ten."

Gardiner giggled. "I never was much good at—"

"Work it out!" Aubrey snapped, then: "Now, get away from there, Tim. Good luck. Thirty minutes. Go!"

He cut the connection. Mrs. Grey dropped the map as if it were heavy. The first telephone number of the Malla Hotel near the Royal Palace added up to ten. He'd understand, eventually. Aubrey sighed, then picked up the telephone again before doubt could enlarge. He jabbed out the number of the Grahame Travel Agency.

Mrs. Grey retreated to the kitchen. He thought of calling out for a whiskey, then felt it would be some kind of desertion of responsibility.

"Yes?"

"Well, Grahame?"

"Ah, sir . . . look, sir, sorry about the mixup, you having to talk to the wife, gets a bit—"

"That is of no importance, Grahame! What have you been able to arrange?"

"Nothing yet, sir. I've got an idea, though!" he added hurriedly, as if Aubrey's anger came preceded by a charge of static on the line. "The airport—"

"They'll be watching the airport, man!" He groaned aloud, clenching his hand, banging it down on his thigh. "He can't go to the airport in plain view of everyone!"

"Sir, not the scheduled flights. Look, Nepal's not our usual beat, but I've been checking. He can't walk out, take too long . . . closedown, you said, so it must be quick." He could hear Mrs. Grey moving plates, stacking dishes, clattering cutlery into drawers; sobbing. "But I thought we could use a private aircraft. People charter them all the time, see the Himalayas from the air at close-hand, you know the kind of thing. There's at least four firms, maybe eight or ten small aircraft—"

"Yes! Do that, Grahame."

"It's almost three-thirty in the morning over there!"

"I don't care how, just do it, man!"

"Sir. Are you in comms with the subject?"

"Insecurely, yes . . ." How could he tell Gardiner the arrangements even when they were made? They *must* be listening in! They were protecting something important, had to be. "Look, Grahame, I need full details within twenty minutes. My man may not be able to get in touch after that."

"Christ!" Then: "I'll try. Valuable, is he?"

"Very."

"I'll call as soon—"

Aubrey cut the connection. Grahame would wonder about the lack of secure communication, but it hadn't to matter. He had been caught *in flagrante,* and he'd find that fact concentrating his mind wonderfully. Aubrey sat back on the sofa and closed his eyes. Danger came like dizziness and he opened them again.

How could he pass the information on, securely? How on earth could he let Tim know his way out without letting his pursuers know, too?

"What did you say? Are you serious, or drunk? One of them *recognized* him as one of his *officers,* and while they were arguing about what to do, Gardiner slipped away? I don't *believe* this!" Brandis was waving his free hand in the air, conducting the room once more. Grins disappeared immediately, heads bent as in a schoolroom from his childhood. Something at the back of his mind, enlarging and slipping into focus like a magnified photograph, made his outburst less than furious. He had had relayed the tape of the last call Aubrey made. "Look, get that place staked out—all right, just *one* man . . . and kick the shit out of that bloody nigger who thinks his officer is something special! Then stand by the car radio! Out."

He tossed the telephone receiver like a ball into the suddenly cupped hands of one of his team. Then he raised his voice so that the whole room heard him.

"Listen to me, all of you! I want the police brought in, now. Get in touch with a couple of the most *reliable* senior officers, and tell them we need assistance. Some tale about one of our people on the loose, walked off with a list of their names or something—proposing to sell to the highest bidder! I don't care who of you does it, just do it!" He turned to Müller, who could not suppress a smirk. "And *you,*" he snapped, "listen carefully. Aubrey is making some weird arrangements to get Gardiner out . . . and he'll have to tell him over the phone. There's no way around that. He's on his own. London can't be giving him help, or else he won't ask them . . . same thing either way. I want the tapes of the calls so far and the next one and any subsequent ones, and I want copies, and if necessary they're going via the satellite to Berlin. *We* can be waiting for our little mouse, like an alleyful of cats. Aubrey isn't *that* clever!"

With a singular lack of imagination, the company was called "Mount Everest Airtours," and its offices were two small huts on the far side of Kathmandu airport, well away from the terminal building. So Grahame assured him. Eight in the morning, a solo flight as far as Delhi, for Mr. Richardson. Price, four times the usual rate because of Grahame's pleading, then threatening, insistence. *Didn't do the subtlest job of persuasion, sir, but you didn't give me time for that . . . probably thinks your man's carrying drugs, hence the price. Got the bloke at home, had an answerphone, thank God, at the office . . . after eight and the deal's off. He needs the plane back same day. More smuggling, I expect. You'll authorize the payment through channels?*

Thank you, Grahame . . . sorry to have spoiled your evening, good night . . .

And now, Peter Shelley. The telephone in Surrey continued to ring. Like the one at the Malla Hotel . . . Tim was missing. He quashed the thought. The clock on the marble mantelpiece showed eleven. Struck and tinkled like musical glass. Four in the morning in Kathmandu. Tim had been paged by a bored night porter, stiff at first then impressed by Aubrey's title . . . but no Mr. Richardson had answered the summons. No, there was no one in the hotel foyer except staff . . . was the gentleman booked in? Aubrey cut the connection without explanation. If they were listening, they had more time to solve his little puzzle—his pathetic little riddle!

"Come on, Peter!" he whispered angrily. He felt tired; exhausted, rather. He stood at the window, watching the lights across the dark expanse of the park, as if trying to read distress signals flashed from distant shipping. A convoy going down . . . Someone picked up Shelley's telephone.

"Yes?" Alison Shelley. She sounded bored, irritated.

"Alison, it's Aubrey."

"Sir Kenneth—yes? Oh, by the way, I was sorry to hear about

your resignation. Peter told me only this evening. What will you . . . I'm sorry, do you want Peter urgently?"

"Have your visitors left?"

"Half an hour ago. I was stacking the dishwasher." She sounded relieved, and indiscreet. Then she chuckled. "His wife is an absolute *pain!*" she burst out. "Why I'm the *little woman* and she's Sonny-Jim's strong right arm, I really don't know!" She laughed, then sobered quickly. "Peter's just come in and he's giving me filthy looks, Sir Kenneth. I'll hand you over."

"Thank you, Alison. Peter?"

"Yes, Sir Kenneth?" Shelley's voice was stiff with repressed irritation at his wife, and suspicion of Aubrey. Under Aubrey's shadow, Peter had only ever dabbled his toes in the politics of the service. Now, he appeared to be swimming strongly with the tide.

"Peter, don't take it out on Alison. Lady Orrell *is* trying at the best of times."

"Yes, well . . . what do you want—sir?"

"I need one favor, Peter—just one. A crucial one."

"I told you, I—"

"Listen to me!" Aubrey blazed. "I'm trying to save Tim's life, dammit, and you're not going to prevent me trying my best! I want you to signal Middleton in Kathmandu, with information I will supply, and tell him to expect a priority *local* telephone call from Gardiner—identifying himself as *Richardson.* You *must* do as I ask, Peter, and you must do it at once! I know how long it will take to establish fully secure signals with an embassy—twelve minutes. It has to be arranged within fifteen." He listened then to the silence on the line, then he heard Shelley's voice, accusing.

"You must have used Travel if you've something arranged."

"Naturally. Grahame doesn't know what seems to be current throughout the service, that I am *persona non!*"

Shelley's voice was embarrassed, and yet there was a kind of relief in it, too, as if he were somehow making a decent exit from Aubrey's life. "What do you want in the signal, sir?" he asked.

Hurriedly, Aubrey told him. " . . . no later than eight, remember. And *Richardson.*"

"Yes, I've got all that. I'll get right on to it. Fifteen minutes, at the outside." He paused, then asked: "Is—is he in real trouble? Professional trouble?"

"Yes, I'm afraid he is."

"Nepal? I—perhaps it should concern us?"

"I have no idea *who* it concerns, Peter. To me, it is personal. If we save his life, then perhaps we shall find out! Now, get that signal in hand . . . and, thank you."

11:04. The clock insisted on his attention as soon as he let the hand holding the phone fall to his side. He breathed in and out deeply, a number of times, as if fresh air was coming through the window. As soon as he relaxed his breathing, urgency gripped him once more. 11:05. Tim *must* be there by now! The darkness outside looked more than ever like deep, lightless water; he felt totally adrift.

He dabbed out the number of the Malla Hotel.

The telephone system had become an inexplicable and dangerous mystery, a huge trap. He sensed Tim's pursuers waiting for this call, the crucial one. He should have delayed it—

He could not speak for a moment, even when he heard someone at the other end, speaking in what he assumed was Nepali, then English.

"Mr. Richardson—please," he asked in a cramped, small voice.

"Ah, but there is no Mr. Richardson staying here, I'm sorry." There was a pause Aubrey could not fill, then: "Just one moment, I—" There was a muffled protest, then he heard Tim's voice.

"Kenneth, I couldn't make it, sorry . . . they wouldn't let me in, had to claim I was a guest, just about to throw me out—" There was some expletive in Nepali, then he said: "Well, Kenneth?"

"Tim, listen, then go. Go into hiding. In ten minutes, make a very brief telephone call from a public callbox to Middleton. He will tell you what to do. Now, get out quickly!"

He listened. Muffled noises, then someone put down the telephone. The sounds might have been those of a struggle. Weariness passed through him, he felt as if he might faint. He walked slowly toward the sofa and sat down heavily. He could do no more. He could hardly think clearly.

He was left with the silent acknowledgment that Tim's danger was a kind of relief, an escape from self. It was saving him from another bout of the paltry spite and self-pity of the past months; ever since his return from Moscow in exchange for Babbington. Saving Timothy Gardiner's life possessed all the effects of a counterfever.

Mrs. Grey poured him a large whiskey. He drank it unregarding, sipping delicately like an old bird at a bowl of winter water about to freeze over. He could not bear the idea that his last official acts were the deaths of Kurt Winterbach and Timothy Gardiner.

Mrs. Grey, he knew, was studying him. He knew also that she would not intrude on his silence.

11:20 now. Middleton would have been alerted. Would Tim have called him yet?

"Look, I've got the Police Commissioner on one line, wanting his hand held and his brow soothed because *Topi* is imminent. I've got a signal to tell me *Field Trial* is on schedule, which means eight this morning, and the team has to be organized . . . what I *don't* have is one Gurkha officer who knows this city better than you do and is quicker at solving crossword-puzzle clues!" Brandis rubbed his hands through his hair in what might, in other circumstances, have been a gesture of satisfied tiredness, then lit another cigarette. His mouth was dry, stale. He coughed, and swung his legs off his desk. The room was busier, his attention attracted to maps, computer terminals, people moving with assured purpose, with confidence of success. *Field Trial* was coming in on time, and that had to be his priority, had to be—despite Brigitte. Fucking-up at this stage, with Babbington and Kapustin and everyone else looking, was not to be contemplated!

He stood up and stretched. "The General," he announced, "may have gone off her head, but we haven't. If she wants this Englishman dead, then it can be done anytime."

"How much does he know, sir?"

"Fuck-all! What *can* he know?" Again, he rubbed his graying hair. The cigarette was clamped between his teeth. "My mistake," he murmured. "I shouldn't have reacted like that in Pokhara . . . my mistake. *That* was the bloody Chinaman!"

"If he does get away, sir, he's bound to talk to Aubrey."

"And who is going to listen to Aubrey? The British won't want anyone to ask embarrassing questions about this place, will they?"

"Let's hope not, sir . . ."

"Müller . . . oh, Christ, all right! Keep looking for him. He'll be going as soon as he can. Whatever the arrangements, they've been made. Stop him . . . meanwhile, the rest of you, let's talk about *Field Trial* and the airport, eight o'clock, shall we?"

• • •

The sun lay as smoothly as a carpet across Tribhuyan airport, and the single long runway gleamed like a weapon. Gardiner rubbed his unshaven cheeks and jowls with hard, cleansing strokes, as if to erase the nightmare of the Kot, where he had hidden until daylight, before hitching a ride in a slow, ox-drawn cart out to the airport. The heaped, decapitated goats' and buffalos' heads, humming with flies even in the darkness, smelling hideously. Police patrols had entered the enclosed courtyard on three occasions, wiping hurried flashlights across the slaughter; as if they were now nervous of the place where blood had flowed so casually two days before. Streams of dried blood radiating from great splashes visible in the moonlight, unreflecting. He could still smell, despite the new air's sweetness, the stink of the place, and shuddered again.

He sat in the shade of a great-leaved tree, looking down at the airport from a long, planted spine of hillside. He was aware of the similarity of his position to that from which he had observed the Germans in Pokhara. That had been the moment when he began the chain of *karma* that now enmeshed him.

He was hungry. A scrap of cheese had been offered and accepted during the ride behind the slow haunches of the ox, its tail mechanically sweeping at the flies drawn by its heat. He had seen no white face he needed to fear; policemen seemed indifferent, casual . . . and yet they had been looking for him, a further proof both of his dangerous importance and of *their* influence in Kathmandu.

Middleton had been respectful, almost awed by the urgency and detail of Travel's arrangements for him. *Just like a closedown op, old boy . . . you must be important to somebody . . . forget my rudeness, there's a good chap . . . good luck.*

Middleton had made contact near Durbar Square. A passport in the name of Richardson, visas . . . more would be waiting in Delhi, including a ticket to London. And Middleton had added, wrinkling his nose, that there would be fresh clothing in Delhi, too. Someone would be in touch at the little private airfield where the Cessna down there, parked by two dilapidated huts and a hangar, would land him.

What? Undeveloped film, is it? Just in case, eh? OK, I'll see it goes in the Bag to London first thing . . . be there tomorrow morning. London time, with any luck.

Gardiner had handed over the roll of film and its undeveloped images of the Germans and the Chinese to Middleton.

He watched the Cessna through his binoculars, and breathed more easily. Studied the gaps in the boundary fencing. Lifted the glasses, adjusted the focus, and looked across the runway at the terminal buildings. The bright spots of police cars, the khaki-colored men. He was convinced there were more police than usual at the airport . . . and perhaps, just perhaps, more of the pinhead white blobs of Western faces, unluggaged and not possessing the hurrying aimlessness of airline passengers.

He began walking like a much older man, down the shallow, dusty hillside toward the airport's boundary fence. The Kathmandu Valley spread away on every side, dotted with the roofs of villages, clumped with small towns. Patan's roofs were polished like mirrors. He felt a nervous calm, like that of a grazing animal cropping grass between constant upward glances into the surrounding veldt.

The Cessna was one of perhaps a dozen small aircraft littering the edge of the runway like thrown-aside toys. Within minutes, he could read the legend "Mount Everest Airtours" along its green-striped flank. The huts near it were visibly more decrepit, the hangar's corrugated roof sagging and rusted, raggedly edged with interrupted guttering. He crossed the narrow road. There was rising dust from a disappearing truck, and the slow plod of a bullock, framed by the cart it was pulling, drawing slowly toward him. He reached the nearest jagged gap in the mesh fencing, ducked, and slipped through. Smuggling was endemic, drug smuggling only occasionally a serious crime. "Mount Everest Airtours" would regard him as less interesting, no doubt, and probably less rewarding, than a consignment of hashish.

He paused, checking the road, the clean sky. 7:50. He breathed with stertorous reassurance. The sky promised, as he looked south toward India, away from the distant peaks climbing between Nepal and Tibet. Weary gratitude made him shiver in the warming air.

His hand prickled in the places where he had plucked out tiny fragments of glass. He looked at it. No bleeding. Carefully, he approached the larger of the two dilapidated huts. A weathered signboard hung askew, empty oil and petrol tins littered the scrubby grass. Closer, the Cessna was dirty and in need of painting. A fuel pump, the smell of the stuff in the windless air. The noise of the morning flight to Delhi running up its engines near the terminal building.

He knew the Nepali lounging in a battered car seat in front of the hut, caricaturing some RAF officer at ease during September 1940. Leather, fleece-lined jacket, flying boots, a white scarf, even a neat mustache. He wanted to smile. Captain Ganesh Gurung, late of the Brigade of Gurkhas . . .

. . . dishonorably dismissed the service five years earlier. The Nepali remained slouched in his battered seat, squinting up at Gardiner, apparently without recognition. Gardiner sensed the foolishness of his half-extended hand. Even more foolish as he murmured: "Gan . . ."

Ganesh raised his body in the seat, idly curious, his eyes still weighing his cargo to Delhi warily. His olive features displayed only a mild surprise that the white man should know his name.

"Richardson?" he asked eventually.

"Er . . . yes."

Curiosity increased. The Nepali studied Gardiner's features. Then he said: "Your name isn't Richardson . . . I did not expect that it would be. I expected—" He paused. "Tim?" he asked more warmly, beginning to smile. The expression seemed erased at once by a darkening of memory in his eyes, a sense of old relations which stung rather than pleased. As if there were disliked others alongside and behind Gardiner.

"I thought you didn't recognize me!" Gardiner burst out, a huge sense of familiarity overcoming him. The previous night and its dangers suddenly seemed more real, for a moment, his escape more miraculous.

Ganesh stood up and held out his hand. "Tim!" And at once he was studying Gardiner's grubby clothes, his unshaven face. "What have you—?" Then he waved his hand. "It does not matter!" He looked at his watch. "Time to go. Have you luggage?" There was a mild warmth and a keen sense of deliberate distance in the Nepali's eyes. He was a more closed, more careful man, Gardiner recognized.

"I didn't know it was you . . . it was—well, arranged from London." Ganesh had bellowed into the shadowy interior of the hut, then slammed the door. They began walking toward the twin-engined Cessna. "So, this is what you're doing now— tourist flights."

Ganesh shook his head. "Sometimes," he murmured. His

voice was noncommittal, chilly. He seemed incurious now with regard to Gardiner. "And you—how are you?"

"OK."

Ganesh had been dismissed, his rights to a pension removed, because he had protected men in his unit after they had attacked and badly beaten a Queen's Gurkha Officer . . . no names, no pack drill. Fifty men were dismissed, and two native Gurkha officers, Ganesh the senior of the two.

"Climb in—unless you'd prefer to sit in the passenger compartment, take the copilot's seat." It did not seem to matter to Ganesh which Gardiner chose.

"I'll sit up front with you."

They walked through the cramped passenger cabin of the 340A. The seats were almost spindly, easily unbolted and stacked—for cargo usage, Gardiner realized. Smuggling.

"Sit there . . . you can use the headphones."

Gardiner sat in the copilot's seat and strapped himself in. Then plugged in the headphone set and slipped it over his head. He thrust the camera bag down beside his seat. As Ganesh strapped himself in next to him, he felt claustrophobically close to the man, uncomfortable.

Ganesh contacted the tower. Identifications and instructions rushed through the earphones, whirling in static. He started the engines. The three-bladed propellers began to turn idly, as if under deep water. Then whirled and shone. The noise deafened Gardiner. The airport, the terminal, the Avro 748 of the Royal Nepalese Airline and the distant Himalayas, larger now in the pale sky, rushed against the Perspex. Ganesh began to taxi the Cessna away from the huts and the hangar. Bounced on grass, rolled on concrete. Gardiner began watching the terminal building, glancing at his watch, the Avro now moving toward the runway. Nerves urged the small Cessna forward, were impatient with its crawl along the taxiway. The light aircraft seemed very isolated, highly visible in the morning, one of only two moving objects on this expanse of grass and concrete. He flinched against the gaze of unseen binoculars.

The Cessna turned, then turned again, slipping behind the tailplane of the larger Avro. He could see faces at the airliner's windows and wondered where his empty seat would have been on that flight to Delhi . . . and recognized the similarity of his method of departure to the one they had expected him to use. Shivered, so that the Nepali beside him glanced coldly across, as if looking at a stranger. They would watch the Avro, if only from curiosity; they could as easily watch the Cessna. The sun glared off Perspex and metal, gleamed off the propellers. Cautiously, awkwardly, he raised his small field glasses.

The Cessna moved slowly forward like a cygnet behind the parent of the Avro 748 and its forty or fifty passengers, none of whom had been of the slightest interest to the people looking for him. He focused his glasses.

"What are you doing?" Ganesh asked him, his tone one of ridicule.

"Just looking!" he snapped back, too quickly.

White faces amid the olive and brown. On the apron near the terminal, on the railinged roof of the terminal with the sightseers and relatives, behind glass. And the police . . . He concentrated on the white men with field glasses and binoculars. He hardly heard the voices of the air traffic controller in his headphones.

" . . . declared an emergency . . . hold on the taxiway . . . Soviet military flight has declared an emergency and been given permission to make an immediate . . ." He saw a fire engine and two police cars begin to move rapidly away from the terminal.

"Damn . . ." he heard Ganesh breathe.

Emergency?

A white hand, waving and pointing. A mouth open in a shout, gesticulating . . . a second white face hurrying into view, hands snatching at the binoculars . . . he could not recognize them at that distance, only know the direction, the exact location, of their consuming interest. Himself.

"Emergency?" he asked, dazed, unable to react to the fact that he had been seen. As he swept the glasses back and forth along the railinged roof, he saw them moving, gathering, making certain, beginning to react.

"Some Russian's got trouble—he's coming in here," Ganesh was saying. "Military flight from Ho Chi Minh City or Hanoi, no doubt. Calcutta on to . . . who cares? We're stuck here until . . ." He was staring indifferently out of the cabin, his hands slowing the engine revs. The propellers gleamed fitfully as they slowed. "There she is," he murmured, pointing. "Looks big. I wonder if he can make it?" He had forgotten Gardiner except as a physical presence.

Gardiner flicked the glasses up toward the sky for a moment, before his situation became utterly unignorable. He focused on the roof once more. They had gone. He felt a cold, stunned shock. Gone?

"Going to be lucky," Ganesh murmured, staring up at the birdlike speck in the sky. The words trickled like cold water. Gardiner feverishly searched the terminal windows, the apron, the police cars, the, the—

There! Two civilian cars, both black and official in appearance, parked side by side. Running men. A sense of panic and excitement. Exhausts pluming, the cars moving off almost simultaneously.

"Very lucky . . ."

"What?"

"Look! It's a big Antonov. She won't have a yard to spare on the runway . . . up there!"

The Russian transport aircraft was lumbering out of the morning sky.

"If he's fully laden, I wouldn't want to be in his place. Or the poor bastards inside with him!" Ganesh's English was colloquial, easy.

Gardiner swung the binoculars along the perimeter fence, picking up the two black cars as they turned and headed amid rising dust along the road toward the Cessna. The fence was fifty yards away, too close.

"Gan—" he began, but the Nepali seemed not to hear him. The Russian transport had enlarged, he could see the red stars and the pattern of the camouflage paint, the aircraft's pale underbelly as it came on toward the runway threshold. The cars halted, dust swirled, obscuring their opening doors. Men emerged from the dust, orientating themselves, faces turned toward the Cessna. The sticks of rifles.

Fire engines and ambulances, the noise of sirens. The gabbled urgency from the headphones of the controller and the pilot. Ganesh's hands clenched with tension and excitement. The Antonov, huge now, seemed too close already, dwarfing the Cessna and the Avro in front of him. Lumbering, overgrown, too large for the Kathmandu runway—

The two men with rifles, one of them leaning against a fence post, the other kneeling, all disguise and innocence abandoned in the attempt to stop him. Something flickered near one of their faces, like a match being struck in the sunlight, then an impact on the Cessna's fuselage and a whining noise. Ganesh appeared startled.

"Gan—look!" Gardiner shouted, turning the Nepali in his seat. The Antonov loomed like a huge shadow, sagging toward the strip of concrete that seemed much too short to allow its landing run.

"There could be a couple of hundred men on board . . . what is it?"

Another impact on the fuselage.

"There!"

The Antonov was rushing down much too quickly. Ganesh turned in his seat as the Perspex near his head crazed like a car windshield on impact with a flying stone.

"What?" Then he growled at Gardiner: "What have you done? Who are they?" A further impact, something punching against the fuselage, then a passenger window shattering audibly, even above the hurry of noise and tension from the earphones, above Gan's accusations and expletives. "Why do they want you? *Who* wants you?"

Impact with the runway, smoke from the Antonov's landing gear, the screech of braking, the whine of the four engines. The transport rushed across Gardiner's view, hurtling itself toward the end of the runway and the terminal building. Too fast—

"They want to kill me!" he shouted. "For God's sake, get us *out* of here!"

The tires on the Antonov's portside burst, and the aircraft lurched, slowing. Then swerved like a racing car across the runway. Grass and mud plowed up, the port wing dipped threateningly toward the ground.

The Cessna's engine note changed, but the noise was all but imperceptible. Ganesh was glaring at him. Something struck the fuselage, and the Perspex was crazed in a second place. The Cessna wobbled, swerved, and moved around the Avro in front of it like a mouse escaping a cat. Ganesh seemed to be staring at him without even glancing ahead. Another bang on the fuselage. The pilot of the Avro looked down at them, gesticulating furiously. Ambulance and fire sirens.

"For God's sake, take off!"

"I can't. I *live* here!"

"It can be straightened out—take off!"

The Cessna was poised at the holding point, on the edge of the runway. Gardiner saw the black smears from the Antonov's tires. The Antonov, the cars?

The transport aircraft bucked like a great animal, swerving

in a vast, tearing semicircle, grass and mud flying, wings still intact, so that it began to face them, threatening and sinister and helpless. The two cars, the gathered men, the two rifles, now perhaps a hundred yards away.

"You *must* take off!"

A panicky demand from the headphones, the Russian's commentary continuing as if he were falling from some high place and repeating disbelief over and over. A peremptory order to Ganesh to stop his engines. Ganesh glared at him again, and again the fuselage banged. Then the Cessna seemed released as the Antonov came to a halt amid dust and mud and smoke from the burning tires. The fire engines closed on it swiftly, foam spurted. Orders streamed from the tower, then curses and imprecations. A police car began moving down the runway toward them.

The men with rifles were swinging to follow the Cessna as it gathered speed. Ganesh's face was carved, intent. The runway sidestripe markings rushed, the central white line wobbling then flicking to one side as the nose tilted up. The headphones demanded ceaselessly. The ground dropped away and, as Ganesh banked, through the mist of relief and terror before his eyes, Gardiner could see the stranded Russian transport and, toylike, the two black cars. Two hundred men had not died, *he* had not. There had been no disastrous accident, no impact of his soft body with a bullet. The two events seemed fused, he was as closely identified with the fate of the aircraft as with his own life. All of them had survived . . .

"You'd better get me out of this bloody mess!" Ganesh shouted, staring ahead, leveling the Cessna. "*British bloody* officers!" he raged.

Gardiner looked down. Two hundred men might have been on board . . . the size, the weight, the length of runway—a disaster averted by the pilot's skill or desperation. The bulk of the thing, dwarfing the now-taxing Avro, dwarfing the two cars which no longer seemed important as the Cessna lifted into the clean sky. The weight, like trying to stop a—

Pokhara—*Pokhara!*

And the two cars and the Germans became intermingled, the scene and himself all one. He knew now why they had tried so hard to kill him. He had photographed them, seen them, *weighing* aircraft. Aircraft too big for Kathmandu and Pokhara.

Transport aircraft that could carry two hundred men and their equipment. Even—tanks.

"My God," he whispered, shivering with reaction as the airport and the huge Antonov diminished behind them. "Oh, my God."

He had seen them preparing for an *airborne* invasion.

PART TWO

Long-Forgotten Wars

"Now my charms are all o'erthrown,
And what strength I have's mine own,
Which is most faint . . ."

Shakespeare: *The Tempest*, Epilogue

7

Flowers of Deliverance

Brigitte felt the music's tension break against her like waves. Her mouth was filled with the stale taste of too many cigarettes. She had no idea of the time. Her uniform greatcoat lay untidily over the back of an armchair and the whiskey bottle was almost empty—like the glass in her hand. The first movement of Beethoven's Seventh symphony seemed full of threat rather than assertion. Her head ached but she made no move to reduce the volume from the hi-fi.

The photographs were everywhere. Why had she believed she wanted to look at them? Reaching for them as easily as for the bottle, or as if Kurt had been a file under examination. The slow movement of the symphony began to plod with a direct menace she seemed never to have heard before. She pressed the hand holding yet another cigarette to her temple, feeling the throbbing in her forehead. Standing still for a moment, she rocked dizzily with exhaustion. Kurt was everywhere in the room, watching her from silvered frames, from opened albums, from sheafs of prints spilling from folders. She was appalled that she had wanted to inflict his memory on herself.

She had not drawn the curtains across. The other Berlin glared behind its Wall. Her own shabbier city . . . she saw it clearly now, despite the darkness, with his eyes. Her toe paused at the edge of an old photograph, her vacuously handsome husband holding baby Kurt aloft, she in uniform. The husband who had hidden his former Nazism in new usefulness amid the rubble of the postwar city, marrying a Jewess to prove his repentance, she marrying him for safety against any future pogrom and for her career. He had died when Kurt was five.

She stepped carefully over the photograph. The music strained against the window, the third movement whirling dervishlike, bellowing out. She remembered her father, on the last stage of their escape from America, having to shout above the awful noise of the old Dakota flying food into blockaded Berlin, smuggling them back into *their* city. Over and over, he had told her they were at last going home, to a land cleansed, a city fit for . . .

The telephone penetrated her profound abstraction. Her head jerked like that of someone slapped awake. She turned, her glance unfocused so that the litter of photographs passed like a fairground seen from a merry-go-round, and snatched up the telephone, recalling the message she was expecting.

She flicked the button on the remote control handset and the music vanished as she acknowledged the secure line, the encryption facility, Brandis' identity as the caller.

" . . . traced him as far as Delhi. Gone to ground, Brigitte. We're watching the airport, railway and bus stations. He can't get out . . . oh, the British and American embassies, too," he added. Then, when she said nothing, he continued: "He must have had help, a cover, new papers, change of appearance, even—"

"How did he get out?" she heard herself shouting, unnaturally.

"A light aircraft took off just as *Field Trial* was coming in."

"*What?*" She was stunned. "Has he talked to London—to Aubrey?"

A silence, then: "We—can't be certain . . . not since he left."

"You realize he's on his way to Aubrey?"

"What can he—"

"He's the man's *ward!*" Her voice was high, strained. She could see Kathmandu airport, the mountains surrounding it, the big Antonov sagging down out of the sky, Gardiner escaping. "He must be working for Aubrey. He must have been *sent!*"

"Doesn't seem like that, General."

"I don't care what you think, Gerd! It has to be the case!"

"Aubrey didn't react as if it was."

"Over the telephone?" she mocked. Her eye fell upon her greatcoat, the empty whiskey bottle, avoided the photographs on the settee and the floor, the gilded frames. Instead she saw snapshots of landscapes and airports, saw *Topi;* and Babbington. Him most clearly. The operation was endangered. "We must assume Aubrey knows a great deal—and can theorize effectively!"

"Then what do you—" Brandis' voice was disbelievingly obedient.

"You have to find him, this boy. Stop him."

"You still want him killed?" Then Brandis added cuttingly: "Your personal feelings?" Rage made her choke, and she clenched her hand tighter around the empty tumbler. *Personal?* She had made it personal. Abandoning duty, clarity of mind. Overwhelmed by Kurt's death. She must not make a mistake here—

—however much she wanted Aubrey's pretend-son as dead as her real son was.

"No . . ." she said slowly. "Find him and take him somewhere he can be questioned. You must find out what his briefing was, what he knows, what he has passed on. Everything."

Brandis seemed relieved. "Yes, Brigitte. He can't get out of Delhi, and I shouldn't think he wants to stay. We'll get him, don't worry—"

"I don't," she managed to retort. "Keep me informed, Gerd. On *everything.*"

She released the receiver as if it burned her hand. Folded her arms tightly across her breasts. The greatcoat with its general's shoulderboards was now more vivid to her than the photographs. She walked on them, hardly heeding. She felt she had teetered on the edge of some abyss and that Brandis' call had pulled her roughly back. Yes, she wanted Gardiner dead, oh, yes, *how much!* She stroked the hard material of the greatcoat, fingered the stars on the shoulderboards, then gripped them until they hurt her palm. Her personal revenge had further complicated this, this *mess!*

Her head began to clear of the whiskey and the empty grief. Gardiner must not get to London, to Aubrey. Brandis must make certain of it. And Aubrey? How much did he know already—what could he deduce? She released the misshapen shoulderboard. Went to the window. Empty, windy streets: the leaves would be blowing across the square from stripped trees in the Marienkirche's churchyard. She shivered. Her head felt cooler against the glass, her thoughts less wild and sluggish. Aubrey.

The boy was unimportant. Aubrey had really killed her son. She would do her duty, and have her revenge. She moved to her desk, dragging the chair close and sitting like a secretive examination candidate, arm crooked around her notepad. She would draft a signal to London *Amt,* and it must go immediately. She began to scribble, a disregarded sense of loss pressing at her neck and the back of her head. . . . bomb . . . no one, Babbington, Kapustin or anyone else, would ever be certain it wasn't the IRA or INLA. A terrorist outrage, like the dozen or more that had already occurred in London. There had been further scares and false alarms . . . yes, it should have been this way from the beginning. She scribbled vigorously, scoring through, amending, adding. Brandis, she became confident, would stop Gardiner. She must remove Aubrey from the game. Duty and revenge. A symmetry, despite the untidiness of the sheet on which she had written. She read the draft of the signal through. She would send it under Personal Code, Action Immediate.

Kurt receded like a slow tide. She exhaled loudly. When this was done, she would have time to bury Kurt and mourn him . . . and confront the empty time left. But she would have done her duty: preserving the security of *Topi.* No one could ask more of her. She underlined the word *device,* almost scoring through the paper. The *device* that would kill Aubrey.

"Yes, *yes,* Tim! Thank God . . . but, where have you been?" The morning had been brilliant, autumnal only in temperature and the scattering of brown leaves blown across the grass of Regent's Park. Aubrey clutched the remote telephone against his chilly face with both hands, his headache and the stifling sense of the flat vanished. "Why didn't you *call* me? What?" The line crackled, the rushing air around him distanced Gardiner's voice.

"Ganesh landed the aircraft at a small field some way north of Delhi . . . we slept in the plane." Gardiner was blithe, his voice as high as that of an excited child. "Just got here—Delhi airport—part of the way on an oxcart! I'm booked on the noon flight home."

"Excellent!" Relief like a rush of passion through his shrunken old frame. His hands quivered, his legs seemed about to give way. He looked around him and shuffled as quickly as he could to the nearest bench and slumped onto it, still clutching the telephone tightly with both hands. "Yes, yes, the photographs have just arrived—they were sent round—Mrs. Grey is out having them developed now . . . what?" Gardiner's excitement made him breathless.

" . . . big transport, one of their biggest—we only *just* got out! I tell you, Kenneth, they're going to invade, I'm convinced of it! Did you hear me?"

Aubrey was confused. "I heard—I don't really understand."

Gardiner hurried on. "Can you clear up our takeoff? Ganesh thinks he might have trouble."

"Yes, yes, of course! But, you're safe, well?"

"What? Oh yes."

More darkly, Aubrey added: "They're not still on your tail, are they? You *have* shaken them off, Tim?"

"Yes, yes!"

Aubrey felt clearheaded at last. The chill air carried the noises of birds and traffic, the heady, sharp scent of petrol. Normality. His neighbor, Mrs. Carteret, was bulky in her old fur stole feeding the ducks on the long, glittering arm of the lake. He smiled. Then wondered what Tim had stirred up, what ants' nest? It would have to wait, despite his sudden, old impatience at a mystery. He must recognize the people in the photographs, make Peter Shelley listen . . .

The ducks congregated eagerly as Mrs. Carteret's wrinkled white hand, glinting with old jewelry, scattered the pieces of stale bread.

"Look, about this Russian aircraft," Gardiner was saying, "I know its tires burst, but it did get in. I *know* it was a trial run for the real thing!" There was a silence in which the ether rushed like the breeze around Aubrey, then Gardiner said, more quietly: "I think they're here, Kenneth!"

"What?"

"Kenneth—they're here! Christ . . ."

"Tim, get out of there!"

"—too late, Kenneth, too bloody late. Look at the photographs—*do* something!" There were muffled gruntings, harsh breathing. Aubrey felt his jaw drop loosely; his grip on the telephone whitened. He looked wildly toward the white-fronted Nash houses and his flat. Then: "Do something!" And the connection was cut.

He could not move. It was as if he had suffered a stroke. Automatically, he raised his hat as Mrs. Carteret passed, still holding the polythene bag which had contained the bread. Rings flashed and the fox stole grinned. He still held the humming, dead telephone . . .

Then it seemed he had to return, as quickly as he could, to the flat. He hobbled to the gate and Park Square West, his hip hurting. Mrs. Carteret was at the edge of the pavement—

—Mrs. Grey was getting out of a taxi, saw him, waved the yellow folder of developed prints. The taxi pulled away. A milk truck trundled, its slow movement dizzying. He felt a pain in his chest tighten and intensify. He had failed to save Tim, failed him. Mrs. Grey's face became concerned. Mrs. Carteret, now beside him, said:

"Shall we see each other safely across, Sir Kenneth?" Aubrey wanted to shout out to Mrs. Grey, share and lessen the sharp pain in his chest. Tim—they had Tim.

Mrs. Grey was waiting on the steps, between the two pillars, yellow envelopes in her hands. A red, unrecognized Ford was no more than yards from her, parked and empty. The milk truck trundled. Aubrey stepped blindly, weakly off the pavement.

The red car erupted into an orange fireball. The light blinded him, blanking out the scene before the shock wave reached him. It seemed to lift him, fling him to one side. The pain in his chest became hotter, harder. Momentarily, he was aware of losing his hold on the telephone and on the shrunken old elbow of his neighbor. He felt himself splashed with wetness, then the blackness began.

There was early winter in the pale air above the Kremlin towers. The red stars were child's toys held aloft on slender sticks. The river was slate-colored and slow. The British Embassy white and distant. Babbington, his back to Kapustin and the colonel from Stavka's *Topi* Planning Group, rubbed his hands together in a warming, washing gesture. His knuckles cracked one by one.

"The Group is firmly recommending no more than three-quarters loading for the big Antonovs. The exact figures are here, if you wish to see them . . . No? What it means is two air-borne companies, not three—two BMDs not three, and corresponding losses in other equipment areas. As for Pokhara, the An-12s will have to be used. Each one of them will be able to take only half-companies and half-equipment, since you wanted them airlifted, not dropped." The colonel's manner was intent, expert, yet somehow detached. As if he, a sophisticate and socialite, had called upon wealthy but rustic cousins. Babbington smiled. The man's expert arrogance reminded him of his own. He turned from the window.

Kapustin was flicking through the digest of material the colonel had brought from High Command. Babbington continued to crack his knuckles. Irritatingly, Kapustin refused to notice the soft little explosive noises. He said:

"The schedule, I take it, Colonel, can be fulfilled?" He waved a hand airily. "We're not expecting opposition of any kind . . . the smaller numbers will even assist the fiction that we are responding to a cry for assistance, but it must be done *on time.*"

The colonel nodded. "We can get four in there, one after the other, and no more. A total of around eight hundred troops, lightly equipped and with minimal transport, but fewer if you decide on heavier weapons or more transport, within an hour." He studied Babbington's face, then added: "The Group can guarantee that, on the basis of *Field Trial,* Comrade General."

"That is your decision, Colonel—that of the Planning Group, rather. There will be sufficient people to hold the key targets until the final arrests have been made and order restored, and sufficient transport to get them to those targets. *You* know how many it will take, not I."

"Very well, sir."

Kapustin murmured, like a dog disturbed in its sleep by raised human voices. Evidently, he felt interrupted in his reading. Babbington and the colonel exchanged brief smiles of complicity and superiority. Babbington knew it was he who was admired within Stavka, especially within the *Topi* Group. It was his daring concept, and his industry and concentration was making the idea a reality. Kapustin was, at best, a necessary evil.

"The radio and television stations, the newspapers, the embassies, ministries, the Palace, the telephone exchange . . . a token force for the main army barracks." He checked them off on his fingers, and Babbington imitated the colonel. Finally, he nodded his approval at the soldier.

"Good. Then we'll take your offer of the An-12s for Pokhara—how many can you get in there?"

"Since they won't be dropped—we're being *invited*—four An-12s within the first hour. Say two hundred men, lightly armed?" Again, Babbington nodded.

"Near enough to our requirements as originally laid down. I think that will do very nicely." He all but sighed.

Kapustin had selected a sheaf of papers clipped into a folder from the heap on his desk and was now reading more intently than ever. Suddenly, he chuckled and barked: "Your pilot doesn't mince his words, Colonel! A real brown-trouser job, flying one of those big transports into Kathmandu!" Even as he laughed, he was glaring over his spectacles. "You're certain, are you?" he bullied, to Babbington's intense irritation. It was like a vicious, deflating comment on a fine lengthy essay. "It would take just one blown tire and a little accident as a result to block that runway for hours. *Crucial* hours."

The colonel's face revealed an impatient contempt which he failed to erase with sufficient swiftness. "Yes, we're certain—"

"Listen to me, sonny!" Kapustin roared, banging the heel of his hand on his desk. The tired old bullying tactics, Babbington thought, his face creased with vitriolic anger at the older man. "The reason the KGB has been so intimately involved in this affair is *not* because Comrade General Babbington is the one who came up with the bright idea . . . or because we *like* working with Stavka. It's because of all the assurances your intelligence people gave the Politburo over Afghanistan. Our nine-year surprise attack!" The colonel flinched as if struck by a hand rather than a voice. "Understand? This time it's not going to go off half-cock!"

At once, he returned to his reading, oblivious of the two livid spots of color over the colonel's cheekbones, and of Babbington's withering glance.

"Comrade General," the colonel began, addressing Babbington, "*Field Trial* was a complete success, even within the very severe parameters you laid down for us. We found out all we needed to know, and our revised estimates are guarantees, not guesswork . . ." He paused, and Babbington was about to reply when Kapustin interposed gruffly:

"Yes, all right—no need to get on your high horse. We're very pleased with you. OK now?" He did not look up once from his reading. Babbington was certain he could see the old man's lips moving silently as he read.

"And those numbers can hold the capital until our friends have secured their hold on the Council and the heir?"

"Against the unlikelihood of disaffected army units, yes. There isn't anyone else, is there, sir?"

Kapustin ostentatiously put down his sheaf of papers and cleared his throat. "*That,* sonny, is what we're banking on—that the Chinks won't come marching in by the million. We would look stupid, wouldn't we now, if that happened!" He roared with laughter.

Babbington saw in the calculating gleam in his eyes, and the set of his heavy frame, the greed for a quick and complete success. It precisely matched his own, however reluctant he was to admit it. After *Teardrop,* and that fiasco in Angola, and a few other choice items of less than glowing color, Kapustin was hungry for a notable, unqualified success: a fruitful, honorable end to a ruthless career. And, when he went, Babbington would be his eventual successor, his promotion sealed by the success of *Topi,* the cheapest colonial acquisition since New York was bought for beads! Brigitte Winterbach and Kapustin would both vacate the stage soon enough, leaving him in *Topi's* spotlight, accepting the applause. It amused Babbington vastly to consider himself as controller of a KGB Directorate. Possibly even Chairman, and with a seat on the Politburo . . .

"Our intelligence," Kapustin continued, "is accurate. Unlike yours in Afghanistan. The Chinks are not coming to save their little slit-eyed cousins in Nepal. You don't have to worry about them, just about your pilots and their individual talents. Their eyesight!" Again, he chuckled. It was a gravelly, almost threatening noise. "You make sure the first Antonov in is flown by someone special. Just in case the control tower still needs securing. You understand what I'm saying?"

The colonel nodded, his cheeks flushing slightly once more. "I understand. The pilot of the first Antonov will be able to cope with—any eventuality."

"Good." Kapustin selected the personnel and equipment lists from the desk and began to study them ostentatiously, running his broad forefinger down column after column. Babbington shrugged for the soldier's benefit, and then announced:

"Thank you, Colonel. Inform the Planning Group that the first civil disturbance will take place tonight in the capital. Small incendiary bombs, leaflets, a large-seeming demonstration against the Council . . . you will, of course, receive reports as they come in. Flying time, by the way?"

"Four hours, maximum."

"Excellent. Security in Indian airspace?"

"With the radar cover of the Hindu Kush and the Karakoram—and no more than an hour. Secure."

The flight path of the airborne force was securely protected by the mountain ranges between Afghanistan and Kashmir.

Trial flights had been done; everything had been done. Babbington allowed himself a feeling of consummation, smiling at the colonel as at an ally if not a friend.

He spread his hands as if in a benediction. He had not, unlike Aubrey, been forced to surrender power. It had been as if he had moved from the white wine to the red with the progression of courses at the same satisfying banquet.

Kapustin interrupted his reverie.

"Thank you, Colonel. That's all. We'll be in touch," he snapped out as calculated insults. He did not look up from his reading.

The colonel stood, nodded to Babbington, who returned the gesture as one of present and future complicity, then gathered his greatcoat and cap and gloves from a chair. He closed the door quietly behind him.

"Right," Kapustin said, without looking at Babbington, "wheel in the Chinaman. Let's hear what he has to say." He threw the file on his desk as if it had been no more than a means of helping him observe Babbington and the soldier. He glowered at Babbington. "Think it's all going to work out nicely, don't you?"

"There's no reason why it should not." There was this basic difficulty in dealing with Kapustin's lunging, vulgar thrusts. Babbington had not, for a long time, had to deal with a— *superior.* A man who did not share access to the same codes of class, upbringing, education. Kapustin was a peasant. It was an irreducible fact of his nature and power. "And you," he continued, "are you as certain of that as I am?" He stroked his beard, head tilted back, striking a pose.

Kapustin grinned. "Maybe," he said. "Anyway, get him in and let's get it over with."

Babbington assented with a nod and moved to a second set of doors and looked into a small anteroom. Lin's face was reflected in the dark, polished dining table on which he patiently leaned his narrow elbows, seeming to stare into the whorls and patterns of wood and polish. He looked up and at Babbington only slowly, like a zoo cat accustomed to captivity and the gazes of flitting human beings. Babbington waved him in, and Lin Yu-Chiang's small, still-young face registered not even acknowledgment. Babbington, despite his long acquaintance with the Chinese intelligence officer, felt distanced, of no importance.

Lin passed close to him, dressed in a drab gray suit of vaguely

Western cut. The smell of cigarette smoke lingered in the air behind him. Babbington closed the doors to the anteroom, watching Kapustin's habitual distrust of Lin gather like a cloud on his broad face.

"Sit down, Colonel." Lin inclined his head and perched on the edge of an ornate, gilded French chair that belonged with the rest of the room's antiques, but which the Chinese made incongruous. "Good trip?"

Lin merely nodded. The patience of machinery. He had been waiting, as if switched off, in the anteroom, beneath framed portraits of leaders and revolutionaries none of whom wore his narrow yellow face and who had little or no knowledge of Lin's culture. He had come out of Kathmandu on the Antonov, after new tires had been flown up with a maintenance team from Delhi. Lin would arrange his own re-entry into Nepal.

"Yu-Chiang," Babbington murmured, sitting in an armchair beside the other two, "is there anything we should know? About Kathmandu, the King—even Brandis and the Germans?"

Kapustin guffawed, but his eyes narrowed with an anticipatory interest.

Lin did not move his body. "I do not think so." His English was excellent. He considered further, then added: "No. The situation as you desire it is obtainable. Brandis has sufficient forces and skill to achieve his objectives." Babbington became irritated with Lin. He wanted to ask him whether he had lost interest, couldn't he show a little enthusiasm! Was this why he habitually spoke disparagingly of Lin to Brigitte, despite their long, mutual treachery? Because Lin always seemed to possess this detached, outsider quality; not reluctant, not aloof, just—nothing?

"No reservations?" he asked coldly. Lin merely shook his head once by way of reply. "And what of Beijing?" Babbington pursued in exasperation.

"They are deceived, as you wished. There is no suspicion of any such move as you contemplate." It was like *listening* to a machine as well as looking at one! Kapustin laughed, and Babbington sensed that his discomfiture was plain on his features. "The Politburo cliques are in a delicate state of balance . . . which should persist at least until the operation is completed." He spoke to the room rather than to either of the men. "The latest wrangling leaves no faction with the power of decision you fear. No one will show the kind of resolve it would need to challenge what you do in Nepal." His voice seemed to have taken on a weary inflection, as if he were reciting an old, disbelieved catechism. But Babbington could not be certain of it. "I assure you of that," Lin concluded.

Babbington suppressed a sigh, his exasperation and dislike put aside. He had had to have Lin there in person, just to *hear* his assurance at first hand. There had been cause for concern, though he had kept the knowledge from Kapustin. During recent weeks, a bellicose faction of the Chinese leadership had appeared to be gaining an upper hand, threatening eventual control of the Politburo. Now he knew it had not happened. *Topi* was safe from any countermeasures from Beijing.

"A drink?" he suggested, the expansive satisfaction of his mood growing.

"Some tea," Lin replied without emphasis of any kind. "Thank you."

"Of course," Babbington murmured, and waited for Kapustin to bark the order into his intercom before he added: "Now, Yu-Chiang, tell us everything that's going on in Kathmandu." His all but unctuous tones made no impression on the calm, pool-like features of the Chinese.

Looking down from the windows of the hospital corridor at the traffic beginning to clot on the Marylebone Road, Aubrey could not stop the shaking in his hands, his arms, his whole frame. Shock, the doctor who had examined him had said soothingly. Anger, outrage, fear, Aubrey told himself, sipping at the mug of hot, sweet tea and refusing to lie down, *just for half an hour.* His hands, clamped around the patterned mug, quivered uncontrollably and the surface of the remaining tea shivered like a miniature pond across which a stiff wind swept.

His head ached, but his chest was tightened unbearably with alarm and distress on Tim's behalf, so that his own slight injuries hardly impinged. Cuts and bruises; a sprained ankle from falling. *Thank God that truck took most of the blast,* they had said. *Otherwise . . .*

Otherwise, Mrs. Grey might have been reduced to the same final condition as Mrs. Carteret, his neighbor. Aubrey shuddered . . . revulsion not shock, he told himself. Mrs. Grey lay drugged asleep in a tiny, aseptic room, the bleeding stanched from her sliced arm, her broken leg in plaster, her burns treated, her eyesight of concern to the specialist. *Thank God for that truck . . .* He could not rid himself of the image of Mrs. Carteret's headless corpse lying on the pavement beside him as he struggled into a sitting position. The fox's head on the old stole had fallen back to lie grotesquely, horribly, where her features should have been. And he had a sprained ankle and a lump on the back of his head! *Glass,* they had said, *a huge, jagged sliver of the windshield. Just like a guillotine, she'd hardly have felt ...*

He suspected he needed the sense of outrage against whichever gang of murderous terrorists had planted the bomb in order to shield himself from his concern over Tim. They had him ... His hands quivered, he felt cold despite the anaesthetizing, stifling heat in the corridor. He encouraged the rage to work on.

Irish bastards, the Special Branch inspector had said. *After the junior minister living next door to you, sir ...* Probably they were. Mrs. Carteret's hat had lain twenty feet away. He had not, thankfully, been able to see her severed head before he was wrapped in red blankets and bundled into the first ambulance with Mrs. Grey on a stretcher, a mask over her suddenly shrunken features, blood moving down a tube into her arm from what looked like slippery meat in a polythene bag. He was ashamed of his lack of concern, his frightened obsession with Tim's capture. *They're here—do something!*

There was nothing he could do. Whatever Tim had stumbled upon in his casual way, it was important enough to—have him killed before he could widen the circle of knowledge. Near him, on a chair, lay the bloodstained yellow envelope containing the developed prints. He could not bring himself to touch it.

"Can't you do something?" he asked again, looking up at Giles Pyott in his fawn overcoat. Giles seemed surprised and even embarrassed by the pleading in his eyes. But nevertheless shook his head, detached and confident.

"Kenneth, I think your lad isn't helping himself one little bit by running away like this. What the devil does he think he can gain by it?"

"Oh, Giles! He isn't running away!"

"Kenneth, you're still in shock ..." Pyott patted the sleeve of the too-big woolen dressing gown they had made him wear. *Make sure you don't get cold, dear ...* "I'm sorry, old friend, but you *are,*" Pyott insisted. "It's a horrid business. And you are concerned about Tim, I appreciate that. But you won't help his cause if anyone else gets to hear your—untenable theories." He smiled, his hand continuing to pat Aubrey's sleeve. Aubrey could not deride the friendship that came perilously close to patronage. Pyott's gray eyes reminded him, tactfully, of his own loss of authority.

"I had to get him out!" Aubrey protested.

"Yes. I rather gather that Orrell is furious with you for using—official channels? The boy's evidently confused. He has been—er, subject to depressions in the past. I want to help him, Kenneth, but I can't if he won't appear. Try to get him to do that, will you?"

Aubrey looked at the folder of prints and saw little more than the already brownish patches of blood. "He seemed concerned at this—transport aircraft."

"Yes. There's a report on my desk now. Pure accident. A genuine emergency. Kathmandu allowed technicians from Delhi to come in and effect repairs. You see, Kenneth, the problem your lad creates—problems, rather. He doesn't help himself by these wild theories about an invasion, does he, mm?" It was impossible to resent the calm, dim-sighted reasonableness of Pyott's disbelief. Aubrey stared unseeingly at the traffic, jerking forward or halting marionettelike to the strings of the traffic lights.

"I see," he murmured. The folder? Not in Giles' present mood. He must study them first, then show him.

"You're all right, Kenneth?" Pyott was looking at his watch. His Ministry of Defence car and driver were waiting on the narrow courtyard in front of the hospital. An arriving ambulance was negotiating the Daimler with difficulty, its driver short-tempered.

"What? Oh, yes . . . yes." He shivered.

"Nasty business."

"Oh, yes. Awful. Poor woman—Mrs. Carteret, my neighbor. Horrible."

As both palliative and valediction, Pyott said: "Look, Kenneth, when you next hear from the lad . . . well, if there's anything *in* anything he says, come to me with it. But get him *home*, Kenneth! This enquiry won't be best pleased if it's kept waiting." He patted Aubrey's arm. "Lunch, as soon as you're fit enough. Must dash—"

"Yes, of course. Thank you for coming, Giles."

"Not at all. Glad—so glad you're all right."

Aubrey watched Pyott's tall, still-erect figure move away down the corridor and beyond the wedged-open fire doors. Then out of sight down the staircase. He was alone in the corridor except for the Special Branch detective detailed to take his statement, *when he felt fit enough to answer questions, of course.* The detective was cleaning his fingernails with a penknife, intently.

Aubrey sighed. Nausea gagged as the headless—*foxheaded!*—body filled his imagination and led his consciousness, as if through some waxworks parade of terrors, to Tim once more. Giles—who could blame Giles? Tim was all but written off by MoD after the Disbandment Dinner fiasco. Assaulting a senior officer. He rubbed his aching, muzzy head. The yellow folder of prints. He felt almost too weak and unbalanced to stoop and lift them. But did so.

They do have Tim, they do have Tim, he repeated to himself. He had told Pyott and Pyott had disbelieved, thinking it the muddleheadedness of shock. But—he fingered the sheaf of prints—could he be made to believe?

Is your lad off his rocker, Kenneth? Pyott's response to the transport aircraft's emergency landing at Kathmandu airport. *Invasion? I hardly think so.* He shuffled through the first prints, finding himself placed on a dusty, light-filled street, foreign and too-brightly colored. And immediately recognized the European in each of the half-dozen pictures of the outdoor café tables. *Brandis . . .* Gerd Brandis. At once, relief that Tim's story was more than mere delusion was drowned by a sharpened, renewed anxiety, almost a dread. Tim for Kurt. She'd recognized the justice of it, the opportunity to tranquilize her rage and grief.

"Brandis," he murmured aloud, as if Pyott were still beside him, still needing to be convinced. "Brigitte's trusted and true *Hauptfeldwebel,* her sergeant-major, Tim . . ." He broke off. The Special Branch detective seemed unconcerned. *Oberst* Gerd Brandis, MfS *Ausland.* If he was in Kathmandu, then it was important; Tim's danger was only too real, his story unexaggerated.

He studied the impassive features of the Chinese. The two men gave no appearance of knowing each other or of even speaking to one another. But they had been, they were, they did, Tim had assured him. Something tickled about the Chinese, as if he should know him, but he did not. Could not remember.

But, he could and would find out. The Chinese was involved, so were locals, even the police, Tim had claimed. All to stop one young man who had taken photographs. The telephone exchange already in their pockets, the recklessness with which they had pursued a man who had no inkling of what they were doing, but had simply stumbled into the clearing where they were plotting . . . what? The police in their pocket, too. Why? To what purpose?

Whatever this business was, it was already well advanced. He rubbed his chin slowly, ignoring the little bleats of betrayal offered at the back of his mind by Mrs. Grey, Mrs. Carteret's corpse, Tim's acute danger. He stared at the halted traffic in both directions along the Marylebone Road. The traffic blurted forward as the lights changed toward the Westway and Euston. Cars, trucks, vans moving. Others parked, littering the narrow concrete strips and curves in front of the buildings opposite. Slowly, as the dust motes of Tim's scattered, unconnected facts whirled in his head, he became aware that he had been staring at one particular black car drawn up on the curve of a driveway fifty yards away; then at a drab green van of unidentifiable make; finally, at a second car, a blue Ford. They had formed a kind of net to hold his muddled thoughts.

He'd also been staring at a face that had kept its attention, in fixed though irregular bouts, on the windows of the hospital. There *was* no pattern to it, but he sensed rather than saw, as the traffic once more stilled in both directions, movement and purpose; purpose undistracted by the pedestrians, by people weaving between the cars. A purpose which had intently observed his window and the departure of Pyott in his MoD limousine. His attention narrowed further. The man beside the green van at that moment had, he was certain of it, walked from the black car with . . . yes, diplomatic license plates. Minutes earlier someone from the van had passed from that car to the Ford, then back again. It was as if they had left silvery, snail-like trails on the ground. The rear windows of the van were darkly tinted, its doors shut. Suddenly, amid all the cars parked in all the driveways and entrances, it was incongruous.

There was some kind of flat metal box on the rear window shelf of the Ford. Neither of the car's aerials were for a radio or car telephone. Beside the metal box was—some kind of small, shining dish.

He felt as if struck on the chest, because he knew exactly, precisely what he saw. His lips worked loosely, as if trying to swallow back words he had not, in fact, uttered. He glanced wildly around at the Special Branch detective, now reading *The Sun*.

They had heard! Had heard his conversation with Giles. Knew what he knew or suspected, what Tim had managed to tell him. The laser must be in the anonymous van. Unable to prevent himself, he touched the membrane of the glass in front of his lips. There, just there, the beam of the laser eavesdropper would be aimed like a gun, picking up each microvibration of the glass as he and Pyott had spoken—as he had blurted out the identity of Brandis! They would have heard the squeaking of the bed that had passed him minutes earlier. Laser eavesdroppers were inaccurate, easily confused, liable to malfunction . . . but he dare not rely upon that folklore. In the Ford, the little dish aerial would pick up the reflected beam of the laser. He strained to look, but could see neither of its occupants wearing headphones. Nevertheless, he was coldly certain. They were that much concerned . . .

. . . because of Tim. The telephone calls.

He felt sick, and pressed one hand to his stomach, the other against his mouth. *Irish bastards.* He shook his head vehemently. No. Brigitte. As if to confirm his conclusions, the man beside the van crossed to the Ford and leaned into it. Brigitte had overstepped the undrawn but understood boundaries of the secret world. Killed bystanders, the ignorant and innocent, in her attempt to kill him.

The nausea began to pass. There might be time—they would have to interrogate Tim, find out what he knew . . . He sniffed loudly, his thoughts racing. He turned to the detective.

"I—er, just want to check on my housekeeper," he announced. The detective looked up, nodded, and returned to his perusal of the sports headlines. Aubrey passed him, counseling relaxation, lack of haste.

Gently, he pushed open the door to Mrs. Grey's tiny room. She lay pale and ashen, looking very old and small in the bed; deeply asleep. A tube in her arm. Aubrey was seized once more by the violent anger of outrage. *She* had done this! *She* had ordered Tim taken. *She* had tried to kill him—*had* killed Mrs. Carteret, whose only offense was an inability to compromise with the late 1980s! He threw off the offending, too-big dressing gown and picked up his overcoat from a chair.

The indignity of the removal of Mrs. Grey's partial dentures struck him, and he clenched his fists, enraged. Brigitte had no *right!*

He had, almost unconsciously, picked up the folder and its prints. He placed them in his pocket, and buttoned the overcoat. He must call Mrs. Grey's sister, so that his housekeeper could be looked after when she left the hospital. Meanwhile, she was safe here. He thought momentarily of the Special Branch detective in the corridor, but shook his head as Pyott's disbelief loomed like his tall figure. If he did not go now, he would be watched and followed . . . he must go, to a hotel, any hotel, at least for the moment. He'd use the rear entrance of the hospital. Slip away.

He looked intently at Mrs. Grey's unmoving form. He must go.

Behind his closed eyelids, he saw the needle bright in his arm. His throat was dry. The sensation of falling, of being held and bundled into something . . . then blackness. He made to move, to open his eyes, but there was some small, cold nucleus to his swirling thoughts that insisted he remain still, pretending unconsciousness. Demanded that he *listen* . . .

He smelled rough blankets and chilly air seeping into what must be a small, darkened room. No, light increased somewhat beyond his eyelids. Daylight . . . but when? How? Where? Another Timothy Gardiner had already opened his eyes, studied the room. He could feel the blanket under his palm now. Smell cooking, spicy and distant. Hear? Nothing. A thin wind, outside, the creaking of a door or shutter. He continued to listen until the silence tautened and throbbed in his ears. Then the cautious, cold Timothy eased open his eyelids.

The stripes of a shutter along one wall. Cold air leaking in and a thin sunlight. He remembered the Germans, walking between them, the airport toilet, the needle, the satisfied smiles, the lurch into oblivion. He felt cold and frightened, his skin prickling with gooseflesh. He fully opened his eyes, and was alone in the room which was close, untidy, almost filled with the narrow cot on which he lay. Where? He sat up and lifted his legs off the stale-smelling bed. His head lurched so that he felt his thoughts spilled sideways. He held his head and groaned softly. The cold nucleus in his mind expanded, was icily angry and aggressive. He recognized his father's nature.

He stood up softly and tiptoed to the small square of shuttered window, easing his nose and eye against the slats. The smell of thin mountain air. Peaks stretching away from him like a strip of unenlarged film. White, enormous flanks, already pinkening with the sunset, to the—the east of him. Four, five, six . . . the peaks of Annapurna. There was excitement at the recognition. He was east of the Annapurna Himal, in Nepal. The mountains stretched away like huge white ships in line astern. He must be somewhere in the Kali Gandaki gorge, perhaps near Marpha or one of the other villages close to it.

He was . . . what? Nearly forty miles from Pokhara, in a direct line . . . days away, days—

—hunger, weakness, fear. The cold nucleus retreated and he was left with the self who had been surprised and caught like a child. He began shivering, sat heavily on the hard cot, hunched into a captive posture. The mountains outside, strips of pink-white through the shutter, hemmed him. No one knew where he was.

Noise, steps on wood. He whirled about, shuddering. Isolation pressed, the ignorance of the rest of the world, even of Aubrey. No one knew where he was or could hope to find him. The footsteps died away. He thought he heard a voice. He rubbed his arms, his face, feeling his mouth loose and wet under the heels of his hands. What did they want with him? What would they do—to him? You're alive, alive, if they hadn't *wanted* you alive, you wouldn't be here! They wouldn't have flown you from Delhi if they hadn't wanted to know!

What? What he knew? Who else knew, how much . . . ?

He jerked as if a current of electricity had been passed through his body as the door banged open. *He* was there, smiling, assured, proprietarial. The German who had wanted him killed and now wanted him alive. He closed the door behind him and opened the shutter, banging his hand against it. He studied Gardiner in the ruddy light that fell across the cot and splashed on the wall, holding his elbow in one hand, his chin stroked by the other. Head slightly on one side; unthreatening. Gardiner stared beyond him at the peaks of the Annapurna massif. They were no longer familiar. They were tinged with capture rather than dying sunlight.

"My name is Brandis," he announced after a long, quizzical silence. "And you are Timothy Gardiner, late of the Brigade of Gurkhas . . . and almost a blood relation of Sir Kenneth Aubrey into the bargain. Your father was, indeed, an agent for British Intelligence. As are you."

Gardiner shook his head. "No, I am not."

"Well," Brandis said, "that is what we are here to find out, of course." The lines seemed stilted, but the voice was serious, as if Brandis had just that moment minted the threats. "Your pedigree would suggest that you are an agent. Your actions rather do the same, do they not?"

"Don't be bloody stupid! I'm an army officer."

"So am I, under certain circumstances," Brandis replied, smiling. He leaned against the window frame and the mountains were diminished beyond his shoulder. He folded his arms. "I'm afraid it won't be easy for you," he announced. "We do not have a great deal of time to waste. I am under pressure. You will be placed under even greater pressure. There's nothing I can do about that except regret it."

"What the hell do you expect me to be able to tell you?"

"More or less everything you know . . . Aubrey knows, the British know. About *us.*"

"There's nothing to tell!" Anger had replaced fear. The threat of violence had become a need for violence. He clenched his fists on his thighs.

"I doubt that. If it turns out to be the case, then I won't have wasted too much time." He looked at his watch. "We must begin soon," he murmured, as if talking of a short, casual journey. Gardiner saw the urgency on Brandis' features. "Yes, you can come in now!" he called. Two men, neither of whom he recognized, entered. At once his arms were pinioned, he was pulled to his feet. "Get on with it!" Brandis snapped impatiently.

Gardiner, as they thrust him through the door, began counting. Each second. Each small parcel of time . . . but his imagination struggled out of the net he was making for it and turned on him. Pain, violence, isolation. Twenty-two—pain, pain . . . three, twenty-four, five, six—violence . . .

The room where they began hitting him about the face and body was like a cellar, cold and empty. Through the blood from a cut over his eye, he thought he saw the face of the Chinaman hovering in the increasingly opaque, unfocused room.

The leather briefcase lay open like a small suitcase on one of the suite's twin beds. A new identity lay neatly parceled in elastic bands—Keith Allen, retired civil servant. Aubrey stood at the darkening windows overlooking Hyde Park Corner with its thick, brake-glaring evening traffic and the solemn, hardly noticed bulks of the Wellington Arch and Apsley House. He had brushed the new, unused documents absently with his hand, like a man preparing to change the cards he held. Money in half-a-dozen currencies, large-denomination notes, a passport in the name of Allen, visas easily inserted if required.

He stared down at the small whiskey he had allowed himself, swilling the spot of liquid gently at the bottom of the glass. He had sent three good prints of Brandis and the Chinese to Tony Godwin, now ensconced in Central Registry. Whether Godwin knew that he had resigned would not matter. Tony would locate and ID the Chinaman. Now, it was time to ring Peter Shelley. He must know something about Tim—anything.

He put the glass down and perched himself on the edge of one of the beds. Soft, warm light fell on his hands as he dialed. A print of Brandis lay on the coverlet, a hard sunlight paling his features. If Brandis was involved, then whatever was happening in Nepal was Brigitte's operation.

"Peter, it's—"

"Sir Kenneth!" Shelley sounded almost matronly, primly shocked and rather annoyed. "Where are you? Why did you leave the hospital like—"

"—a thief in the night?" Aubrey's anxiety made him impatient with Shelley. "Peter, there's little time for that. Please don't make any attempt to discover my whereabouts. I have my own reasons."

"But you need the service's—facilities?" Shelley asked almost bitchily. "Oh, very well. There'll be no trace."

"Thank you."

Shelley burst out: "Orrell is absolutely *furious*, Sir Kenneth! This whole business with Travel and Grahame. I—I'm being sent to Washington to mend fences over the affair in Florence . . ." His anger tailed off, becoming a bruised, sullen silence.

"I'm sure you'll do a splendid job, Peter." Then he became ashamed at his spite, and added: "Peter, I'm sorry, but Tim has disappeared. I must have news of him. The pilot who flew him out, where is he now?"

"Squealing to our man in Delhi! We're going to have to bail him out and smooth things over. As for young Gardiner, he's simply gone AWOL. The pilot claims he's just hopped off. Avoiding coming home to face the music, from what I gather."

"Peter!" Aubrey was shocked by the specious credibility of the explanation. The mirrors in the large bedroom of the suite revealed him isolated and disbelieved even before he spoke. "Peter, I'm—certain that Tim is in great danger. You see, I—"

Shelley intruded with: "Sir Kenneth, I have to catch this evening's flight. Is there something you want from me?"

A bland, blank wall. Orrell stood behind Shelley's voice, silently approving, content to play his masters' political games and utterly at their bidding. A watercolor sketch of the hard disbelief of people like Roth in the CIA. He felt himself beached and stranded, a curious sea-creature thought extinct.

"I don't think you understand," he protested.

"About Gardiner, you mean? He's caused everyone a great deal of trouble, Sir Kenneth!"

"But he's in grave danger!"

"I very much doubt that." Impatience tempered with indifference.

"Then you won't help me?"

"I don't see what you can expect us to do."

Aubrey swallowed. His chest and stomach felt watery. The room seemed to surround him with huge shadows. "Have a pleasant trip!" he snapped and put down the receiver angrily. His throat was dry. It was all but impossible to believe Tim was still alive, to cling to the comfort of his speculations in the taxi on the way to the bank to collect the briefcase and his new identity.

They must be keeping him alive as a lever . . . even to find out what he knows, what I know! Now, that idea seemed to slip into the shadows of the room like cigarette smoke and dissipate. He stood up, restless for action, but merely switched on the television.

News.

" . . . though no one has claimed responsibility for the bombing, the Anti-Terrorist Squad's senior officers are convinced it was the work of one of the factions of the INLA. Bomb materials recovered from the wreckage have, they say, the hallmarks of that particular organization . . ."

Savagely, he switched off the set, raging at the impotence that he felt in himself. He could do *nothing.* The images of his flat with its scorched façade and shattered windows faded on his retinae. The junior minister who lived next door was presumed to be the target. He had glimpsed the man, and his daughter, the moment the image on the set vanished. Sara, wasn't that the daughter's name?

The telephone rang. He started guiltily until he remembered Godwin, then snatched up the receiver.

"Yes?" he demanded breathlessly. Action, activity, something to do—

"Sir—Tony Godwin."

"Tony! Have you something for me?"

"Christ, that bomb, sir!"

"Never mind that now."

"Why the hotel?"

"Tony!"

"Sorry, sir . . . yes, I think I've got something. There's bits of his file scattered everywhere, so I haven't seen all of it by any means. A lot of recent material's not available, can't think why—"

"Yes, Tony?"

"Oh, sorry again. His name's Lin Yu-Chiang, and he's Ministry of Public Tranquility all right. Army intelligence sometimes, too. He's never risen higher than Colonel, but that's obviously a cover. He was in Hong Kong until a couple of years ago, doing something menial. Mixed up with security for that whole deal with the PRC over the colony, I gather. That's just gossip, though."

"I see." Aubrey was disappointed, and out of breath. As if he had run after a bus or train, only to miss it. "How far back does the file extend?" He felt he was concentrating on Colonel Lin now as a means of masking his anxiety regarding Tim. His own danger had temporarily subsided.

"He was in Malaya, that's certain. Late on during the Emergency, but he was there . . . then Beijing and various foreign postings. Like the printout, sir? I can send it round on the q.t. if you like."

"Thank you, Tony. And his recent activities?"

"Ah, that's under Foreign Office now, not us. He must either be important, or very unimportant . . ."

"The Foreign Office has a special interest in this Lin, or dealings with him? I don't understand."

"I could make a written request for the file, sir."

"Don't do that. I'll take that on. Address the printout here, would you—Keith Allen is the name."

"Right, sir. Was it the Irish, sir?"

"What? Oh, perhaps . . ."

"If you need any help, sir, you know the number."

"Thank you, Tony."

"Take care—" But Aubrey lowered the receiver and cut the

call, abstracted, staring at the notes he had scribbled on the bed-side pad. Lin, the Foreign Office—and *Brigitte?*

He felt ashamed of the ease with which Tim's danger receded into the back of his mind. But, if the Foreign Office ever kept files on intelligence agents, they were always copies, not the file itself. Especially one involved with the East Germans. He dialed Alex Davenhill's flat. The Knightsbridge number continued to ring, and he began to tap his foot impatiently.

"Alex?" he asked, remembering over the years the number of young men who had answered Davenhill's telephone.

"Yes? Kenneth! My poor dear . . . I was just on my way out! Oh, dear, I heard the news from Humphrey Appleby this morning—they've forced you to resign!" All pretense was dropped from his tone. The affectation of a highly camp manner denoted concern, even honesty. "That dreadful man Orrell and his awful *wife!* What have you done to me, Kenneth?"

"I'm sorry, Alex. I couldn't find any way of—holding on."

"I understand, my dear. God, some of our masters are so *crass* it takes my breath away!" Then he added, more simply: "Why have you upped and disappeared, Kenneth? What are you up to?"

"I need time to think—a problem."

"I understand. You think I can help?"

"Thank you. How is, er?"

"I'm still being faithful to Bill. Well, almost. But it's doctors' certificates on first dates these days, Kenneth."

"Alex, what do you know of Colonel Lin Yu-Chiang of the MPT?"

There was a pause. Aubrey felt his fingers intertwining themselves superstitiously. Alex Davenhill *could* help, in his position as SIS Special Adviser to the Foreign Office. But would he? He must have the file—at least, be aware of its contents.

"What's your interest, my dear?"

Aubrey resisted the little tide of concern that pressed him to blurt out what had happened to Tim. Cautiously, he said: "Pro-fessional, I think."

"Oh, then there's no need to worry. Lin is strictly kosher. He—helped coordinate security throughout the Hong Kong negotiations . . . here, there, everywhere. Nice chap. Bit on the quiet side. He liaises with us . . . oh, of course, you're wondering why we have his file!"

"Partly that."

"Is he the reason you dropped out of sight? If so, you needn't worry about Colonel Lin. One of us. Well, not one of me, but certainly one of us!"

"I see. He's gone legit, then?"

"Definitely, my dear! Very useful, very trusted in Beijing, which is always a help. The only blot on his character was the fact that at one time he liaised with an old friend of yours."

"Who?"

"Andrew Babbington, who shall be nameless."

"What?"

"Oh, don't worry about it, it wasn't the poor chap's fault. Andrew was top dog for security, after all. Who else would he liaise with to protect the Foreign Secretary in Hong Kong and his own top people over here? Not his fault at all."

"No, of course not." There were small, cramped pools of light around the bedside lamps and a strengthening darkness beyond their glow. Aubrey felt chilly, his mind spinning a pattern without proof but which seemed justified. "So, the Foreign Office can vouch for Colonel Lin?"

"*I* will, if you like."

"That's fine, then. He's out of court as far as my little problem is concerned."

"The worst thing, of course, was he was always staying at Andrew's *house!* So embarrassing after Andrew popped over to the other side. That was all during the 'New Territories' arrangements—you know, the Nepal arrangement . . . ? Of course you do. Look, Kenneth, I absolutely must fly. Pavarotti's singing in *Ballo* tonight. Can't miss the curtain, dear!"

"Alex, this business about Nepal—" he began.

"Must fly! Our friends are getting very sticky about turning up late. Apparently, it's up to us to put bottoms on seats and convince the Arts Council the Garden needs all the money in the world! Logic slightly cockeyed there, but never mind. Love, Kenneth—anytime you need a shoulder to cry on—'bye!"

"Alex!" But he was gone, the receiver humming. "Damn!" he exclaimed. "Oh, *damnation!*" They were *all* involved in it! The unholy Trinity. Brigitte, Kapustin at the First Directorate, no doubt—and *Babbington*. Lin had to be a double, and had been even before they unearthed Babbington's treachery. He was liaising, all right—with Brandis! What did they intend in Nepal? "New Territories," was it? What did that mean?

He all but reached for the telephone. Alex would have left

by now. Alex . . . ? Alex must tell him more. He had friends, but not authority. Alex would listen, he would help. But how much help could he give?

"Damnation," he breathed, his chest constricted. Tim seemed like a pawn, an eye for all the eyes he had put out. God—
—what would they do to him?

He walked into the lounge, flicking on the television to distract himself from his foreboding, switching on lights so that they blazed out, dimming the city outside the windows. News, still . . .

" . . . just receiving reports of a number of bombing incidents in Kathmandu, the capital of Nepal, home of the world-famous Gurkhas . . ." A map of the long, sausage-shaped country sandwiched between India and Tibet—Russia and China, to be exact, he thought fiercely. " . . . more than twenty small devices, a number of dead and injured . . . accusations surround members of the pro-Western faction on the King's council of Ministers . . . King, of course, is suffering from an inoperable stomach cancer and is close to . . ."

His mouth dropped open. He saw Tim as a small, still point on which rested . . . this!

It was the answer, it was what Tim had stumbled upon. A change of government in Nepal . . . a Soviet government in Nepal!

Tim's life was irrelevant to them.

8

The Grain of Seed

The whole building which had once housed the Senate was a museum, and the fact irritated Babbington like a skin complaint he could not rid himself of. His cramped, dingy offices were two short corridors away from those Lenin had occupied between 1918 and 1923. It was an example of Kapustin's humor, though the Russian peasant had referred to the choice as expressive of the respect and gratitude felt by the KGB toward the English Comrade General.

Dingy, bare, cramped, untidy. A low ceiling, the beams darkened by age and cigarette smoke and countless open fires. The grate was empty now, except for powdery woodash. Again no one had come to light the fire, and he rubbed his hands, his breath clouding the grimy window through which he could look across bare, gaunt trees toward the long façade of the Arsenal. The idea of the room as a metaphor rubbed against him. An attic of power, the low leaves of a king's palace; the servants' quarters. He was unimpressed by the proximity of Lenin's offices; just as he was unaware of the monochrome photograph of the revolutionary on the cracked plaster of one wall of the office. Ridiculous to be organizing the annexation of a country from this place! He snorted in a mild, almost neutral self-ridicule.

The taciturn guard was, inevitably, in the corridor outside. He switched on the kettle and shook the coffee jar. Grains rattled in a lonely fashion. Nescafé, at least. He had requested a percolator. Someone had stolen the one he had transferred from his flat. It was ludicrous. The image this place supplied to the vanity of his inward eye enraged him.

He opened the digest of material he had collected from the security desk on the ground floor, checking over the reports from Kathmandu. Bombs, a violent demonstration, looting, the police restoring order late and with difficulty . . . rumors, as were required, of right-wing elements in the country, as yet unspecified and unnamed, seeking to overturn the Council. He plucked his beard often, as if silently punctuating the signals and reports.

Eventually, he completed reading the Kathmandu reports coming direct from Brandis, copies only now to Brigitte in Berlin. That idea, at least, was pleasurable. He began examining any other files in the morning digest. Skimmed his eye across them after fanning them with a broad, long-fingered hand. Felt settled, more at ease. *Topi* was working well—

Bomb . . . London . . . Regent's Park area? He hardly noticed it with the forebrain. But the street, the exact place, registered with his memory.

. . . Aubrey's address . . . Park Square . . . Aubrey.

Chilled and heated in the same moment, all well-being dissipated, he scanned the report from London. IRA, but London Station had no warning, no indication . . . junior minister . . . yes, they had noted the address, but only noted it—appending yet another report confirming Aubrey's resignation! No mention of Aubrey being injured, or of his whereabouts. He flicked over the sheet, studying the attached snapshot, taken presumably from the gardens of Park Square. Windows broken . . . ah, yes, the housekeeper in hospital, nothing on Aubrey. He clenched his fist. What did it mean? IRA—why would they hit Aubrey anyway? The junior minister was insignificant, hardly worth a paragraph in any paper relying on tits for its circulation! Was Aubrey the target? London Rezident had scribbled the comment *No Irish connection or motive—any action required?* He plucked his new beard, staring down toward the hundreds of cannon ranged along the front of the Arsenal; captured from Napoleon during the hideous retreat of 1812. How might this be connected . . . was it connected? He admitted both his obsession with Aubrey and his paranoia concerning *Topi*'s security. There could be no connection between Nepal and this bomb in London. Yet it concerned Aubrey, who must have been the target of the bomb. He felt the violence of his hatred for the man well into his chest, making breathing an effort. It was as if someone had tried to cheat him by making an attempt on Aubrey's life.

Who had made the attempt? *Who* considered Aubrey a legitimate target less than two days after his forced resignation? *Not* the KGB!

So, he would signal London Rezident and have the matter investigated. Much as he disliked Priabin, that arrogant, ambitious survivor and youngest general in the service. Kapustin had acquired him, by Nikitin's direct intervention, after his return to Moscow Center to be feted. That had been in the spring. Already, the man had the plum London posting so that he could, in Kapustin's words, *begin to learn about the real work, the real play!* Priabin had survived one huge disaster during his career, was as slippery as a cartload of monkeys, and clever . . . and still only forty. Oh, yes, he was certainly a rival . . .

. . . but he was useful enough to check on this bomb business without alarming MI5 or Special Branch. Aubrey . . . only old Brigitte, the spider woman herself, had ever hated Aubrey as much or more than he, and even she did not have his own hatred of England. Aubrey and England. Babbington tried to rid himself of his sense of his country and his former place within it. He had already gathered disciples around his ruthlessness, but he was still not at home in Moscow, inside the Kremlin walls.

He excised the thought with an effort of will. He stared at the ranks of long-captured cannon and sensed again the onset of winter. He thought of Brigitte Winterbach, the old Jewess, the hating old Jewess . . .

No, she had no immediate cause. Not now, not at this crucial time. His sense of *Topi*'s smooth acceleration would not come to him. Instead of satisfaction he felt the bomb in Park Square niggle and itch. Almost as a reflex, as if scratching, he snatched up the telephone.

"Signals . . . yes, London, fully secure. *Now!*"

He knew, through the pain, that he had said something. Not something forced or beaten from him but contained in a defiant, raging cry. The Chinese had flinched, Brandis' face had become less detached. His eyelids were a screen where red flared like explosions along an horizon. Something . . . *I know! Aircraft— transports—I know, you bastards!* The animal-like rage had betrayed him. His body still seemed to flinch and tense and fold as it had done against their fists and boots. The bruising and whatever might be broken was like a heavy, suffocating weight all over his body, creating recurring agonies. Sometimes, the pain rushed over him like a breaking wave and withdrew as if dragging stones across his skin.

. . . throwing Nepal to the army like a bone to a dog . . . your people's fault! Brandis had been yelling at him, his face distorted, as if he, too, had lost all consciousness of place and purpose; screaming at each other like man and wife locked in a mutual domestic hatred. *They're leaving the place to the Chinese and we can't allow that—blame them for what's happening to you!*

Brandis, too, had been hitting him then, for a time. *Your people shouldn't have given it to the Chinks!*

He could not open his eyes properly. They watered with the effort. He shuddered at the damage they might have inflicted already, and the damage to come. He was terrified of more pain, hard though it was to imagine greater physical torment. It seemed he could not touch any part of his body. He was afraid to let his hands inspect his injuries in the darkness of the room. He groaned, but the noise seemed a long way off and drowning. He let the blood and saliva dribble from the immobile corner of his swollen mouth. *Fuck off, fuck off, fuck off!*

Eventually, he had been returned, knees scraping along bare wooden floors, toes dragging like brakes, arms pulled almost from their sockets, head lolling, to this dark, close little room to wait until they were ready to question him again. He saw the sentences describing his situation stutter as if from a poorly operated typewriter along that margin lit by flashes of pain. Dim moonlight filtered through the closed shutter; there was a faint noise of shuffling feet outside on the veranda. The moonlight, blurred and wet and pale, fell tiredly down the wall like the light of a failing torch. He groaned aloud and the noise was a little nearer, it belonged to him.

He felt a raging hatred. He touched at his eyes, his mouth, swollen lips and cheeks, his bruised chin and the caked, dried blood. Damp hair . . . his ribs, each one detonated by his fingers into another explosion of pain. Groin, thighs, arms, hands, fingers . . . he still possessed his fingernails.

Cool, pale moonlight, chill, thin, sweet air. Balm . . .

. . . the wise man makes an island for his soul which many waters cannot overflow . . . self-possession, he felt that. But no sense of peace because the moonlight was like a thin, ragged curtain at a blank window. He ended his tense, careful examination

of his pain. Broken ribs, internal injuries? He could not tell. *Hate is not conquered by hate, but by love* . . . He felt detached, the Buddhist words and ideas floating in his head without magnetic attraction either to him or to each other. Something had happened to him within the beating. Something unlooked for and frightening. That yelling, that insane screaming until his throat ached. *This body is frail like a jar, make your mind strong like a fortress and fight* . . . No, it wasn't like that, it was aggressive not wise, a rage that awakened his injuries to renewed violence. It was—his father, his father as Aubrey had always described him and as he had always sensed him to be. Richard Gardiner, the most dangerous man . . . *watch for anger of the mind* . . . *those free from hate* . . . It meant nothing. The *Dhammapada*'s teachings were like tedious sermons, unreasonable and ignorant restraints. His eyes were wet. The disconnected, jumbled aphorisms revolved slowly in his head. His rage coursed through him like icy water, chilling even the heat of his pain.

His father was no longer a shadow in the room with him, but had somehow entered him. His anger was like an insane passion for a friend's wife, and he felt powerless to resist it, to do anything except employ it or be used by it. *Hate harms human nature.* He felt the ache of his disbelief, his loss. Tears—

—anger. *All beings tremble before danger, all fear death.* They would kill him, once they knew all he knew, knew that no one else knew or believed. The statement was clear in his mind . . . *when a man considers this, he does not kill or cause to kill* . . .

And that was it, winking out like the last grains of light from a long-exploded star. Gone. He sniffed loudly. His mouth, nose, and eyes were wet. Gone. There was nothing left of his beliefs. There was only anger, and calculation. He shivered. There seemed a huge darkness looming at the back of his mind. Then a fresh wave of pain and its accompanying rage diminished his perspective. Smells of the room, the pale light on the wall, slatted, the shuffling of feet . . . the time! He lifted his left arm achingly, and squinted until the luminous dial of his watch gathered into focus as if he were looking at it through poor binoculars. Midnight . . . one? Nearly three in the morning. He had been unconscious or semiconscious for hours!

Then he heard Brandis' voice again, yelling in his head. *Aubrey's disappeared* . . . *why? What did you tell him, what does he know? Tell me, damn you, tell me!* There were no other words, no other voice. Brandis had little time available, he had promised that. They would be back soon.

He tried to sit upright, his head lurched and his whole frame ached in protest. Four times, four, until he was able to place his feet lumpenly on the bare floor and hold his head in his hands. He ignored the body's protests, its weariness and weakness, sitting as tensely as he could, as if prepared. Sitting was enough for the moment; the illusion of strength. His eyes blinked away red pain again and again.

He could move only with difficulty, but there was no doubt in his mind, no fear. Whoever came would have a gun. Food? The land was littered with tiny villages, sources of food. A compass? He knew where he was already, where he must go. But, the gun. He wanted a gun. His hands were shaking as he clasped them together in front of him. He knew he had been robbed of all his beliefs, his illusions. He wanted only to expend his rage in violence against them—Brandis, the Chinese, all of them.

Dmitri Priabin, the KGB's London Rezident, was enjoying himself in Regent's Park. The girl, whose hand he held as they strolled, looked utterly unsecretarial, but that was mostly makeup and new clothes. She was no actress but she sufficed to complete his cover. Just another item, like his denims, the dark glasses, the loose-sleeved collarless shirt and diamonded slipover. The too-long hair. Of course, Special Branch knew what he looked like and knew his function at the Embassy. Par for the course. But he was confident, even careless, that they would not assume that the still-young man with the pale, red-haired girl was a general in the First Directorate. Almost, it did not matter. There was no danger in this. He could have sent a minion, but had not.

He squeezed the girl's hand, sensing her nervousness. A glazier was already at work on the broken windows . . . yes, that was Aubrey's flat.

He murmured something calming to the girl as they passed through the gates toward Park Square. Police in uniform, others plainclothed. Parked cars, minor roadworks that were probably a cover. And a man looking unaccustomed to the small dog on the lead he held. The center of gravity of the scene was the flat belonging to the junior minister.

He sensed eyes and binoculars move, pause, pass over and beyond them. The girl shivered, despite the sunlight and her sweater. He cautioned her, firmly squeezing her arm so that she winced. Then he put his arm around her, his other arm crooked so that he held his worn leather jacket draped down his back. He was unarmed. Yes, they were watching Aubrey's flat just as intently as that of the junior minister.

They strolled across the road to the opposite pavement. The girl's arm was hesitantly around his waist as they passed Aubrey's flat and the debris of glass and metal that remained on the pavement and in the gutter. Scorch marks. The façade of the Nash house was scarred. Where was Aubrey now? He shook his head, kissing the top of the girl's head, appearing to whisper to her. Not his business.

The girl seemed to relax as they moved away from the flat and the Special Branch surveillance. It was difficult to say, but he had seen no obvious signs of East Germans or anyone else apart from the British. Aubrey had evidently disappeared, just as he had reported to the Center. He took his arm away from the girl's shoulders and brushed his hand through his hair. A cloud hid the sun, and then it flashed out again—

—flashed, too, on glass behind glass, something focused from an upstairs window further along the row of white façades. Someone watching comings and goings. He stood looking up, languidly brushing his hair with his hand, waiting to be observed. He smiled, removing his dark glasses. The binoculars that had glinted sunlight from the window above the *For Sale* notice withdrew. A face hesitantly appeared, one he vaguely recognized. He waved. Two bemused, embarrassed expressions, like those of small boys. He waved again. A hesitant hand returned the gesture guiltily.

Yes, they were both on the strength of the East German Embassy. His people had even used the older, thinner of the two! He nodded his head ironically and moved on. Her role completed, the girl now strode at his side, rubbing her sweatered arms against the chill of the returned breeze.

Priabin stopped at the first telephone box on the Marylebone Road, paused to recollect the number he wanted, then dialed. Almost at once, the call was answered.

Without bothering to identify himself, Priabin said: "I want to know why some of your boys are interested in Kenneth Aubrey." He spoke slowly and distinctly. "What their interest is and how far they're carrying it. I think I need that information quickly. By—oh, three at the latest, even though it's a Saturday."

He put down the telephone. Dust and petrol on the breeze, as if summer were not quite over. Hurrying cloud, the first few spots of rain. Dark leaves curled in the gutter, rustling past his feet.

"Come on—we'll get a taxi," he said to the girl.

Once more, Aubrey glanced into the rearview mirror, as surreptitiously as if he had not been alone in the car. The same gray Renault, three years old and unremarkable, was still there, two hundred yards and two cars behind him. Events were accelerating. The presence of the Renault informed him that there was no course of action that was not dangerous or already exposed to surveillance. They must have seen him renting the car, or picked him up leaving London. Weariness and a sleepless night assailed him, as if the car had run into deep water.

Special Branch had been in the hotel foyer; he had avoided them. None of the morning staff on the desk could identify him from his photograph, presumably, since they had not registered him. Alex Davenhill's Knightsbridge flat had been under discreet surveillance. He looked into the mirror once more. Now, the Renault was one car and a mere hundred yards adrift of him.

The road was straight, level, the countryside high-seeming and virtually treeless. Stony fields. Cotswold names on the road signs. Down Ampney. He was between Cricklade and Cirencester. He had to talk to Davenhill, just briefly and in the fond hope that he might avoid the encounter he dreaded with Babbington's wife. He had to know how intimately Lin and Babbington had been involved in each other's lives and with any unwritten accord that might exist concerning Nepal between HMG and the People's Republic of China. Vague, often-expressed sentiments floated in his head like motes of dust . . . *oh, the Chinese will make good landlords, no need to worry about them . . . safe hands, and all that* . . . a remark half-overheard and ignored at his club, just recently. It might be HMG's official view, the view of the Foreign Office, or the PM and SIS, for all he knew. But Babbington was a confirmed traitor and Lin was evidently a double agent. And both of them had been intimate with whatever agreement or accord might exist. He *must* know what it involved.

Radio news . . . He glanced into the mirror. The gray Renault was as steadily behind him as if he were towing it on a long, invisible rope. " . . . Foreign Minister of Nepal, as he left London today to return to Kathmandu, claimed that news from his country had been exaggerated, and that the army and police were in control of the situation . . . the Nepali Foreign Minister had been in London recently to negotiate the amount of compensation to be paid to ex-Gurkhas and to Nepal in the wake of the disbandment of the . . ." He clicked his tongue against the roof of his mouth, smiled sardonically.

"They intend it, I know they do," he said aloud, as if to convince a skeptical audience.

" . . . on the stock market—"

He switched off the radio.

The road began to dip. He was not quite able to ignore the low, green buildings and the open spaces and the wire and the regimental badges at the gates of the army place on his left. He was forcibly reminded of Tim, even though he had quashed all significance in the radio's reference to the Brigade of Gurkhas. He must be alive, please God he must be. His life was the length of a piece of string; the length of his interest to them, the length of his silence. He had to believe that . . . did believe it.

The Renault was now behind a BMW, keeping its secure distance. It seemed to lag behind the urgently moving thoughts as real as events in his mind. He clenched and unclenched his hands on the steering wheel, the very act of driving the car unfamiliar. Alex was weekending at his cottage with someone new and casual. Bill had been sulkily unhelpful. Aubrey wanted to face Davenhill, not merely talk over the telephone. He had to know about the thing they called "New Territories." *Anything* he learned might save Tim's life. If he could make them listen.

He slowed the car. Ampney Crucis on the signpost. He turned right down a narrow sideroad, the car bumping on the poor surface. Breathless, he waited. The Renault turned cautiously after him. His mouth felt dry, his body quaking and old. It was so stupid of him to have let them find him too easily!

The fear passed, like a spell of dizziness. Minutes later, he stopped the car outside a cottage's white gate. Around the whitewashed cottage trees stiffly, twistedly climbed a shallow hill to become a copse, isolating the place and drawing the eye to other dotted cottages scattered through the landscape's gentle tide. The small, quaint village was behind him; the Renault had drawn into the pub's carpark. Church towers rose out of clumps of woodland, cattle were scattered over fields like scraps of colored paper after a wedding. The air was fresh, the breeze chill. Alex Davenhill was in the garden, digging with an intent and ineffectual fury at a stubborn, overgrown vegetable patch. Old leaves and stumps littered the path near him.

Aubrey opened the gate. Its creak made Davenhill look up. He stood upright, some unidentifiable root in one muddy hand. There was an instant calculating surprise on his handsome features. He dug his spade into the earth and rubbed his hand through his gray-flecked, tightly curling hair.

"Kenneth—my dear!" he called, clumping toward Aubrey in rolled-down boots, a bright sweater, mud-stained, and corduroy trousers. "Quite the gardener, eh?" he asked mischievously. Unabashed by Aubrey's chilly, serious face, he kissed the old man lightly on the cheek. "Swear to God you won't catch anything nasty!" he laughed. Then he added, his features darkening: "My dear, you look positively *hunted!*"

Aubrey controlled the involuntary twitch of his head in the direction of the carpark. "Just—reaction, I expect," he murmured.

"Mm . . . well, dear, you were quite the talk of the Crush Bar last night. Far more interesting than Pavarotti to our circle of acquaintance. What *are* you up to, Kenneth?" He studied Aubrey more in hope than expectation, while Aubrey smiled his most innocent smile. "I mentioned our little chat to Geoffrey Longmead, who hadn't enjoyed the first act anyway, and he almost swallowed the lemon in his G and T!" Davenhill laughed aloud. "Then he warned me off . . . in all seriousness, he warned me away from you." He hesitated, then added: "Well, you'd better come in."

"I don't think I will, Alex, thank you. Just in case I might put temptation in your way. Give you the idea and opportunity of a telephone call."

"Oh, Kenneth!"

"Nevertheless, Alex, we can talk perfectly well out here. *Will* you talk to me? Off the record?"

"Do you have any idea what you're doing?" The words became as leaden as parts of the sky. The scene seemed caught and blown by the wind as it strengthened. Trees, cattle, church towers, cottages were only a semblance of place. Davenhill's question had stranded him in an unknown, alien landscape. He shivered.

"No. For the present, I simply know that I need to know exactly what the accord over Nepal entails. Will you tell me that—and trust me to use the information *sensibly?*"

Davenhill was silent for a few moments. There was a distance between them, but also the credence there had always been. Then Davenhill nodded.

"I don't pretend to plumb your depths, Kenneth, I never have. But, I trust you. Over that disgraceful *Teardrop* business—well, I just wish I hadn't been in Washington all that time! I did try to tell anyone who would listen . . ."

"I know. I'm grateful."

"Kenneth, yours is the most subtle and elegant and old-fashioned mind I've ever encountered. You still believe things the rest of us long gave up, like Santa Claus and country." Davenhill smiled disarmingly. "What you're up to can't be important, but you're absolutely bloody stubborn and only the truth will persuade you it wasn't worth learning. So, what do you want to know?"

Aubrey realized Davenhill had decided to abandon a set of instructions he had been given.

"I'm preparing for—and trying to avoid—calling on Elizabeth."

"I'm not surprised!" Then: "What do you want to ask her?"

"How deeply was Babbington involved in this business called 'New Territories'? What *is* 'New Territories,' exactly? That is your question rather than hers."

Davenhill rubbed his chin and raised his face to the sky. Dark gray clouds seemed to be drawn toward the sun as if by a magnet. "Looks like rain later, almost certainly. Shan't get all this dug before then . . ." He continued in the same absent tone: "Longmead would be furious. *He* was more involved than anyone, really. Oh, you know how it was. It just grew out of the negotiations to return Hong Kong to the People's Republic of China in '97—hence the nickname it acquired, 'New Territories.' I think Longmead put the idea to HMG, who were really looking for someone to take over Nepal for us. Once the Gurkhas were no longer our responsibility. Like selling a recently deceased relative's house, you know? Some woodworm, dry rot, furniture's junk, but the place could be attractive to the right buyer . . ."

"And what did the Chinese propose in exchange?" Aubrey inquired.

"Trade, mostly. A lot of very large contracts for British firms. Extra guarantees over HK after '97. The usual sorts of things favored by Longmead." Davenhill's smile was withering. "The upshot is that China will have effective control of Nepal within a few years. Better them than the Indians or Russians, it was felt. Can't say I disagree with that part of it."

"I see."

"Well, you knew the rumors, Kenneth. It can't come as much of a surprise, surely? Best thing in the circumstances. Does it *matter,* really?"

"I—perhaps not. But what of Babbington and Colonel Lin, Alex? Where are they in the picture?"

"Andrew, as I told you, was responsible for security whenever any important Chinese were here. Lin did the same for the Foreign Secretary and anyone else going out to HK or Beijing . . . well, Lin and Andrew would normally cooperate in HK. Yes, it certainly looks like rain . . ." He lowered his face and smiled at Aubrey. "It's really all settled, you know. It's not just some madcap scheme of Andrew's, there's nothing sinister in it. It's policy, do you see? The truth about Andrew doesn't make a ha'porth's worth of difference, Kenneth."

"And that's all you're prepared to tell me?" Aubrey divined. He had been listening to a prepared statement; not Davenhill's own . . . or perhaps it was. Prepared, nevertheless. To them, all of them, he was simply an infernal nuisance; a dog who kept bringing the same old bone back into the drawing room— Babbington. They thought him obsessed, and maybe he was. No, Davenhill would not understand. None of them would, unless he had incontrovertible proof.

"I'm—not sure," Davenhill admitted. "Since I don't know what's got into that clever old head of yours. Unless it's the current situation in Kathmandu . . . and that's little or nothing to worry about, I gather. Just a flux, a fever because of the King's death. That's from the horse's mouth, their Foreign Minister, who's just gone home with a sackful of HMG's money to pay off the Gurkhas! Everything's under control, he assured Longmead and the Foreign Secretary. You're not worried on that score, are you? That boy of yours been filling your head with some new nonsense, has he?"

Carefully, Aubrey shook his head. "No," was his entire response.

"Good. The army and the police can handle anything out there—there really isn't any opposition over there, you know."

"And that's Foreign Office gossip and Gospel, is it?"

"Absolutely. *Is* it to do with that rather beautiful young man you adopted, or whatever? I knew a very nice American boy once who simply adored his brother's guitar playing!" Davenhill was at his most masked. The dialogue was, effectively, at an end. "I rather gathered Tim was in the shit. Could he be behind this wild-goose chase?"

Aubrey wanted to share Tim's danger and his anxiety. But it could not be shared, he could not halve his trouble in that way. Davenhill was asking on behalf of others, Longmead and the Foreign Office, Orrell, all those who might be—distressed, made uncomfortable?—by his inquiries and general unpredictability. He felt contempt. What a *pity* he had ever uncovered Andrew Babbington's treachery! The old arrangement would have been so much more *comfortable* for everyone!

"Not really," he said quietly. Davenhill's eyes watched him brightly.

"I see." Davenhill was disappointed. There would be nothing to report. Then Davenhill said: "I won't say a word. But you're going to have to go on to Elizabeth, you know. I can't help you further. I only know that Lin stayed there often, that's all."

Aubrey replied sharply: "Thank you, Alex. I'm sorry to have spoilt your weekend!"

"You haven't!" Davenhill snapped back, his lips pursed. Then, more softly, he added: "You can trust me, Kenneth. I will help, if needed."

Aubrey felt shamefaced. "I'm sorry."

"Making waves won't be appreciated, Kenneth. I *can* tell you that much."

"I see. Heavens forfend that I should *upset* anything!" He clamped his hat more firmly on his head as the wind plucked at him. He squared his shoulders. "Goodbye, Alex. I'd appreciate your silence."

"You have it—Elizabeth may complain upstairs, you know . . ."

"Not before I've spoken to her. Goodbye, Alex."

He walked toward the gate, careful of the little traps of uneven crazy paving and frost-lifted flagstones. It was all so ordinary! The Foreign Office was wearing blinkers again! Handing over countries in exchange for exports now! A pity the Russians

didn't appreciate the neatness and finality of HMG's solution
to the little problem of Nepal!

The sky rushed with dark rainclouds and the wind cried in
a lonely, high-pitched way. He shivered with cold. The Renault
was still in the pub's carpark, one of its occupants leaning
against it, watching him leave, cigarette smoke whipped away
from his face by the wind. They would follow him to Babbington's place.

Very well, let them! He was angry now. In a frightened, edgy
way, with concern for Tim flushing over and through him like
small eruptions of fever. But he was angry!

Somehow, she avoided the men in bemedaled uniforms with old,
chilled features; avoided, too, her daughter-in-law, passing her
weeping, helpless weight to the arm of one of her bodyguards.
She reached the car with fresh mud on her black shoes, her fur
coat held tightly around her as if the breeze tugging the few
small clouds were an icy wind. Brigitte Winterbach leaned heavily against the car door that her driver had opened. Pieter's face
watched solicitously from the limousine's rear seat. On his lap,
a portable screen and its keyboard were attached to the car telephone.

She breathed raggedly, as if her exertions had been a race
against the welling grief which she had suppressed throughout
the funeral. Dirt rattled and clumped onto the coffin behind her,
making her shudder. She slid into the car, her driver's hand
firmly guiding her elbow. She dragged off her fur hat; strands
of frizzy gray hair fell against her cheek and temples. Uniforms
and topcoats passed the window as if in procession. Faces peered
in and at once looked away from her bleak, carved expression.

Words and idents stuttered across the screen balanced on
Pieter's knees like a salesman's open briefcase. They remained
like a neon advertisement. Eventually, Pieter murmured apologetically:

"Comrade General . . . I think—this needs your decision."

"What is it?" Her voice was tired and small.

Pieter offered the portable keyboard and screen like a box of
chocolates in a cinema. "Report from London *Amt* . . . Aubrey.
They're reporting his position."

She waved a hand and he retained the screen. Words after
idents. Fully secure comms. EYES ONLY. *Cirencester . . .
Davenhill . . . headed back toward London, M4 . . . Newbury,*

*Berkshire . . . left motorway for A4, A4 for village of Bucklebury
. . .* and the times of those small, worrying events.

"Confirm!" she snapped, glancing wildly out of the window.
Aubrey must know or suspect *everything!* That boy they were
holding and beating in Nepal must have convinced him! Her
hand fluttered at her mouth. The mound of earth was decreas-
ing, the sextons moving rhythmically. The soldiers and mourn-
ers had scattered as if the breeze had moved them. Cars turned,
accelerating. *Bucklebury!* The screen went blank, and then the
words reappeared, identical, confirming the signal. Aubrey was
making for Bucklebury—Babbington's country house in Berkshire. He was going to see Babbington's wife.

She had not believed that he would see or guess the links between herself and Babbington, and even Lin. But he did! The
time shone out from the screen. 2:15! Aubrey had reached Bucklebury more than half an hour ago . . . he was with Babbington's
wife! *Further orders?* the screen asked. The cemetery was almost
clear of cars now, the mound of fresh wet mud almost replaced
in the hole into which Kurt had been lowered.

"Comrade General?"

"Be *silent!*"

Aubrey was a terrier, a dog bred for ratting. He would not
let go of this now unless his grip were forced open; unless he
was stopped. He would expose the whole operation, blow *Topi.*

Brandis had not been able to make that boy talk, but the boy
had talked to Aubrey, spilling everything and convincing that
clever, suspicious old man. If Babbington thought her to blame
for the uncovering of *Topi,* then he would destroy her. Now, Aubrey could be killed—not out of grief or passion, but out of duty,
with no element of revenge. Yet it would *be* her revenge.

"Tell them to eliminate him—today. Quickly and efficiently.
The method does not matter. An accident would *look* well and
close the matter more innocently. Just tell them to do it."

Pieter was silent for a moment, then he said simply: "Yes,
Comrade General," and his long fingers began typing at the keyboard.

Brigitte lit a cigarette and watched a kneeling old woman in
the chill breeze beside one of the headstones. She placed the
flowers carefully in a mossed, empty jamjar. Brigitte's head
began to ache.

●　　　●　　　●

The rain swept like long, draping curtains across the lawns and the terrace. Urns and statues glistened where they were not mossed. The trees bordering the grounds and screening the house from the road were distant and black against the low, scudding cloud. There was a draft coming through the French windows at which he stood, uncertain, still wearing his overcoat and holding his hat in his hands. He felt like a tradesman who had presented a bill there was little hope of having settled. He was acutely aware of Elizabeth Babbington seated across the room from the windows, just as he was aware that the occupants of the Renault must now be inside the boundary wall, beneath the dark, massed line of trees.

Were they still merely watching? What would Brigitte decide when she learned where he was? What would *Babbington* decide? He turned from the window. Lady Elizabeth Babbington had admitted him reluctantly, but with curiosity rather than malice, and as soon as she had shown him into this drawing room, she had returned to her seat in a bay window and to the watercolor on which she was working. In the past Aubrey had always been surprised, perhaps unkindly, that a woman of such snobbery and with such a closed, almost bigoted mind, could demonstrate a degree of ability such as she showed. Her watercolors were noted. This room had featured in a Sunday color supplement only weeks ago, with Elizabeth seated where she sat now, caftan-dressed, untidily coiffured, almost bohemian. She disliked him as much as she had detested her husband, her principal attitude to Aubrey one of disbelief that her husband could ever have been outwitted by a verger's son.

She seemed indifferent to his presence. "I hear you're preparing for a new exhibition, Elizabeth," he remarked, turning his hat in his hands, staring out into the late autumn rain and the darkening afternoon.

"That's right. Can't live on the stipend that bloody man sends us, can we?" Her voice was gruff, as if she smoked heavily. The money, of course, had always belonged to Babbington, the inheritance of a two-generations-before business tycoon. Elizabeth's class had been her dowry, grafted onto the education and status bought for Babbington's father and passed down to him. She was the Babbington family's final assumption into the ethereal sphere. Babbington's money was mostly abroad. HMG winked at the checks that arrived punctually at this house and which maintained it. She snorted in derision. "I warned him I'd never move from here," she added.

Aubrey shook his head, amused. He turned to her. Her strong, large face and broad forehead were paled by the dull light from outside. Her bearing, voice and manner were at odds with the delicate, decisive movements of the brush. "Will you answer some questions for me, Elizabeth?" he asked. She had not inquired as to his motives for arriving on her doorstep, being shown in by her butler.

"Depends," she replied, frowning with concentration.

"It won't hurt you further."

She looked up, eyes glaring. "You've a bloody nerve, Kenneth Aubrey!" Her voice was without malice. There should have been anger, vulnerability of some kind. Instead, Elizabeth Babbington watched him out of her background and class. "You want my help—ask me questions?" There was no emphasis placed by emotion where it should have been.

"It's why I've—intruded," he offered. She snorted with contempt. "It can't hurt—Andrew, I can at least offer that—"

"—comfort?" It was as if she had wiped her feet on the word and its attendant idea. "Him?" He contemplated her watercolor for a minute or more. The wind had shifted slightly and the draft through the windows increased as rain spattered against the glass. "I've given him up, as you should have realized. He failed."

Aubrey wondered whether she had produced a cocoon out of old habits, former attitudes. Married beneath her . . . men aren't to be trusted . . . never surrender yourself, my dear . . . He looked up at the center rose of the ceiling, and its elaborate frieze. Babbington had given her only what she had a right to expect, and which she now retained. Antique furniture and ornaments littered the drawing room, flotsam on a strange and private beach.

"I'm sorry."

She tossed her head. Gray hair fell untidily about her face and she brushed it back with a hard motion of her hand.

"I do not understand how he could have been defeated by someone like you . . . though he was always weak through his vanity."

"May I ask my questions?" he prompted.

She studied her work before answering, then waved one hand dismissively. "If you must."

"It concerns one of your houseguests—from before Andrew . . ."

"Went home?" she supplied archly. "To that Godforsaken place!" She laughed. Then she looked at him quizzically. "Why did he?"

Off-balance, Aubrey replied: "I—don't know. I really don't know what the attraction was, Elizabeth."

"Well, who are you interested in?"

"A Chinese gentleman—his name was Lin."

"Lin?" She shrugged. "How long ago?" She was already studying her work once more, bored and indifferent. Her face softened, though it frowned with concentration. Years and habit fell from it. Then she was her old self again as she looked up at him.

"Perhaps two years ago, maybe three. More than once. A colleague of Andrew's during the Hong Kong negotiations?"

She began painting again. "Chinese everywhere, then," she remarked, frowning. "Is this really of any importance?"

"It—may be."

"Why can't you people leave me alone?" It was not a complaint, merely an observation. The hockey match was over, why the postmortem? She had always despised Babbington, he realized that more clearly now. "Very well, I remember Colonel Lin. He stayed here. Andrew fussed about the man's food. I asked him whether take-away wasn't good enough." She laughed again, the same hard noise. "Anyway, the next best thing to take-away foods for whole weekends at a time!" She glowered at Aubrey. "Richard and I did laugh at Andrew's capering around the little Chinaman, I have to admit!" Her son would have laughed, of course. Perhaps her son was the reason for her contempt for Babbington? The son was a buffoon.

He said: "Quite. Have you any idea what they discussed? Why Andrew *capered* for the Chinaman?"

He was standing almost beside her now, his initial qualms subdued. She looked at her watercolor rather than at him.

She shrugged. "How should I know? Richard thought Andrew must have a Hong Kong bank account he was trying to protect." She looked up. "I expect the answer was smaller and more sordid than that. Andrew *liked* playing your silly games!"

"No more to it than that?" he asked. "Were they alone together a great deal?" He felt wearied by this armored woman. She had no interest in him or his questions.

"I suppose so. I didn't watch them."

"Was there anything they seemed to wish to keep from you? About which they were secretive?"

"I doubt if they were buggering each other! Andrew at least was normal in that department."

"Nevertheless . . . ?"

"I'm tired of this, Kenneth Aubrey—tired of you." She yawned contemptuously. "I tired of Andrew a long time ago." Her eyes flashed as she glared at her painting. Aubrey felt that she had wanted to get out, but Babbington had kept her in an old and disliked role because she must be the suitable wife of the man he wished to be. In her painting she *had* found an alternative, a persona he would not allow her to fulfill. He suddenly felt sorry for her.

"The Chinaman," he urged.

"Christ, the bloody Chinaman!" Her tone and even her vocabulary seemed freed from some restraint. "The same little bloody Chinaman who turned up in the middle of our first proper holiday in years—my painting holiday in Malaya!" She stood with her back to him, declaiming to the rain beyond the bay windows, her arms gesturing like those of a conductor. He shivered at the touch of discovery, and remembered he had not even read the file digest Godwin had sent to the hotel. *He was in Malaya, late on . . .*

So was Babbington! During the latter stages of the Emergency, in the late fifties, as a rather junior MI5 adviser to the police out there.

Elizabeth intruded. He felt he understood her now. Since Babbington's unseemly departure, perhaps she had blindingly glimpsed freedom. Then the crushing weight of the past rallying around had stifled that vision. Her watercolors sold now out of her husband's notoriety and the patronage of friends. She was more than ever not herself, and never would be.

She continued, as if to herself: "I managed to get away a lot, I suppose . . . perhaps his arrival kept Andrew occupied. He didn't interfere with me, at any rate."

Aubrey was no longer listening. Babbington and Lin and Malaya. Last year, and in the latter days of the Emergency. The thought insisted, Lin could have become Babbington's creature that long ago, been turned that far back.

Carefully, all excitement excluded from his voice, he said: "Elizabeth—when you work on a new subject like Malaysia, for

example, I presume you must take hundreds of photographs?"
He was surprised at the breathlessness with which he awaited
her reply.

It was noisy, fifteen years out-of-date, and Priabin delighted in
every moment of it, hardly able to keep the wide grin from his
mouth. A free rock concert in Kensington Gardens, within
sound of his embassy, to support some royal charity. There were
long-haired, middle-aged men wielding guitars or plunging at
ranks of electronic keyboards. To Priabin, there was the frisson
of the unpermitted, the censored. Names and faces and gyrations
that had belonged to a fenced-out life and the occasional smug-
gled or copied record or tape. Or American radio broadcasts
eavesdropped between the jamming. These were the unicorns,
the mythical beasts, of his youth.

The man walked beside him as they patrolled the Round Pond
and the fringes of the crowd, smelling sweet, forbidden smoke
and hearing gales of laughter, clapping and cheering which
seemed intended to exclude them. He evidently disliked both the
noise and the public openness of the meeting place. Rather like
a parent, he seemed to want to drag Priabin away. Priabin simply grinned and listened, his attention divided.

"Yes, yes," he all but shouted, secrecy preserved by the ascending, intensifying cry of a guitar solo and the cheers that accompanied it. "Yes, but why them?"

"They don't use them to take the cars out to keep the batteries
charged!"

"And they don't send them out without liaising with me first!
Remember that, Johannes." A Wet Team . . . what on earth was
she doing? The solo reached an orgasmic, chilling climax, then
organlike chords on the keyboards. The music whirled around
him and in his head and memory. He was still smiling. "And
they're working strictly to a direct order from Berlin—from the
spider lady?" Johannes nodded, wincing at the raucous music.
"You can't find out *what* orders they have?".

"Not this time. My seniority cuts absolutely no ice with the
Wet Team. Or with Brigitte, either!" He seemed on the point
of hurrying away. The scent of sweet smoke on the wind and
the glimpse of policemen studiously ignorant. Yells for the keyboard player climaxing his solo.

Heat of the Day. Priabin's favorite group, long disbanded and
now reunited and even richer . . . and even better! He continued

to smile, like a ventriloquist's dummy whose expression could hardly be expected to alter. And yet he was concerned now. He would have to report to Babbington, and at once.

"They saw Davenhill talking to Aubrey, then followed his car to Bucklebury—you're certain it was *that* house?"

"Gossip . . . jokes about it. From the duty team taking their reports. Look, no one knows they're a Wet Team. It's supposed to be surveillance, that's the story!"

"But the spider lady isn't taking the chance of any delay, is she?" Priabin observed. The water seemed rippled by the waves of music rather than by the breeze. A few ducks congregated in agitation on the far side of the pond, mere dun-colored dots. The swans had fled, temporarily, lifting away against the rushing gray sky. "She will make her move if she thinks whatever Aubrey is doing has become dangerous. No delay while she sends for the hit men, they're already at the scene!" He had to talk to Moscow. This confirmed that Brigitte had bombed Aubrey's flat—she must be mad to be out to kill him!

And now Aubrey had gone to Babbington's country house. To see the man's wife?

Heat of the Day finished the number. Whistles, a roar of approval, clowning from the stage amid the smoke and lights. Cries for a favorite piece, the announcement concurring. A small part of him felt warm with satisfaction. They were going to play "*No way back.*" Though, he realized with a sharp disappointment, he could not stay to listen. He must tell Babbington—and do it now. He had no idea what Babbington would make of it, but it had to be important! Important, too, presumably, to stop Brigitte?

Of that, of course, he could not be certain.

"Thanks, Johannes. You get off now, and keep in touch. Sorry to spoil your weekend!" Johannes evidently did not believe him. The band drove into the brick wall of sound that was the suite's opening section. He felt a pang, then added: "I'll want to know as soon as you know," he warned. "However, I think the Center needs to know first."

There were none of her watercolors or oils in Babbington's study. Presumably, had there ever been any, she had removed them. The landings and corridors laid a trail of paintings that petered out at this door which she seemed reluctant to open and pass through. The room was cold, unused. She rubbed her arms beneath the shawl she had thrown across her shoulders and then pushed back her hair. Rain streaked the windows. There was an empty neatness about the room, a heavy desk that impressed but was devoid of papers, sparse bookshelves, wood-veneered cabinets. A room not much used, even in the past.

Elizabeth Babbington studied Aubrey as if still in the process of reaching a decision. Her arms were folded, her eyes mistrusting. When she spoke, however, her question surprised him.

"What is he up to now?" It was as if he had brought home a child of hers often in trouble previously.

Aubrey shook his head. "I—really don't know."

Her face was disbelieving. She laughed, then said: "You really are The Cat That Walked by Himself, aren't you, Kenneth Aubrey?" Her tone was mocking, and yet not utterly without warmth.

"I'm sorry?"

"Kipling," she explained.

"The cat that walked by himself through the wet wild woods—on his wild lone, or whatever it is . . . that's you, all right!"

Aubrey smiled, all but blushed, then said: "Do you really think so, Elizabeth?"

"Oh, yes, I really think so," she replied.

"The—er, photographs?"

She sniffed loudly at his impatience and pummeled warmth into her arms. "I don't like this room, never have. Once I'd finished with the snaps—they were for color and light as much as anything else—he locked them away in here. One of these cabinets." Suddenly, she sighed deeply, and her face became suffused with anger. "Will you do your worst to stop him?" she insisted. There was a real hatred shining in her eyes. "Will you spoil things for him as much as you possibly can?" She demanded it in the tones and with the grim solemnity of some awful initiation ceremony.

"I—can promise to try," was all he said by way of reply. "Does it mean that much to you?"

"I didn't think it did, but perhaps it does." She waved her arms around the room, toward the windows. "I realize I'm too old to change, break out. I haven't the nerve for it, anyway." She glared at Aubrey. "But *I* didn't build the bloody prison!" There was a vast contempt in her flushed cheeks and her hard stare. It was a mirror of an expression he had habitually seen on Babbington's handsome features. They were alike in many ways, and entirely incompatible. He remembered now that she had left Babbington once, early in their marriage, and wondered whether she had sought then not an affair but a different life. Yes, she lacked the nerve. Even as a young woman, she had come back.

She sighed again, and the anger seemed to evaporate, leaving her still.

"Oh, I'll dig out the bloody photographs, and then perhaps you'll go away! I feel—unsettled when you're around, Cat That Walks by Himself."

She unlocked one of the cabinets, and began flicking through files.

Prompted by a surge of renewed anxiety, Aubrey drifted to the windows, picking up a pair of field glasses lying on Babbington's desk and refining the focus.

It took him minutes to locate them, while Elizabeth Babbington sorted files and snapshots on her knees in front of the cabinet. A shadow beneath shadow, the dark, shiny-wet trees and something quick and shiny moving through them. Then another.

The rain ran down the window or leaped against it, and the sky was early-afternoon-already-evening, but he saw them. He thought three, but could not be sure, only cold and afraid. Urgency, now, and he was unused to it. The window misted from his increased temperature.

" . . . they searched thoroughly here, I must have been using these at the time—they took most of them away, I remember." She had relaxed, he was a friend come for coffee and required as little attention. Cold, streaked window, the glasses misting, the shiny oil-skinned figures slipping from bole to bole.

Strangely, out of context, the sounds of a horse's hooves on gravel. He saw the son, the unpleasant Richard Babbington. It seemed like an additional threat that he should canter along the drive and then disappear toward the stables; a half-drowned face set in unlearned arrogance and the horse smoking with effort in the rain.

"Here you are, this is what's left." He turned to her. She seemed at peace, having arrived at some obscure truce with him and with herself. She pressed the folder into his hands. The figures beneath the trees had been moving with a purpose, one that was not surveillance. He could not even begin to think about it.

"Thank you." His voice was shaky.

He glanced down. Snapshots, the light tropical, the blue water of a swimming pool hard, unreal. Like her oils on the stairs, like Hockney's. He raised the glasses, and a shiny oilskin flicked beneath branches. Chilled, he looked down at the sun splintering off the swimming pool.

Babbington in profile, the Chinaman bending over him as if to whisper in his ear. Elizabeth had caught them only as a foreground. The faces in the snapshots were not watching the camera. Probably they had been unaware of her. For her part, she had evidently been interested in the light off the pool and the palm that overhung its glittering water. He flicked to the next snapshot. Scene . . . scene . . . scene . . . His temperature rose on his cheeks, but his body was cold, just as if the window no longer excluded the wind and rain. Scene . . . Babbington in sunglasses, a waiter carrying drinks on a tray, small and Malay. Richard, the son? Probably not. The daughter, yes, Elizabeth, less expertly taken. Scene, scene . . . Babbington and Lin again. He felt warmed by proof or at least the beginnings of proof.

He looked out of the window, and began to listen for the son's approach. Field glasses. Glint of wet metal. A rifle—he could not catch his breath. His heart pounded weakly like an old drum.

The shining gun beneath the dark wet trees, the moving oilskins. They were *not* surveillance. Brigitte wanted to end it, now or very soon, and was recklessly insistent: the rules had gone. He *did* have something, Babbington and Lin, in his quivering grasp. He flicked through the snapshots even more urgently. Felt hot.

The gun glinted again beneath the trees, a stick of dull metal. Long barrel; sniper. He scuttled away from the naked window.

Snapshot—a woman with gray hair in a multicolored frock and low shoes, approaching Babbington and Lin, the blur of an unfocused waiter in the background. Footsteps in the corridor outside. The woman . . . oilskins beneath trees . . . the *woman!* Brigitte squinted at the edge of the snapshot, easily identifiable. He had the proof! The unholy Trinity together in one picture.

Confidently as in a melodrama, the study door began to open. He glanced toward it almost in the same moment that he once more raised the glasses to his eyes. The man with the gun and two further shapes, arranged so that anyone coming along the long avenue of oaks toward the gates would coincide with their crossfire.

And then Richard Babbington entered, the arrogance of his face like a fitful bulb rather than the steady lamp of disdain his father displayed. His hair was lankly pressed down by the rain, and his riding boots were muddy. His mouth was open, and he glared at his mother, then at Aubrey. A face used to scanning restaurants.

Elizabeth Babbington had begun to quail and retreat even before he spoke. "Ma, what is *he* doing here? Why are you talking to that old bastard!" His face was crumpled with hate, as he strode across the study toward Aubrey. "What's this?" he demanded, snatching the bunch of snapshots, dropping many. Addressing his mother, whose face no longer reflected anything but her son's expected image of her. "What have you given him?" He flung the remaining snapshots across the room. "You—get out! Get out of my house!"

The chill of the window behind him seemed to penetrate his coat. "The pictures—" he managed to say.

"You're taking nothing from this house! Haven't you done enough? What the hell are you doing here, you old bastard?" He grabbed Aubrey's sleeve and began dragging him across the room. Elizabeth said nothing, hardly looked in their direction.

He was tugged toward the study door. The scattered snapshots lying on the floor, as insignificant as the son's wet bootprints now.

"No!" he said.

"Yes! I'm bloody well chucking you out, Aubrey! You've no business here, with us!"

9

Patriots and Expatriates

He felt the anger of a schoolmaster confronted by a recalci-
trantly clever pupil; Brigitte must be insane! Moscow's Saturday
afternoon gawkers and worshipers moved across the flagged or
cobblestoned pavements beneath his high window, stroked or
mounted cannons for the sake of keepsake snapshots, gawped
up at buildings which reminded them of the Tsars and the old,
bad past. Brigitte intended *killing* Aubrey—had already tried
once! The woman had lost all sense of perspective, for God's
sake.

Damnable old crone, *why?* He tugged painfully at his beard.
All she had succeeded in doing was goading the bloody man into
a renewed effort of suspicion. What the hell was he doing in
Bucklebury? And what in God's name would Elizabeth tell him,
what material would she spin for him out of contempt and hatred? That bloody boy had been allowed to set Aubrey on the
trail of *Topi,* and now the silly German bitch was trying to *erase*
her earlier mistakes first with a bomb and now a Wet Team!

The room crowded, its ceiling low, dark with cigarette smoke
and neglect. Aubrey was on the move and there was a sensation
of something crawling across his skin, so that he shuddered. Aubrey had gone to his house! Each of Priabin's sentences over the
secure line were part of a large, ominous shadow threatening
the security of *Topi.*

"Yes, yes!" he snapped. "Yes, stop them. They must be
stopped!" More equably, he added: "To have him killed now

would arouse suspicion. I don't want that, Priabin. *No one* wants that."

The pauses and the clicks and the rushing of ether, then the flat, decoded voice of his rival, the oh-so-young General. Tourists walked in drab columns and colors past the cannons outside the Arsenal. The breeze tugged hard, pale winter across the sky.

"I understand that, even though you've told me very little. I don't understand what she's up to. No one in England would believe in an accident to Aubrey."

"*You* must assume responsibility for surveillance on him. I want to know—*must know!*—what he does, who he sees. Do you understand?"

Brandis' report lay open on his desk. Brigitte's sergeant-major had decided on which side his bread was buttered. Timothy Gardiner, Aubrey's ward-or-whatever, had stirred up the hornets' nest. Aubrey had set off like a terrier and straight to Elizabeth! Via Davenhill. Babbington felt things loosen in his hands, like the reins from a horse that had pulled free. It *must* not be . . .

. . . then let it happen, this accident to Aubrey. He shook his head, as if someone in the room were pressing this action upon him. No, Aubrey still had friends, people like Davenhill and Shelley who doubtless knew where he was, what he sought. He must be stopped, but not yet and not in England.

Watch and wait, then.

He began to relax, unclenching his hands, stretching away tension. "How long has he been at Bucklebury?"

"We don't know—"

"Then find out!"

He looked at his watch, then at the unreliable clock on the wall surrounded by cracks in the plaster. Three exactly, on Saturday afternoon in Berkshire, at his former home. Elizabeth would have been at home, probably alone.

"I'm trying to." Priabin sounded irritated even through the mask of the decoding device. "What exactly do you want from me?"

"Call off her dogs, at once. Use whatever means you have to, but do it. Then take over."

"Very well."

"Then get on with it, man!"

He cut the connection immediately, as if doubt and error leaked through the line from his former country. Late afternoon darkened outside. A minute past, two minutes past three in

Berkshire, and Aubrey was talking to a woman who would certainly talk to *him*. He tugged at his beard, his new persona. The past still bound him, and he resented such knowledge. *Topi* was at risk. Aubrey would discover what happened in Malaysia last year, was bound to uncover those meetings.

Three minutes past three in Berkshire.

There was rain on his bare head and striking against his cold face. The son's grip was fierce as he thrust him against the side of his car, then bundled him into the driver's seat.

"Now, just bugger off and leave us alone!" Richard Babbington yelled, his face crowding close. "Do you hear me, you old bastard?" he raged. "Bugger off and don't come back!"

Aubrey jerked his hand away from the door as it was slammed shut. Rain streaked the windshield, which was clouding with his breathlessness and trepidation. He could see Elizabeth's figure in a doorway, arms across her chest as if to keep warm, her features chastened. Her son strode toward her across the noisy gravel, still shouting. She seemed to flinch, then vanished back into the house. The door banged shut and the courtyard was suddenly quiet, except for the rain tapping like fingers on the car.

He watched, appalled, as his shaking hand fumbled the key into the ignition. He flicked on the wipers and looked at his watch. 3:05. He wiped at his face as if to dry or reshape it. They were waiting for him at the end of the avenue of old trees. They would stop the car and take him away quietly somewhere and dispose of him like so much household refuse.

He put the heater on fully, to clear the mistiness from the windshield.

The snapshots were lying on the carpet of Babbington's room. Babbington and Lin in Malaysia, last year . . . a hotel in Penang, he had glimpsed the location scribbled in Elizabeth's carelessly bold handwriting on the reverse of the photograph. And Brigitte, too . . .

And Tim. The idea bludgeoned against him that he had left Tim's safety, his life, lying on the carpet in Babbington's study. Those photographs . . .

Then his own danger bullied every other consideration aside. Brigitte's people were waiting for him. Seven minutes past three. He should go back into the house, demand to be allowed to call the police. He knew the son would not let him inside. He felt he could do nothing to fend off the inevitable, not even sit here in the hired car. They would only come looking. Make a nuisance? Make them call the police?

Babbington's son would simply order the staff to get rid of him, or do it himself with vindictive relish. He could not even make sufficient nuisance of himself to save his life.

He shivered with cold. The noise of the heater was unnerving. The windshield was clearing only patchily. He withdrew his hand from the steering wheel; its companion clutched it in his lap as if he had been wounded. His stomach churned.

He heard his breath sobbing raggedly, as if drinking the air thirstily. The windshield cleared. He blinked away a mistiness from his eyes. Fastened his seat belt, locked the doors. Turned the key. The engine barked explosively. The tires creaked and grumbled on the gravel as he turned the car. Richard Babbington watched him with a satisfied smile from a second-floor window; as if he knew they were waiting for him beneath the trees near the gates.

He steered the car like a tired, wounded bull out on to the wet, ocher drive. 3:12. His heart was beating wildly. The wipers flicked aside the large droplets of rain falling from the trees. The heater kept the windshield clear of his tension. Dark . . . he had turned on the headlights because they would hear him coming anyway. Gleaming fat tree boles glancing back the headlights. Leaves scuttering across the drive. He was a hundred yards from the gates and the road past Babbington's estate.

As he turned a bend in the drive, he saw a car drawn across the open gates and his foot touched the brakes instinctively. The car lurched, then proceeded at its funereal pace. He did not know what to do—he was *incapable* in this situation!

A figure in oilskins stepped onto the drive from beneath the trees. Then a second. Two guns. A third man was bent half-into the parked car, head hidden, the shoulders of his coat dark with rain. Two rifles. Two men waiting. Unreal, like cinematic images rather than a threat. One gun raised at the windshield.

He stopped the car and took his hands from the wheel. They were shaky and damp. He rubbed them together. One of the two men began walking nonchalantly toward the car, smiling. It was finished, absurdly, unreally—like *this!*—but it was finished.

The doors were locked, the windows shut. The engine running. It was ridiculous to consider escape. Ten yards away, and the man turned his head as if at a shout. Yes, the figure near the car had come running into the drive, arms waving. Hesitation, an angry reply, the second man with a rifle looking from one to the other of his companions.

His old head struggled with defeat, with what he saw. The three men were arguing together now, as if he were irrelevant. The one who had come from the car was red-featured, his arms gesticulating, his lips working. The two men with rifles were quarrelsome, contemptuous. His hands reached slowly, uncertainly for the wheel. His heartbeat loudened in his ears. His hands closed on the wheel. A change of orders? Some delay, some misunderstanding?

His foot touched the accelerator. The argument was resolving itself. He was aware of the small, flat briefcase on the back seat, the money it contained, the credit cards and passport in the name of Allen. It was as if someone else was in the car beside him.

He pressed down on the accelerator and the wheels spun, the back of the car swinging then straightening. The men turned in surprise toward him, but they moved aside rather than raised their guns. They were still arguing, questioning each other as to what they should do. The passenger side banged and scraped along the body of the Renault as he swerved around it and bumped and skidded out into the road, hardly able to control the car. The men behind him were running, the closest of them already holding the microphone of the car radio to his lips, the other two throwing their rifles into the back of the Renault. But not pursuing, *not* . . .

He was aware that he was sweating profusely, his whole frame shook as if with an ague, but there was that simple, irrefutable *delight* in having escaped! The Renault was still motionless as he turned the first bend in the road alongside Babbington's boundary wall. Elizabeth's prison wall.

Money, passport, credit cards, visas. He began to know what he must do, even as he watched the rearview mirror intently. He turned the car left, heading for the motorway. Not Heathrow, they would expect that. Somewhere else. Birmingham, Manchester, even Glasgow. Any flight to anywhere. Even though he knew precisely his eventual destination.

The road behind him remained clear except for the lumber of a slow-moving tractor and heaped trailer. Shreds and wisps of hay blew in the wind like hairs. The road ahead was empty, a signpost told him it was less than two miles to the M4. He could be in Birmingham before it was fully dark. The airport there, then—

And then he began shaking with reaction and had to continually swallow the nausea that rose into his throat and burned there at each relieved heaving of his stomach.

"There's no trace of him, General." A calculated detachment in Priabin's admission. "What—what do you want me to put in motion?"

Babbington was standing just outside the pool of light from the standard lamp in one corner of his office.

"How can one feeble, friendless old man just disappear?" he demanded, addressing the encryption unit on his desk rather than the disembodied voice at the other end of the connection. He felt tired. Aubrey's escape penetrated like a thorn burying itself deeper in his flesh. "Have you *no* idea where to locate him?"

"He hasn't returned to London—nor to his cottage, nor to friends. Hasn't contacted anyone, as far as we can ascertain."

"He knows something! He has deliberately disappeared."

"Scared?"

"Not *just* scared!" *Topi.* Aubrey knew more, much more, than he had even suspected mere hours ago. He nodded in confirmation of his thought.

"If you could give me more information?"

"Leave this to me!" Babbington snapped. "Continue your search, and report regularly to me, here—now, good night."

Babbington crossed to his desk and switched off the unit. He picked up his tumbler and sipped at the whiskey. Reports from Kathmandu littered his desk . . . the army and police there were being bullied by the Foreign Minister for more action to quell the unrest now that he was back from London with his begging-bowl full! The pro-Soviet faction's leaders wanted to press ahead with the disinformation campaign against the Foreign Minister—but not yet, not just yet. Tonight, more rioting and looting. Newspaper allegations tomorrow. He waved his hand in a complex, dismissive gesture. He admitted to himself he was avoiding what he knew he must do, and do quickly.

Sighing, he picked up the telephone receiver, jabbed out a number. A businessman abroad, calling home. His lips twisted into mockery at the thought. *She* had told Aubrey something; would have delighted in so doing. *She* had sent Aubrey boring into the woodwork. A report on the King's health caught at the corner of eyesight.

British surgeons again examined the King . . . palace rumours talk of a coma—drugs, perhaps?

He sensed the operation's gathering momentum. A huge locomotive rushing down a long mountain slope. Power, success. He was filled with pleasure. *Topi* was like the Cresta Run now, all exhilaration and speed. He was impatient. Aubrey must be stopped. Would be. Brigitte would be made to handle the matter, to expiate her—*stupidity*. He was just one old man without influence or power, with suspicion for a creed.

Rather than one of the servants, it was his son who answered the telephone.

"Richard—your father," he announced.

He remembered other calls, the faint sense of the ridiculous in making them, the humiliation of Elizabeth's rejection and his son's outbursts of self-pitying blame and insult. His own response of contempt, threat, the purse-strings used like jesses to keep them from being free of him, to retain his command of them.

"What do you want?" Sullenness was like a habit of speech.

His authority remained unpunctured. "Aubrey was there today—don't bother to ask how I know, I know. What did he want?"

Money hung on the ether between them; Richard's pocket money, so that the careers barred to him were unnecessary, a luxury he could forgo. Whatever room of the house he happened to be in, there would be palpable reminders that his money came to him from Switzerland by his father's largesse. *His* money kept them at Bucklebury, and old friends winked at the payment of bills, the bankers' drafts, the large checks and the bonds and stocks—all increasing their obligation to him.

"I—chucked him out. Look, I don't know what he wanted, do I?" It was all but a whine.

"You didn't ask?" Babbington sneered.

Truculently twisting on the hook, Richard said, "No, I didn't!"

"He spoke to your mother." It was not a question. A certainty. He clenched his hands, tugging at the receiver's cord. He repeated peremptorily: "Did he speak to your mother—alone? Answer me, boy!"

"I suppose so." Richard was half-drunk, he realized. Always.

It was as if the son were the exile, waiting in some foreign watering-place for his allowance to arrive by post.

"When was he there?"

"This afternoon. I was out, otherwise—"

"Yes, yes! What time?"

"I got back about three. He was here then."

So *close?*

Had he made a mistake, not letting Brigitte's Wet Team take care of that bloody old man? He shook his head. If Aubrey was alive, he was still alone. Dead, he would have found friends, aroused suspicion.

"Put your mother on."

"She doesn't want to talk to you."

Babbington sighed theatrically. "Put her on." There had been a time when she had been able to hurt him, revealing her shame, her rejection, even that futile attempt at reshaping her days. But not now. His money, her continuing old life, had tamed her like a horse; she was between the shafts of her past fifty years and she knew nothing else.

A pause, then: "Yes, Andrew?" Good. Her voice was pretend-weary, pretend-bored. The acting tricks of a long-played role. Their son, of course. She could not distance herself from him, and therefore could never do other than remain the woman *he* knew. But hardly loved. "Look, I've got a stinking headache. Will this take long?"

"My dear," he murmured with blatant irony, "forgive me for disturbing you, but I must ask what you discussed with our mutual acquaintance today."

"Very well." Affected boredom. "He seemed very curious about that damned Chinaman you kept bringing to the house."

"Lin?" He managed to control his voice.

"Yes. You don't know that many Chinamen, do you?"

"What exactly did he want to know?"

"He became very interested when he discovered the little bugger turned up in Malaya last year."

"You told him *that?*"

"He saw my snaps."

"He *what?* Has he still got them, for God's sake?"

"No . . ." she drawled, evidently detecting and enjoying his discomfiture. "Richard chucked him out. They're still lying all over the carpet in your study. Anything else you'd like to know?"

"No!"

"There are some heavy repair bills—part of the roof needs replacing, and some wet rot—"

"I allow you enough to keep the place up!" he snapped, his hand punching his desk. "Be satisfied."

"Are you keeping well, Andrew?"

He slapped the receiver down on its rest. There was no need for courtesies. They would always talk to him. He had bought that assurance over and over.

Aubrey was going to Malaysia, nothing was more certain. He stared at the telephone. He could not leave, take care of this himself. Kapustin must have no inkling . . . *Topi* needed him.

Brigitte, then. Brigitte could clean up the mess she had first spilled!

The sun streaming down onto the tarmac of Penang's Bayan Lepas airport made Pieter squint. It dazzled off the flanks and tailplanes of aircraft, off the glittering sea which was darkly pooled, as if from dozens of small spillages of oil. The brightness made it all but impossible to recognize her as she came down the passenger steps. Then he made out a drab cotton frock even his own mother would never have chosen. She was shading her eyes with her hand as she walked across the hot, ink-shadowed concrete toward the terminal building, and he realized she was looking up at the observation windows. He waved, but she did not seem to see him. Beyond her, the sea hurt his eyes, color lost in glitter and flashes as urgent as distress signals. She drew closer and became clearer, like a desert traveler emerging from a heat haze. Her hand luggage consisted of a single Interflug flight bag from the DDR's airline. She passed almost beneath him into the air conditioning of the terminal.

The coast of the peninsula, fifteen miles across the ache of light on the sea, was hazily dark with jungle. Then the luggage trolleys were towed across the view by a yellow tractor, and Pieter left the huge, dusty window and moved through the terminal's crowds. Relatives and friends and mere onlookers congregated outside Customs. His eyes perfunctorily scanned the knots of people. The two Malays who were working for him, a few white faces, none of them of interest, and Gelber, who had flown up from Kuala Lumpur *Amt* on the same flight Aubrey had caught. Gelber had picked up the old Englishman at the airport, stuck with him, finally followed him out to his hotel on the beach. He still looked flushed with excitement as Pieter nodded to him that Brigitte had arrived.

Ten minutes later, Pieter watched her emerge from Customs with that inevitable surprised look, as if the waiting crowd had gathered just for her. She looked very tired, even more unkempt than when he had left Berlin. Her grief was more set upon her face, but also more of an habitual expression, not fresh or renewed in recent hours; for that, he was thankful. He waved his newspaper and she gratefully caught the gesture. He took her suitcase, which dragged behind her on tiny wheels like a child's overlarge stuffed animal.

"Where is he?" she asked at once.

"Gelber followed him out to one of the hotels along the north coast." Gelber fell in behind them while the two Malays seemed caught up like debris attracted to a passing comet.

"He booked in?" Pieter nodded. "Who has he seen, talked to?"

"He spoke to someone called Scudamore, from the hotel, making an appointment for this afternoon."

"Scudamore?"

"We think he's—or was, anyway, in a similar line of work to ours. I've sent a request for identification to Berlin, General."

The sunlight outside the tinted glass doors struck against their eyes, the humidity and heat slid across their skin as heavily as a towel. Brigitte shaded her eyes quickly, as if concealing her features from a hidden camera, as Pieter waved his newspaper in the direction of a large green Volvo sedan. It pulled forward toward them. Brigitte seemed revived by its promise of shade and coolness, as well as by Gelber's proximity and his own. Pieter considered the dumpiness of the old woman's shadow on the concrete. In the hard, bright light, he could see more clearly the wearing action grief for her son had had on her.

"He's contacted only this one man?"

"Yes, General."

"Then—" She hesitated, then shook away his supporting hand as he attempted to assist her into the rear of the Volvo. Her features were concentrated, as she brushed absently at her dress and spoke in a clear, gruff voice. "Then he had found nothing so far, he knows no more than when he arrived. There is time."

She attempted to tidy stray locks of frizzy gray hair as Pieter slid into the car beside her. Gelber climbed in next to the driver, while the two Malays made their way toward the old yellow car they were using. Even within the darkened car, Brigitte's features were strained. She *was* old. And pursuing an even older man, mostly for personal reasons. She was motivated by revenge, not duty. Perhaps it was all that was left to her?

Pieter realized, then, that Babbington had been very clever. He had given Brigitte the task of eliminating Aubrey. In her grief, he could never have trusted her to do any other job efficiently. This one, however, she would make certain of.

He heard her murmur: "We will wait—see who he sees, learn what he learns . . ." She was patting his knee in time to the rhythm of her words. " . . . we must be certain—absolutely certain, he is working alone, who he has come to see. When we know all that, we can kill him and whoever else it may be necessary to dispose of in order to put out this fire." Her old, bony hand gripped his knee, all but making him exclaim in pain.

She would see this through, that much was certain.

His rage appalled him. Its cold clarity of reason, its confidence, even its ability to surmount the pain they had inflicted during a second day of interrogation—all served to remove him from himself, as if he had shed a skin, or a chrysalis. His anger had even been able to calculate and observe when they took him out into the wind and doused him with buckets of icy water to make him talk. When they had finished, he could not feel his hands, could not close them into the fists he desired to form; could not prevent the chattering of his teeth, the ache in his bones or the agony of reawakened blood after they had flung him back into his room. For hours, his whole body had shuddered in an ague of cold, his head whirling and pounding with the endless, endlessly repeated questions. Even then, he had been aware of the cold, clear center of his mind which frightened him as much as a diagnosed, malignant tumor.

He must have slept, he realized, stifling a groan, feeling the hardness of the cot beneath his palms. The slats of the shutter were dark. He raised one arm wearily and held it close to his face, stilling its tremor with his other hand, squinting at his watch. Five, seven . . . ? Six . . . dark shutter. Six in the morning. Before dawn. He was still *here!* There had been no opportunity, no instant when surprise would have given him advantage and a weapon. He had had to endure the beating, the drenching, the questions just to wake in this room again! His head throbbed.

They had had no drugs. He still had not confessed the extent of his knowledge or betrayed the fact that no one was acting on his knowledge. They were still obsessed with what he really knew, who else knew . . . still interested in keeping him alive.

Yet they'd let him sleep. Perhaps they'd been unable to wake him? Now, before the little recaptured strength was used up, he must escape. *Would,* not must. There was no room for doubt. Eventually, a doctor would come to examine him, just as on the previous morning, or a guard—someone to taunt him with food or merely observe his condition. At the moment of the door's opening, he would begin his escape. He did not consider how long he could hold out. It was of no significance. He would not be there to be broken.

He watched the door. The one question that dominated his thoughts was simple—would whoever came be armed? Would there be a gun? There must be. He was ravenously hungry, but did not feel weak. They had given him water to drink, once he started fainting. Before that, he had licked it off his hands and shoulders even as they threw buckets of the icy stuff over him. He could not remember whether he had intended the repeated fainting; he preferred to think he had.

I'll help you get away. One of them sidling up, whispering. Brandis himself, perhaps? *Tell me and I can save your life . . .* even while the questions bellowingly overlapped, as if angel and demon sat on his shoulders with their separate temptations. Tell us and it stops, tell us and you will live. *Fuck off, fuck off, fuck off, fuck off!* His throat was sore from yelling.

She'll want you dead . . . she hasn't realized how much she wants it yet, but she will. Who was *she?* Some woman in authority over Brandis, an enemy of Kenneth's? He could not remember. It was only a threat, nothing more. *An eye for an eye . . .* just a threat. *Son for son . . .*

I'll help you get away.

Don't need help. Just a gun. Short, precise, cold thoughts, which satisfied him like cut and polished diamonds. 6:10. The room was gray now. Almost first light. His body was shivering almost rhythmically, but only with the night's cold. He listened. Footsteps outside.

There was a moment of hesitation, as if he stood outside himself and saw not just the marks and shiverings but the thing he was becoming, that feared and detested image: his father. Then it was gone.

What does Aubrey know? Tell us *what you told Aubrey, tell us, tell us . . .*

Brandis' voice faded, rushing away down a long tunnel as the door-handle turned. His breath caught in his chest, his headache retreated. And then his body felt weak and treacherous. The German smiled—the one with the insinuating rather than the bellowing voice—his hands holding a tray. Spicy food, his mouth salivating like that of a dog so that he all but dribbled. The shock of company in the room, the shock of his weariness, his stiff legs, each bruise protesting, his headache now thudding. A cup of coffee was lifted, then delicately poured onto the floor. The smile broadened. The coffee moved as if on some slowed-down film, a thin brown stream, individual droplets splashing slowly back up from the floorboards, absorbing his entire attention. His stomach protested violently. His hands lay limply on his thighs. Then the plate, a stew of some kind, bread very white even in the gloom, the smile white in the gloom—

—groaned aloud. Laughter. The stew spilling in a slow gray tide over the edge of the thick-rimmed plate, his cupped hands moving to prevent the spillage, the German's mouth forming words very slowly which echoed in his head as if shouted in an empty building, his legs very weak, the stew spilling on the floor with an extended, bass roaring noise, his hands loosely bunched, the German dropping the plate with a flourish of success, his first step more like a lurch, the German's face—

—slower, even slower! His hand rising in front of him, the tray being dropped, the German's hand moving very quickly, reaching into his jacket—gun, *gun*—second step, third lurching movement, his own voice sounding meaningless, the gun beginning to come out, his foot slipping in the stew on the floor, his two hands in front of him, the dimness of the room and the glint of metal coming at him—

—collision. He could hardly feel his own fist, hardly feel its contact or the second blow against the German's face. Two more, but so slow, slow . . . the noise of the gun a small tinkling, the slither of the German's body down the door into the spilled stew . . .

Speed. He was scooping up stew on his hands, dabbing bread across the floor like a sponge, eating, swallowing, wiping his hand, wiping the soggy surface of the gun, eating coffee-stew-bread, his head spinning, a slow ache returning to his knuckles.

He gagged on the food, but kept the bread down and stood

upright. The rage surged in him. There was a smear of something dark on the white blob of the German's face: blood worn
like a beard.

Obsessively, he continued wiping the gun on his shirttail. He
smelled his own energy and fear and cunning: his feral self. His
father. *Our Father which art* . . . that father had always looked
like his, with remote gray eyes and no smile, impatient, perpetu-
ally angered. He moved to the shutter and listened, seeming to
know how much time had passed since the German had entered
the room. Footsteps but no voices. One man. The smell of a cigarette in the chill pre-dawn. He looked down at the gun, clutching
it like a prize, bringing it closer to his face until he could recognize the small pistol as a Beretta Mo 84. His fingers stroked it
like a dog's coat. Thirteen rounds, thirteen. He whirled around,
almost losing his balance, his head lurching. Knelt and fumbled
in the German's pockets—only thirteen, no spare clip.

Sixty seconds. He moved to the shutter, hardly aware of the
room now or of himself. Tested it with his hand, then hesitated,
breathed in, banged the shutter open—

It swung creakingly open but time was not slowed down now
and it swung back painfully against his elbow as he leaned out
to left then right—left, *left!* Shadow along the veranda, near a
climbing plant. A cry of surprise, he pushing the shutter open
with the painful elbow, the gun held two-handed and almost
smothered in his grip, cocking the pistol, squeezing, squeezing.
Two deafening noises echoed in his head. The shadow leaned
wearily against the plant, then fell, and he seemed already halfway through the open window as the body settled. His feet thudded onto the veranda. He staggered into a run as noises rose behind him. Stars, a gray horizon, the lights of villages scattered
like glowing seeds.

He reached the body. Dark stains on a light jacket. He
stopped, falling to his knees, searching the pockets, finding the
spare clip, unable to locate by eyesight or touch the gun which
must have fallen away from the man's loosened grip. He found
something hard which crackled and spluttered, and thrust the
small walkie-talkie into his pocket together with the ammunition clip. He climbed unsteadily to his feet, orientating himself,
the noises behind him more urgent as he ran out from beneath
the roof of the veranda and at once began careering down a long
slope toward the gorge of the Kali Gandaki. Annapurna's peaks

ranged away ahead of him while Dhaulagiri loomed gray-flanked behind him to the west.

The lights of the villages around him. The stars becoming dim in the slowly-graying sky. The noise of the river in the hidden gorge. Familiar villages . . . Marpha lay huddled behind a ridge, a few early lights glowing, the flat-roofed houses and hotels and lodges mere lumps like sleeping cattle. He knew which way he must head. Down into the gorge and pick up the trail south, toward Tatopani.

Something noisy as a bee whirred near his ear. He was aware of the whole vulnerable area of his sweating skin. His heart bumped in his chest and his throat was raw and hot from his dragged-in breaths. He glanced behind him, needing to reassert the foolhardiness which would help him to run blindly on across the sloping pasture. The light shone out from the isolated lodge and he could see shadows crossing and recrossing the lights from doors and windows. Flashlights wobbled and glimmered. He could hear orders, recriminations, threats, and felt exhilarated and fearful. The slope was taking him out of sight of his pursuers. The breeze chilled him. He felt only the imperative of survival.

Then he stumbled across a narrow goat-track which wound down the sharpening slope. He heard the noise of the river in its narrow bed. The stars had almost disappeared in the strengthening gray of the sky and the moon was dim and old. The mountains became more real, no longer gauzily vast. Within minutes, he could see the white-flecked rush of water below him as the goat track joined the main trail along the gorge. They would know he must come this way. He had only darkness and the small distance of his head start over them. The river's noise was like the churning of a paddle-steamer's wheel.

Marpha was just to the north—should he make for the village? He turned, his body urged to do so by a new weariness. He clenched his hands. *No!* The country was arid and becoming yellow beyond the village as the gorge climbed toward Jomosom and then Tibet. He turned south, jogging down the trail, his breath roaring in his ears like the noise of a seashell. Above it, he heard trees creak in the stiff dawn breeze and the rush of the water. There was no elation at escaping, only the leadenness of distance, of isolation. Trees were perched high and strange on the bare flanks of the gorge, as if wrecked there by a sudden sinking of the riverbed. The valley widened ahead of him as it dropped down toward Tukche and Larjung. The land was smudged with forest and pasture, streaked with irrigation. The mountains to east and west were white now, their peaks touched with pink-becoming-gold. The approach of daylight seemed as swift as he imagined the pursuit behind him; faster than his own flight.

He knew the place . . . where was it? Near here, surely? He studied the floor of the valley. There was a log bridge just south of Marpha which would take him across the river to the easier trail on the other side. If he crossed, he would make better time.

He looked behind him, but saw nothing in the gloom. Only high up, storks and eagles flying against the white flanks of the mountains, awaiting thermals. They were not much bigger than dots.

The bridge was below him. The river was full with the last of the monsoons and flowed across its logs as if swamping an inadequate dam. The water rushed, gray-white. He realized he was thirty hours from Pokhara. The knowledge caused him to stumble, almost fall, and the small faltering of his stride made him feel weak. A hot tremor passed through him. Breathing loudly, trying to calm himself and shut out all sense of distance and time, he began climbing carefully, slowly, down a goat track toward the floor of the gorge. Six-thirty, no, already later . . .

He was exhausted as he reached the gravel and rocks on the valley floor and began picking his way across the river's debris toward the bridge. He could see nothing on the almost-dark slopes above. He glimpsed an ammonite as he paused, neat and small as a cake set in a boulder. He was alert, cautious, crouched as he reached the bridge and began wading through the rush of the river, one hand gripping the rope handhold, the small pistol still in the other. His trousers were at once soaked to the knees. The water was deeper than he thought, the logs slippery beneath the surface. He tottered, slid and edged forward, looking behind him, around him, his vulnerability flooding back. His thighs were wet as the river buffeted around him. His body remembered the drenchings of the previous day and shuddered, protested at the stinging, hurrying water.

Convulsively, his hand tightened its grip on the rope as his feet slipped again on the submerged logs He heard the cry of a large bird somewhere above him. Then his feet went ludicrously from under him and the river pushed him across the logs, threatening to loosen his grip on the rope or pull his arm from its socket. He coughed, swallowed water. The water lifted him, dumped him back on the logs, lifted him again, then ducked him. He struggled to his knees, blind, coughing, thrusting the pistol into his shirt, so that he could grip the rope with both hands, straining against the river's force.

The first bullet soundlessly plopped into the water near him, but he heard the second whirring past his head. He looked wildly up toward the side of the gorge, and saw small, gesticulating, running figures—like rescuers to a drowning man! Then another bullet and another. He could see the tiny flashes of flame from the rifle. Someone—had to be Brandis—was pointing, urging, probably screaming he be killed. The river, too, seemed malevolent, increased in strength, dragging and lunging at him, trying to loosen his grip on the rope.

He thrust himself to his feet and struggled forward, trying to hurry, his feet slipping, his hands burning on the rope as he slid them forward. His nerves cried out because of the clear, vulnerable target he made. Another bullet wailed near him; there seemed a renewed rush of the water and his feet slipped. He tumbled—the gun! He grabbed his hand against his shirt. The river tugged his other hand from the rope in a moment, spun him around as if he had been shot and threw him across the bridge into deeper water. His hands slid over the logs and he was hurried away, helpless in the current, his hands still clawlike as if expecting the rope or the logs to be within reach.

He was thrown along the river's narrow course, hurried into a tunnel of darkness and noise.

10

Scenes of Former Glory

There was urgency now, pressing at his back as he got out of the taxi's cooler, false air into the damp towel of afternoon humidity and the coast's hard light. The temperature clung to his hands and face and pressed his new, German clothes tightly against him. A car had followed him from his hotel. The suspicion that he had been observed at Kuala Lumpur while he waited for his flight to Penang, observed again on his arrival, was now a reality. He was alone and old, sensing with a dull certainty that whoever was behind the tinted windshield of the car just drawing to a halt a hundred yards further down the dusty coast road, had been sent by Brigitte. Whatever he had to do and learn had to be done and understood and acted upon quickly. The acute sense of personal danger rippled outward until it encompassed Timothy, who fell like a heavier stone into the pond of his concerns. The idea that they had already killed Tim was as difficult to shrug aside as the humidity and clung as fiercely to him.

Light baked the headland and the sea, enameling both. The sprawled bungalow in front of which his taxi had stopped was in need of repainting. It overlooked a small, secluded cove near Telak Bahang, where the white columns of hotels rose distantly, smudging the hot sky like rising smoke. They were well beyond the small car that had followed him out here from Batu Feringgi and his air-conditioned hotel. He paid the Malay behind the wheel, and the taxi then turned and diminished back along the road. As the dust settled on and around him, he was alone with the other car and its tinted, blind windshield.

He pushed open the creaking gate. A burnt, yellow lawn, dusty bushes and clumps of garish flowers littered the garden. A sprinkler threw a peacock's tail of spray into the sunlight. The bungalow murmured of untidiness and modest affluence, and seemed to resist his intentions for its owner.

Yes, still alive, French had told him over the telephone from Birmingham Airport of one of the names in Godwin's file, *Penang, I'm certain of that, Kenneth . . . still get the odd Christmas card. As to his helping you, not so sure . . . odd bugger, truculent, cut himself off entirely. Might resent you turning up.* Aubrey sighed. Scudamore, a name that meant nothing other than its appearance in the file. Scudamore had been one of the people who had assisted with the early interrogation of Lin after his capture near Ipoh during the fag-end of the Emergency. Thirty years earlier. It was all he had—except that he was staying at the beach hotel where Babbington and Elizabeth had stayed the previous year, and where Lin and Brigitte had been, too. It was all so thin.

Tim intruded, thrusting him up the path like a hot, quick wind. He rang the bell, the dried-out boards of the porch creaking beneath his nervous shuffling. The temperature was no different beneath the porch. Flies hummed as loudly as if around the carcass of something. A Malay opened the door.

"My name is Aubrey. Mr. Scudamore is expecting me." Scudamore's manner over the telephone had been reluctant to the point of abuse. Aubrey had forced the meeting.

"Selamat tengah hari," the Malay murmured, gesturing Aubrey inside, into cooler shadow. Aubrey removed his straw trilby.

A fan moved sluggishly beneath the ceiling of a large, open room. The Malay, evidently Scudamore's servant, led him through open, sliding glass doors onto a wide veranda at the rear of the bungalow. Cane furniture, deep shadow, Scudamore lounging in one of the chairs, his eyes at once assessing Aubrey in an echo of old professionalism. Scudamore had long been running to fat and ease. He brushed one hand through overlong gray hair, then around his jowl. A well-iced drink was clamped in his other large hand.

"Thank you, Rahim. Bring the *Tuan*"—his eyes gleamed with mockery—"a drink. *No* ice." The Malay disappeared back into the bungalow. Aubrey's head flinched around as he thought he heard the slamming of a car door. "Yes, you're Aubrey," Scudamore conceded. "Sit down, why don't you? Make the place look untidy." There was still a distinct Northern accent, Lancashire perhaps.

"Thank you." He sat heavily, as if the humidity had extorted his energy. The green-blue of the sea was hazed now with soft gold. He placed his briefcase beside the cane chair.

"Best time of the day to be in the shade," Scudamore remarked, and waved a hand airily. "Best view on Penang." The Andaman Sea was empty to the north and west, except for a single faint smudge of smoke on the horizon. The small curve of white sand below the headland on which the bungalow perched was deserted. The Malay returned with a long, iceless drink. "Don't want guts-ache, do you?" Scudamore offered mockingly as Aubrey took the glass.

Insect noises in the silence as he sipped his drink, the calls of hidden, exotic birds, a flash of red and blue and yellow in a tree. Peace impressed as heavily as the heat and Aubrey clearly understood Scudamore's resentment of his intrusion. But, there was little or no time left to him.

"Superintendent French," Aubrey began, only to be interrupted by a snort from Scudamore accompanied by a toss of the head. His hair flopped on either temple, over each ear. He resembled one of the more disreputable Europeans from an early Conrad novel of the Far East, Aubrey decided. "Superintendent French gave me your name. Confirmed, rather, that you might be able to help me. He gave you a glowing testimonial. I need your help rather urgently," Aubrey concluded limply, unsettled by the other man's indifference.

"So you said over the phone." He brushed his hair away from his ears, swallowed at his drink. "That was all a bloody long time ago, Aubrey. You must be clutching at straws to chase all the way out here just to talk to me. On the off-chance. Look at you. You're no spring chicken to be traipsing round the world looking up ex-coppers, are you?" Scudamore laughed loudly. Aubrey stared into his glass. The man was unruffled, as untroubled by his visitor as one of the clumps of flowers or one of the bushes in the scorched, mock-English garden. Was there anything left of the Special Branch officer French had lauded?

"You're like a fictional detective whose name I can't remem-

ber," Aubrey remarked. "Fat, vulgar and a drinker. Are you
clever like him, too, I wonder?"

Scudamore's eyes narrowed within their creases of fat and
age, but his body hardly stirred in the chair. Then he laughed
again.

"Cheeky sod!" he bellowed, swallowing more of the drink. Ice
rattled and Aubrey envied him his acclimatized stomach.
"Look, Aubrey, you're an important old bugger, too important
by half to do your own legwork. So, what's up?" His eyes narrowed again. Was it only habit, or sunlight—or had the fat
man's curiosity begun to awaken? Aubrey waited, sensing himself probed, prodded, weighed much like a baby at a postnatal
clinic. A small tickle of excitement stirred in the pit of his stomach, as if he indeed had ice in his drink and it had begun to upset
him. "I wonder what you want? Jim French was very cagey over
the phone when he told me you were coming—but then, I expect
you were cagey with him, right? Is it the Fifth Man . . . or have
we got to double figures yet? I don't read the papers much,
though I do listen to the World Service enough to know you
were right up shit creek without your paddle only months ago!
More trouble, is it?" He nodded. "I thought so. What the hell's
it got to do with me? Eh?" He finished his drink. "Rahim!" he
bawled. "Fill my glass!" Then he subsided into silence. The
Malay came and went, returned with a clinking glass. Scudamore continued to study Aubrey.

Aubrey watched the fair-haired young man in shirt and light-
coloured slacks walking on the sand below. His were the only
footprints in the cove. They were as heavy and dark as if some
great, ponderous creature had passed. Scudamore eventually followed his intent gaze.

"Who's *that* cheeky bugger?" he bellowed, climbing noisily
out of his chair. "It's *my* bloody bit of beach, that!" He stood
upright, but on the point of shouting said to Aubrey: "Is he with
you?"

Aubrey shrugged. "Not exactly."

Scudamore grimaced, then nodded. Cupping his large hands
around his mouth, he yelled: "Oi, you—fuck off! You're tres-
passing on private property! Go on, bugger off!" Down on the
beach, a hundred yards away from them, the young man was
watching them through binoculars. Then he raised his hands in
a gesture of noncomprehension. Scudamore waved his arms. "I
said this is private property!" he roared. "Fuck *off!*" Once more,

he waved the young man back along the beach. The trespasser began to retreat the way he had come, his second set of footprints as ominous to Aubrey as the first. "Go on, on your bike!" Scudamore growled. "Bloody trespassers—if I wanted people on my bit of beach, I'd sell it to one of those bloody hotels, wouldn't I?" He glared at Aubrey, then tossed his head and smoothed his hair away from his ears. *"Tourists!* Except he isn't, is he?"

Aubrey shook his head primly. "No, I don't think he is."

"But he's not one of yours . . . same line of work, though?"

"I think so."

Scudamore's curiosity seemed aroused. It was like a blood test, proving they had been fathered by the same parent and were brothers under the skin.

"OK," Scudamore said, "what's going on?"

"If I might begin at the beginning?"

"Suit yourself," Scudamore shrugged, drinking again. "Just make it interesting, eh?" He smirked. A parrot cried mockingly, hidden by trees.

There seemed to be voices, intermittent and distant as if remembered rather than heard. A rushing noise, an iciness that numbed and buffeted. Even before he opened his eyes, he began coughing, retching out the water in his lungs. His eyes came startled open. The clouds rushed against a slaty, cold sky . . . which then seemed more blue, less cold. Water stung against his face. Color of cliffs, brown; color of sky, blue, clouds white. Color of water, gray and white. He could almost give the wind howling up the gorge its own dark, hurrying color. The voices continued to puzzle rather than alarm him as his body registered new bruises and abrasions. He was curled against a boulder, white water heaved and thrust around it. His hands clung clawlike in crevices, his feet were braced against rock. Slowly, the pistol assumed its recognizable shape in the small of his back. Something pressed against his thigh. The voices seemed to be coming from there.

He absorbed the landscape. More than a mile downstream from the bridge. His thoughts skittering across the tumble and pain and collisions of his struggle prompted more retching, and a thin dribble of water and bile from the side of his mouth. Now, the slaps of the river as it twisted and thrust through a narrow part of the gorge and over shallow rapids revived him.

Helicopter. He lifted his head, turning it wildly. The wind

hurled against his face, he slitted his eyes and saw the distant, lumpy shape of a Puma settled on the eastern bank of the river. Smaller moving shadowy lumps of its occupants on—yes, both banks, trailing gradually downstream toward his hiding place. The voices clicked, spluttered near him, as if from men drowning in the current. He touched his thigh. The walkie-talkie in his pocket must have been switched to Receive as he was washed along the river.

He ignored it. Raised his head again, studying the distant, slow-moving figures bent, like old men, against the wind at their backs. They were looking for his body. Not expecting him to have survived the current, the rocks. He looked at his hands. Lacerations. Clothing torn, his face aching as feeling returned. He had survived . . . just. His arm was skinned raw. His body hurt now, as if some anesthetic had lost its effect. He groaned through chattering teeth.

The wind had sprung up as it did every midmorning. He saw the rotors quivering in the wind, the airframe shivering. Bent men, moving slowly. He had time.

The gorge narrowed between outcrops of tougher rock. Creaking trees bent over the river, over a litter of covering boulders. The goat trail was up there, on the western bank, high up the cliffs. That was what he had to find. The gorge opened out ahead of him, toward Tukche and then Larjung, where it was at its widest, the river lakelike, less dangerous. He stared at his hands and arms with a kind of disbelief, hardly feeling relief, or anything. Except the rage inside the tightly wound shroud of bruises, aches and lacerations.

Move—

—groaned aloud, almost wailed, lost his grip, was flung against a rock and knocked breathless, gritted his teeth to prevent himself crying out, clung on.

He moved his feet slowly, exploring footholds; moving, changing the grip of his hands, bracing himself, watching the shadowy bent figures moving up both banks. Jumped once, knocked himself breathless, clung on. He dragged himself behind the closest litter of rocks to those in the river, slithering on his stomach. Blood ran thinly, diluted almost to colorlessness. He spat and coughed out water. Lay still, exhausted. The voices.

He drew the walkie-talkie from his pocket. Still working underwater like a Walkman! Listened . . .

. . . slowly, words becoming sense: *no way, he couldn't be.* It was in English, the accent German. *Just keep your men looking. What?* Change of voice, accent, the discomfort of an Oriental speaking English. *Time is not on our side, we should return. Not yet! I want to see the body first! You cannot ignore the news from the capital. I damn well can, Lin! And I will. But . . . No!*

Gardiner listened to the silence that crackled after the words. He had to press the tiny radio against his face to prevent the howl of the wind from whipping the voices away. He watched clouds hurry, the pale blue of the sky, the rustle and creak and sway of branches above him. The Chinese was there, too, with Brandis. The cold-faced Chinaman from the other side of the wire in Hong Kong. Lin. His anger focused. The Chinaman who had received back hundreds of poor devils who'd tried to get out of the PRC. *Lin!* He squeezed his eyes shut, seeing the face in night shadow, through night glasses. He sighed. Lin was responsible for what had happened to him.

Reports trickled through the walkie-talkie. Nothing to report, nothing here, no sign of the body. He rolled onto his stomach and slithered across the rocks and stones into the shelter of low, scrubby bushes. He watched them moving steadily toward him, while he recovered, awaiting the anger to prompt him, allow him to continue.

Eventually, he began to climb the shallow cliff-face, slowly, breathlessly, up through the struggle of twisted, wind-moved trees. Lin, Lin, *Lin* with almost every breath.

The walkie-talkie accompanied his progress like loudspeaker announcements of other events at the same athletics meeting. His clothes dried in the wind, his bruises were slapped and scraped by the movement of branches, even leaves. The pistol must be drying by now . . . please God, drying, *usable!* He ground his teeth together. He rested, breath exploding, body shaking. Deep in cover, fifty feet up the cliff from the floor of the gorge. The river already beginning to possess the appearance of an innocuous stream. The radio—

. . . *more important than—Damn you, no! I shall have to . . . Don't threaten me, Lin!—I must, if you neglect the imperatives, Kathmandu requires our— Fuck Kathmandu!*

He could see Brandis, he thought, but not the small, slim form of the Chinese. In the Puma? They bickered on. Brandis was raising his arms, waving them in anger. *There could be no more than a single day before Moscow has to—*

A man below him!

—*damn Moscow!*

Turn off the bloody bloody—

—*risk everything, the whole operation?*

Turn it off! His clumsy fingers found the button, depressed it even as the Nepali beneath him began looking about, puzzled, for the source of the voices. He held his breath, cramped with fears.

The soldier scratched his head. Another walkie-talkie, carried by an officer, crackled and twittered and the soldier relaxed. Gardiner let out his breath slowly, his chest tight, his heart thudding as if to alert the two men now directly below his hiding place. The trees and bushes rattled against his body, remarking his presence.

He was shaking, he realized. He clutched his arms across his chest, rocking slightly to and fro while the tinny, unreal voices bickered over the officer's open walkie-talkie channel.

Then the orders, Brandis' reluctant agreement, his figure moving off toward the shivering Puma—and the name, growing like a hidden disease suddenly become a tumor appreciable by touch. Hard to believe, shocking.

Babbington.

. . . *he is arriving tonight, Brandis.*

Babbington—*him!* He remained still, feet braced against a thick, twisted branch, figure concealed by heavy foliage, the Nepali officer and two soldiers now clumped together fifty feet away and below. Brandis walking bent-backed as if defeated toward the waiting helicopter.

. . . *we must be there, things should be under control, before he arrives. Do you see that, Brandis?*

And Brandis had seen it, taken the point, capitulated. Babbington. His gaze remained on the Puma, its rotors now beginning to turn as if struggling through deep water rather than the wind. It bobbed like a young bird uncertain of flight. The orders snapped out, were acknowledged. *Find that body, or him, find, find . . .*

Then no more of Brandis or the Chinese, only quick Nepali orders and reassurances. The Puma wobbled into the air, turned unsteadily on its axis, then it was hurrying past him and on down the gorge like a small bird carried into exaggerated speed by the wind's force. Its noise diminished so that the voices over the officer's walkie-talkie became apparent once more, then the Puma was quickly hidden by the gorge's flanks.

Urgency hurried his heartbeat. He was shivering with excitement and anger. He looked at his quivering hands, then felt at his back for the pistol. Examined it, feeling its dry shape. Should work—

He pointed it down, toward the Nepali officer now standing over the two soldiers, who were breaking open rations, eating something. An easy target. His finger began to squeeze—should work, should—easy target, squeeze—

He rubbed his face, replacing the gun in his belt. He must get up to the goat track, follow that down toward Tukche, then on to Larjung, Lete, Ghasa—*must!* He had to survive if he was to report, explain . . . catch up with Lin. Babbington.

The officer walked away to the riverbank, talking continually over the walkie-talkie. The two soldiers relaxed further into semirecumbent comfort. For them, he was dead, merely undiscovered because of some trick of the rocks or current. He eased himself upright against rock, enclosed by trees. Began to climb, their meandering voices below louder than the river's noise. The wind rattled the leaves, masking his own noises.

He reached the goat track, winding between covering rocks along the flank of the cliff, toward where the gorge opened out like a different country. Dhaulagiri loomed to the west, huge. He groaned and exhaustion posed itself to assume control of him. The helicopter was less than an hour from Kathmandu— he was still more than a day from Pokhara. Whatever time he made, he was a whole day behind them.

He crawled some distance, as if burdened by realization, then looked back. Men settling into unsupervised, fearless relaxation. They did not expect to see him; they would not. Lin's face, Babbington's name. He rose to a crouch and began to move more rapidly from cover to cover along the dipping, rising, twisting thread of the track, the wind at his back like hands attempting to tip him off-balance, down the cliff. Then the track twisted around the flank of the cliff and he could no longer be seen from the valley floor. He began jogging as quickly as he could.

The valley opened ahead, the river became lakelike with the reflections of clouds moving on its gleaming surface like hurrying vessels. Foothills. Eagles high overhead. Fields, cultivation, the roofs of Tukche. He was hungry but his exhaustion was content to remain quiescent.

Lin's face, Babbington's name, his rage.
A day, a whole day—

Scudamore seemed unimpressed, slumped in his chair so that
his waist and thighs bulged over and around it; possessing the
sloth and intelligence statues of the Buddha suggested. He had
not interrupted Aubrey's narrative on even a single occasion.
Aubrey heard his own voice fading into silence.

" . . . may prove important to establish that these people were
here together, with Babbington, last year."

Scudamore's features adopted an insolent boredom. Aubrey's
irritation was pressed into expression by the scant regard paid
to his narrative. He snapped waspishly:

"And I have come to you, Scudamore, because you seem *exactly* the sort of person who would make himself known to bar-
persons and hotel undermanagers and cocktail waitresses, and
as such you would make an *ideal* assistant in my enquiries!"

Scudamore's face darkened—the man was so, so *immovable!*
—then his eyes glittered more brightly for a moment before he
burst into laughter.

"You're a cheeky old sod, and not half as clever as you think
you are!" he rejoined, his jowls quivering with what Aubrey assumed was genuine amusement. Then Scudamore creaked forward in the fragile-seeming chair. "You're worried about something, all right. It's not just an *enquiry,* as you put it. What's
up? You in the shit again?"

Aubrey felt himself flush, and Scudamore's features revealed
a satisfaction. Aubrey hesitated, then risked a shake of his head.

"Not personally," he offered.

"Look, *Sir* Kenneth Aubrey, I know all about you and Babbington. And if all you're interested in is tying him in with some
old Kraut tart and a Chink in Penang last year, then you're the
bloke trying to blame the man next to you for the smelly fart
you've just dropped!" Again, he roared with laughter. "You
don't have a shred of authority to be out here. You got my name
out of a pal of yours. You'd be making other noises if that wasn't
the case. You're *begging!*"

Scudamore was perspiring freely, but made no effort to wipe
his face and neck. Aubrey dabbed gently at his own forehead
with his already crumpled handkerchief.

"Listen, *ex*-Chief Inspector Scudamore," he enunciated carefully and with a chilly, subdued hostility, even as he obscurely

warmed to the man, "at the moment, I am dealing with more shits than I know how to shake a stick at. I am not interested in any private agreement you think you've drawn up with the world in general. Whoever gave you the impression you could *retire?* Donald French has a high opinion of you. I can see for myself how badly in need of revision that opinion is!"

Immediately, Scudamore snapped back: "Christ, Aubrey, you're an old man—why not act like one? Anyone would think you were twenty, bustling in here, making demands."

Scudamore's armor appeared impenetrable. Aubrey had no wish, no wish at all, to mention Tim—would he need to? Would the personal have any more appeal than the secret past? He decided to continue insulting the man.

"Old? Like you, I presume? Whiskey and slippers and servants! Drink and complacency are both cheap here, Scudamore! This is just another Algarve or Sussex coast for you." Aubrey smiled, catlike. "You don't read newspapers, you ignore the television. I'm here to tell you, Rip Van Winkle, that it's time to wake up again!"

Scudamore, hardly disconcerted, shook his head. "I voss only obeying orders!" he snapped in a heavily caricatured German accent. "Those days are over, when I wasn't allowed to ask why. French has a high opinion of you, too. He didn't try to call in debts, neither have you. But you'd better tell me exactly *why,* or you can fuck off now."

The veranda now possessed a bluish light. Insects hummed. Aubrey debated. It was like nakedness, this candor demanded of him. But he needed Scudamore . . .

Aubrey sighed, spread his hands, and said: "It *is* personal. A young man—" Scudamore leered. "No!" Aubrey barked, his features savage. "My—foster son, I suppose you would call him. Or my son," he added in a quiet whisper. "He is not an agent, not professional. Babbington has him—or as good as. I must do what I can to get him back, get him out."

The silence was filled with insects, the distant radio, the chopping of the kitchen knife. Scudamore rubbed his chins. Eventually, he murmured: "Christ." Settling back in his chair, he added: "I bet you've never been so bloody honest in your life before," then made an apologetic face in response to the anger Aubrey displayed. "And that's all you want—proof they were here together last year? You can use that?"

"I think so. It is all I can hope for."

"Christ." Scudamore laved his loose face with both hands. "You don't want anything on Babbington from way back, then?"

"Is there anything?" Aubrey asked eagerly.

Scudamore shook his head. "I shouldn't think so. I remember that bugger Babbington. Right clever-dick he was. And the Chink, after he was caught. Slimy little sod got away. That's about it."

"I never thought there would be," Aubrey said with studied acceptance. Careful. It was as if Aubrey's effort at candor had become addictive, and he struggled for a moment against further honesty. He was dealing with a clever man whose manipulation would not be simple. The present—last year at least—was simply a bait. The last days of the Malayan Emergency were where Aubrey believed the real truth lay, during the months when the British Army finally defeated the Communist guerrillas in Malaya, after more than a decade of trying. Somewhere back in 1958 or '59, Babbington and Lin had become allies, sharing their mutual treachery. But Scudamore's being caught willingly on that hook would be difficult to achieve. He had offered the reformed alcoholic one small drink. But, was the man really cured? Or could he be re-addicted?

Had his damned curiosity vanished in the creases and rolls of fat?

He repeated: "No, it's last year, that's the key." He thought he glimpsed suspicion in Scudamore's gaze, but then the man nodded. Aubrey kept relief from his expression.

"I won't ask if it's dangerous, despite our friend down on the beach. You'd lie anyway. Still, it can't be that rough, otherwise you wouldn't be here . . . one wrinkled old man?" He laughed with the same rough, callous noise that seemed habitual with him. He continued: "You make me laugh, Aubrey, you really do. I'd kick you out, if I knew what was good for me." His stomach thrust hairily through the strained front of his shirt. "Always the same old game, eh? Now, you want to give Babbington a boot up the arse for what he nearly did to you. Oh, I believe you about this boy you adopted or whatever. But, you want to stuff Babbington as much as anything!"

Aubrey smiled in admission. Good, there was amusement, but curiosity, too. He said, simply: "True."

"I thought so. Dog with a bone." He sighed loudly, slapping his hands on his vast thighs. "Oh, all right, I'll give you a hand—

just so long as you remember that it's just a couple of old farts *pretending* to be spies, and not the real thing! It won't take much more than a few phone calls and a couple of visits anyway . . . Sidney Wei, for instance, he might know something," he added, thoughtful at once. "Yeah, not a lot of work. But first, I want to know who the trespasser on the beach might be and what his angle is. OK?"

Aubrey sensed the car doubtless still parked down the road and its occupant. Saw Scudamore's age, the ease with which he might become impenetrably complacent at any moment, then he nodded. "Thank you. And—very well, I'll tell you who I think he is and who he represents."

He looked down on the schoolyard in the quick, gathering dusk, and remembered the place filled with young men from the hills, ringed by onlookers, small knots of officers and NCOs gathered, himself among them. Recruitment camp for the Brigade. Easy tears pricked, prompted by memory and exhaustion. He felt alone, drained of his abiding anger; a former, incapable self. The clusters of houses that constituted Tatopani were slipping into evening; lights glowed out, the smell of cooking, and himself outlined on the hill, exposed. He slumped into a sitting crouch, arms wearily folded across his knees, head forward. The huge flank of Dhaulagiri was orange-pink and darkening toward icy blue.

There was only danger, and the fear of recognition and capture. He had skirted the police checkpoint at the edge of the village. Its occupants had been reinforced by soldiers. Perhaps they now accepted that he might have survived. To Nepalis he was a Queen's Gurkha Officer, something considerable and brave. He tossed his head mockingly at the idea and looked at his raw arms and scratched, dirty hands, torn shirt and trousers gaping at one knee. And the Nepalis knew the country, knew where best to await him.

Here?

Hunger was nauseous. His body shivered with the evening's new chill. He was more than half a day from his destination and all he could think of was food and sleep. Warmth of some kind, however meager. The chill of their icy-water douches flung at him and the cold of the river had remained inside.

Beyond Tatopani, rhododendron forest covered the slopes. There were cultivated fields, bright masses of flowers after the ending of the monsoon. The mountains seemed more distant and less awesome. He was in the shadow of bushes covered with orange berries, and a black juniper that straggled about the hilltop. Beyond the village, the gorge narrowed like a final trap, and he could see the suspension bridge and then the valley of the Ghar Kola and the route toward Pokhara. He groaned. Envisaging the country he must travel was daunting even as it taunted him with its familiarity.

He needed food now, some rest. Shelter. There were ex-Gurkhas in the village whose names he knew. Best hope; only hope. He pushed himself into a squatting position, breathing heavily at the tiny exertion. Remained still like that, on all fours like an animal, until his dizziness passed. Animal, father . . . his father's code name had been *Wolfsbane,* but he had always seemed the wolf rather than the cure. His breathing quickened, then became easier. Simon and he had made an unspoken pact never to become like their father—dangerous, forbidding, barely suppressed. Now, he *was* like him. He had never before admitted the kinship, even though he had always been the twin who showed temper, who was punished. Simon had always retreated into silence while he stamped his foot for both of them. Now, he accepted the likeness with Richard Gardiner because it had kept him alive . . .

. . . and made him cautious as he straightened and began descending the slope toward the schoolyard's shadows. He crossed it, remembering young boys with numbers painted on their chests, desperate to outdo one another, to be accepted into the Brigade. Then the site of the recruitment camp was behind him and he was suddenly into the village, the hot springs smoking at the side of the quick river, the hikers littering the streets, the smell of cooking making his stomach churn. He thrust the pistol and the walkie-talkie deeper into his pockets, covered their bulges with his hands, adopted a casual slope of the shoulders, and slouched down the dusty, noisy street. The sense of people and their exclamations and laughter and murmurs hurting just as if his hearing had become painfully acute. Making him wary, too.

Then he began moving more swiftly, drawn by the lights of hotels and shops. He brushed against backpacked hikers, and an idea possessed him which he did not analyze. Women carried burdens of food or children, one with a gas canister on her shoulder. He hurried toward the Namasti Hotel where Simon had lain for two whole days, drugged and at peace. Wires trailed out from beneath the eaves of the low building—telephone wires. Their presence made his mouth seem dry with eagerness and he wiped his dirty hand across his lips. The calls he had made to Aubrey, one after the other . . .

Two hikers, a man and a woman, were splashing each other, naked and hilarious and probably drunk, in the concrete bowl of the hot spring that had been imprisoned in the center of the village. Other hikers laughed with or at them, drank from cold-misted bottles. Bending almost without pausing, he snatched up a disregarded backpack, rolled tent, pans, a tin cup which he hushed against his chest before hefting the bundle onto his shoulders. He hunched against its weight and mass, sensually delighted with its fullness, its possibilities of equipment, food, dressings, clothes. Pleased with its effectiveness as a disguise. He stepped onto the veranda of the hotel and into its glowing interior. Now, his injuries, the dirt, his torn clothing, would be expected and unsuspicious.

His legs felt weak. The weight of the pack, he told himself, or tiredness, only tiredness.

At the hotel desk, a Nepali in shirtsleeves watched him in a careful, disdainfully English way which amused him. The hotel had evidently ascended in self-regard since Simon and he had used it during their only camping trip together. Gardiner moved past the desk, disregarding registering guests, toward the two telephone booths in the shadows beside the main staircase. The smell of oranges, lemons, other fruit, even though he was indoors. Shivering with excitement and nerves, he shut the folding door of the booth behind him, picked up the telephone, feeling himself squashed against the coinbox—coinbox!—by the pack. He had no money!

The dangling pans attached to the pack rattled against each other, the cup tapped at the glass of the booth's door. He flushed with hot self-ridicule. Jammed into the telephone booth with a stolen pack, without money, without—! Bloody, bloody stupid! Weariness pricked at his eyes and made his legs and hands tremble. He felt panic mount inside him—panic and the same ineptitude he had felt when Simon had seemed deranged, upstairs in this very hotel, before he realized it was LSD not fever. He had panicked then, terrified and incapable of making a simple phone call. Now, the same thing.

He stared into the tiny mirror above the coinbox, beside the printed list of numbers. A hollow, weary, young face stared groggily out at him, unshaven and dirty.

He picked up the receiver and dialed the operator. Waited. He began, slowly and irresolutely, to watch the small, cramped hotel foyer and the reception desk. And the door. His breathing became calmer. The ridiculous pans and cup tapped and tinkled, a grotesque of a hiker's equipment but almost amusing now. He wiped his forehead.

The operator . . . reverse-charge international call, he explained in Nepali. He gave the number, aware immediately that it was a number they might suspect, had traced before. The reception desk, crowded with hikers, and the uniform of a single, new policeman, lounging. Other backpacks made his less noticeable. Yes, yes . . . he hesitated, then gave Aubrey's name as the subscriber. Yes, yes—quickly, please.

A second policeman. Conversation with one of the two Nepalis behind the desk. Quietness settling on the hikers booking in.

He need only say—Babbington's involved, he's here. He wanted to say, *help me,* but knew nothing could be done. He would have to make his own way out. Babbington's here—I was right, wasn't I? That gave him a fierce satisfaction. Bottles on the reception desk, the policemen drinking Tiger beer. Shrieks from outside, as he listened to the distant clicking of the connection, then the ringing of Aubrey's telephone. At once, his temperature jumped, his heart lurching, as he watched the arm movements of the drinking policemen, the shuffling hikers moving toward the staircase with their keys. The ringing of Aubrey's telephone was slow, ponderous, like a recording played back at the wrong speed. Come on, come on, Kenneth—Babbington's here!

Soldiers. Two Nepali soldiers entering the hotel, guns slung casually, eyes uninquiring but uniforms threatening like the closing of a door. Greetings from the policemen—Aubrey's telephone unanswered, its ringing almost lost in static—beer ordered from the rushed, shiny-faced Nepali behind the desk, Aubrey's telephone ringing out clearly in the gap of static, his left leg beginning to tremble, the pans rattling softly against each other like a signal to the soldiers and the two policemen whose eyes were sliding over the hikers, over the shadows of the foyer, the glass of booths . . .

Aubrey's telephone, then the operator.

"No reply, caller."

"Keep trying!" he blurted in a high, unnatural voice. "Please," he added more carefully.

"Very well, caller."

The ringing again, seemingly more distant, ineffectual. Where was Aubrey, where? Immediately, he thought—trap? Were they keeping him waiting? No, he could hear the telephone ringing— could they fake it while they traced his call? They knew his number, knew he was in Tatopani—

His mind seemed shaken loose even as his awareness narrowed to the foyer, the hotel door, the group of uniforms at the desk. Fears flickered across his need to survive. The soldiers detached themselves from the desk and the policemen. Began lethargically to inspect papers—the pans rattled behind his back like snickering laughter. He had no papers! One, two—ring, ring—three, cursory, indifferent glances at permits and passports, perfunctory nods of acceptance. Ring, ring—he could see the flat, the London evening gathering outside the windows, or was it still afternoon? The telephone remained unanswered. Four passports, five.

Put it down. Ring, ring. He could not. The ringing was mesmeric, a way of keeping open the trap he felt had already slammed shut.

"Still no reply, caller, do you wish—"

Spell broken. He thrust the receiver down. He eased open the door of the booth, his own smell suddenly intolerable as he became aware of the smoky atmosphere. The smell of food was intolerable, too. The noise of unworried people, the rattling of the implements dangling from the pack.

Shadow, a narrow passageway beneath the staircase, cooler air on his hot face, darkness beyond frosted glass. He all but stumbled out of the rear of the hotel and down the steps into a noxious-smelling yard. Drains, urine, rotting vegetable matter. A chicken scuttled away. Distant laughter, presumably from the hot spring and the naked tourists. The pans comforted, regular in rhythm like cymbals, as he scuttled into a twisting lane, then emerged from the cluster of shops and hotels and houses. The lights of the village seemed to hang in the darkness like warm stars. He knew the address he sought. There was no one behind him, no noises in the alley other than those of a thin, snuffling dog and the scurrying of a rat. There was no significance for him in that small pursuit. He felt lighter, and the pack seemed to weigh less. There was an exhilaration in escape, even in danger, a pleasure in risk which had become addictive, as if he was a racing driver or war photographer.

He hurried on through the backstreets, thumbs tucked into the straps of the pack, mind racing. He had discarded self-dislike, self-loathing, and accepted his present mood without judgment or condemnation. Aubrey's not being there when needed had confirmed some change in him.

He seemed to outdistance fear as he hurried. This way, turn right—no, left here, down this alley where the smell of rotting vegetables and open drains led him like a map. Right here. Left, and the smell of fruit and dung. A dog's quiet whining, or perhaps the voice of its dim dreaming. A radio, the big stars beginning to gleam out. He knew this place, knew what he required of it. Food, shelter, assistance. Purchased by acquaintance or threat, it did not matter, just so long as they became available.

Here—

A row of low bungalow-style dwellings, the pale sheen of concrete and cinder blocks. Lights powered by a gas generator from behind thin curtains. Wooden tiles on the sloping roof. Evidence of money, the ex-Gurkha's payoff after disbandment. He hardly hesitated before knocking loudly at the door. He slipped the small Beretta from his pocket, hefted the pack to comfort so that he could move quickly, if necessary. The door opened.

"Birandar—" He could not be certain he actually voiced the name of the corporal, though the man's unsuspicious face began at once to re-form into surprise and then respect and then confusion through which an ugly sense of enmity started to reveal itself. Birandar, in the uniform of a Nepali policeman, recognizing his former officer at his door, beginning to realize what he had been ordered to do by his new superiors. Birandar's wife paused behind him, in the middle of the one main room, her curiosity minimal. Birandar . . .

The Beretta rose into the ex-Gurkha's view. The smell of spicy cooking, a meal prepared and being served. Birandar's wife held two bowls in her hands as she paused, looking out into the darkness. Gardiner moved the gun higher in obvious threat as the Nepali's mouth opened.

It seemed to Aubrey that he stood a little apart from himself and saw an old man dressed in a suit twenty years too young for him, his trouser bottoms rolled to his calves, shoes and socks in one hand, stick in the other, patrolling the edge of the sluggish, murmuring tide. He found the image of himself uninspiring. *I grow old, I grow old . . . bottoms of my trousers rolled,* he recited with a grim mockery. Prufrock to a T!

His hatred of Babbington had led him to this place, and to this frame of mind. His loathing gripped like a coronary pain. He was worn out by concern and hate. His last energies seemed to have been finally spent, he had been bankrupted of determination by the effort of persuading Scudamore to assist his wild scheme; he was left with little else but an omnipresent old age, more pernicious in its effects than the jet lag. And the thin leak of revenge like a corrosive fluid over stomach, heart, mind. If Tim was dead . . .

After some moments, he continued the thought. If Tim was dead, then the unholy Trinity would pay weregild for him. Blood money. Even if he had to adopt a belief in Tim's madcap idea of a Soviet takeover in Nepal to do it, he would ruin them. It was a time of détente, of the re-emergence of the old privateering intelligence services. No big operations, just personal scores to be settled. He and Babbington and Brigitte and those who worked for them both. Even Kapustin. Old scores and new plots.

And justice for a boy surely now dead.

The sea was sheened with moonlight, the edge of the tide like a lace collar stretching away from him. The ridiculously young pale suit seemed to shine in the darkness. Monkeys screeched invisibly, night birds called and squeaked. There might be watchers in the dark, but the thought of them made him realize he was too weary for personal fear. The car had not been there when Scudamore had roared off toward the lumped hotels along the coast in his old, dusty Jaguar. The lights of the bungalow above him were as distant as those of a ship.

The World Service news bulletin had spoken of more violent rioting in Kathmandu, dozens of dead. The juggernaut of whatever Babbington had planned was running out of control. Perhaps Tim had been right. Privateers and freebooters. Toppling small governments in obscure places. Open accusations had been leveled at the Nepalese Foreign Minister of bribery, corruption, plotting, embezzlement, of being behind the right-wing riots—arms dumps, agreements in secret, funding the riots . . . accusations now made openly by the Prime Minister, the leading mem-

ber of the pro-Soviet faction on the King's Council. The juggernaut was rushing down the hill—did they really mean to invade?

And if they did, he could not stop them, not unless he could
expose Babbington, Lin and Brigitte as a trio of conspirators.
China must know of it, HMG, too. If he stirred the pond vigorously enough, the mud would rise, people would have to notice
it.

If someone could prove Lin was a double for Babbington!

Someone was calling him, a distant noise. Vaguely aware, he
looked up toward the bungalow. A shadow, blocking out much
of the subdued light behind it, was shouting and waving impera-
tively. Aubrey sighed, expecting nothing. Scudamore's impatience drew him toward the winding steps from the beach. Carefully, he brushed his feet and put on his socks and shoes. Then
climbed laboriously upward, halting often, gripping his stick and
the handrail convulsively. His breath wheezed. Babbington had
learned to play the Russian and American intelligence game to
perfection, he thought. I never did . . .

" . . . never did," he gasped, reaching Scudamore at the top
of the steps and only then realizing he had been muttering his
thoughts aloud. Attempting a deferential smile, he announced
rather breathlessly: "The intelligence community used to be
somewhat like an exclusive girls' school, Scudamore, it really
did! We were rather privileged and somehow cut off. Now, we
do our masters' bidding, to the letter—giving away whole countries or taking them for the sake of export orders!"

Scudamore steadied Aubrey, and frowned at him. "What the
bloody hell are you chuntering on about, Aubrey?" He seemed
unreasonably angry. "Aren't you even interested in what I've
been doing?"

"Yes, yes, of course. I apologize."

"Anyway," Scudamore exploded, "I've found out fuck-all, so
it doesn't matter a bloody toss! Fucking useless! I've tried
everyone—hotel, airline office, police even. Of course your mate
Babbington was here—but not the other two. There's no bloody
trace of them!" They stepped up on to the dark veranda. Rahim
hovered. "Bring me a large bloody whiskey, Rahim—Christ, I
need it!" Scudamore bawled. There was something apologetic,
even abject, about his bluster.

Aubrey sat gratefully in a cane chair, and murmured: "So,
there would seem to be no way forward?" He felt a disappoint-

ment, but it was masked by his need to maneuver Scudamore. The past, the past, he willed at the man. Volunteer!

"What?" his companion snapped.

"I said—I can't see how we can pursue this matter, not here, at least. Can you?"

"Are you getting cold feet, Aubrey? After getting me stirred up, are you going cold?" Aubrey remained silent, a tickle of excitement in his stomach. "I was followed all the way. Some Malays, not the young bugger who was down on the beach. No interference, just watching me. Anyway, you haven't answered my question. I'm all keyed up, and that's what you wanted. Hours of fucking about to no purpose—sweating like a pig and getting really annoyed! So, what *now?*"

"There doesn't seem to be any way," Aubrey murmured, quelling anticipation.

"Bollocks! There's always a way. If you *really* want to stuff Babbington, that is?" He leaned heavily on the table as he poured their drinks, swallowing heartily at his glass as soon as he had done so. Then he said: "This old German bint you keep on about—Brigitte. Is she important?"

"Vital."

"Ugly, is she?"

"Not handsome."

"Ah," Scudamore sighed. "I've been thinking about her, especially getting nowhere . . . didn't dawn on me for quite a while." He leaned forward and turned up the lamp, his face becoming a landscape of hills and shadows. "Then an idea came to me." He bent down with a grunt and hauled an untidy heap of torn and faded brown envelopes onto the table, almost knocking over the lamp. Light and shadow wobbled weirdly. Aubrey maintained an inexpressive mask on his features. His stomach churned. Insects banged against the globe of the lamp. "That's why I dug these out. No bloody Chink and a German bint are going to stuff me, Aubrey, even if they've got you in a knicker-twist!"

Scudamore removed a leatherbound album from the bottom of the heap and began to leaf through it, tracing each fixed snapshot with his large forefinger. Then he halted and turned the open page toward Aubrey. He stabbed with his thick finger.

"That her, by any chance?" he asked in half-triumph.

Aubrey took the heavy album, smelling of mildew and age, and studied the mounted, liver-spotted photographs, all of them

monochrome where they were not already sepia. A clearing, a
village, Malay and Chinese faces. Young British soldiers in
baggy shorts, grinning and squinting in the sun. A woman hovering in the background of one or two of the shots. Aubrey put
on his spectacles, pushed the album into the pool of light, and
peered, holding his breath. Please let it be, please—

National servicemen, ironically Gurkhas, too, and other men
in police caps and shorts. He recognized Scudamore, almost as
paunched as now. The heavy, bleaching sunlight lying on everything. Huts, half-naked villagers, Chinese in shirts. The woman
in the background could have been any age, from anywhere.
Anonymous—the date was 1958. Brigitte would have been—
nearly thirty, no longer the young woman he had pursued across
England and all the way to Berlin with her father. The lamplight
flickered in drafts and the wings of suicidal moths. He squinted
at the moldy photographs.

"A naturalist, she said she was. Had all the papers. Bit of a
local character. The natives thought she was touched. Shouldn't
really have been there—my chief had a fancy for her collection
of moths, though, so she stayed. There wasn't a lot of trouble
then, not even that far north. She didn't bother anyone. But she
was a Kraut, and Lin was there—"

"Brigitte!" Aubrey exclaimed. *Brigitte.* He sighed aloud.
Scudamore grinned triumphantly.

"It is her, then?"

"I—I'm almost certain, yes."

Scudamore took the album again, turning it to himself. He
flicked pages, then handed it back across the table.

"You'll recognize that bloke, in the middle of the front row?"

Babbington, of course. Scudamore, too. A police soccer team,
arms folded, Babbington with the ball between his knees. All
of them young, all grinning.

"That's two of 'em," Scudamore announced. "And the third,
the Chink. They were all here in 1958!" It was announced with
an air of discovery and self-congratulation. Aubrey smiled quizzically. Scudamore was hooked—there *was* an answer here!

"I see . . ." he said slowly.

"Oh, for Christ's sake, Aubrey, what bloody more do you
want as a starter? If you want them tied together, then why stop
at last year? They were here *together* thirty years ago!" Again,
Scudamore banged the table and the lamplight shivered. A res-
cued moth flew off into the darkness. "You're a blockhead, Au-

brey. Look, *we* captured the Chink, Babbington was in contact with him *then*. The German bint was hanging around. Can't you string those facts together for your purpose?"

"I'm very grateful . . . where does it lead?" He felt like an exhausted swimmer suddenly swept toward a rescuing shore by a huge current.

"Look, Aubrey, don't be dense! We captured your bloody Chinaman in 1958. Babbington helped to interrogate him. The German bint used to hang around the village where we arrested the Chink! What more do you want to be going on with?" He swallowed the remainder of his whiskey and refilled the glass. "I tell you, Aubrey, you and me are going on a little trip tomorrow. We're going to talk to people who *remember* 1958, not just last bloody year!"

Babbington—Lin—Brigitte . . . all three.

Thank God for Scudamore's bloody-mindedness.

11

Ghosts in an Old Theater

Serious, serious, serious . . .

The inadequate word raced and whirled in his head as the wind plucked at his shirt, and seemed to drain his arms of strength. The belly-light from the Puma splashed across and through the girders and wires of the bridge. The noise of its rotors banged and drummed off the steel, set the taut wires humming. Serious . . . They knew he was alive now, knew *almost* where he was, and which way he must come . . .

. . . across the suspension bridge. There were soldiers and police at either end. The river was blanched and chilly far below in the gorge, occasionally slithering in the spilled light from the Puma. His arms ached, his feet seemed numb as they searched along the narrow girder beneath the bridge. His fingers clung to the parallel girder about his head and the wind buffeted.

The mountains gleamed with mottling snow in the moonlight. He looked down then swiftly up again, shutting his eyes against the sudden glare of the searchlight as it washed across rivets, wires, girders. He was crouched like a small ape beneath the bridge, as taut and straining as the wires holding the narrow platform above the gorge. The lights of Tatopani were fuzzily distant. The Puma strolled with easy contempt away down the gorge, its lamp revealing the thin white parting of the trail along the cliff. He sensed hearing return, the rush of water like static, then the footsteps and voices from either end of the bridge as his hunters shifted and murmured like nervously grazing animals. The wires hummed.

Serious . . .

He had fled from Birandar's doorway, had already turned one dark corner before the man's voice had been raised, crossed two noisome courtyards before the first whistles had cried and called to one another, before the first running footsteps. The pack had banged heavily against his back, his breathing had been labored, his legs weary, his strength ebbed by the confrontation with Birandar's uniform. The Puma, which must have been returning from Kathmandu when the alarm was raised, had appeared only minutes after he had reached the bridge—

—and heard and seen the shadows of the soldiers beneath the pylons at the end of the bridge, and scuttled into the cover of rocks beside the trail, shivering with fear. Police behind him? He forced himself to move, edging slowly along the cliff below the trail until he reached the bridge and could clamber silently out onto the girders running beneath the wooden planking. Then he had forced himself to crawl out over the gorge.

To hang there now as the helicopter retreated, leaving his legs foal-like, weak, and his hands unfeeling as they gripped the girder above him. The river rushed below, noisy. The mountains seemed cold like the water. The Puma was little more than an insect-buzz.

He breathed deeply and regularly, calming himself. Moved forward a few crablike paces, then three, four more. The helicopter's drone seemed louder, as did the casual voices from the far end of the bridge. He scuttled—his foot slipped. His arms seemed pulled from their sockets, then his fingers lost their grip. His chest slid painfully against the lower girder, his left arm crooked against and over one of the supporting wires, his right hand caught the edge of the girder as his legs swung in space. The river's noise was louder, the wind stronger. The pack pulled at him. He struggled back onto the girder, hearing the rotor noise above the furious beating of his blood, as the Puma returned up the gorge. His hands were bleeding and he seemed on fire beneath his armpit and across his chest.

He moved as quickly as he could hand over hand, one foot before the other, buttocks almost dragging along the steel. The searchlight from the helicopter danced off the cliff, illuminated the trail, the water, then the skeleton of the suspension bridge— catching him! Light slid over his body like cold oil, then dripped over the bridge and onto the water. The Puma swung in the air like a kite tugged by the wind and returned, draping its white lamplight slowly across the planking, the individual wires, each girder and support. He could not move, like a rabbit in headlights, could not . . . *did!* The light missed him, slid on. He forced himself the last yards, against the fear created by the raised voices, against the knowledge of heads peering over the wire mesh flanking the bridge's roadway. They can't see you, can't!

A face peering down, caught by the Puma's lamp like a target. He had risen, was clinging to the edge of the bridge's wooden roadway, only a few feet from the man's boots. He held on with one hand. The other hand fired, the Beretta flashed and boomed. The face vanished; for a moment there were hands gripping the wire mesh like those of a desperate prisoner then they, too, were gone. Uproar. The Puma had flicked away, further along the bridge. He heaved himself onto the footholds set in the pylon, clinging to its chilly, saving metal. Moments of confusion, use them, no one else has seen you—

The searchlight illuminated the dead soldier. Three of them around the body, footsteps running along the planking. He clambered up, his legs trembling, then swung onto the end of the bridge, beneath the skeletal archway of the pylons. The Puma's light seemed to have paused above the dead body, then it swiveled and searched like something maddened by pain or anger. He crept away—five paces before he began to run, obeying blind panic. The pack bumped, he stumbled more than once as the downward slope of the trail threatened to overbalance him, but careered on oblivious to noise, awaiting the return of the searchlight. He paused and turned only once, to see the white walking leg of the lamp stamping hurriedly to and fro along the bridge, then alongside its span. The helicopter seemed more than ever a maddened insect, bloated and enraged.

Twelve hours, twelve, he could afford no more than that, even exhausted. Five hours of daylight, minimum. They might know, from Birandar, where he was heading. Brandis might have guessed, or the Chinaman. They'd seen him near Pokhara, they might be waiting—now they all knew he was alive.

The trail sloped into the first of the giant rhododendrons. The stars disappeared, together with the big, pale moon. He caught only glimpses of the mountains and of the Ghar Kola flowing thinly below. He had to survive for half a day. Reach the village—and help.

He must keep running . . .

After the torrential monsoon downpour, the place steamed like an image of his impatient frustration. The kampong contained a few traditional wooden houses raised on stilts, but was mostly a collection of concrete boxes, the compound gravelled and largely treeless. Chickens, a few goats, an alien, denuded, gray landscape half-hidden by the sun drying out the earth. The village north of Ipoh seemed to have been tumbled out of a box of child's building blocks onto this leached, treeless landscape blotched with abandoned mining pools and horizoned by skeletal machinery. Aubrey was unable to reconcile the tin-mining township with any conventional image of Malaysia. The jungle might never have existed.

Scudamore consulted the village headman, the shopkeeper, other Malays and the occasional Chinese in rapid bursts of local dialect. His red face was a badge of his frustration, and symbolized Aubrey's own. The smells of the village wrapped him as the ground steamed. A distant rumble, presumably from one of the huge tin dredgers they had passed on the highway before reaching this place. The sun was high. Flower gardens lay like welcome mats before each of the tiny houses, but their garish colors served only to make the place more incongruous after the jungle pressing against the highway from Butterworth. They had crossed the channel to the mainland and driven a hundred miles in Scudamore's old Jaguar—for this! This . . . nothing: silence, lack of memory, a forgotten time. Aubrey felt hot and weary.

Scudamore's hands waved to emphasize his questions. Heads shook, pondered, shook once more. Aubrey chastised himself for surrendering to the appeal of ancient, sepia snapshots in a moldering album.

At the edge of his peripheral vision, slow, huge buffalo wandered toward the river, two turbaned Sikhs marshaling them with thin sticks. Washing fluttered limply. The spicy smells of the midday meal being prepared. It was all but impossible to believe that Lin had been here, that this had been one of the last areas to be cleared—by Gurkhas!—in the last days of the Malayan Emergency. Lin had been sent across the border from Thailand by the insurgent leaders to stiffen resistance, reorganize the terrorists against the clearing-up operation that was steadily moving north through the peninsula. Here? In this strange, almost untenable amalgam of Malay kampong and Chinese mining township? Yes—just the kind of place to hide, to re-form, rearm, move out from.

And no one, apparently, remembered him! Angrily he stamped across the clearing and its drying gravel toward Scudamore as he leaned over a small group in the shade of the headman's stilted wooden house. Bright skirts wrapped around thin loins. Two Chinese in the group, too.

"Well?" he demanded peremptorily. "Any *luck?*"

"No," Scudamore replied, his face heated, flies landing and buzzing. He wiped a large hand at them. "Listen, it's a long time ago. I'm having to fill them in, for Christ's sake! They weren't trained in Intelligence, were they?"

"But, they can remember nothing? Surely—"

"Look, Aubrey, *I* know Lin was here, so do you—so, probably, do some of them." Brown faces watched the two white men with what might have been studied indifference. "But they're suspicious, man! They want to know why we want to know— what harm we mean them. Asking about the Emergency still isn't *innocent.* We might be police agents sniffing out Communists! They're as paranoid about the Red Menace up here as they are in Singapore!" He threw his long arms into the air. "If they remember me, I *am* a policeman as far as they're concerned!" He lowered his voice, reprimanded by the impassivity of the faces around him. "I'm trying to explain *me*—and how I left the Branch. Then, I'll get around to your bloody Chink—OK?"

Aubrey looked at the old men's faces in the bluish shadow of the wooden hut. Although distanced from them, he felt somehow similar. Old men, chasing a shadow from thirty years before. He looked away uncomfortably as Scudamore began speaking in rapid, slithering Malay once more. Beyond the concrete and wooden houses of the village, a few straggling palms, the intrusion of tussocky grass; the gray, leached gravel everywhere. Limestone outcrops made the landscape even more lunar, irreconcilable to the heat and humidity. The sun burned. The huge, lumbering dredgers and their distant noise. Then, in the blue, hazed distance, the foothills of the Cameron Highlands, reaching up out of the valley of the River Kinta. A world of Hill Stations and a different, imperial past. The image suggested the village as a backwater, similarly lost, like his own search for Lin.

Aubrey walked into the shade of a twisted, broadleaved palm, motionless in the heat, and waited. Ten, fifteen minutes . . . flies and murmured talk, and mounting impatience; the thought of Tim only just kept at bay . . . no, not even that. Merely within bounds. Twenty minutes.

"That's fuck-all use, that is!" Scudamore announced, reaching Aubrey's patch of hot shade and lighting a cigar. Blue smoke coiled lazily. "Christ, I sometimes think they can't remember yesterday! No idea what yesterday is—*conceptually,* that is," he added with heavy sarcasm.

"You found out precisely nothing, then?" Aubrey burst out.

Scudamore mopped at his face with a very creased handkerchief. "Bloody waste of time," he replied.

"Then why are we here?" Aubrey demanded. "What is the purpose of this—this wild-goose chase, may I ask?"

"Christ, you don't half piss me off, Aubrey."

Aubrey blenched. He said, carefully, apologetically: "I'm sorry, Scudamore. Unforgivable—" And turned away, leaning heavily on his stick.

"Before you say it," Scudamore murmured, tossing his head and giving a chuckle that might as easily have served as a warning growl, "I couldn't get more out of them if I had an hour alone with the use of a rubber hose." He sighed. Aubrey watched the shadows beneath the wooden house, and saw the glint of amused eyes, the huddled smiling of a shared joke. They were two old white men arguing in front of the natives; quite ludicrous. "All I got was that they remembered the Chink, and the old biddy. Yes, they knew each other. Lin is remembered being seen with her. But there's no bloody proof, and your mates in London aren't going to take *their* word now, are they?" He waved his hand toward the house.

"I suppose not," Aubrey replied, looking toward the hills and receiving no aid whatsoever. "Anything else?"

"Not much. They can't remember dates—they're not important, even to the two Chinese. Lin did come back here, after his escape. Then he vanished. No, before you ask me, the German bint had left long before that; took off, I don't doubt, as soon as we copped Lin. Presumably, Lin went back over the border where he'd be safe."

"So, nothing tangible connects them?"

"No—nor with your mate Babbington."

"Damnation."

"Apparently, Lin came back with a lot of money—"

"What? How much?"

"They've no idea how much, he passed some of it around. I don't think to these people, though. It's not important. They may have got it wrong."

"Then what do we do *now?*" Aubrey demanded, his hot, fearful anger returning with an added vehemence and desperation.

Scudamore slapped his big hands against his thighs. "Go to bloody Ipoh, I suppose!" he barked. "Ask around, look through all that ancient stuff I threw in the back of the car before we left. I've got pals who were in the police in Ipoh at the time— we'll find something," he offered finally.

"I don't know whether we have the time!" Aubrey burst out, waggling his stick like an inoffensive weapon. "I should be *doing* something!"

"Look, Aubrey, you're powerless to help the kid, or do anything, unless you've got something on Babbington. Unless you can stir London into a tizz. I'll try to give you that, but I didn't promise and I can't do it in five minutes!"

Aubrey breathed deeply four or five times. Then, reluctantly, he nodded. "Very well, Scudamore, very well. If there's nothing more here, we'd better be on our way." He looked over the desolate landscape, then up toward the Highlands. They had not been tailed, as far as he could ascertain, and there had been no sign of surveillance on Scudamore's bungalow when they'd left at first light. "To Ipoh, then," he concluded.

He floundered through the mud, the rain streaming from his lank hair, streaking his face, soaking his clothing. The pack had been abandoned—hadn't it? Its weight still seemed there. He had eaten the food from it, used some of the clothing which was hardly his size but which he needed to combat the icy cold that was spreading outward. Latent cold not latent heat. The sweater he had donned was pounds heavier with the soaking rain. He was cold, so cold now . . .

Oak forest, cultivation, the long edge of a ridge, the mountains looming in and out of the cloud and mist, then masked by the rain. There had been no portable stove in the pack and that was when he had first flung it away down a wooded slope, and scrambled after it, not wanting the maps but needing the can opener and the glutinous, nauseous soup, and the can of peach slices and the biscuits and chocolate with an Indian wrapper . . . the water, too. He had gagged, kept the food down, drunk the water . . . and left the pack and its maps. He knew where he was going!

Socks! Groaning, he had returned to the pack and changed his socks. Dawn had filtered through the forest as he had struggled to get up, move on, now leaving the pack reluctantly, like the body of a loved pet. He had taken the water bottle and the binoculars like mementos.

Gardiner wrapped his arms across his chest as he floundered on through the mud, head bowed, the slippery, churning ground joggling in his hazy vision. He had kept away from people, avoided all the villages since Tatopani, marking them off uncertainly in his mind and skirting around, above, below them. Not resting, not allowing himself to sleep.

Occasionally he heard the helicopter like a threatening noise in a dream. He could hardly alert himself to the dangers of this more open, cultivated country. In the main, he was little more than a flitting shadow from the air. He could not see the mountains, hardly see the ridged, lunar landscape as it fell away to his left, the bomb crater created after the rice terraces had been harvested. There was only the rain, his smoking breath, the noise of the water and his splashing footsteps. He did not know whether the Beretta remained thrust into his waistband or had long ago worked loose in one of his frequent falls. It could be miles behind him. He did not have the energy to pause, to reach behind him to discover its presence or loss.

He hardly possessed the strength to take the next lumbering, weary step. He attuned his harsh breathing to the movement of his deadweight limbs, and sounded like a distant buffalo offering challenge.

He could not discern the hands of his watch and renounced the attempt . . . midday? The sweater weighed on his shoulders, dragged at his arms as they hung numbly at his sides. Rain ran into his eyes every time he tried to lift his head. He thought he was still on the trail, that he was less than ten miles from the village. The huge, still whirlpool of the descending rice terraces seemed to begin to move in a slow, hypnotic circle—something to plunge into and be drowned. His head began to spin with it, sickeningly.

He struggled to move his legs . . . then he realized he had fallen once more, was on his knees in the mud. The spinning of the rice terraces slowed, eventually halted. His breath smoked more regularly, steadily. The rain seemed heavy enough to hurt his head and neck. The sweater soddenly imprisoned him. He tried to rise—could not, tried once more, could—not—! He thrashed at the mud with his fists like a child in temper, his face lifted to the rain, his mouth open, howling . . .

. . . which brought them running. Nepalis. He glimpsed low huts ahead through a swing of the rain's curtain, glimpsed moving figures, groaned only once and slid onto his side and lay in the mud, curled fetally.

"It is him—yes, *him!*" he heard distantly. An excited gabble of voices as dark, small faces surrounded him. "Yes, I am certain of it—him!" Calls, cries, pleasure.

They had him, then; it was over. His hands kept slapping at the mud like the twitching of a wounded animal.

"But, what *exactly* do the doctors say?" Babbington, staring out of the window of the East German Embassy down toward the brown, rain-speckled water of the Bagmati, cracked his knuckles loudly in the silence following his question. He concentrated on the unmoving set of his shoulders, the angle of his still head. His stomach revolted with anger, with the sense of being thwarted. "Are they to be asked to put the King out of his misery or not?"

He turned at that point and was gratified by the flinch that twitched across the frame and features of the Nepali Prime Minister. Then the Oriental shrug with which the man responded to his question infuriated Babbington.

"Tell me, Prime Minister," he asked, "will the Queen ask that the King be put down or not—to save him from further suffering?"

"Her Majesty is very distressed."

Brandis' small grin was a further goad of Babbington's loss of temper. "*I* am distressed!" he snapped. "You assure me the boy-King who succeeds is putty in your faction's hands, you assure me the King is dying, that civil unrest has reached a point of crisis—but *when is the bloody man going to die?*"

The Prime Minister's dark features blanched, there was a vivid enmity in his eyes before they became hooded.

"I do not know," he said. "It surely cannot be more than two, three days." Again, that infuriating shrug. *Mañana,* or whatever name it had here, this lack of urgency. Lin's face was inexpressive in a shadowy corner of the office. Babbington turned again to the window, holding up his hand, checking off his fingers with his back to them.

Umbrellas in the downpour, the dulled gold of alien, barbaric roofs, the dark muddy river and the wet fields beyond the towns. *This* place? He almost wondered, for an instant, why they wanted it, why *he* wanted it.

"The police have been enthused," he began with a pronounced ironic drawl, "there will be the most savage rioting tonight and tomorrow. You have your timetable—" Three fingers aloft now, haloed by the gray shine from the window. "You will arrest those you blame, including the Foreign Minister," he continued, raising a fourth finger, spreading his hand like a photographic enlargement, "then you will ensure that the unrest continues so that you may appeal to *friendly* Soviet forces to assist you in restoring order." His whole hand spread, ready to close and grasp. "Therefore, only one thing is missing—the exact time of the King's death!" He whirled round theatrically. "Do I make myself clear? The doctors *must* do their part in this. The timing must be exact." He smiled coldly.

The Prime Minister's podgy, small frame wriggled on his chair like that of an accused schoolboy. The man's face was almost white with shock. Then he nodded. "If it can be done—"

"It will be done. Tomorrow." The Prime Minister began to shake his head, but Babbington was nodding his firmly. "Whatever kind of deity His Majesty may be to you, Prime Minister, he is only another man to his various tumors . . . something to feed on. You will be killing nothing which is not already dead. The cost is immaterial—but confidentiality is everything. Make certain it is done. *Tomorrow.*" He held the Nepali's gaze until the man nodded. "Thank you, Prime Minister—you may leave us now. I'm sure you have a great deal to do." He waved the Nepali to the door. Brandis closed it behind the Prime Minister, grinning openly now.

Babbington cracked his knuckles successfully once more. "And next?" he asked like some traveling masseur. "The police chief? Who else needs their spine straightening for the events of the next forty-eight hours?" He seemed affable, but as soon as Brandis appeared to relax, he snapped: "Where is that damned boy of Aubrey's? Why can't you find him?"

"We will, rest—"

"You'd better! I've given the Prime Minister a thirty-six-hour timetable. I don't want to alter that. It *can't* be altered. In two

days, our units will be on those wet, stinking streets down there.
I don't want that boy running around shooting off his mouth—
do you understand, Brandis? You and your bloody general had
better not cause any change of plans, not at this late stage!"

Watching Scudamore shuffling through the boxes of old notebooks, papers and files, his anger was aroused not so much by
that activity, pointless as it seemed, but by the image of Babbington somehow escaping him, retiring into thick, impenetrable undergrowth. He could almost hear his hard, mocking laughter.
He got up and walked to the window, a rectangle of orange as
the sun set over the town. The rattling and shuffling of paper
was like the noise of distant, ironic applause. He rubbed his chin,
staring across the Kinta and its rush-hour bridges thick with
traffic, toward old colonial buildings and elegant mansions. The
town was a vivid image of an imperial past. Buddhist temples
jutted like scattered, ornamental shells up through the crowded
buildings.

Scudamore's old police cronies had all been a waste of time:
retired, complacent, forgetful. The authorities either would not
release any documents they had, or they had been mislaid or
destroyed. Scudamore had attempted to ring Sidney Wei in
Kuala Lumpur, without success. Unavailable at his hotel . . .
*Sidney must have had some of the money, oh, yes, he was tied
in with your Chink, all right. He was part of the cell working this
area; slipped away when Lin was nabbed.* He found it hard to
believe Scudamore's assertions, and looked down at the drink
in his hand. Urgency trembled in his wrist and fingers—no, call
it impatience.

"So," he announced, "all we know is that one of Lin's guards
must have been bribed to let him escape. Am I correct?"

Scudamore cleared his throat with a growling noise. "Don't
sound so much like a bloody teacher marking my homework,"
he replied.

"For Heaven's sake, Scudamore, this has been a *monumental*
waste of time!"

"Sorry," Scudamore replied sarcastically. "On the other
hand, you didn't have any ideas of your own, did you?"

"How did Lin get out?"

"Like you said, one of the guards—I wasn't involved by
then."

"Who was?"

"Babbington." Aubrey heard taunting laughter from the thicket of the past where Babbington had hidden himself.

"Then how, precisely, were *you* involved?"

"I arrested the bugger and brought him back here. With a Gurkha bodyguard."

"And?" Aubrey enunciated carefully.

"I was present at his initial interrogation—want to see my notebook, Inspector?" he added mockingly. He held it out toward Aubrey, who shook his head. Scudamore added: "He wasn't saying very much, anyway."

"And how long was he held?"

"Weeks—two or three."

"And interrogated by Babbington?"

"Mostly. Some others, the MI5 lot attached to the Branch out here—usual system."

Aubrey put his free hand into his pocket, and felt the medal. Cross and attached ribbon. The Military Cross, Tim's medal for saving the lives of two Gurkhas wounded and pinned down in Brunei. The medal that had given him a longer leash, kept him in the army, and would have kept him in it now. The reluctant hero. He snatched his hand from his pocket as if the metal burned.

"Christ, I'm pissed off with this," Scudamore muttered. "Look," he added awkwardly, gruffly. "I'm sorry I dragged you out—"

"Never mind that!" Aubrey snapped. "Where did Lin get his money, if it existed? Tell me that."

"How should I know? Those people in the village would be impressed with a couple of quid in those days."

"Was this a couple of quid?"

"They saw a great deal of English money—none of them had any of it. I'm not sure that's true of at least one of the old Chinks, but that's what they said."

"English money?" The river was red, the bridges dark shadows, the crowds and vehicles sluggish like the water, flowing homeward.

"English money."

"Was there an active Communist Terrorist cell in Ipoh by that time?"

"No, we'd got them earlier. They gave us our lead to Lin."

"So, the money came from somewhere else—where?"

"Your German tart?"

"Possibly. Or Babbington? But how? If it was a large sum, a bribe—thirty pieces of silver—then how did Babbington get it? From Brigitte, from funds? And why in *sterling?*"

"True. They'd have paid Lin in local currency, or East German marks, roubles, his own currency. Sidney Wei would know, I'm sure of it."

"Oh, *bugger* Sidney Wei!" Aubrey snapped. He turned on Scudamore, his glass jabbing at the air in front of him. "It's *you* I want answers from! Wake up your sleeping intelligence, Scudamore, your country needs it!"

"Piss off," Scudamore replied without malice. "OK, it's awake. What now?" He was pouring another large Scotch into his glass, seated in one of the two armchairs in the suite's small lounge. The air conditioning purred like a cat.

"Now, how *much* money, I ask again."

Scudamore held his hands three or four inches apart.

"They said—that much."

"The color?"

"What? Oh, white. Like paper, white man's paper money. Old-fashioned fivers?"

"Possibly. It *was* a deal of money, wasn't it?" He paused, then added: "I don't see how Babbington bankrolled Lin out of his own resources, nor Brigitte with that much in sterling. So, where did it come from?"

Scudamore shrugged. "Babbington hadn't been here five minutes, anyway. Mind you, he made a lot of friends and few enemies . . ."

"You mean he *borrowed* the money?"

"Don't be daft. But he was popular, trusted."

"He was always the latter," Aubrey remarked bitterly.

"Aye, maybe." Scudamore massaged his loose features with his huge left hand. "No, of course he didn't borrow the money, but he was out here to make a name for himself, all right. Lin fell in his lap—in more ways than one, according to you. So, he took charge of the interrogations."

"Was he getting anywhere?"

"No idea. I suppose so. A few arrests followed, supposedly on information obtained from Lin. A few small fry. Then, Lin upped and hopped it."

"With a great deal of money. Bought by Babbington. But, with whose money . . . ?"

The silence extended between them, without tension. Scudamore flicked idly through papers, rummaged files, turned the leaves of his notebooks, their leather covers mildewed. Aubrey pondered Babbington, envisaged quite clearly the long process of persuasion, bribery, corruption. Lin had gone over for the money . . . not to London but Moscow. Perhaps at first he believed it *was* London. Later, Brigitte would have revealed the truth to him. Perhaps she had begun to turn him even before his capture, and Babbington had simply continued the work? What had she been? Babbington's control? Perhaps she had been in the Perak region testing him, monitoring? Lin had fallen into the spider lady's hands just as Babbington had. An agent inside the increasingly hostile Chinese intelligence services—another ladder-climber like Babbington. She'd been clever, and lucky . . .

"Old times," Scudamore remarked. "Bloody shame. I liked the lad, even if he was upper-crust and a bit snotty."

"What *are* you talking about?"

"Suicide—while awaiting the outcome of a court-martial."

"Who? When?"

"Oh, no one you'd know, just a lad. Subaltern in the Gurkhas—" Aubrey's hand quivered. "Shame, really. Those were the good days, see. We'd had the regional political commissar spilling out names for money—*Malayan* money—for more than six months. He put the finger on Lin when he came over the border to attempt some reorganization in Perak. Everyone was pleased as punch. Hardly any fighting left to do. Then this poor young bugger kills himself. Terrible stink, don't y'know . . ." He resorted to the heaviest of irony in what seemed an attempt to mask freshly remembered regret.

"What happened? To whom?"

"The usual upper-class-twit story. Gambling debts, hand in the till to pay them off, all discovered, shock-horror, charges brought, disgrace to the Brigade and his white-haired old mother, hangs himself in his cell the night before the court-martial's verdict." Scudamore sighed as he fingered the dry old pages of his notebook. "I was interrogating him while your mucker Babbington was having his fun with Lin."

"I see," Aubrey remarked indifferently, distracted from his fierce, contemplative anger at Babbington.

"He might have got off, even though it was a lot of money. He did have an alibi . . ." His voice tailed off, and Aubrey found the man staring at him, his mouth opening slowly like that of a fish in a tank, redfaced and bloated. "He had an alibi from your friend Babbington, which I *broke . . .*" He looked down at his notebook as if he were an actor who had dried in rehearsal and required the script. His finger moved ponderously. "I smelt . . . a rat. Babbington changed his story when he was re-called to the witness stand. The boy hanged himself the same night." He whistled.

"What is it—" Aubrey began, then asked: "Money? How much money?"

"Most of the payroll for two battalions of Gurkhas about to be sent home."

"Stolen? By a subaltern?"

"He had the keys, he was responsible. And his debts were huge. Perhaps he saw a way to go on gambling, with the Queen's money? He made it look like someone had broken in and ripped open the safe. He even had some of the money in his quarters, poor sod. They never found the bulk of it."

Aubrey cleared his throat, then said heavily: "They were certain—*you* were certain, he stole the money?" Scudamore nodded angrily. "Then why were you so sympathetic, Scuda-more? You don't strike me as possessing a rich vein of compassion."

"Bollocks," Scudamore murmured. "I just felt sorry for him. He was like a bloke having a nightmare. Couldn't really cope with it."

"But you thought him guilty."

"It couldn't have *been* anyone else."

"And now, thirty years after the events, you're not sure? Come, Scudamore—really!" Aubrey used scorn like a thin, sharp knife, prodding the fat man who was sitting tensely for-ward on his chair, hands clasped across his huge thighs.

Without looking up, Scudamore said: "Babbington admitted that he'd been trying to shield the kid. But he couldn't rest, his conscience wouldn't—"

"And that's the only *important* thing you've said!" Aubrey remarked with a kind of triumph. Babbington with a *conscience?* "How close in time were these events? Lin's escape, the young subaltern's suicide?"

"Within—oh, a couple of weeks." He consulted his notebook. "Yes, that's when he killed himself. Your Chink escaped ten, eleven days later. Maybe as little as a week."

"I see."

"But, it couldn't be, Babbington tried to save the poor bugger, not drop him right in the shit!"

"But he *did* drop him in it, eventually, didn't he?"

"Poor sod's name was Standish—just like *Boys' Own Paper,* he was. Everything stereotyped, even his bloody so-English, so-Empire name! Just a shit-scared kid who liked to gamble. Now, they'd get him to smuggle heroin to pay off the debt. How do those bloody schools turn 'em out like that, unprepared for the naughty world, eh?"

"You don't know the alibi Babbington gave him?"

"In his company."

"What did he eventually say to the court-martial?"

"I don't know." Scudamore shook his head vigorously. "I haven't got the transcript of the interrogation, or the charges, or statements from witnesses! I don't know how much more money there was. I'm just remembering. All that's in here is just a few scribbled notes and a couple of dates." He looked apologetically at Aubrey. "Not bloody much, is it?"

Aubrey calmed his breathing before he spoke. Thirty years ago—Babbington's *need* for a great deal of money. He could imagine Lin's proposal—I'll work for you for money. Make me rich and I'll do it. And Babbington suddenly knew how to lay his hands on a great deal of sterling!

"I know," he announced, "who will have the records, Scudamore—Ministry of Defence. Standish, did you say? Very well." He knew that until they could talk to Scudamore's Chinese acquaintance, Wei, nothing else could be done, time had to be occupied. Better this than—

—the medal like a hot coal in his jacket pocket, Tim's young features insisting in the dark at the back of his head. Gurkhas, subalterns—the strange, unexpected pattern. He hovered at the window, vacillating between self-ridicule and desperation. Almost began shifting his weight from one foot to the other.

"I must telephone—" he began, then the telephone rang.

Scudamore snatched up the receiver. "What?" he growled. "Who's there?" He waited. "What? Gone? Christ, don't waste my time! And up yours too!" He thrust down the telephone observing: "Bloody jumped-up wogs on the desk!"

"What was it?"

"Someone asking to be put through from the lobby. Then they disappeared. Joker!"

"Go down and get a description, now that whoever it is knows our room number. Quickly. I'll call London in the meanwhile. Oh, get on with it, Scudamore!"

"Right . . ."

Someone checking on their room number. Giles Pyott must help—*must!*

"I needed to have the room number!" Pieter protested, his lips narrow and his face blanched by the sting of her anger. He waved his hands as if fending off a worrisome insect. "We can only tap into the switchboard, not the room. We had to know which calls, if any, were made by—"

"And to achieve that you warned Aubrey we were this close to him!" Brigitte retorted. Her face was near to his as she sat crouched forward and he turned to look over the front passenger seat of the limousine. She waved a hand at the tinted window, across the street toward the hotel. Even inside the air-conditioned car, there was a pervading smell of dust and petrol. The sun slanted low against the windshield, making her squint. "You warned him," she reiterated.

"How will he know?"

"He'll know."

"General, we've bribed the boilerman, *not* the manager. He's let us into the cellars. Our people had to know which *room* to tap into!" He rubbed his hand nervously through his fair hair. His face was brick-red from the sun and embarrassment. The car's Chinese driver stared unmovingly into the sunset.

Brigitte suddenly felt some thread of tension snap, cutting her adrift on weariness, and she slumped back into the leather of the rear seat.

"Can you tap in?" she asked tiredly.

"Oh, yes."

"Good." The traffic moved sluggishly past her, the crowds on the wide pavement seemed as slow as some queue for meat. "Good . . ."

She could, with only the smallest effort of imagination, smell the river. Glimpses of old, colonial buildings and wide thoroughfares as they had driven into the town. She disliked—at the moment hated—Ipoh. How much did that fat old policeman know or recollect? She recognized Scudamore as someone at the periphery of her time in Malaya as Babbington's field control. His first tour of duty overseas after he had come over. Then there had been Lin, whom she had cultivated and Babbington had bribed. Scudamore could know nothing of all that, of course. Yet she could not be certain. He had been here, just as they had been.

Kurt lingered like a stranger at the edges of her mind, doubtful of his welcome. She saw him in his garish, greedy colors, arrayed in bribes. Like Lin, she admitted. *I will, if the price is sufficient.* Money was always the easiest insult and the easiest persuasion. So, they had hooked Lin. The money had been more powerful, she admitted, than the brief affair she had had with the Chinaman immediately before his capture.

She laughed aloud, scornfully, startling Pieter and making the driver's shoulders twitch. *Her,* a Venus-trap! But, she hadn't money, not in the right currency. Babbington had had to find that.

"Drive," she ordered. The car drew away from the curb, slipping into the viscous traffic-flow. Pieter turned his back on her.

The village was safe. Now that they had removed the old Chinese who had been part of the final cell, who still kept some of those old English banknotes. She saw the frail, small body spin and twist like that of a lean diver out over the cliff edge, saw the splash in the oily gray water of the abandoned pool, and shuddered.

Necessary . . . like the deaths of Aubrey and Scudamore. Once she discovered what they expected to unearth.

Returning to the village had been strange, unearthly, somehow. Questioning the Malay elders, the Chinese shopkeepers, the Sikh herdsmen. No one recognized her except the one old Chinese who had been one of them. And, of course, he would help, he would come with them, yes, and he would repeat everything that had been asked, yes . . .

As always, there had been that dumb, accusing, final surprise on his wizened face as they dragged him to the edge of the quarried cliff and flung him over. She touched her lips nervously. She wanted to ward off bad luck. Perhaps that was why she had been so angry with Pieter? Because the old Chinese had been *so* old, *so* vulnerable?

There must be nothing, no one, no links, Babbington had said. *Nothing from thirty years ago he can unearth or use. Stop him.*

She sighed. In the end, that was all that mattered.

Pieter was speaking into the car telephone.

"Yes, yes—good—called who? Repeat that. Yes, O-double-T, got it. And the message?"

Eventually, he turned in his seat and passed her his pad. She read his hasty, underlined scribble. *Pyott.* Giles Pyott? Yes, at MoD in London. Breathlessly, she read on, then reread, exhaling noisily at last. She hardly recognized the name Standish. Babbington had been mentioned. Court-martial . . . it was the money. Somehow, through Scudamore, Aubrey had stumbled upon the money! Would London take any notice?

"Get the full message!" she snapped in an ugly, cramped voice. *"Now!"*

The money! In the briefcase beside her, a small bundle of white five-pound notes, taken from the old Chinese they had killed. *That* money. Pieter was gabbling into the telephone.

"Get back to the hotel!" she growled at the driver. "I want to hear that tape Gelber's made."

He turned from the unconvinced, detached expression on Ganesh's face and caught sight of his own in a broken mirror, lit by the quivering warmth of an oil lamp. His anger ran in his blood like a fever. His eyes glittered feverishly above dark stains and hollowed, aged cheeks. The stubble of his beard made him appear villainous, even fanatical. The skepticism of the other occupants of the room pressed against him with an almost palpable force. He turned once more to face them—Ganesh, the old NCO, two others who had served in his regiment, including one of the younger ex-Gurkhas who had found him near Lumle and brought him back to the village on a makeshift stretcher, unconscious and rambling.

He spread his arms in appeal. "Will you not do this thing for me . . ." He paused, then added with a quiet desperation: "For the old times—and for yourselves?"

Ganesh remained motionless near the door, leaning against one of the stone walls, his face unaltered in its half-amused skepticism. The old NCO was shaking his head as if in sadness; the two younger Gurkhas seemed intrigued, even challenged. But, they would do nothing without the old man's approval, and would probably be subdued by Ganesh's cynicism and rank.

"But, this talk of invasion, Captain Timothy—" the old man began, puzzled and somehow adrift. He shook his head to emphasize his doubts. "It is difficult to believe, what you say." He raised his hands, palms outward, in a signal that he had no wish to offend.

"Crazy," Ganesh murmured, a slight smile emphasizing a growing contempt.

He rounded on Ganesh. "Where the hell do you think I disappeared to, Gan? I've told you what happened, and why it happened! They *panicked,* don't you understand?" He was quivering, as if icily cold again and lying in the rain on the cold mud while people he did not recognize surrounded him with babble, then care. "This Chinese knows the whole thing—the whole scenario! I have to get him to tell me . . ." His voice tailed off and he slapped a dismissive hand through the air in Ganesh's direction. The broken mirror, sharding his narrow, dark features, reflected a disbelief like that on the faces of the Gurungs in the room.

They had been ex-Gurkhas who had found him, not his pursuers, men being trained to become farmers at the British agricultural project near Lumle. *His* men, like the one here now. They had brought him to the village—back home.

"You *must* help me!" he burst out, surprising them. Ganesh began shaking his head, arms still folded, face impassive, and Gardiner snapped: "For God's sake, Gan, *grow up!* This isn't a game! Why they want your country—*my* country—I have no idea. You've been sold out by Britain, so maybe they just want to walk in—but they're going to do it, I know they are!"

Once more, he turned away from them, from the febrile excitement of the two young men, from the puzzlement or indifference of their elders. He was making no headway, he would be unable to persuade them. He crossed the room quickly, and went out into the cool, fresh evening, the moon splashing light against the stone walls, glistening the big tiles on the roofs. Music, the smell of cooking lingering, the dribble of water somewhere, the faint noises of sheep. He listened and looked as if he were no more than a tourist, suddenly deposited in that place. His detachment from the place, his being corralled away from it, pained him.

"Captain Timothy?" It was the old man.

"Yes, my friend."

"Walk with me."

"Yes."

They patrolled the village's main street. Tiled roofs, a few thatched with reeds. The smell of bread being baked. Voices, the flitting of long-robed women carrying sacks or baskets. Eventually, the old man said:

"This thing you say will happen."

"Yes?" His voice was impatient and he regretted his tone.

"It could be prevented?"

"I think so." Though he spoke quickly, he found himself unable to dissemble.

"What you want the young men to do is to become soldiers again?"

"Yes, I suppose so."

"And you know they would do it, eagerly. Many of them are still disappointed they saw little action in the Falklands." The old man did not smile, though his voice was light. He continued to stroke his chin, a rasping noise in the quiet. "And it would be a matter of pride, of course—there is always pride. They would be Gurkhas again, for a time."

"Yes." Gardiner thrust his hands into his pockets, and dropped his chin onto his chest, watching his feet intently.

"Your scheme is a wild one."

"It's the only scheme!" he burst out. Then, more quietly, he added: "Look, old friend, all I'm asking is that you help me capture *one* man. Simply that. You don't have to believe the rest of it until you hear it from him!"

"And if it is all true, what then?"

"Then we can use him to tell others!"

"Britain will not help?"

"If it's the Russians, they will—*might,* but there'll be enough of a stink to make them pause. Don't you see that?" His arms were waving, his face was close to that of the old man.

"Perhaps," the old man replied, unmoved it seemed. "Major Ganesh does not believe a word of it," he continued.

"And you?"

"I am not certain, either way."

"Then help me to do this—please."

They continued walking in silence, toward where the lake slowly enlarged between two hillocks and the ground fell away in a long slope down to its shore. Lights from the shops and hotels strung along it like beads, the surface of the water shining like a polished mirror, cracked by the wake of a small boat.

Eventually, the old man at his side spoke. "You are asking them only to be what they are," he announced. "But you, Captain Timothy, what has become of you?"

"It doesn't matter."

"Ah." He was silent for some time, both of them looking

down toward the lake. The murmur of distant music of indistinct nationality. Then: "I should prepare the village for the burials and the *arghun* afterwards . . ."

"It will not come to that!"

"You cannot be certain, Captain Timothy. Nor can I. It seems a long time since we last stood here . . ." He sighed. "You say there is not much time. Come, then. How many young men will you need?"

"Thank you."

The old man shook his head. "The young men will thank you, I suspect," he said.

He felt a breathlessness of mind, as if his thoughts were a voice attempting to speak coherently after violent physical exertion. Scudamore's description, obtained from the desk clerk, of the young man who had called from the lobby, was the same as the man on the curve of beach below Scudamore's bungalow. The man who had followed him on Penang. His proximity unnerved Aubrey, and brought with it the insight that Brigitte was close at hand, too. He knew, in a manner he could not question, that she was here, that she had been sent by Babbington. There was little or no time left. He was standing in the juggernaut's path and he had to *act!*

Especially on what he had learned from Giles Pyott.

"Yes, Giles, yes—I see. No, I'm sorry, Giles, I can't tell you that, not at the moment. Yes, a tragic business all round, if that's the case, yes . . ." Scudamore was looking at him open-mouthed, still as a Buddha yet tense in every limb. Aubrey's hand convulsively jerked the cord of the telephone in time to his words and those of Pyott. Eleven in the evening, midafternoon in London. Warm light enfolded them both. The rest of the suite was dark around them. "Yes—that much?" He released the telephone cord and scribbled on his tiny pad. "Yes, I think there is doubt, Giles—but no, I can't say why, not yet!"

"Kenneth," Pyott said heavily, "I've dug over a lot of old ground for you. The transcript was missing, as I said. I had to get in touch with young Standish's senior officers—those left alive—various colleagues and even a couple of military historians! I think I've earned the right to know, don't you? Besides, Kenneth, any mention of your *bête noire,* Babbington, makes me begin to wonder what you're up to—whether you haven't got hold of the wrong end of the stick." He added darkly: "You haven't, have you?"

"I don't think so, Giles, no." Aubrey soothed. The litter of a room-service meal lay abandoned at the edge of the warm pool of light, its trolley gaunt.

"Then give me some answers, Kenneth—such as, what is the significance of Malaya thirty years ago?"

"I—want you to hear the whole thing, Giles, not just part of it."

"What *are* you up to?" Then, more formally: "You really shouldn't be engaged in anything and I shouldn't be helping you, Kenneth. This *is* obviously to do with the crazy ideas of that young man of yours, I take it?"

"Yes."

"Nonsense, of course. I've looked into it. There's nothing in it, Kenneth, no sign of any buildup, any planned offensive against Nepal."

"Don't be so damned hidebound, Giles!" Aubrey barked. "Just because MoD says something isn't going to happen, it doesn't guarantee it!"

"Kenneth—"

"Giles, you've been very helpful. I mean that. As soon as I can tell you anything, I promise you I will. Then you must act swiftly."

"What are you trying to establish?"

"That Lin the Chinaman, Babbington and General Brigitte form the planning committee for the Soviet annexation of Nepal. And that all three of them are on the same side!"

"The Chinaman, Lin? Ridiculous." There was a long silence, then: "Can you prove any of this?"

"Well done, Giles—skepticism triumphs over Queen's Regulations!" Aubrey chuckled. "Not yet—I hope to, very soon. If I prove Lin is a Russian double, will you take all appropriate steps?" He realized that the worm of doubt, quiescent until now, had awakened and was twisting in his stomach. He had to be certain Giles would listen!

"*If*—then yes, I will. What else will you be able to prove?"

"That they planned it last year—in Penang. That Lin was turned by Babbington—"

"Not with the money that . . . ?" Pyott's voice was small, appalled.

"I *think* so. Lin was bought somehow, we already know that

much. If I can prove it, then the role he has played in Nepal becomes suspect. The Chinese might then—"

"Yes, Kenneth, they might!" Pyott was strangely angry. "Very well, I'll listen to you, and I'll make sure others listen to me." He paused, then added: "The King's on the last leg of his journey, the final lap, Kenneth, that much is certain. If his death is any sort of signal?"

"It may be."

"The rioting, the accusations and counteraccusations, all getting worse in Kathmandu—"

"Then can't you do something *now?*"

"No one would listen!" Pyott growled. "Bring me proof, Kenneth." Aubrey heard his breathing quieten, then Pyott said: "You know young Standish's suicide broke his mother's heart? She died only months later. I found that in the files today, too."

"I—I'll be as quick as I can. Thank you, Giles. You've got those telephone numbers, just in case we have to move around?"

"Yes."

"Goodbye."

He cut the connection and all but flung the telephone receiver toward Scudamore, snapping: "Get hold of that Chinese chum you talk so much about, and check this figure with him!" He slapped the small pad into Scudamore's grasp, then walked toward the window. He heard Scudamore begin dialing.

There had been no news of Tim, Pyott had assured him. Tim was—gone. The darkness glared with neon, Ipoh was any city anywhere, garish and filled with tawdry promises. The warm stars were all but obscured. Aubrey allowed Tim to drift once more, and his impatience at Scudamore's voice and noises became a wild anger at his own impotence. It had taken Giles hours, but he had unearthed the details. If the money tallied, then he *had* Lin and Babbington and—Brigitte.

"Sid, you old bugger—how are you?" Scudamore bellowed into the receiver. Aubrey whirled round, hands clenched tightly in his trouser pockets. "What?" Scudamore's eyes were cold within the mask of bonhomie that covered his features. "Sure I've been trying to get you! How is Miss Feng, your secretary? Is she enjoying KL, too?" Scudamore roared with laughter at the reply. His braying and the false hilarity of the conversation infuriated Aubrey. He wanted to shake Scudamore, shake the telephone and Wei at the other end of the line!

"Listen, Sidney, a confidential question. No, not one of your dodgy investments, something much older than that. What? No, it doesn't mean trouble for you, not really." The levity had gone from his voice. "Sure, all the way back then. Look, I'm not *collecting,* Sid—just enquiring for a friend." Scudamore's face was chilly in the light. "Yes," he enunciated carefully, as if about to charge a minor felon, "it's about *those* old days. No, sure I said it was all forgotten, yes, it was a crying shame I ever retired to Penang, but there we are Sid, old boy—tough titty! Listen, Sidney—when Lin came back . . . yes, after he escaped—Sid, you put the fucking phone down and you put it down on the rest of your life, son!" He was breathing hard, his fist banging softly, repeatedly, on his huge thigh as if on a muffled drum. "You *know* I can," he said. "Now, let's be friends, eh? Just tell me how much money he came back with. No, not your share. Of course you had a bloody share, Sid, how else did you get started after the Emergency? You were *broke* in '58, a wanted man!" He winked outrageously at Aubrey, grinned wolfishly and looked around him for the Scotch bottle he had put aside when Pyott's call had been put through.

Aubrey poured him a whiskey, his hand shivering with anticipation. He returned to the window, his back to Scudamore now, like a child unable to contain its excitement on a birthday morning.

"That's more like it, Sid." Could he hear the scratch of his pen on the pad? "You sure? No bullshit?" Scudamore whistled. "Where did he get it, Sid? What? You certain he didn't say? Mm. OK, thanks, Sid. You back in Penang tomorrow? Why? Thought we'd have another little chat, that's all . . . and good night to you, too, Sid!" He roared with laughter once more and slapped down the receiver. "Silly sod!" he observed, still laughing, then gurgling as he swallowed whiskey. He held out the pad to Aubrey, and said:

"As near as dammit, eh?"

Aubrey studied the figure offered by Sidney Wei. All but identical with the one from Pyott. He swallowed with difficulty, then slowly, deliberately, he picked up the telephone. The line clicked. Identical. Babbington had robbed the Gurkhas to pay Lin, and thrown the blame on Standish. He must have. He must tell Giles at once, get more—

Why had the line clicked?

He put down the receiver as if it had burned his skin. "There's a tap on this telephone," he announced. "Now, she knows everything we know. She knows about *Wei,* dammit!"

12

After a Long Illness . . .

The sun pressed down into Durbar Square like a heavy weight, and was broken into glittering fragments when caught by the litter of glass from smashed or exploded windows. People moved slowly. Hot anger like the glare of a flashbulb robbed his senses each time he looked out from the ruined offices he had chosen as his headquarters.

His hands ached as they mended; his other treated cuts and bruises insisted now more than ever they had done the previous night. He did not feel tired, only lightheaded. It was difficult to concentrate without preparing for the effort.

In the street and the square beyond, colors clashed and jostled, clashing, too, with the atmosphere of Kathmandu; like carnival dress after all celebration was done. The hundreds of stylized portraits of the King looking out over the square from every vantage seemed drawn, ill. The costumes were like slowly moving flags, their wearers now cautious strangers in their own city. Each time he looked down, the bile of his anger rose into his throat and his knuckles became white as he squeezed the scorched windowsill. There was a tension out there in the square that was hotter and more stifling than the sunlight.

The walkie-talkie on the glass-littered desk coughed out ether and Tim Gardiner snatched it up, his eyes hardly leaving the movement of a monk's holy saffron through the crowded square. Ganesh, still wearing the leather flying jacket, stroked his small mustache like an actor and watched Gardiner's movements with sardonic amusement; and a new, reluctant interest.

"Yes?"

The heavy sunlight gleamed, enhanced the glow of green and red and blue costumes, caught gold and other metal. The monk moved with almost painful slowness through the crowd toward the pagodas and the white, carved animals roaring silently at each flank of a temple's steps. Golden lions sat beside a small, ornate door. The monk seemed unmoved by the debris and distrust of the square, floating like a bright cloth apart from the tensions, and the impression angered him. It was as if the monk were ignoring . . .

"What? Repeat that."

"He is heading for Durbar, Captain Sahib. He has left the trishaw—"

Clots and tumors of people in Durbar Square, surrounded and loomed over by fifty ornate temples and countless statues of gods and animals.

"Which way is he coming?"

"Pie Alley, Captain."

"How long?"

"Some minutes only, Captain Sahib—he is alone."

"Good. Well done, Corporal. Keep him in sight."

He switched off the walkie-talkie and lifted the heavy binoculars to his eyes, focusing on the narrow, twisting shadows across the square at the entrance to Pie Alley. Lin had been tailed from the Chinese Embassy—to here? Why? And why alone? Behind him, he heard Ganesh light a cigarette and inhale loudly. He continued to watch the alley hungrily. The saffron robe of the Buddhist monk had reached the entrance of the Taleju Temple and passed between its white, painted-faced lions and through its drunken, ornate doors out of sight. The royal line's own temple; a prayer for the dying King . . . ?

Lin—

The small Chinese emerged from the inky, dusty shadows into Durbar Square. He squinted at once; otherwise his face was inexpressive. But it was him. Gardiner's breathing was hurried. He saw the corporal and the Gurung with him come into the square side by side, then split up, both of them keeping the ambling, somehow purposeless Lin clearly in view. Both men wore shorts and their Brigade-issue uniform pullovers. Why was Lin dawdling? His pace robbed Gardiner of his urgency, too. It seemed like a travesty of what should be happening. The corporal was looking up toward the shattered window, his walkie-talkie in his hand. Lin continued almost as slowly as the monk across the square, into deep shadow, out into hard sunlight, his small figure drab amid the colors of the crowd . . .

. . . which now possessed that sense of mass, of a potential mob, grouped and gathered around the Trailokya Mohan Temple or drifting toward it as if they were expecting an orator. Yes, the crowd, or at least a large part of it, was clotting over on that side of the square. A goat wandered with as little purpose as the Chinese, a cow ambled, chickens scratched in the dust. It was as if Lin had become one with the easy, bright lethargy of Durbar Square. A Buddha's painted eyes, compassionate and surmounted by the mystic symbol of the wise third eye, stared down at him from the face of a bell tower, a *stupa* containing Buddhist relics. Small amid the statuary and carving and the pagodas of other temples. Something plucked at Tim Gardiner's thoughts, but was whirled away by the small breeze of tension he felt shivering through his body. The two Gurkhas moved at an easy stroll behind Lin.

He climbed the steps to the Buddhist *stupa* beneath the Siddhartha's compassionate gaze. The crowd continued to drift— as he quickly swung the glasses like sliding oil across the square—toward the platform in front of the Trailokya Temple, which remained unoccupied even by small traders and souvenir stalls. As he swung the binoculars back, he glimpsed hikers backpacked and dazzled, the clutch of chickens, the goat, the flash and ripple of bright costumes. The occasional holy saffron.

Lin paused in the doorway of the Buddhist *stupa,* looking up at the unblinking, painted wisdom of the Siddhartha's wide eyes, then moved beneath the arch of the small, pagodalike doorway. A Buddhist temple . . . ? Unnerved, he snatched up the two-way radio.

"Corporal—wait until he emerges, then stay close to him."

"Yes, Captain Sahib." He watched them position themselves so that they could keep all four entrances of the *stupa* under observation, then they settled into idle, unsuspicious waiting.

Gardiner scanned the square, but could detect no sign of protection for Lin. The man had been alone, and he was visiting a Buddhist temple. What did it mean? If it had been a shop, any other kind of building, Gardiner would have suspected that Lin had spotted his tail . . . but somehow, not now.

"He's gone into the *stupa,*" he announced to Ganesh.

"There are Chinese Buddhists, too—as well as English," Ganesh replied. He exhaled with customary noise.

"I know! But, *him?* Doesn't make sense, does it?"

"Why worry? He'll be spotted coming out, won't he?"

"Yes." Gardiner rubbed his chin, holding the binoculars in his other hand. He was genuinely puzzled. Lin had now become more of a stranger than ever before.

It was little more than ten minutes before Lin emerged from the *stupa,* and it was as if the Buddha's eyes picked up his slight, drab form at once, staring down at his narrow shoulders and cropped head. The two Gurkhas slipped into the same ambling pace as the Chinese moved across the square toward the now-expectant crowd . . . the glint of glass, the glint of metal, there? Yes, a knife. *Kukris,* too, and clubs. It was as if he expected Lin to ascend the platform and address the crowd, so much so that he was surprised when the Chinese slipped past the crowd's fringe and entered the adjoining Basantapur Square, heading toward Ganga Path. The two young, small Nepalis in army boots followed. Gardiner exhaled a deep sigh.

Orators on the platform; an absence of police. He rubbed his hair and said: "Is he in sight?"

"Yes, Captain Sahib."

"Don't lose him."

A growing absence of color in the square, the predominance of black coats, white shirts, baggy trousers, the occasional patterned, loose blouse. The women had vanished, their bright costumes like flags captured and removed. The tension was like a temporary membrane stretched across the broken glass of the window. A waving fist, bellows through a loudspeaker, a cry from the crowd-becoming-mob.

"Trouble's starting any minute now," he murmured as Ganesh joined him at the window, still smoking. The Nepali nodded.

"Knives, clubs, ugly faces. The right mix."

The speaker on the platform was waving his arms, declaiming in a bull-like, magnified voice, making the wave of violence build, then break, build again. The tempo seemed to increase with each conductor's wave of his arm. His companions on the platform encouraged the crowd with similar semaphores.

"Where are you, Corporal?" he snapped into the walkie-talkie, whose static gushed like someone out of breath.

"Captain—we are now in Sukra Path, sir. He is turning into a sidestreet." There was a noise of breathing, the sense of quicker movement, then the whispered: "He has turned into one of the dirtiest streets in this damned city, sir!" He remembered the Gurung from the hill village disliked Kathmandu, its noise and dirt and oppressive odors. "He is still in our sight, sir."

"Be careful—but follow."

"Yes, Captain Sahib."

"When are you going to close in on him?" Ganesh asked quickly, the former sarcasm once again in his voice.

"You think I should do it now?"

Ganesh shrugged. "It doesn't matter to me, only to you."

"Don't you believe what's happening down there?" Gardiner asked angrily, pointing through the window. Already, fragments of the crowd had been flung off like sparks from the orator's bonfire. Then the whole crowd swayed, broke, surged across the square, scattering stalls and goats and chickens and children. "Look man—*look!*" They flowed through the square, into adjoining Basantapur, down Pie Alley and toward Indrachowk, wild and yet somehow purposeful. At once, the shattering of the first glass and a burst of fire from the shadows of Pie Alley. Their yell faded below the broken windows. "Christ, Gan, can't you see this is only the *start* of it?"

Ganesh looked at Gardiner, his eyes shiftily unsure, his fingers plucking obsessively at his mustache and lips. He was shaking his head, but the reaction seemed outdated, disbelieved.

"I—don't know."

"He has gone into a house, sir," he heard from the walkie-talkie.

"What?" he replied, startled.

"He has gone inside, sir."

"Can you avoid being seen in the street?" When there was no immediate reply, he added: "Find someplace from which you can keep watch—and keep in touch!" Lin was installed somewhere. Who was he meeting? "Well, Gan?"

"Well what—Tim?"

"You're not sure anymore, are you? That I'm off my rocker, that is?" He grinned, unexpectedly.

"It depends."

"This has to be some kind of meeting place."

"Does it?"

"We'll *see!*"

Brandis was still inside the East German Embassy down near the river. Two Gurkhas were watching for him, armed with a vivid description. The German's face was etched on his memory; he had taken a perfect print from the plate.

"What now?" Ganesh asked, lighting a cigarette and blowing smoke into the sunlight slanting in and making the room glow. The light wove a roll of bluish smoke.

"We'll wait and find out who he's waiting for."

Ganesh sighed, but Gardiner sensed the excitement, however unwished, beneath the affectation of indifference. A camera lay on the desk near a brown, dried stain which revealed two smudgy fingerprints. Insects buzzed and glass fragments caught the light like salt spilled everywhere. Ganesh had supplied the camera just as he had supplied the small radios. He had pilfered quickly and effectively in the days before being dismissed from the Brigade.

"OK—we wait."

Gardiner turned back to the window. The square was almost empty. A cow trotted nervously, as if riot came to it on the light, hot breeze. The chickens had gathered into a small, pecking knot once more. Women in bright colors. The noises of the riot, a gout of flame from a sidestreet, the shattering of windows and wood, an occasional scream. It was unreal, but only as a nightmare is unreal, he thought. He shook his head. His anger saved him from introspection. *Damn* Brandis, and Lin, and Babbington.

There was smoke hanging in the almost-still air above Freak Street.

The walkie-talkie.

"He has left the Embassy, Captain Timothy."

"You're sure it's the man I described?" he asked with urgent excitement.

"Yes, sir. He is on foot and we are following."

"Don't lose him—there's a riot taking place!"

"He waited until the mob had passed further down Tripureswar, sir, before he came out."

"OK. Keep him in sight."

"Why are you waiting for them to meet—*if* they do?" Ganesh asked, nodding toward the camera. Gardiner returned his nod.

"Yes. I want to prove they're tied in—*before* we lift him."

He breathed in deeply, exhaled slowly. All those hours of pleading and persuasion, then the planning, had brought him six Gurkhas from his old regiment—and to this. His hands closed smugly into fists.

"He's going to meet Lin, I know he is."

"You hope he is."

Gardiner shook his head. "No, I *know* it."

He noticed the litter of leaflets now in the square. Hundreds, possibly thousands, like dirty, drifted snow. Most of them, he knew, proclaimed that the Foreign Minister's faction on the Council—the anti-Communist grouping—were behind the riots. And people were already beginning to believe the disinformation. Kathmandu was a frightened, unstable place.

"Captain Sahib . . ." the corporal whispered from the radio beside his hand on the windowsill. Ludicrously, he whispered, too, as he acknowledged, "Police, Captain. Three cars. In this narrow, filthy street, sir. There are no uniforms, but we are certain. Outside the house."

"Where are you?"

"An upstairs room of a house opposite. It did not cost much to bribe the woman. Her father lived here, but he has died—"

"What are they doing?"

"Someone has got out of the biggest car. A man saluted him, he must be important . . . he is going into the house while the others are spreading out along the street."

"Be careful!" he warned. "Miss nothing—we're on our way." Then he snapped, more loudly: "Nakam, where is the German now?"

"Ah, Captain Timothy—he is near the vegetable market. He is heading for Dharma Path—"

"Then he's making for the house!" Gardiner called across to Ganesh, who shrugged. "Don't lose him, Nakam!" Then, remembering, he added: "Out." At once, he snatched up the camera and its spare lenses in their cases. "OK, Ganesh, we're on parade."

"You're too eager, my friend."

"No!" He clenched his fists as if preparing to strike Ganesh. "No," he repeated more evenly. "Lin, Brandis and a senior police officer. It might be just what we need."

"A few photographs?"

"If we can prove—look, the whole *secrecy* of this thing is its strength and its weakness. If we can *show* they're being secretive, then they become suspect."

"Show? Show who?"

"*Anyone!* Aubrey is going to need proof to convince people. He'll want to know how, and when. Proof could be anything, anything at all." He opened the door of the office and began stepping gingerly down the uncertain, damaged staircase to the ground floor where the wall of the building was missing and sunlight filled with dust motes hung like a heavy, golden curtain. "Just don't be a bloody cynic, Gan! Christ Almighty, you're *in!*"

"I know."

"Then bloody act like it! It's your bloody country, chum!"

"And yours, apparently . . ." Ganesh murmured.

The square was silent, waiting. The leaflets stirred under their feet. Beyond the square, a rabble muttered at the denunciations of a speaker on the steps of a small, ornate temple. A golden tiger roared noiselessly at his side. Gardiner felt himself immersed in the tensions of the streets as they hurried through small, reeking squares and pressed through the narrow alleys north of Durbar Square. Gardiner checked the exact location of Brandis' tail, the precise house in which the surveillance of Lin was stationed. The alleys and streets were familiar. There was talk of the King everywhere as they passed. The hot, close, smelling alleys seemed to be swiftly boiling under pressure. He was gripped by the acceleration of events and his own sense of action. He had the Gurkhas and Gan now.

He halted Gan at the corner of a narrow street of cheap hotels and poor shops. A green Mercedes. There was the sense of conspiracy in their lack of uniforms and an arrogant certainty of success in parading such a car at a secret meeting. Young men in linen suits of Western style. Guns, doubtless. Two long-haired Westerners in faded denims, Nepalis in black-and-white, as if little more than a background.

"We can't just walk down the street."

"All these places have courtyards, back entrances. I suggest we look." Gan smiled, but then swallowed. His eyes were bright, eager. Gardiner nodded.

"Come on."

A dirt-paved lane, a thin dog, a sleeping, ancient man. A broken trishaw, cardboard boxes, rotting vegetables and a litter of empty egg-boxes. Gardiner counted along the grubby terrace, nodded with satisfaction and pushed open a creaking, drunken gate. A cramped courtyard serving perhaps four of the houses. An old man looked unexpectantly from his slumped occupation of a rickety chair, then ignored them as they passed into the narrow passageway and climbed unsafe, filthy stairs to the second floor. Corporal Aitasing was waiting for them like an expectant relative. The radio in Gardiner's hand crackled loudly in the silence of the landing. A fly buzzed.

"Yes?" he whispered hoarsely.

"The German is on Sukra Path, sir."

"Good. Be careful as you get closer, the house is being watched. Out." He looked at Aitasing. "Well?"

"There is a good view. They have not closed the shutters. The Chinese and the police officer—two others, on guard."

"You have done well, Corporal." A moment of mistrust, even dislike, before Aitasing nodded and gestured Gardiner and Ganesh into the cramped, littered room. Aitasing's companion was watching through binoculars and did not turn his head. Gardiner felt his grip on the camera's strap tighten. There was a sense of conspiracy taut as a wire in the foul-smelling room with its soiled bedlinen and litter of books and ancient furniture. "What are they doing, Harka?" he asked, his hand on the Gurkha's narrow shoulder. It did not flinch at his touch.

Harka lowered his binoculars. "They talk, sir. Argue, I think. The Chinese is angry, anyway, more angry than the Nepali, though he doesn't shout." Harka grinned with even white teeth. His face was pockmarked from a childhood infection.

"Let me see, Harka." The Gurkha handed him the glasses. Tensions crackled in the room's still, fetid air. Sunlight coming through the slats of the shutters tiger-striped the walls and floor and the dark, serious, detached faces around him. He bent his back, adjusting the focus of the binoculars. Army issue; something else filched out of the Brigade's wreckage. He peered through the gap between the two ill-closed shutters. Something was scrabbling behind the cracked plaster. The floor of the room leaned like the ground in a drunken excursion.

Lin's small, precise features emerged into focus. Gardiner felt satisfied with the secrecy of his surveillance. Lin's eyes were small, black, angry coals, his whole frame was tense. Two light-suited men at the door, without feature or stature. He nudged the glasses across the open window opposite. Bald head, loose jowl, small narrow eyes, an expensive gray suit. Large, plump hands gesticulating, emphasizing.

The features of Kathmandu's chief of police. Timothy Gardiner gasped, even though it was little more than a suspicion confirmed, a hope fulfilled. Despite his concentration, he could hear their argument only like a conversation from the other side of a thin wall. The chief of police; worried, angry, frightened. Something was wrong—

The door behind the two light suits opened. Brandis. His hands quivered holding the binoculars, the lenses of which seemed to mist with his excited tension. Brandis, the man who had tried to kill him. And Lin. And the chief of police. Brandis at once commandeered the situation, his face vivid with impatience, head turning from side to side as if adjudicating. Nodding, shaking his head, hands spreading in calming or denying gestures, becoming more and more emphatic. He could not lip-read, and the mutter of the pantomime across the narrow street infuriated him. The chief of police mopped his shining forehead with a large handkerchief, Brandis' smile was sardonic, Lin's features were quiescent. The two light suits remained motionless near the door. Brandis began making points and emphasizing them on his fingers.

"Harka—camera, please."

Quickly, he changed the camera's lens, checked the film, adjusted the focus. The three faces. The tip of the barrel-like lens touched the shutters and they creaked. He held his breath. Then he paused. Brandis, Lin, and the chief of police . . . movement. The motor whirring on like a fly spinning into death on the windowsill. The room was hot, smelled of decay and damp and rat droppings. The chief of police and Brandis together, Lin alone . . . Brandis and Lin, the motor whirring. Lin and the German, Lin and the German, Lin and the chief of police . . . The hot, dark room. Lin and the policeman, Lin and Brandis, all three of them, all three in focus . . . the room lightened at a creak, as if—

The tip of the lens had pushed against one of the shutters and it swung open. The sunlight streamed in, over his face and hands and their whiteness. Lin, Lin . . . the motor still whirring, his heart thudding, Ganesh calling out—

Lin's pointing arm. Brandis' twisted, suspicious face, the voice of the policeman. The two light suits hurried out through the room's door.

"Listen, Sidney, just do as I tell you, eh? Don't go near your office! Just get along to the Lone Pine Hotel out on Batu Feringgi—yes, the one on the beach, and ask for Mr. Allen—got that?" Scudamore was sweating freely. Improbably, almost ludicrously, both of them were thrust together into the cramped telephone booth; the door had, with difficulty, folded shut behind them. The glass was misted with their heat and nervousness. "Mr. Allen, that's right . . . what? *Why?* You want to know why, Sidney?" Scudamore stared down into Aubrey's eyes, his face red.

"Tell him."

"Sidney—an old friend of yours is in the area. She's sure to look you up." Aubrey nodded in uncomfortable approval. He wanted a shower or a bath, *he* wanted to be back in his air-conditioned hotel room. Instead, there was this breathless, uninterrupted journeying, their drive through the jungle and the night to Butterworth, their need to decide how best to protect Wei. "Who?" Scudamore was perversely enjoying himself, taunting Sidney Wei. "I'll tell you who, Sidney! Do you remember the nice little lady who used to hang about with your lot— yes, all that time ago. Your mate Lin knows her well. German bint, she was." He was grinning broadly. "Ah!" he exclaimed. "That's her!" He put his hand over the receiver.

"Panic job from Sidney, I think—he's just soiled his trousers." The man was actually *reveling* in Wei's discomfort! "What's that, Sidney? Look, there's no need to turn nasty! I'm doing you a favor. *I* didn't stir this mess up, Sidney—that's very unfair!" Scudamore's almost ghoulish enjoyment was like an irritant on Aubrey's skin. His clothes clung to him, too. The narrow booth was hot, their proximity ridiculous!

"We're in Butterworth *now,* Sidney, waiting for the ferry! Won't be more than an hour—what?"

They had sneaked out of the hotel in Ipoh, taken an all-night, circuitous route through the foothills of the Cameron Highlands, then headed west after south before turning north through alien, marshy country near the coast, muddy tracks alongside rivers and paddy fields all the way to Butterworth. A strange, phantasmagorical journey that seemed to have no conceivable connection with his concerns, his urgency, their danger.

Now, on the Butterworth waterfront, the palms still and the scents of petrol and oil and fish hanging heavily in the air, it did not appear that they were under surveillance—as far as two old men could determine. But Wei must be warned, must be got away from home and office. Brigitte knew the name, would remember the man, would be coming to Penang for him just as they were. Wei was the single witness, the one accusing finger.

"Look, Sidney, they know about *my* place, it's not safe for you to go there—" Aubrey shook his head vigorously in agreement. "—you park yourself in Mr. Allen's room until we get there, OK?" Scudamore's soothing tone had little less abrasiveness than his mockery or anger. Then he shrugged before placing his hand over the mouthpiece of the phone. "He won't play. Oh, he'll talk all right. I know too much about him for him not to. But he won't go to your hotel, insists on my place . . . ?"

Aubrey clasped his bottom lip between his teeth. He glanced out, and studied the approaching ferry. Two and a half miles across the water—they could practically *wave* to Wei from here! In less than an hour they could be at the hotel. Did it matter—

"Very well!" he snapped. "Tell him you'll collect him at your place within an hour! Tell him to be *careful!*"

The booth was at once stifling, oppressive. He folded open the door and stepped out, suddenly shivery with doubts. Wei would have protection, they'd promised him that, now and for as long as necessary. Scudamore had promised him immunity from everything short of rabies. He had agreed to talk because Scudamore could cause trouble for him and his various businesses . . . and Wei did not have Triad backing or protection and was therefore exposed to their blackmail.

And he *would* talk!

Aubrey studied the queue for the ferry, which was sliding closer as if to butt the quay with its fat waist and hips. No, no one he should be wary of or conceal himself from. Where was she, then? he asked himself immediately. She had Wei's name, she knew what they had said, he and Pyott, she knew about Scudamore. She knew enough to force her hand. He remembered Kurt, lying broken on the cobblestones. Now, she could have her revenge, tidying up a professional loose end.

Wei would say—they'd have to persuade him to London, of course—that Lin had been bought, that Brigitte and Lin were tied in together in Malaya, that Babbington was tied in with both of them through the money. Once that stone had been thrown, the doubts would ripple out across Whitehall's pond, affecting MoD, HMG, the Foreign Office, Nepal . . . Tim . . . ?

He shook off the thought which battened like a mosquito, stinging and feeding at once. Wei had to stay alive, to furnish the proof.

Scudamore joined him, breathing heavily, but his face was still wreathed in a smile of superior, mocking pleasure. The ferry

docked and passengers began to spill down the rickety gang-
ways.

"All right?" Scudamore asked.

"What? Oh, yes—all right," Aubrey replied. "Where is she?"
he demanded, hardly realizing he had spoken aloud.

"What? Oh, her . . . still looking for us in Ipoh, I expect! Don't
worry, it's in the bag. Sid'll play ball with you. Don't worry!"

"Come on—out—out *now!*" Ganesh shouted into his face, his
hand dragging at Gardiner's shoulder.

Without thinking, he yelled back, oblivious of the faces at the
window opposite. "What about the bloody Chinaman? I *want*
the bloody Chinaman!" Orders in Malay from across the gap
between the two houses, a voice growling in German. Aitasing
and Harka stared at them as if at strange, warring beetles. He
looked across the narrow street, and saw Lin making for the
door, to be elbowed aside by the chief of police. Brandis leaned
heavily on the windowsill with the contained, confident anger
of a neighbor threatening litigation. Then the German smiled
and drew his forefinger quickly across his throat. Footsteps and
the banging of doors. "Stop them, Gan—stop them!" he whispered urgently.

For a moment, Ganesh hesitated, and then his eyes seemed
to glow as he nodded. "Harka, Corporal—don't let them
through the front door!" The two Gurkhas left the room immediately. Gardiner heard their light footsteps on the creaking
staircase, then heard the front door being charged or kicked
open. He clutched Gan's arm. There was another noise, too, like
that of a distant and strengthening wind. Brandis had disappeared from the window. He smelled petrol as the Mercedes'
engine fired and the car screeched away, grinding some part of
its frame against the stone of a house. Cries? "Come on,"
Ganesh urged. "Now you've begun it!"

He dragged Gardiner across the room and to the head of the
staircase. Two light-colored suits sprawled in the passageway,
torn and stained with big, irregular daubs. There were *kukris*
in the Gurkhas' hands. The doorway was empty.

"Pick up their guns!" Ganesh ordered, then: "The rear, come
on!"

One of the suits shuddered, there was a low, awful moan before stillness. Ganesh and he clattered down the stairs and fled
through the house into the yard. The old man was still in his

rickety chair, even as they pressed through the drunken gate into the alley—

—empty! That noise like a growing storm, and louder, more destructive noises and cries behind them, but the lane was clear. All four of them ran together, the unnoticed camera now banging against Gardiner's thigh as he held it by the strap. His face was hot and there was a small, tight, stonelike lump of triumph in his chest—he had them on film!

He plunged rather than stepped into the street and it was already too late. The storm-noise broke like a wave and he was cramped and pinioned by hurrying bodies. Banners, placards, huge pictures, staves and clubs whirled around him. He was engulfed by some tributary of the riot he had seen stampede from Durbar Square. He looked wildly around and saw Gan and the two Gurkhas caught up, too, thrust along by the flood of people; yelling, screaming, brandishing weapons, exuding the smells of violence and rage. Ganesh was ten yards away already as if drowning in another wave immediately behind his own. Then the river turned in its course and rushed against the black limousine that had drawn up in the narrow street where they had been observing the house. The riot broke momentarily against the dam of the car which almost blocked the street, and its force seemed spent.

Brandis—

The mob clambered, slipped, seemed to wash over the car and the German and the two new white faces that must have been summoned with the car, and—

—Lin, ducking his narrow frame into the back of the limousine. There was no sign of the chief of police or the green Mercedes. The tightly wedged mob struggled free of the car's impediment, or became wedged and more enraged. Brandis was clearly unnerved. Lin was already invisible behind tinted glass. The other two Germans, hands close to breast pockets, seemed at a loss. The noise increased. He heard the smashing of glass, a groan. People screamed for relief rather than in rage. He looked around for Gan, the air pressed from his lungs, but could see neither him nor the two Gurkhas. His arm was trapped, he seemed unable to move. Then Brandis saw him and forgot his own fear in a grin of pure pleasure. His arm pointed, Gardiner could not hear what he shouted.

The Germans could. Gardiner tried to struggle, a man yelled into his face, someone struck him with the pole of a torn banner.

The limousine seemed all but buried by clambering Nepalis, by a shroud of dirty white shirts. A woman fell, soundlessly. The heat of the packed and jostling bodies was like that of a furnace. The two Germans were wading through the chest-high water of the riot toward him, clubbing men out of their way with the barrels of their guns. Brandis had struggled onto the roof of the car and was yelling from cupped hands, pointing and yelling . . .

He dragged in air as the pressure on his chest eased. The noise of the crowd was like a firestorm. His legs shuffled irresolutely, not under his volition. He held on to the camera with one pinioned hand. The car's windshield broke audibly, smashed in. Brandis' face was violent with anger, there was a flash of returning fear—then everything was concentrated on Gardiner.

The closer of the two Germans was ten yards away, then less as he thrust and clubbed a man out of his path. He saw Lin dragged from the limousine and someone tug at Brandis' ankle. Lin was hoisted, then tossed like a doll from hand to outstretched hand, his face a mask of terrors.

Brandis kicked out, and a man's face turned red. Gardiner felt his arm grabbed, twisted—he turned, expecting Gan, but it was the other German, who must have found some easier shallow of the crowd through which to wade, and he saw the gleam of a knife—and the gleam of the man's quick, intent smile. The crowd bayed at a terrifying, numbing volume. The knife flashed out at him and he tried to twist away. The man pressed closest against him screamed and clutched his side, slipping only a little in the press as his legs buckled. Smoke from somewhere began to fill the alley and the screaming became higher-pitched. There was a huge thrust of people back toward him, dragging him away from the German who still held his arm. The knife probed for him again.

Brandis—still on the roof, the car like something beached now as the crowd moved back from the fires that must have started in some of the narrow houses. He tried to move the arm from which the camera dangled. Lin? The knife probed. Where was the second German? Knife again. Where? Brandis, alarmed, jumped down from the car's roof. The German was squarely in front of him then, as if the crowd were schoolboys who had moved back to make a ring for their small battle. He lashed out with his foot, catching the German across the shins, making him wince, making the knife lose force and direction. Kicked again and missed, but was able to drag his arm free of the man's grip.

He was running backward now, off-balance, with the surrounding crowd hurrying him away from the two Germans. His vision was clouded with sweat. Gan . . . ?

He staggered over a body lying at the corner of the alley and the wider street and fell, the camera clattering down beside him. And the street suddenly seemed emptier, as if he had been left by the riot to fend for himself. It was a thin crowd now, hurrying away. The two Germans were moving in. Something grabbed his arm, hauling him to his feet—both arms, so that he struggled and yelled but could not break away—

—Gan.

And a small Chinese seated, head bleeding through the fingers that held it, slumped against a doorway. Lin's drab clothing, and the Germans becoming more cautious, until Brandis screamed at them to help Lin, bring Lin, get Lin, *get him!*

Harka stabbed at the closer German, who dodged but was cut open at least to the flesh, his suit and shirt gaping, then was whirled and thrown off his feet by the last remnants of the mob. Gardiner moved to Lin, drew his hands away, saw the dazed face, dragged him upright and pressed the Chinese against him. Brandis and the other German watched as he rounded the corner, increasing his momentum to match that of the last of the crowd, then allowing himself to be moved by them as if he had boarded a vehicle, Lin's feet dragging and stumbling as he held him. Gan behind him now, and the others . . .

The Chinaman's face was close to his own as they were spilled by the crowd, already losing momentum, into the ornate square of Indrachowk. Temples, roaring, silent, golden lions, Garuda and other gods. The ebbing of the mob into exhausted silence. Gardiner grinned at his prize. Lin's bloodstreaked face was palely sallow, reflecting the exhaustion Gardiner felt himself. Worn, weary, aged. It was not the face Gardiner had expected to see.

"Come on!" Ganesh shouted in his drumming ear. "Let's get him out of sight."

Police whistles now, and new, uncertain movement in the crowd. Sirens and the roar of approaching trucks. A statue of Shiva in a wall niche with a huge, erect phallus, his *lingam*. He stumbled and righted himself against a stone carving of Garuda, half-human, half-eagle. Fruit from overturned and wrecked stalls littered the square, most of it crushed; torn and trampled bales of cloth scattered everywhere in untidy heaps.

Then Ganesh thrust the unresisting Lin into Corporal Aita-sing's arms, and he and Harka flanked the Chinese as they hurried from the square in the direction of Kanti Path and the Annapurna Hotel, where the rental car waited in the hotel's underground garage: Lin's feet dragged and shuffled. Gardiner swallowed, then grinned at Ganesh—and waved the camera he still gripped by its strap.

"Done—*done it!*" he managed to shout above the noise of his own breathlessness, and that of the nearing sirens.

The glint of sunlight from glass or metal—there, just there, where a parakeet plunged out of the trees, its cry like a raucous alarm. Scudamore squinted, trying not to look directly toward the clumped palms and undergrowth the headland wore like an untidy, too-luxuriant wig. The sunlight flickered again across slow-moving leaves, there was dust in his eyes and the light hurt coming off the white paint of the bungalow. Then—yes! The glint of glass, the movement of light sliding across green before disappearing; binoculars dipping, being taken away from someone's eyes. Scudamore lumbered through the wooden gate, the picket fence shivering with his effort.

The garage door was ajar and Sidney Wei's BMW nudged into slanting sunlight. They were watching the house! Oh fuck it, fuck it, *fuck!*

"Sidney!" he bellowed as his weight thudded onto the veranda into hot shadow and the buzz of flies. Too late, you should have been cool, played it calm, you silly bugger. "Sid, for Christ's sake, get out here you stupid bastard!" He banged on the door. He had blown it now, there wasn't any time and he was out of breath and his heart had begun panicking and his back felt cold where they must be watching it. *Shouldn't have panicked!* Rahim opened the door, and Scudamore merely bellowed into the hallway: "Sid, get your arse out here now, for Christ's sake!" He glanced wildly behind him, knowing that that, too, was another mistake in a growing catalogue of errors. He was too *old* for it!

Wei appeared beside Rahim, his face grayer with forebodings. Scudamore dragged at his arm immediately, his breathing hoarse and ragged in his ears, hurting his chest.

"Come on, Sidney, old son—we're getting out of here!" Then he added out of fear and panic: "I *said* you shouldn't have come here, you stupid fucking Chink! They were *watching* the place when you arrived!"

The trees, the trees . . . Nothing? He kept a firm grip on Wei's sleeve, creasing the expensive seersucker jacket. Wei's face attempted the calm registration of mild offense, but his eyes were quick, darting everywhere.

"What do you—" he began, but his voice trailed away, as if bleached by the heat and light. Dust stirred through the clump of trees, there was the roar of an engine and the squealing of tires.

"Oh, *shit!*" Scudamore wailed.

The car, a grubby, mustard-colored Datsun, slewed out of the clump of darkness on the headland and threw up a fountain of dust as it straightened on the road only hundreds of yards from them. The Jaguar beyond the white fence seemed a much greater distance away. Sidney Wei's face had collapsed into a hunted expression, wild-eyed, thin-cheeked. Scudamore had seen hundreds of faces like Wei's during the last days of the Emergency; surrendering faces.

He dragged at the Chinaman's arm, got him to the gate, and waited for an instant, holding his breath. It seemed the Datsun with its blind, tinted windshield was doing the same. Then a radiotelephone aerial waggled like a signal of the car's panicky acceleration.

"Oh, Christ, come on!" he bellowed against Wei's cheek, thrusting the small, slim man into the passenger seat of the Jaguar, hearing his well-cut suit squeak against the leather. He rushed around the hood—hot to the touch—fumbling for his keys, slamming the door as he squashed into his seat, breath exploding.

Come on, come on—

The engine caught first time, he let out the handbrake, thrust the gearshift forward and accelerated, tires squealing, a blind brownness in the rearview mirrors. He swung the car around on the handbrake with deft, old movements that made him smile in a mirthless grimace. Wei buckled his seat belt with nerveless fingers, his complexion chalky, his body slumped into the seat almost below the level of the windshield. Then the Datsun and the Jaguar faced each other like wary, poised animals.

Should have been more careful, should have insisted, shouldn't have let the silly bastard come here . . . The litany continued in his head, but its voice seemed obscured by excitement and tension; he was not afraid, but exhilarated, and in a manner he had not encountered for thirty years. Wei's hollow-cheeked, sweat-sheened features beside him increased his sense of the past, of old dangers, moments of terror. "Sit tight, Sidney!" he bellowed exuberantly, not feeling the burden of his weight, the heat of even small movements. He was deft, quick again.

He thrust his foot down on the accelerator and the old Jaguar leaped forward toward the Datsun—

—whose passenger doors were opening, all three of them, and small, bright-shirted bodies were emerging, and enlarging as he bore down on them. Small black sticks in their hands, frightened, alert faces, the dust whirling up from the road and obscuring the sky as he shuffled the wheel through suddenly wet palms and skidded, swerved, attempted to evade them. One gun coming to bear. The white man alone among the Malays was the young man who'd been on his beach . . .

Almost past them, the rear of the Jaguar swinging against the flank of the Datsun and rending it with a tearing cry which might have been the shriek of one of the Malays caught between the two cars, then the dust was again behind him and so was the Datsun—that gun leveling? All the others had been shocked, too slow, too late—that one gun?

The rear window fell inward, the car's frame responded in shudders to the impact of bullets, he felt icily chilled by the sense of something thumping into the rear seats.

Wei was slumped in his seat, safe, his face still white. The dust behind him obscured the Datsun and the Malays and the white man. He could hear nothing except the exertions of the engine and his own heart. Then the road seemed to open, the sky became colored with pale blue and the sun glinted off even the dusty paint of the Jaguar's hood as the car accelerated. There was more shooting, but fainter. Christ, he'd done it! Fucking well done it!

The dust settled in the rearview mirror, the Datsun seemed stranded, then sluggish, then it turned and began to pursue them, a mustard-colored miniature of no consequence. They wouldn't catch him now—

"Not bloody likely, eh, Sid?" he yelled at the top of his voice, exulting. Bloody well done it! "Oh, Christ, Sid—get a smile on your bloody . . ."

Red where white should be, peeping between the lapels of Wei's suit. The face chalkier, the body's posture without bones like a jellyfish. Scudamore tugged open Wei's jacket with a cry of desperation. Red, damp, no—not damp, sodden—across his chest, the head lolling doll-like. Scudamore groaned and wiped his sticky hand on the material of Wei's jacket, his stomach revolting and his thoughts outraged.

He had no time to discover whether Wei was still alive. Or the source of the pain in his own side. He pressed his heavy, suddenly tired foot down on the accelerator, keeping the pursuing Datsun at a distance, then losing it as the road bent into dark trees. Aubrey . . . fucking well dump *this* in Aubrey's lap! he thought, blinking his eyelids rapidly, his grip tightening on the steering wheel. Angry, so bloody, bloody angry!

Haunted by the palpably inferior? No, not haunted, he affirmed to himself. But why then was he so evidently mindful of Standish? Flying north from Gandhi's India across the barren, yellow-brown expanses of Soviet Central Asia, Babbington looked meditatively out of the cramped little porthole in the fuselage of the military Ilyushin. Outside the aircraft, the daylight of the same day it had been when they had lifted out of Delhi's haze. He strangely *wanted* time zones, even the prospect of jet lag, the sense of thousands of miles of journey, of distant yet attainable destination. He rubbed at his beard with surprising energy as if to erase some disguise and break through to a former self.

Why this cold touch, this sense of Malaya and that silly, malleable young man who had killed himself thirty years before?

His meetings with that gaggle of senior intelligence officers and civil servants and a brace of politicians in Delhi had served to confirm, in the most pleasing way, the necessity of *Topi*. Gandhi was losing favor and control, even over his own party. India was slipping from the Soviet Union's side like an ill-trained puppy. Nepal must be made—secure. The Politburo would be generous in praising and rewarding his foresight; all this could be used, ensuring the succession to Kapustin.

So, why this disquiet over Malaya?

A mere boy in a lieutenant's uniform was approaching his seat with a copy of a message in his hand, having emerged from the signals room behind the flight deck.

Brigitte. His stomach tensed involuntarily and he was angry with the sense of fearful anticipation in himself. Brigitte, the spider lady.

From Ipoh. *The contacts traced, identified, eliminated.* Good, good. *Lin, Standish*—a premonition, his thoughts of him? *Sidney Wei identified, to be eliminated—Scudamore . . . ?* He was puzzled for only a moment, then remembered the name, the man. Aubrey was using Scudamore, who knew things, could remember Standish.

He rubbed his frown and placed the signal form on the seat next to his own. Aubrey's ploy was patent. He was attempting to expose *his* part in *Topi,* the links between himself and Lin and Brigitte. It might make the stupid Americans lean their gross weight on the UN, even HMG might be stung to some kind of puling protest. The Chinese, of course, would threaten, stamp feet, bully. In total, it might be enough for Nikitin and the Politburo to hold back, draw breath—*wait!*

Cancel *Topi?*

By a curious and shocking irony, it was as if Aubrey intended that Standish, thirty years dead, should slip through the net, and come to judgment on him, point an accusing finger in his direction.

Message form. *Déjà vu,* the strangeness of an identical sheet, identical apologetic look on the young officer's face. He glanced at the first sheet beside him, just to make certain he was not somehow dreaming . . . no. He snatched up the form and read hungrily, his mouth dry.

Brandis . . . Lin? He rubbed his forehead as if wiping a misty glass to see more clearly. Lin—gone? Gardiner? Fragments of the message hurtled like meteors. Lin had been *kidnapped by Gardiner and others as yet unidentified. Search proceeding with utmost manpower and urgency . . .*

. . . request further orders. Situation report follows. Rioting to climax tonight . . . in view of disappearance further orders necessary.

He felt breathless. He opened his shirt, tugging at the high neck of his sweater as if loosening a cord. Incompetents, inferiors—they dogged him again! His career seemed not a pattern, only glimpses and flashes of momentary success.

The King, he read on, *tonight. Dose administered . . . broadcast for assistance to restore order—*

His sole was grinding on the carpet between his seat and the one in front. Think, think—!

His breathing became easier. Cold, quick clarity of enmity.

Aubrey eliminated *first,* at once, together with Scudamore and Wei. Yes, tidying-up quite neatly and finally. Lin?

Find Lin, have him back in hand—or eliminated, like Aubrey. He was *not* losing control of the situation, it was simply that his success was as yet qualified, in the balance. But *he* held the scales, the weights. The rioting must go on and on until Lin was accounted for. *Topi* was the ever more crucial pivot of an even greater success. The thought warmed him.

Signals to be transmitted—in reply to these. Orders—the first one being, *Kill Aubrey at once.*

The suitcase and briefcase lay on the bed, still emanating the haste with which he had packed them. Aubrey sat on the edge of an armchair in the small lounge, repeatedly expressing his mounting tension with birdlike peerings through the open bedroom door at his luggage. He clutched his whiskey glass in both hands. The light outside was like a gleaming white sheet drawn across the veranda. He felt unnerved, as if expecting at any moment a dark shadow to be haloed against that fierce light. He should never have let Wei go to Scudamore's bungalow, should never have sent Scudamore after him.

He paced the veranda berating himself, despite the heat and the little black hanging bunches of slow, noisy insects. He rubbed his forehead, swallowed at the whiskey, stroked his chin but could not cease moving, cease squinting out toward the almost colorless mirror of the sea and the small, indistinct dark shapes that wavered in its shimmer. The hotel's jetty, the small launches and their crews, the few fishing boats drawn up picturesquely, the few reckless bathers bobbing in the heat.

Scudamore, Scudamore . . . where were they? He glanced at his watch. Time was too elongated already; they were overdue now.

He returned to the imperceptibly cooler lounge and its drawn-out sigh from the air conditioning. He slumped into the armchair and automatically patted his pockets. Wallet, tickets, credit cards, passport in the name of Allen . . . habits of a serene traveler.

The watch on his moving wrist went in and out of focus and the time crawled and yet seemed quick because they were late. His very nervousness made him feel drowsy. The air conditioning and the murmur of insects seemed to mingle with some unrecognized noise . . . Subliminal. A noise in dreams, like a bell or siren; demanding . . . what?

He snapped awake, shuddering despite the heat. The continuous noise of a car's horn. Going on and on. He thrust himself upright with quivering hands and weak wrists, grabbing for his stick. He scuttled to the door and opened it. The volume of the noise increased and was challenged by human voices. He heard—

—telephone in his room? Horn. It seemed the greater demand, playing upon his anxieties in an almost hallucinatory way. The telephone could only be the hotel desk, asking about his luggage. He skittered the few yards to the foyer of the hotel and saw the old gray Jaguar slumped against a palm tree with torn-up roots and a drunken lean. In the Jaguar a face pressed like old, grey clay against the windshield, turned sideways, the face distorted. Another face behind the smeared, dirty windshield, lying back as if asleep on the headrest of the passenger seat. People crowding the carpark, moving hesitantly out of the shade of the big awning over the doors, a clutter of bright print shirts and frocks and darkened flesh. Wei—it must be Wei—was in the passenger seat, Scudamore's was the crumpled, clayey face pressed against the windshield, his heavy body squeezing the steering wheel and car's horn. Both faces were still.

"Mr. Allen!" he heard someone call but it wasn't his name and so he ignored the foreign accent.

"Excuse me . . . please, excuse!" He struggled through the hot, sometimes slippery bodies, his strength ebbing at a terrifying rate. "Excuse—please, excuse me! I must . . ."

He dragged open the driver's door of the Jaguar. Scudamore's face was turned to him, eyes staring, lips wet. There was saliva on his chin and a creeping, wet redness on his shirt where it strained across his midriff. Aubrey touched it as if to stanch the bleeding, then drew his hand away with quick shock. Wei was evidently dead. Others crowded behind him now that he had broken the spell that had stifled their movement.

"Please, get back!" he shouted in a high voice. "Give them air, room!"

Scudamore's vast flank heaved like that of a downed bull, shudderingly.

Moved?

He tried to push at the big frame but it would not move back into the seat. The noise of the horn continued, now like a wail.

Scudamore's chest and side heaved again and again. More saliva; more blood. Aubrey pushed at Scudamore again, almost groaning with effort—and then Scudamore straightened his arms with what seemed a dying effort and lurched back into the driving seat, his hand at once pressing onto the wet, red shirt.

"—thought you'd . . . never come, you daft old *bugger!*" he bawled, as if the words were forced from him by the action of a bellows. "Fucking done for Sid!" He could not whisper. Aubrey had leaned forward like a priest expecting some final communication, but the voice and the man's hot breath both roared in his ear. He jerked away, staring open-mouthed at Scudamore, who was looking ahead through the grimy windshield, concentrating with the fury of a child, his voice that of a bad actor, ranting. "Waiting—must have followed him there—*shit-this-fucking-hurts!*"

Scudamore went on shouting, and now there was another noise. "Shot Sid and fucked me up too! Christ, it's *all right* but it *bloody well hurts!*" It was a siren. There was an ambulance, or the police, coming. Hold on, he thought. Somehow, he could not touch Scudamore, not even his shoulder. "Up the bloody spout now! Just what they wanted! Got the notebooks?" He suddenly turned his head and stared balefully at Aubrey, who nodded at once with the urgency of an accused child. "Then get the fuck away from here!"

"There's an ambulance coming," Aubrey murmured through his horrified disappointment, staring across Scudamore at Wei's ashen, still features and the bloody suit he was wearing.

"Is there a Datsun around?" Scudamore bellowed by way of reply.

"What?" Aubrey glanced about. One—yellow, engine running, Brigitte's blond young man standing beside it. "Yes," he whispered.

"They've started . . ." Scudamore lowered his voice, his breathing lunging, his hands quivering on the steering wheel. He stared almost sightlessly into Aubrey's face, pushed close to his own. The shouting had been less horrifying than this rattled breathy whispering. "They'll kill you now, without a second—thought . . . so, fuck off out of it!"

"Ambulance—"

"Bollocks! I'm not dying, just bleeding like a pig! I—I've got you an *audience!* Don't you see? They can't shoot you here, you silly old sod! Bog off while you've got the chance! Go on, *go on!*"

One hand shooed at Aubrey, almost comically. Aubrey glanced up the slight slope of the hotel's drive toward the Datsun, dusty and ungleaming in the hot sunlight. The blond young man hesitated, then began to move down the slope. Aubrey looked back at Scudamore's pasty complexion and his reddening shirt, and saw that he was squinting in the same direction. "See!" he crowed in a weird whisper. "I bloody well *told* you! Now the bugger's coming for you—fuck *off!*"

The crowd remained drawn back like a curtain opening on the little drama around the Jaguar. He stared for an instant at Wei as if willing him to awake from some hypnotic trance, then patted Scudamore's arm.

"Oh, bugger off . . ." Scudamore whispered in a voice that indicated he had lost interest, almost consciousness.

The young man was coming steadily down the slope, balanced like a matador, his hand beneath the unneeded jacket. Aubrey's glance whisked across the knot of hotel staff and guests.

"Get this man—" he began, and then the blond young man was dodging aside to avoid the assault of the ambulance as it blundered onto the hotel drive, tires screeching. Again, he patted Scudamore's arm, mouthed his thanks silently, and then turned away with the aid of his stick toward the doors of the hotel.

He thrust at the earlike wooden handle, then bullied through the doors as if in pursuit of the strength he had already expended. The air conditioning caused perspiration to spring out on his forehead. He glanced back through the tinted windows of the foyer and saw the somehow dead, silent scene outside . . . the Jaguar, the slowing ambulance, the again-crowding circle of guests and staff . . . and the young man, two-dimensional beyond the glass yet clearly menacing.

He—what? His room? He stared around him in alarm. The young man moved through a reduced, shadowy world, the only vivid thing in it. He could hardly distinguish Scudamore being removed from the Jaguar. His room! As if running for a burrow or lair . . . shadows, the hurting, splintered light from the sea and the bobbing shadows of boats, the hotel launches. He fumbled his key into the damp free hand in readiness.

"Mr. Allen!"

Who?

The clerk scurried as if on castors across the foyer toward him. Aubrey flinched.

"Mr. Allen—a telephone call . . . you must answer it, it is most urgent!" Allen? Himself.

"I—I—there's no time, I'm sorry, please excuse me, I do not have—"

"This really is most urgent!" The Chinese clerk's features were prissy with redness. Order was collapsing. "The call is *international!*"

So?

"Please excuse me!"

The clerk clutched his arm. "The caller's name—*please!*" Aubrey stared at the clerk. "The caller's name . . . he was certain you would wish to take the call—your room, you did not—"

Tinted, deadening glass, the German only a few paces from the doors, Scudamore's arms waving feebly in protest as he was slid into the ambulance on a stretcher. No one felt any urgency toward Wei. He shook the arm that held his own.

"The name!"

"Mr. Gardiner—"

"*What?*"

"Mr. Gardiner."

Refusal to believe, utter, surprising relief, a tight thankfulness gripping his chest and making breathing difficult.

"My room—that man, there! Do not give him my room number—transfer the call—my room!" He was uncertain how much of the flurry of his thoughts he had made audible, but the Chinese clerk nodded his acknowledgment and began moving away, satisfied.

Move—his legs were shamefully weak, his heart pattering like that of an alarmed bird. The German was at the doors, peering through them to locate his quarry, someone impatient for a shop to open for business. You must move now, he told himself quite calmly, firmly, and managed a step, then another, leaning heavily on his stick and deliberately not looking behind him. He left the foyer, then hurried, no longer observed, forcing his key into the lock, opening the door of his suite—the phone ringing . . .

It had been Tim, when he had ignored it! The realization seemed vast. Tim, Tim. He snatched up the receiver.

"*Yes?*" he heard his breath force out, his head still spinning.

—Tim alive! The knowledge was like bouts of heat against him, over him. Thank . . . God.

"Kenneth! Surprise, surprise?" Those other telephone calls from Kathmandu while he tried to save Tim's life—the same boyish, high excitement now. Where was he? "Got your number from Pyott—tried every one of your friends, been trying for hours—*got him,* Kenneth, knew you'd be pleased!" There seemed little or no sense, the explanations rushed by him—like his own scattered, flying thoughts. The German, his weak legs, quick breathing—he should not sit down, be taken unawares—glanced at the door again. Tim—was alive. Even that much was hard to realize in a rational way. "Really got him, knew we would—he's not saying anything . . ." The boy's babble soothed now, like a child's excitement bringing a parental warmth of feeling.

"Tim, where are you?"

"What? Oh, didn't I say? Pokhara—rioting here, too. Post Office—he's back in the village. Don't worry, he's safe until you get here. You must come, open him up . . . knows everything, I'm certain—"

"How—how?"

"Alive, you mean?" Gardiner laughed. "Got away—*just!*" Glance at the door, the shadows on the veranda. Listening for a hand on the doorknob. His own danger receded, his caution becoming automatic. "Long story—tell you when you get here—"

"We must meet—"

Tim was safe—he was convinced now. Door and window reasserted themselves, his danger flicked back into his mind. *He* was endangered now, not Tim. Tim was alive and well.

"Don't be ridiculous, Kenneth! You have to come *here!* There isn't much time—the King died two hours ago, they announced it on the radio. It *has* to be the trigger! The King's dead and I've got *Lin*—you have to hurry!"

Door, window . . . a knock? Yes, a knock on the door, the rattling of the doorknob. A louder knocking.

Lin!

"Yes, Tim, at once," he whispered fiercely. "I have to stop talking now—no, don't worry! Yes, immediately!" He put down the telephone softly, unbetrayingly. Snatched up his cases almost without noticing he had gone through to the bedroom. Dragged them at his sides, stick tucked beneath his arm, out onto the veranda and into the humidity's assault. His thoughts were scattered again.

The King of Nepal was dead. Tim was right. It had to be the trigger, as Lin would know. There was little or no time, but he must make the attempt. Banging on the door behind him, then a high, protesting voice, perhaps that of the clerk who had demanded he answer Tim's call. The light and humidity were like a transparent wall into which he blundered down the veranda's three shallow steps onto fine sand and the crunch of small shells. His suitcases were vastly heavy, his stick under his arm awkward, his brow wet and his shirt creeping with sudden moisture.

Slowly, the hotel's launches and crew and the fishermen came out of the running, melting shimmer ahead of him and took on form. He lowered his suitcase and waved his stick to attract attention, then glanced behind him. No one had emerged through the windows of his suite. There was still time—

—no time, the King was dead. Long live—Babbington.

He must try!

A Malay took his suitcase. "I have paid my bill," he primly assured, but the man seemed indifferent. The heat clamped down and the scent of the sea was stale, like that of unwashed, perspired-in clothing. He was helped aboard the small, slim launch, and thought of those the Venetian hotels used . . . and of Brigitte and Kurt and Tim in the same instant.

Then, as the launch's engine caught and roared and the small vessel bucked and moved, he thought solely of Babbington and Lin.

The young German stood on the beach, shading his eyes, attempting to make out whether it was he or a stranger in the launch. The breeze cooled him.

PART THREE

For Kings and Countries

---

*"Had I but serv'd my God with half the
   zeal
I serv'd my King, he would not in mine
   age
Have left me naked to mine enemies"*

Shakespeare: *Henry VIII,* **III, ii.**

13

"There are men steady and wise . . ."

It might have been a broadcasting company's control room reporting some great occasion of state, or a police station's operations room, even to the faces of wanted men and suspects ranged in monochrome along one of its walls. Its stale, metallic scents of electricity and febrile excitement were invigorating rather than enervating—at least to him. Reports jumped and crackled into the room from a dozen sources monitoring the rioting in progress on the streets whole floors above them. Babbington looked at each of the hugely enlarged photographs of members of the King's Council, some recalcitrant senior army officers and policemen, a group of civil servants, some media executives—all of whom would be subject to arrest during the first hours after the Antonovs landed.

He had ordered his aircraft to return to Kathmandu rather than merely signaling Brandis or Brigitte. He hardly admitted the sudden but complete sense of being cut off, of needing to be at the center of things and not thirty-five thousand feet above the deserts of Uzbekhistan . . . and the center was here.

Nevertheless, there was another face on that wall, that of Lin, and he could not avoid being held by its impassive, somehow aloof features and the strangely dead look in the eyes. Below the photograph were maps, colored tape that stretched and climbed like a geometric plant across the wall, pins, written reports. It was a net that Lin had slipped through. He turned decisively away, arms folded across his chest, and surveyed the room. Success sprang out from VDUs, faces, the swiftness of movements, the gabble from receivers. His breathing was easier.

The Nepali Prime Minister was seated with Brandis in one far corner of the long room, ill-at-ease, fidgety. Brandis seemed to be trying to attract his attention with a large, opened map and a tracing forefinger, but the Prime Minister appeared like a plump child in a high chair unwilling to swallow some pap served up to it.

"Russian Embassy . . ." he heard, and smiled. The necessary staged demonstrations and flag-burnings outside the Soviet Embassy, to allay suspicion. "American Embassy, they're over the gates . . ." "Airline offices . . ." Each time the small, fat Nepali twitched—as if harm were being done to him! The room vibrated like an orchestra, he its conductor. "Place is on fire good and proper . . . a couple of dead at least." It was the night after the King's death and the end of the first day of Diwali, the Festival of Lights. No mourning and little ceremonial. Babbington smiled. He knew little about this place, God alone knew that, but even he knew enough to appreciate the irony of Diwali's first day, when crows were honored and fed as the messengers of death. And tomorrow, when they burned the King beside the river not hundreds of yards from where he was now, dogs would be honored as the dead's guardians. And the third day would see lamplighting to the Goddess of Wealth. A great day for gambling, so they claimed. Superbly brutal, the festival's ironies. "The Annapurna Hotel, cars overturned, shops being looted—chaos all along Durbar Marg . . ."

He crossed to Brandis and the Prime Minister, smiling. Shook hands briefly with the Nepali and was aware of the dampness of the man's palm.

"Prime Minister—you have forced our targets to resign?"

"Yes, except for Tamang, who refuses." His brown eyes were apologetic, even fearful, a look that was becoming habitual. "There are people loyal to him—he has his own army bodyguard now; his arrest, when it is time, will be difficult—"

"But not impossible." Babbington's hand was heavy on the Nepali's shoulder. Brandis grinned briefly. "No, you have done well thus far, my friend." His eyes glanced toward a buff folder tagged with a green plastic strip, and Brandis nodded as he handed it to Babbington, who opened it and flicked at its contents before handing it to the Prime Minister; who received the file like a powerful electric shock. "There. The details of the money Tamang received from the British over and above the amount he brought back in compensation, the number of the bank account in Switzerland, everything." Brandis was openly smirking. "You know what to do with the—information?"

"Yes, yes of course," the Nepali replied, swallowing, looking at the folder with something that might have been distaste. He even let it rest on his lap while he wiped his hands on his lapels. "Tomorrow, as soon as the cremation is over, I must announce this discovery on television and give interviews to *Rising Nepal* and the other newspapers. It will be done."

"Then move immediately to arrest our beloved Foreign Minister," Babbington added in a professorial footnote.

"Yes, of course."

"*Regardless* of how many men he has surrounded himself with."

"Yes . . ."

"And the heir to the throne? What news of him?"

"I was granted audience earlier this evening—" It had all the detail and lack of imagination of an extract from a policeman's notebook! "His Majesty desires that order be restored among his people—by whatever means are necessary, including assistance from our *friends* in the world. Those were his words." There almost seemed to be a *sir* on the point of utterance at the completion of any statement the man made. The idea was absurdly pleasing.

"Good, good." The teenager in the Royal Palace was anti-British, mostly because of the Gurkhas and "New Territories." In that sense he was reliable. Anti-Indian, anti-Chinese, anti-British, a bouquet of prejudices that had driven him into their arms like a bride! He had, of course, been promised the moon regarding aid, authority, independence. The young man, hardly more than a boy, chose to believe those promises.

Nepal was in his—their grasp. His fist closed and unclosed behind his back. Only Lin, came the cold thought, could hurt or balk them. Where was he?

"Brandis!" he snapped, beckoning the German away from the Prime Minister. Brandis walked beside him through the thicket of radio reports, clattering keyboards and the babble of excited voices. "What have you from your people in Pokhara? Regarding Lin?" Anxiety hurried his words. "It was your belief that they would take him to Pokhara."

"Yes—and I'm still certain of it." He crossed to a desk and

snatched up a sheaf of reports, scanning them as he returned to Babbington. "They know which village," he murmured. "They've talked to the headman, who knows nothing. They're turning over Pokhara as quickly and thoroughly as they can, given that—"

"Given *nothing!*" Babbington whispered fiercely, leaning close to Brandis. "All this is *for* nothing if Lin is spirited out of Nepal altogether and talks."

"Then go for the operation *now!*" Brandis replied. There seemed a challenge in his features and the bulk and set of his body.

"I can't do that. Lin telling his story afterwards is almost as damaging as his being believed before *Topi's* lights are all on the operations board. Can't you see that, Brandis?"

Brandis shrugged. "For you, maybe—General."

"For *everyone,* Brandis. What we require here is a stable *fait accompli,* not some situation capable of reversion, something seen and castigated as an *invasion,* a situation subject to pressure—the fruit of some *plot!* Those days are over for our services, Brandis—though I sometimes wonder if either you or your general realize it."

"It's your operation."

"Thankfully, yes." He surveyed the room, then added: "We're putting our people in power here, keeping up appearances." He glanced across at the Prime Minister, studying the buff folder's contents like some particularly difficult homework and dabbing his broad, creased brow with a white handkerchief. "Has he," Babbington asked, "sent those placatory cables to Washington, London, Peking, Delhi and all points east and west?"

Brandis nodded. "Yes. I checked that. Everything's going to be all right, order will be established. I gave him the various wordings to use."

"Good." This *was* the center. He had been right to turn the aircraft around and come back—at least for tonight. There was Kapustin to beware of and the Politburo to be humored, thus he could spare only this one night more away from Moscow. "Good . . ." Lin looked down and for a moment was only one face among many.

"Where the hell is he, Brandis?"

"They'll have taken him into the hills above Pokhara, probably. Or he could be in one of those lodges near the lake. Look, General, we'll find him." His face hardened. "All right, we shouldn't have *lost* him in the first place!" he growled in reply to Babbington's unspoken accusation. "Or lost that bastard Gardiner, either—I *admit* it!" Gardiner's face was there, too, but he'd been able to ignore his youth and callowness. "He's stopped running now. We'll get him. He'll get nothing out of Lin, anyway. He's an amateur."

The transcribed, decoded message handed to Babbington by a young man with an ominously apologetic expression caused him to glance down immediately. The salient points shone out like stars.

Wei dead. Aubrey disappeared. Wei's office, home destroyed . . . Triad cover-story. Scudamore in hospital, guarded. Orders required . . .

. . . money, connection with Lin, village, Ipoh . . .

The room seemed vast as a cathedral and breathing difficult. *Aubrey disappeared . . .* He read on. *Launch from hotel . . . Georgetown, Singapore flight!* His chest was tight now because of the rush of realization. Aubrey—flying from Singapore—was coming here! That bloody boy of his must have been in touch, crowing he'd got Lin in the bag and wanting the *great man's* help in opening the reluctant tin! Of course—

"Important?" Brandis asked, puzzled.

"Your bloody general has let that feeble, disgraced old man through her fingers!" Babbington snapped.

He looked sidelong at Brandis, who was already hesitantly loyal. There had been little sparks of rebellion and former loyalty, but the man *knew* who would be credited with *Topi's* success! And he was hungry for Brigitte's job, of that Babbington was certain. So, Brandis could both use and circumvent Brigitte.

He said: "Your general needs to be here. And you, Brandis, may not need your general. Do I make myself clear?"

A moment of pure contempt crossed the right side of Brandis' mouth before calculation removed it. For an instant the eyes glared with dislike mingled with his old loyalties, then the German nodded. Babbington filed the reaction against some possible future value it might possess.

"Yes. You make yourself clear."

"Most importantly, *your* future rests on the single issue of Lin's survival," Babbington all but purred. The room was now an adjunct to his authority. The reports seemed breathless. *Burning . . . looting . . . newspaper office . . . hotel . . . house arrests, petrol bombs, right-wing involvement. Riot, looting, police holding back, army units ineffectual.* He could not prevent a smile. The orchestrator of chaos. "Just make certain of your future, Brandis, by making certain of the futures of our mutual friends, Lin and Aubrey! Do I make myself plain?"

"Oh yes, you do—Comrade General." Brandis' facial muscles had stiffened or been dragooned into acceptance.

"Good."

Riot, burning, looting, bodies, the reports went on with the now incessant chatter of copying machines.

"What?" he suddenly roared. "What was that signal from Pokhara?" He pointed toward the woman seated at the desk where the Pokhara search was being coordinated.

"The Englishman has been sighted, at the main Post Office. Just waiting . . ."

"Brandis!" he shouted at the top of his voice. "Here!" To the woman, he snapped: "Tell them to do nothing—understand? Nothing—just watch him!" Brandis reached Babbington's side. Babbington waved the report in his face. "They've managed, your clodhoppers, to locate Gardiner in Pokhara. Just make sure, would you, Colonel, that they do nothing *final* for the moment, merely keep him in sight!"

Brandis' cheekbones were blotched with red as he did no more than nod before turning away with the woman toward the group dealing with the hunt for Lin.

Aubrey was coming. The boy was waiting for a signal of some kind, otherwise he'd never risk the Post Office or waste time there. Forty-eight hours. He must signal Alma-Ata and the Planning Group in Moscow at once. Two-hour readiness from this moment.

"Orrell has checked into this whole business very thoroughly, Giles, I have to insist on that." Longmead's tones were those of a satisfied cat, a purring insistence. He linked the fingers of both hands in front of him and then placed them as a net behind his head. His jacket fell open on his vest and the fob of his pocket watch. His eyes searched and reassured over his glasses which were pulled down onto the tip of his nose. "Their man—what is his name? Ah, Middleton, yes . . ." He was shuffling through papers on his desk. "Mm, Middleton, that's it—he's very reliable. He's prepared to wager his career on this being nothing but the madcap idea of that rather *unsound* young man, Gardiner." His eyes were engaged only in anticipating agreement.

Lights shone out from the Foreign Office across Downing Street, hazy beyond the Cabinet Office's yellowed net curtains. Pyott felt the intense reality-unreality of the place, the Cabinet Secretary, the conversation. Plausibility wore at his concern like water on a stone.

Longmead continued in his measured, unhurried way: "I have cables here—" His hand indicated the desk then returned to hold the back of his neck comfortably. "—from the Nepalese Prime Minister, and from Tamang, the Foreign Minister—and God knows those two aren't the best of friends! In essence, both cables claim that the situation in the capital is strictly temporary. They seek to *reassure*, Giles—so I don't think *we* need worry, do you?"

Pyott, seated rather formally before Longmead's carefully littered desk, prevented the nod that was an all but automatic response.

Longmead smiled.

"My main concern," he announced wryly, "is which Royals to send out there to the State funeral . . . even though the old boy will be cremated with a rush in the early hours of tomorrow!"

"Geoffrey—" Pyott began, concerned that he could not distinguish between doubt and loyalty in his own mind.

"Yes, Giles?" Longmead sat more upright, then leaned his elbows on his desk, his fingers interlaced once more. A kindly, compassionate marriage-guidance counselor. Pyott resented the man's chameleon-yet-obvious changes of insinuation. The assumption of confederacy—well, he could do nothing about that. They had been in the Guards together just after the war and, though Pyott had never liked Longmead, he was not as quick or peremptory as Kenneth to dismiss the man as a fool. Aubrey had positively *gloated* at Longmead's embarrassments over that ridiculous spy-book case. "What really is your problem, Giles?" the Cabinet Secretary added, smiling.

The trouble was Pyott felt himself drawn with the gentlest inexorability into camaraderie with Longmead. Aubrey became a figure of—of not-quite probity, prone to exaggeration. The brilliant maverick had come to seem, well, little more than eccentric. And he and Longmead had *both* much regretted the disbandment of the Brigade of Gurkhas. Longmead had fought against it at some more-than-minimal risk to his relationship with MoD and the PM.

Finally, he and Longmead were bound together as inheritors of a similar sense of honor and tradition, one which Kenneth had never fully shared and had often flouted, even ridiculed. And yet he was here, pleading Kenneth's case, concerned for Nepal, suspicious of plots and plans.

He said with some embarrassment: "Are you *certain*, Geoffrey? I mean, is there room for doubt?" He, too, was leaning forward now. To anyone else, they would have appeared like conspirators whispering in a Club smoking room.

Longmead shook his head. "I'm not *certain*, Giles." His glance as he adjusted his glasses and they flashed back light from the ceiling was almost amused, mildly remonstrative. "What real evidence for this nonsense is there, Giles—ask yourself that question, my dear fellow!"

Pyott shifted uncomfortably in his chair. *He* had asked for this meeting, *he* had come there troubled, alarmed by the parallels between Timothy Gardiner's wild story and the mounting disorder in Kathmandu. Prompted, even goaded into this conversation by the boy's excited telephone call, his desperate urgency to locate Kenneth. It was as if he, too, had contracted the illness. Nurse Longmead had cooled his fevered brow!

"I—" He spread his hands. "Geoffrey, I believe in Kenneth!" And there you have it, he thought with a small ache of betrayal. Believe *in*, not necessarily believe . . .

"All of us do," Longmead purred. "Cleverer than so many of us. Streets ahead of most of us in matters like intuition, smelling a rat, making connections." It was hollow praise, almost contempt. The hands indicated the desk and the papers and the trays and files. Work, they suggested. Logic, application, detail, a wearisome attention to facts. Real, solid virtues, unlike those Aubrey possessed. Pyott felt himself all but mesmerized by power, by the activity that murmured beyond the walls of the office, the occasional interruptions of aides and assistants. He was less and less able to credit the theory of a man who was already no more than a memory there. "Dear Kenneth, still so—what? Impetuous, I suppose?"

"This business of the Chinese—Lin?" Pyott persisted with the sudden energy of a drowning man.

Longmead shook his head. "Ah, I anticipated you there, Giles—after your telephone call. Again, Orrell assures me—really *assures* me—that there is absolutely nothing to it. Colonel Lin's connections with Andrew Babbington are the merest accident. And all very right and proper at the time. No, I'm afraid there's no comfort for Kenneth in starting that particular hare." He took his watch from his vest and studied it for a moment.

Anticipating his dismissal, Pyott prompted almost in desperation: "I wish you'd look into this, Geoffrey—" He broke off at the quick glare in Longmead's eyes.

"Giles, I am sickened unto *death* by our precious intelligence and security services!" He cleared his throat, his tone only temporarily becoming more equable. "At least with some of them. For *them,* the conspiracy theory of history is no more than a starting post! Kenneth Aubrey is a disappointed, *bitter* man. Just remember that, Giles. The PM and HMG have been reassured that the King's death over there will have a calming effect. Order will be restored. As to this *ludicrous* theory regarding Colonel Lin, I wonder you, of all people, Giles, could give it even a moment's credence! Have you thought at all about your own position, should your support of such a wild theory become—more widely known?" There was no trace of threat in the tone, but the words were enunciated with stonelike clarity.

"I see," Pyott murmured, rubbing his mustache.

"No, you don't see, Giles. Your loyalty to Aubrey is well known—as is your intelligence. I'm only suggesting you use the latter to examine the former." Longmead sighed. "I'm afraid you must excuse me, Giles. I'm having to work on this damnable arms limitation treaty they're mauling in Geneva. Endless digests for the PM, expert testimony, you know the kind of thing." He stood up with a convincing display of reluctance. The burdens of high office seemed to cause him to stoop. "Well—" he held out his hand—"I appreciate your concern, Giles. Quite understandable. We'll meet again soon—oh, at the defense budget review session next week, surely?"

He had come around his desk, his hand was on Pyott's shoulder, steering the tall soldier toward the door.

"Goodbye, Giles—so glad we could have this little chat."

Pyott walked the familiar corridors toward the Cabinet Office's Whitehall entrance slightly bemused, strangely reassured. Longmead had simply shone a bright light on his bogies, revealing them to be merely children in Halloween masks and white sheets. Kenneth—it was impossible to avoid the thought now— was simply getting old.

He buttoned his greatcoat and strode out down Whitehall toward his club. If Kenneth got in touch, if there was fresh evidence—solid fact, not mere theory—then he would press to see Longmead again and argue the case as best he might. But now he remembered vividly Tim Gardiner's wild excitement over the telephone, his delight in mystery, his sulking refusal to inform and his desperation to get hold of Kenneth . . . who had similarly rushed off into the blue, it had to be admitted.

It all had to be discounted. Pyott nodded to confirm his decision. Unless he came back with proof of something.

He smelled the river, dust and the exhausts of cars. Strangely, the scents whetted his appetite and he increased his pace, his umbrella striding jauntily beside him.

He scurried like a mouse through the sudden, oppressive heat and humidity of the Delhi night which was alive with new, strange smells and noises. The concrete of the airport apron, with the terminal lights gleaming onto the rapidly vanishing wetness of an evening shower, smelled headily of fuel. His eyes darted in examination of the deeper shadows, looking for Ganesh. Tim's plan . . . *there's rioting in Pokhara now, and they must know you'll come . . . you can't land at Kathmandu—Ganesh's plane, Delhi . . .* yes, Tim. But he could not distinguish Ganesh from the mechanics and stewards and loungers and even what might have been beggars and homeless.

A hand grabbed the sleeve of his jacket and he tried . o move his stick in defense. *Come,* he saw clearly mouthed, *Mister Allen.* They turned aside in the shadows beneath the portico of the entrance and he was hurried—Ganesh making no attempt to take his bags or make allowance for his struggle with them and his stick—down narrow alleyways, past numbered glass doors, illuminated signs. Then long lines of sheds and hangars with light spilling from them and the whalelike shadows of parked aircraft. He almost stumbled over a sleeping form wrapped in dingy white cloth—like a discarded bale of damaged cotton—in one of the alleyways where the smells of the place increased and oppressed.

Haste had enlarged his indecision, his lack of control of his circumstances. There were light aircraft dotted about the concrete, the pervasive smell of aviation fuel, the rumble of cargo and commissary trucks, the swifter passage of bright yellow baggage carts. Cardboard boxes leaned against the sides of hangars, figures lay or murmured or moved in the shadows. There was a silence in which someone coughed rackingly, again and again.

His own breathing was harsh and Ganesh, studying him with
what might have been a detached kind of disappointment, took
his briefcase and cabin bag.

"I have made no promises regarding my abilities!" Aubrey
snapped, regaining his breath but leaning heavily on his stick.
"Now, where is this aircraft of yours?"

To his surprise, Ganesh smiled and nodded. "Over there," he
said, pointing.

"Then, shall we go?"

It was, at least, the illusion of control, and must suffice for
the present. It veiled his sense of himself as a scurrying, heedless
mouse. Brigitte would know where he was gone. Either that or
Babbington would order her to follow him, knowing *exactly* his
destination. Brandis must be mounting a desperate, thorough
search for the kidnapped Lin. It would be a gathering of wildcats; *all* the wildcats, waiting for him. For the present, they'd
eaten all the rats in Europe's dilapidated warehouse and now
the pickings were in Nepal.

"Well, let's get on, shall we? There's little or no time to
waste!" His waspish, snappy little detonations continued to
soothe him.

"Here," Ganesh announced with evident impatience at the
old man. "Be careful how you climb in, at your age." His English, Aubrey realized, was fluent enough for sarcasm.

Ganesh flung the briefcase and bag into the tiny cargo space
and slammed the panel shut and locked it. Then he held Aubrey's arm, having climbed onto the wing, and shoved him into
the narrow, coffinlike cockpit of the Cessna. Ganesh jumped
down and began inspecting the belly of the aircraft, then lowered
himself into the cockpit, strapping himself in and indicating that
Aubrey do the same. Ganesh looked at his watch, his map, then
tuned the radio to air traffic control's frequency. He slammed
the cockpit hood shut over their heads, and masked the stars
with the Perspex.

"I bribed a few people," Ganesh remarked casually, "to look
the other way." It was as if he expected Aubrey to reimburse
him immediately. Aubrey ignored the remark and Ganesh
turned his vocal attentions to air traffic control. Reference to
his flight plan, his slot time, permission to start his engines. The
noise deafened, making the whole aircraft rattle and shudder;
he felt genuinely insecure as the Cessna began to taxi slowly
away from the cargo terminal.

White face through the murky cockpit Perspex. White face. He turned his head, straining to be certain . . . *there,* where the irregular row of lights marked that tiny, appalling suburb of the airport—a figure stepping out into more light. A European, with an Indian beside him pointing toward the Cessna. The bribes had not been sufficiently generous.

His stomach plucked. All the wildcats, he recollected. No longer a fanciful image. Babbington's authority, Brandis' skills, Brigitte's hatred, all of it focused on him. He wished, suddenly and intensely, that Tim had agreed to try to get Lin out of Nepal. He'd argued with the boy during at least two of their telephone conversations before his flight—from Georgetown, KL, then Singapore. *Use the Gurkhas to smuggle him out . . . no, he's safe here, well hidden!*

All Tim's resistance now meant that he was rushing headlong toward those dangerous, hungry cats.

The runway lights sprang out ahead of them in a diminishing perspective. Aubrey shivered.

The stillness was that of an aftermath, as if their occupation of the country had already been accomplished. Smoke from dozens of small fires smudged the pale dawn sky above Kathmandu. The body of a dog floated on the brown surface of the river. There was the litter of the rioting, too, drifting past the embassy on the Bagmati: boxes, a shattered, scorched window frame, spars of wood, spread, dull cloth, and two male corpses in sodden white. Patan's roofs on the other side of the river were haloed with the first touch of the sun. Brandis, leaning on the sill of the open window, smelled fire and rot and freshness, and sensed the electricity charging the whole scene. It was no more than a strange pause in an unremitting, violent contest.

He breathed slowly, deeply, his attention focused on the small, somberly dressed group assembled on the riverbank below him, at the bottom of a flight of stone steps. The only color in the scene, which was as still as an etching against the waters now turning gray, was the robes of the priests. He saw the sleek head of the Prime Minister and other members of the King's Council; the chief of police, a few senior army officers. And the widowed Queen.

The pyre was untidy with straw and kindling, the body on its bamboo platform wrapped in white, its face thin, wasted, calm. There were no spectators along either bank, only army units, as if the city were deserted or struck by plague. It was easy to imagine Russian military vehicles trundling through the place.

Brandis was tired, his temples thudded with a dull headache. He felt crumpled and soiled like his clothes, and he had not shaved. Gardiner was under surveillance. His telephone calls must be to Aubrey. He had to be allowed to move, free for the present, because there was no trace of Lin. And if Aubrey was coming then he, too, must go into the bag. Brigitte was en route. Brandis rubbed his cheeks with both hands as if washing. Brigitte—was a problem. He did not wish to stand in her shadow, not now that Babbington had effectively indicated her —*temporariness*. He wanted to move against Gardiner immediately, but Aubrey was the prize that would ensure his succession to his general's office.

He sighed. His respect, even affection for the old woman was undiminished and he envied the unsentimentality of animals fighting to lead their pack, even though he knew that Brigitte was a broken reed since her son's death—

—death. The young, new, pliable boy-King walked around his father's body three times, carrying in front of him the butter lamp to be placed on the dead man's face. The priests, Hindu and Buddhist, went about their business with what might have been awe. The Queen stood between her Prime Minister and Tamang, who seemed to be studying the small events preceding the cremation as intently as if reading omens. The cremation *ghat,* the flat area at the foot of the flight of steps, was crowded, silent. It might have been the funeral of an executed criminal for all its lack of pomp, rather than the ritual surrounding the death of a King-deity.

. . . wish that he be cremated in the manner of the humblest among his people . . . on the banks of the Bagmati with only his family to mourn him . . . The King's daughters, his younger son, and the few politicians and senior officers who had elbowed their way in, Brandis observed mockingly. Otherwise, the King's wishes had been obeyed, people had abided by the instructions contained in the Queen's television and radio message. The boy-King placed the butter lamp on his father's wasted face. Something in the ritual troubled Brandis like an insect sting *. . . asks that he be allowed to slip away from this life as our lord Siddhartha stole away from his palace and his concubines at night, in the disguise of a beggar . . .*

Brandis folded his arms. Very pretty, very Buddhist. His attention concentrated on the reality of the scene below, the new King. His features seemed to betray impatience, even disapproval. Of course, there would be countless memorial celebrations and rituals before the coronation. Two visits for royals and heads of state and foreign ministers. If they came, of course, with *friendly Soviet forces* still on the streets, maintaining order. Brandis chuckled softly. And yet there *was* something in that simplicity below him that caused discomfort.

The flare of torches, the sudden, quick crackling of dry straw and kindling. A shiver and backward step shared by everyone crowded onto the *ghat.* They wouldn't, of course, shave the young King's head or that of the Queen, nor would either of them bathe in the river in an act of purification. But there was enough to satisfy the dead King about the manner of his departure. The flames spread and licked up about the shroud. The heat haze smeared across the river and the temples of Patan, making them seem insubstantial.

The Prime Minister—good move—dipped a bowl into the Bagmati's brown-gray water and offered it to the boy-King, who ritually washed his hands, as his mother did immediately after. Tamang's features, in profile, seemed intent, even disdainful. A lock of hair was cut from the boy's head by a saffron-robed Buddhist, then from the Queen's dark hair. Satisfying the ritual. The fire, catching hold of flesh, burned blue and flared up greedily. The smoke above it darkened. Patan shimmered behind the heat.

Babbington, he knew, wanted Aubrey almost as much as Nepal, though he had never said as much. Brigitte wanted revenge, too. But Aubrey's head had to go to Babbington on a plate. The darkened smoke roiled and quivered like something alive as the King's spirit joined Yama, the god of death, merging with the divine.

Brandis felt obscurely threatened by the smoke. There was no nauseating smell in it yet, but a breeze pushed it insistently toward his window. Abruptly, he shut out the scene, even lowering his blind so that the first sunlight spilling across the sill became striped on the carpet. He moved across the room, arms folded, his chin cupped in one hand.

More people on the airport here—*and* people at Pokhara? Gardiner was there and had made no move . . . but, Brandis admitted, he might know he was under surveillance. In which case Aubrey *would* come through Kathmandu. They hadn't been able to tap into Gardiner's calls from the Post Office, not in time.

Just to be certain, increase the surveillance on Gardiner. He *had* to meet with Aubrey and take him to Lin. He looked at his watch. Brigitte's flight was due in before noon. Better meet her with due ceremony and a full report. The untidy, tired old woman appeared at the edge of his thoughts like an infirm relative for whom he was responsible, but he dismissed the silly thrust of sympathy that accompanied her. He glanced toward the slatted window. He could just make out the dark, bluish smoke, spreading out in a small, flat cloud as if there had been an explosion of chemicals down on the riverbank.

He kept the binoculars Ganesh had thrust into his hands trained on the terminal building and the perimeter fence of Pokhara's small airport; otherwise, they would enlarge the vast mountain peaks even further and already they were almost appalling in their size and beauty. They caused his sense of danger to recede and diminished the curious amalgam of tension and exhilaration he had felt as they had begun to descend toward Pokhara. Perhaps it had been when the Cessna dropped below the peaks that he had really noticed them, felt them hurry toward the tiny plane as, fragile and wobbling, it touched down. The Himalayas seemed about to swallow them.

Then Ganesh had thrust the binoculars against his chest almost angrily, as if blaming Aubrey for his situation. *They shouldn't be there, but make sure.* His heart thudded noisily and his mouth was dry and tasted stale. Ganesh and the radio gabbled at each other. His eyes pricked with tiredness and he constantly had to blink or strain them wide to keep the terminal, the tower and the perimeter fence in focus. The glasses felt heavy, his wrists fragile. Who was he looking for—were all Germans blond, all white faces those of Russians or East Germans? Ridiculous. They could be here, he reminded himself, armed with a description of the aircraft and its pilot and passenger. That white face in the darkness, watching, oblivious of the heat, his attention fixed and held by the Cessna as they had left Delhi.

Ganesh and the tower made their courteous, international farewells and the Cessna began to taxi. Aubrey's glasses swiveled, slid across mostly brown faces, mostly airport vehicles, overalls, uniforms, bodies at expected business.

Then Ganesh said: "Up ahead."

Aubrey turned, and a straggling group of huts jumped into enlargement; fuel pumps and an old Land-Rover, an untidy row of light aircraft, an ancient American car, boxes and fuel drums. A disheveled, narrow-faced unshaven boy was slumped over the wheel of the Land-Rover. Aubrey slid the glasses past the young man, then jolted them back. *Tim!*

Tim's altered, worn, concentratedly angry features completed Aubrey's sense of being trapped. He felt old and weary and afraid, and this angry young man now staring at the approaching Cessna wanted something of him he had no idea how to give. He had to break Lin, get him out, back to London, make those who must, listen. He doubted he could do it.

Then Tim waved, standing up in the vehicle as the Cessna drew alongside it. He was grinning. The binoculars were damp in Aubrey's grip as Ganesh thrust back the cockpit hood. The air was cool against his hot cheeks. He stood up very gingerly, gripping the cockpit edge, heaving himself awkwardly out onto the wing—

—to see the grin on Tim's face fade, become darkened as if a light had been switched off. His eyes had hardened. They stood confronting one another, Tim squinting up at him, his disappointment and doubts as evident as if he had spoken them. Aubrey quailed momentarily, and then was angry. Deeply angry. Faced with his tiredness, the challenge presented by Lin, he found Tim thinking ill of him. He felt an unreasonable and self-justifying heat well into his chest.

"You need not judge me entirely by my present appearance!" he snapped. Tim's eyes were shielded by a hand raised across his brow as he stared into the sun. His lips, however, narrowed. "You're not exactly elegantly turned out yourself!" There was bruising half-hidden by the stubble of beard and swollen flesh on his jaw and near his mouth. Aubrey sensed Tim's recent experience and something attempted to elbow his anger aside. But he was too ruffled to allow it to do so.

Tim's hand was firm as he helped him down from the wing. Ganesh slammed the cockpit cover shut and locked it, then jumped down beside them. His presence interrupted nothing; rather, to Aubrey, it seemed to provoke further distance. And an awkward silence. Tim seemed older and Aubrey felt the patronage experienced by someone in his dotage at the hands of a healthy adult. Tim's disappointment refused to clear from his features. God alone knew what hopes he had built up.

"You had a good flight?"

"Thank you. Just a little tired."

"Too much running around in Malaya?"

"They almost prevented me from getting here," he blurted. "Your call was—at the very last moment. They were *there*, Tim!"

Tim rubbed his forehead as if puzzled or embarrassed. Then he said: "They don't seem to like either of us very much, do they?" And grinned self-consciously.

Then he gripped Aubrey by the shoulders, embracing him roughly, squeezing his arms tight against his sides; disconcerting the old man, affecting his breathing.

"Thank God you're here!" Tim said gruffly, releasing him. Tim was one of the few he had ever permitted to really touch him, he realized. His cheeks felt hotter than the day provoked.

"You've got him safe?"

Tim nodded. "Oh, yes, he's safe enough. I was spotted at the Post Office, of course, calling you, but I gave them the slip, I'm sure. There'll be someone here, no doubt. I think we should—"

"Yes," Aubrey replied eagerly. "Has he talked at all?"

"Not a word. He doesn't even ask for food—I've left him for you."

"Exactly right. Very well, let's be on our way."

He moved, stumbled slightly—weariness or relief that there were no barriers between himself and Tim—and the young man's hand at once held his weight, righted him. Tim's gaze assessed for a moment, then he smiled disarmingly.

"It's up to you now, Kenneth," he murmured.

"Yes," he replied. As he climbed into the Land-Rover and Ganesh swung his weight easily up behind him, he realized he was no longer perturbed at coming hours and events. Challenged, yes . . . exhilarated. He wanted movement and bustle now. He rubbed his eyes as Tim started the engine and turned the Land-Rover.

"Anyone taking a special interest, Gan?"

"Can't see anyone."

"We'll take the scenic route and find out." Tim was almost blithe. Dust coated Aubrey's sleeve as it rested on the doorsill.

"Hasn't he said *anything?*"

"Who, Lin?" Tim shook his head. "Silent as the tomb. But he *knows!*"

There were little columns of smoke over Pokhara.

"There's trouble here?"

"Some rioting and looting, a lot of agitation."

They drove through the gate in the perimeter fence and turned north toward the town and the lake. The hot air rushed against Aubrey's face and he squinted because of the dust.

Tim turned to look at him. "The King's dead—why are they waiting?"

"Because you have Lin—and because of you, and myself." He glanced around him with renewed caution, slipping easily into a practiced, habitual cast of thought and behavior. "If they had him back, ourselves too, then they would go ahead. Really, we should get him out, away from here altogether," Aubrey said with an effort.

"It's too difficult now!" The Land-Rover bucked over a rise and dipped its nose toward the gleam of the lake. They began passing straggling lodges, small bungalows and hotels. Hikers in boots, stooping beneath backpacks. Beggars. "While we keep him here, he's safer. I know this area better than they do, we've got people who will help here." He stared at Aubrey, who eventually conceded with a curt nod.

"Tell me about him," he said, gripping the dashboard and the doorsill firmly, his old body shaken by the road's potholes and deep ruts. The lake looked hot like some huge recently cast metal plate. The air was hazy, the mountains had become indistinct. Aubrey leaned toward Tim, listening intently.

They skirted the lake, unfollowed, and climbed into the hills beyond its shore. The sun made Aubrey feel welded to the hard seat. Lin remained at an indefinable distance as Tim talked, even when he described his own discoveries in Penang and Ipoh. Maddeningly, the Chinese remained without substance. They passed through the village. Men waved at Tim and Ganesh, stared at himself. In only a few more minutes they slowed beside what might have been two barns. Two Nepalis in shorts and army pullovers and carrying guns squatted beside the door of the smaller building. The handbrake rasped on.

The two Gurkhas saluted Tim and seemed at once to inspect Aubrey as he clambered awkwardly out of the Land-Rover. He brushed dust in a fine cloud from his suit, slapped his hat against his leg then replaced it after wiping his grimy brow.

"Do you want to wash—a drink?"

"Some water—and something for Lin. Food, too—we'll share

something, I think." He ignored the mountains now, as if he were moving along a familiar corridor to a known room.

"OK. Corporal, any reports?"

"There are more people joining the search, Captain Timothy. No one has come asking questions here yet. My men have as many as possible under observation."

"OK, get on the radio and get me an update." He squinted at the sun. "Midday, Kenneth. Do you want to start now?"

"Yes," Aubrey replied, breathing deeply and straightening his stance, even adjusting his tie and grimy collar.

"I'll arrange some lunch, in that case."

He arranged Lin in his mind as if his hands were tidying a file on his desk, then walked steadily toward the door of the smaller hut. The armed Gurkha watched him with intent, dark eyes. He paused, then opened the door.

As he closed it behind him, the room seemed dark, close, very hot. Light came through one small window which was heavily shuttered and a few cracks in the wooden walls and the tiles on the roof. Lin occupied a tiny corner of the room, as if concealing himself. As his eyes grew accustomed to the gloom, Aubrey saw highlights from copper utensils, a narrow bed, rickety chairs and a plain wooden table. An unlit lamp on the table. Lin seemed abstracted, hardly curious, as if his were the eyes having to accustom themselves to the lack of light.

"Colonel Lin Yu-Chiang?" Aubrey asked, then continued: "My name is Aubrey—which you may already know. I'm sorry to find you in this situation, but you probably understand very well the necessity for your confinement." There was a clean white bandage plastered to the top of Lin's head. Aubrey approached the table, drew out one of the hard chairs and sat down facing Lin, his hands clasping each other on top of his walking stick. He smiled benignly. "I'm here, of course, to ask you some questions," he announced almost breezily. "You understand their urgency, I'm certain."

"I have been brought here by force," the Chinese announced slowly, his body remaining still, his hands folded in his lap. "I have diplomatic status in Nepal. As you are no doubt aware." His tone seemed expressionless and yet at the same moment mocking. There was a statuelike self-possession about the man. Aubrey's lips twitched as at the racing of a clock.

"I doubt that, Colonel. Oh, of course you *had* such status, I agree. But I think you would be disowned by your embassy

the moment they came into possession of certain information."
He continued to smile. "Like your close and long relationship
with Andrew Babbington?"

"That acquaintance is well known. It was necessary in my duties."

"Ah, your duties. Such as those during the Malayan Emergency, I presume you mean?" Aubrey's smile was brilliant. Did
the man's eyes gleam out quickly, just for a moment? Aubrey
felt refreshed, employed to purpose. "I'm certain you take my
meaning."

The door of the hut opened. Lin's cheeks seemed to flinch as
his eyes switched their focus to Tim, who carried a wooden tray.
The smell of spicy food and rice, the gleam of water in a pitcher.
Two smeared glasses. Tim grinned at Lin, then at Aubrey.

"Thank you, Tim, that will be fine." Tim's inquiring glance
went unanswered and he left, closing the door behind him. The
room seemed cooler now that the hot light from outside was filtered again by the cracks and the shutter. "Lunch, Colonel?
Some water?" Aubrey filled a glass and bent forward, setting
it down in front of Lin. Then he filled a bowl with rice and some
kind of hot-smelling stew which made his stomach wake and
grumble. Lin ignored the food and water. Aubrey filled his bowl
and ate, his posture relaxed, his expression bland. "Really very
good, if a little overspiced—mm?" He seemed to become absorbed by his eating. He sipped delicately at his glass of cool
water, indifferent to its effects on his unacclimatized stomach.
As he ate, he threw off remarks in Lin's direction.

"Malaya. Thirty years ago . . . Heavens—that long? You were
an associate of Andrew Babbington even then, Colonel. White
five-pound notes, I believe." His eyes watched Lin in little, sharp
birdlike glances as he ate. Eventually, the Chinese picked up the
flat spoon and began eating, the bowl and his actions now a mask
against any expression on his face. Urgency gripped Aubrey and
he wrestled with it. "Poor young man who was blamed. Ah,
well, the price of Andrew Babbington's acquaintance so often,
of course . . . as with you, here, *now* . . . splendid food, mm?"
He smiled. "It took some digging out, of course, but we managed
to unearth it, all that ancient history." He waved the hand holding the spoon. "Ipoh, Penang—Sidney Wei." The silence buzzed
with flies, his arm as it leaned on the table made the surface of
the water in his glass quiver in a reflection of his tense imitation
of calm. "Now," he announced carefully, "Sidney Wei—did you

know him under that Anglicized name? I doubt it. Sidney Wei was communicative—*is* so still, and prepared to assist."

He looked up from his empty bowl and the glass with its now calm water to find Lin's eyes glaring, his face not quite masked. Reflections chased one another. Lin had been incommunicado since before Wei died. Wei alive was a real, solid threat to his thirty-year treachery.

"I knew him as that, yes," Lin admitted. "It is the only thing I have so far understood, Mr. Aubrey—but yes, I do understand the name."

"And what it means? That he *remembers,* Colonel. He *knows.*"

Aubrey drew a crumpled packet of cigarettes from his pocket and offered one to Lin, who disdainfully refused. Aubrey lit a cigarette, drew heavily, and smoke rolled across the low ceiling and around beams as he exhaled.

"Remembers? Knows? I do not understand you."

The room seemed filled with the stifling midday heat, yet Aubrey's equilibrium endured despite the temperature. Lin appeared like a carved figure: no hairline cracks in the surface composure, that Buddha-like squat. Aubrey flexed his fingers on the edge of the table, ignoring the hurry of the clock that had begun ticking in his head the moment he had closed the door of the hut behind him.

"He remembers many things, Colonel. Your arrest, your escape—your return burdened with money. All of which he is prepared to speak of—to whoever will listen."

Lin looked up as if a hand held beneath his chin had forced him to do so. "Why is all this of such importance to you, Mister Aubrey?"

Aubrey studied the tip of his cigarette and without looking at Lin, murmured so that the Chinese had to tilt forward to hear him: "Important to you, I should have thought. Not exactly in your contract of employment with the MPT or whatever it was designated in those dim and distant days, mm?"

"I doubt if such—" Lin stopped himself.

"But it would not be good news in Beijing, I strongly suspect."

"I suspect bluff, Mister Aubrey. And urgency. Your situation is . . . temporary."

"After which, you feel, none of this will matter?" Aubrey remembered news items relayed by Ganesh and Tim—riots, looting, the army hardly apparent on the streets, the police slow,

just spectators. "Perhaps not, but I'm really interested in your—
seduction by Andrew Babbington, Colonel. I have a consuming
interest in everything concerned with Andrew. It does seem
rather *tawdry,* wouldn't you say?" Lin's cheek had the momentary appearance of having been slapped hard. His eyes narrowed
but their betrayal was minimal. He was still not drawn into the
play. Tim had left Lin in the dark, no one had spoken to him
even though he had been fed, given water. Bandaged, too. He
had been made a prisoner, his capture evident and inescapable.
But he had not even begun to inwardly collapse. The clock hurried once more in Aubrey's head. "Wouldn't you agree? Tawdry?" he prompted.

Lin simply shook his head, a minimal gesture. Aubrey felt the
man retreat, felt Lin's inward clock hurrying, too. Temporary,
he had said.

Aubrey shook off a wave of tiredness and the gritty sensation
behind his eyes, and drawled: "And the woman? Our mutual
friend, Brigitte?" Lin looked up quickly. "Ah, I see the name
means something to you even after all this time!" He leaned forward on his chair. The heat stifled. "Look, Colonel, I shall put
all my cards on the table. I admit to not knowing what will happen here—yes, I must do that, but what I do know—and can
prove—is that you were *bought* thirty years ago. You betrayed
your service and your people for money. And I can also prove
that you and Babbington and the woman met in Penang last year
to plan whatever it is you intend should happen here. All of the
information will be made public, or will be withheld, dependent
upon your cooperation or otherwise. Could I be plainer?"

The silence seemed to squeeze at him, constricting his chest,
while the heat broke against his exposed skin in little, fiery
waves. Lin studied his hands in his lap. Aubrey forced himself
to remain impassive.

Why did he feel Lin looked like a man clinging to the edge
of something by only his fingernails and yet hardly moved by
the experience? He was *affected* by the degree of Aubrey's
knowledge, and yet *unmoved* by it. All that information—
Standish, Babbington, Wei—was as silly and irrelevant to Lin
as an outmoded manner of dress. Lin must be frightened, he
knew he was alone, in danger, he must believe Aubrey had
proof . . .

And yet, none of it touched him.

Then Lin said quietly: "You could not speak more plainly,

Mister Aubrey. However, it does not matter, not at all. None of it."

Aubrey waited, but Lin merely stared past him, over his shoulder toward the slatted, hot light coming through the shutter—as if slowly blinding himself. Aubrey studied Lin's impassive features. And his peculiarly dead eyes. It was early—it ought to be too early to make any kind of judgment in an interrogation. Nevertheless, he was convinced of his intuition. It *didn't* matter to Lin. It really didn't matter, any of it. He was somehow already defeated and therefore beyond threat.

And as a result, he couldn't be broken . . .

14

A More Than Secret Life

You were always a plain, dull woman . . . Not Kurt's voice, though with something of his dismissive tone. No, it was her husband's memory upbraiding her, quite out of time and place . . .

. . . or was he? His mockery must have been evoked by something she sensed about Brandis, something more closed and wary. Perhaps the small shock of mistrusting Brandis had reminded her of her husband. She sensed herself evaded, circumvented, and Aubrey's proximity rubbed like nettles against her hard, wrinkled skin; his unknown whereabouts thudding like a migraine.

"The boy is here, but you lost him," she accused Brandis. His eyes flashed momentarily, but recognized her tone. Good. He was still afraid of her and therefore capable of being subdued, whatever promises Babbington might have made him. "*Where* is Aubrey, Gerd?" she persisted, almost mocking him. "That is, you *are* assuming Aubrey is here, together with the boy?" She waited, her face half-turned to where the police station's windows looked out toward Pokhara's dam and the swollen stretch of lake beyond it. Pieter would be watching Gerd's features for her.

She snapped her glance back at Brandis, who hesitated only for a second before nodding.

"Aubrey's here. I'm certain of it."

"Not staking your reputation on it, Gerd?" she goaded.

His eyes narrowed. He was weighing her against Babbington. Her proximity appeared decisive.

"If you like, I'll stake my life on it, General."

"That shouldn't be necessary."

The fan suspended from the ceiling moved the flies about the room a little less lazily than under their own efforts. She felt hot and drained. They had the remainder of that day and the first half of the night to find Aubrey and Lin and—

—eliminate them. Babbington's inference to her was clear. No doubt it had been a direct order to Brandis. Get rid of the inconvenient Chinaman. Until midnight . . . after that, the rioting and killing would have gone out of control—into meltdown. The aircraft must come tonight or perhaps not at all. Tomorrow, other countries would become concerned, even involved; other groups might rally.

She felt the operation's urgency as her own. It prickled on her skin, however much she regarded the still lake. "Somewhere in the area yet to be searched," she murmured. The maps pinned to the walls were colored with a hurriedly shaded red, indicating the creeping advance of the sweep search. Police and army units, even helicopters, under their control—

—*her* control.

You're a survivor, Brigitte, I'll grant you that . . . Her husband's voice. To distract herself, she tried to snatch at the peace suggested by the lake; she did not succeed, because Aubrey and her father crowded behind her feckless, handsome, ex-Nazi husband. Perhaps it was Gerd's shift of loyalties? The stain on the maps was slipping upward with a thorough capillary action along both shores of the lake toward the villages and hills beyond the town—where she was certain Aubrey would be. The lake held no peace for her. She could see only its further shore, and Aubrey and Lin.

Aubrey's bald spot as she looked down from the train window while he talked with a German officer . . . Lin in Malaya, his strangely inexpressive face above hers as they copulated. Her husband's dismissive smile; Kurt's dismissive shrugs and smiles. *You'll always do well,* Winterbach had said to her once, when her career had been threatened by an upheaval and she might have been swept aside or away. *You've got the face for it.* Her Jewishness, her present aging self had begun to show by then. Her husband's verbal cruelty had increased to match the decline of her features into somber plainness.

Brigitte shook her head. Winterbach disappeared with a mocking smile, but Aubrey and Lin remained, though more shadowy. Aubrey had saved her life, Lin had been her lover.

They both had to be eliminated before midnight, and she felt nothing but a vestigial conscience over the matter. *You'll always do well.* At least on this occasion, she would. Especially if she dwelled on images of her screams as her father lay shot in the snow, the tire-stained, ridged slush slowly leaking into redness, as bright a red as the stripes on the pole that marked the crossing point into the Russian Sector of Berlin. Aubrey had begun running toward her but she had fled until she collided with the rough material of a Russian greatcoat. Someone had held her as she screamed and sobbed. Aubrey had knelt by her father's body.

She turned away from the lake. A grille pattern placed over one of the maps revealed the crisscrossing flight of one of the two Puma helicopters. She rubbed her forehead. Brandis' face was anticipatory, even submissive. "What do you know about the boy, this Gardiner?"

"I don't—"

"He has friends here, evidently—among the natives." She glanced around the office at the Nepali policemen and soldiers, manning radios, studying maps. Then up again at Brandis, her features contracted and waspish. "*Where,* exactly?" She crossed to the largest, most-reddened of the maps on the walls and began tapping it with a stubby, rigid forefinger, as if poking a subordinate's chest to emphasize her displeasure. "In which of these villages? Which one? He has gone to earth, but where, Gerd? You should *know!*" Brandis' face was inexpressive.

She studied the map. Name after unpronounceable name, dozens of tiny villages. She took her wire-rimmed spectacles from their case and leaned toward the map, squinting, her mouth pouting angrily. Brandis remained silent. She clicked her fingers—there was a degree of pleasure in doing so—and waved him impatiently to her side. She jabbed the map. "Move them north of the lake, Gerd. All of them, and the helicopters. *Everyone.* He must be in one of the villages, and there are more than a dozen of them." She sensed the daylight beginning to ebb. For the first time, she looked at Brandis, and saw a common urgency bind them, at least temporarily. "Aubrey is in one of these villages, and Lin is with him. We don't have any time to waste. Give the orders, Gerd."

He merely nodded. "Hurry it up!" she added to his retreating back. His shoulders flinched infinitesimally, in front of the natives whose heads at once returned to maps and dials and graphs.

Watching his cropped gray head and wide shoulders slip obediently across the room, she felt she controlled the situation. Aubrey was—well, simply at rest somewhere, simply the pursued. She was the more dynamic, despite the encumbrance of her griefs and memories and guilts and their passing parade through her thoughts. Her father working on Project Manhattan in Chicago and then Los Alamos, the strangers who contacted him, the secrets he told them, Aubrey pursuing them across England until dollars had bribed the pilot of an old Dakota to take them into besieged Berlin—1948 . . . her father dying a few yards from safety and Aubrey smirking over his body.

She rubbed her arms beneath her cardigan, but they were not really cold. She was in command. Here, Babbington did not issue orders, she did. And, given the few hours that remained, she felt more certain of success now than ever she had when pursuing Aubrey through Malaya.

"Listen, Comrade General, I know you can dazzle Nikitin and the rest of those boobies on the Politburo with that claptrap about a *new era* in intelligence operations—but *I'm* not convinced. It smells too much like vanity to me!" Kapustin's eyes taunted, seeking the first flush above his cheekbones, the beginnings of anger in his eyes. Babbington struggled to maintain an impassive expression. "OK, politicians want to play spies and spies want to play politics—it's the way of the world!" He waved his arms as he walked across to the window. "But to me it's a bit like buggery—not natural!" He whirled around to face Babbington, the afternoon light outside making him little more than a bulky silhouette out of the middle of which came his snorting, derisive laughter. "Well?" he challenged. "Well?"

Babbington studied his fingernails, irritated with the gesture's juvenile insolence even as he performed it. Then he said: "I thought the meeting went very well."

"You thought!" Kapustin snorted once more, waving his arms above his head, then slapping his hands against his thighs. "It's going to go like clockwork, that's what *you* thought!" Babbington looked toward Kapustin, his lips pursing—he attempted to smile. "Look, Andrew, you are the acolyte who will one day

stab the high priest, we both realize that. This operation—*Topi*
—is your examination. If you pass it, blessings flow. You think
you will pass with honors. But I warn you, you'd better find your
Chink *and* Aubrey today or your success is up the spout!" In
shadow, Kapustin was much younger, more threatening. "And
I'll come down with you," he added heavily. "There are prizes
for everyone in this. You understand that but do you *feel* it?
You, me, the Politburo, the army, the KGB . . . everyone gets
a pat on the back, a warm glow inside. And cheap at the price!
But *where* is Aubrey, where's the bloody Chinaman? Where's
that damned boy they let slip through their hands? You haven't
even moved against Tamang yet . . ." He moved closer to Babbington so that his features jutted granitelike out of the shadow
and his eyes gleamed. "Let me tell you what's going on in the
real world, Andrew. The Chinese are making enquiries about
Lin, London has at least been tickled into dozing instead of sleep
by Aubrey. The Americans are concerned and are pressuring
Gandhi for some answers about his northern neighbor . . . all
that is stirring. Unless this operation takes place within the next
twenty-four hours, then it isn't going to be clean and quick and
neat anymore—just expensive! Understand?"

He walked away to the tall window once more and the office
assumed its former, habitual spaciousness. Babbington felt his
throat dry, his certainties tilted, the warm satisfactions of his
report to the Politburo dissipate as if in a chilly breeze. He
cleared his throat but became reluctant to speak. Eventually, he
announced:

"I think you're taking an extreme view, Dmitri." He raised
his hands, palms outward. "There are some—a few—diplomatic
noises, but little more than that. Some feathers have been ruffled, a few people smell something in the wind. Dmitri, they
don't give a *damn* about Nepal! Half of them would rather *we*
were there, not the Chinese." He got up from the chair and
crossed the room to Kapustin's desk.

"Don't sit down behind it yet—it's not yours, for the moment," Kapustin instructed with heavy irony from the window.
High clouds pulled and hurried behind his large shadow. Babbington prickled, then smiled to himself, his fingers resting on
the green leather surface of the desk.

"Heavens forfend," he murmured. "Dmitri—you have to remember that Aubrey has precious little influence in England any
longer—he has *none* elsewhere in the *real world*. He is a small

fire and one which has not broken out directly next to the ammunition store!"

"Just make certain it works." He sounded, to all intents and purposes, like a sulking child. "Understand?"

"I understand," Babbington replied to the leather of the desk, seeing little more than his spread fingers forming a miniature cage. He sighed audibly. "I can tell you only what I told the Politburo—"

"Christ, you're being diplomatic!"

"—what I told the *Politburo,*" he repeated heavily. "And that is that Aubrey and Lin will be disposed of by tonight, nothing is more certain. The *weight* of the operation would crush them anyway, its noise drown their feeble voices." Suddenly, he was blazingly angry. "For God's sake, don't you *realize* that, any of you?" His fist banged on the desk. "The aircraft are at readiness, the troops could be on board within thirty minutes—it's a four-hour flight to Kathmandu! The Nepalis will stand aside while we restore order. What better sort of guarantee do you want than to know the result of the race before you place your bet?"

He felt the quiver of his lips, almost felt the paleness of his features. His eyes stung with rage.

"All right, Andrew, all right," Kapustin mollified, patting the air in pacifying gestures with his hands. "I never realized you were such a zealot." Kapustin grinned. "Even if the cause *is* yourself and nothing larger." He approached his desk and sat down heavily behind it. Babbington was perched on the edge, one leg swinging, his hand again a small cage on the green leather. Kapustin rubbed his loose jowls. "All right. I believe *you're* confident, at least." He sighed and made his hand, extended in front of him, quiver. "There are unknowns, however," he observed tiredly.

"Because of Aubrey?" Babbington asked disdainfully.

"He's cleverer than a cartload of monkeys!"

"And old and tired and alone."

"You said that days ago—now there's the boy and even the Chinese for all I know!"

"Dear Kenneth is *stuck* in Nepal. He won't get out the way he got in. That Nepali pilot's plane—doesn't function any longer." Babbington made a vast effort to control his contemptuous anger, and continued: "There's him, the pilot, presumably Gardiner, and perhaps some Nepali villagers. *We* have Brandis,

Brigitte, Lin himself, the Red Army's best *spetsnaz* units, the government of Nepal *and* the new King! You're getting too old, Dmitri, your nerve's gone!"

"I almost wish you'd fall flat on your arse, Andrew, just for the pleasure of seeing your injured look." Then Kapustin shrugged. "All right, get that bloody boy Colonel in here and let's have an update. We'll see if he's as confident as you are." His smile disarmed, suggesting they remained allies, still needed each other. "*You* get Lin in the bag by midnight and *I'll* have those troops in Kathmandu by tomorrow morning."

"We must make certain of Aubrey before—" Babbington began, but Kapustin was shaking his head. "We must!" Kapustin continued to shake his head slowly.

"No," he said. "Tomorrow morning, at the latest." His face was impassive.

"You can't impose such a timetable just like that!" Even if I have done so on Brandis, he thought.

"*I* can't. Nikitin can—and has."

"What?" Babbington breathed, his chest tightening. "What do you . . ."

"Mean? Nikitin sent for me this morning—*before* your appearance in front of the Politburo. Whatever you had said to them would have made no difference. He's got the jitters, not me. There have been ambassadorial enquiries, a few rumors are in the wind . . . only to be expected. But he was promised secrecy and his disguise is wearing thin. OK? Now you know. Tomorrow, or never."

"He can't stop it now!"

"Read our constitution, Andrew. He can, and he almost certainly will. He has a lot on his plate at the moment. A summit in Washington, a tour of the Far East, placatory noises when he goes to the People's Republic, his image in the West as a man of peace and probity. A *fait accompli* he can explain away—a *plot* he doesn't need in his lap! Andrew, if this shows any danger of becoming a fuck-up, he'll go back to hoping he can buy the place with aid and rely on Gandhi to go on keeping an eye on our interests there. *Now* do you understand?"

Babbington immediately left the desk, hurrying his fury into the shadows near the window. They *couldn't*. They would not . . .

He ground his teeth, oblivious of Kapustin's presence or attention. *Aubrey* . . . Brandis claimed he must be holed up in one of those bloody Gurung villages west of Pokhara. He felt his own future urgently outstripping him. It couldn't, *simply couldn't,* depend on Aubrey?

But, if it did, then Aubrey was a game—

"—not worth the candle!" he heard himself say aloud.

He simply could not hurry, couldn't . . . Everything, absolutely—*everything,* depended on Lin. He couldn't hurry whatever his own danger, whatever the press of events and the lack of time. His feet were trapped in thick, glutinous, clinging mud. He couldn't hurry, couldn't—

—awake. A buzzing like that of a fly near his head. The radio's noises had intruded again and again into his futile attempts to rest. Each time he dozed, each moment he was awake, he felt events rush, and the strain of his own inability to hasten. He blinked his eyes and sat up. There was straw on his jacket and trousers, and he brushed its strands away. The larger of the two huts smelled of animals and dusty straw and lubricating oil.

A Gurkha was cleaning a rifle near him. Tim was standing, hands on hips, watching him, his attention evidently directed toward the radio though his eyes were on Aubrey. The radio continued to buzz—

—radio? He thought not, as his head cleared of tiredness and stress. The buzz of a helicopter, some distance away. Tim guessed at his attention and tossed his head.

"The same one they used to look for me, by the look of it."

"Is there anything else, any sign of—"

Tim shook his head. "Not yet. They're away from the lake, though . . . and coming west. It won't be long."

Aubrey stood up with the aid of his stick. He felt dispirited rather than tired, the two hours of his interrogation of Lin clinging like cobwebs in his head, making even reflection indistinct. Lin was somehow beyond Aubrey. He had all but admitted the truth of Aubrey's version of events in Malaya, and yet it all had had not the slightest effect on the man's composure. Was it composure, though?

Tim was studying Aubrey, hardly attentive to the radio's dribble of reports and sightings and monitorings from the scattered Gurkhas keeping the search under surveillance. Helicopter . . . police unit . . . Land-Rover . . . on foot, army patrol. Rifles, guns . . . ten, twenty, thirty . . . moving west, west . . . Aubrey shrugged and attempted to move quickly toward and beyond Tim.

"A word with you, Kenneth."

"Yes?"

"Outside."

No, it wasn't composure, he decided. Rather, it was trance-like, an almost hypnotic removal of his self from his immediate surroundings like someone bedridden and close to death. More than mere, expected Oriental detachment, an impassivity of face and body. He looked at his watch. Four-thirty. And shivered slightly as he sensed the hurry of time and the bottled-up tension in the young man beside him.

"We're running out of time!" Tim burst out, his hand waving at the daylight, the distant noise of the helicopter. "We haven't got time to waste being *nice* to Lin anymore!" His face was suffused with blood, his body rigidly tense, the cordlike veins and muscles standing out.

"What do you mean, Tim?" he asked primly. He hardly regarded the heat of the afternoon, the light splintering off the distant mirror of the lake, the eye-hurting snow on the peak of the Fishtail Mountain. Gurkhas lounged. Tim's stance made it impossible to think of them merely as Nepalis; they were soldiers. "I don't think I understand—"

"You understand me! You spend two hours in there with him and the result is bugger-all! How long do you think you've got? I'll tell you in case you don't realize, Kenneth, you've got sod-all in terms of time!"

"Tim!"

"Oh, don't pull the innocent on me! You must have used other methods a hundred times before!"

"No!" His face was hot now, his body quivered. "You will not lay a *hand* on him—do you understand me? I haven't time to explain, but it would not do the slightest good. The man in there is *impervious!* He can't be reached easily, if at all. The Chinese practically invented torture, Tim! You think it would work on him, of all people?" He was leaning forward, all but hunched over his stick, his breathing coming quickly, his whole concentration directed toward dissuasion.

Tim turned his back on Aubrey, exclaiming: "How the hell would I know? I just know *your* way is going to take too long!" He turned toward him again. "They must realize I have friends in one of these villages—they must guess I would come here, within a few miles, at least. That's why they've skipped the rest of the lakeshore, why they're on their way now! Can't you see that?"

"Then you have not the time to beat him, wake him, beat him a second time, allow recovery and fear to grow in the lonely dark, beat him a third, fourth, fifth time—how long were you in *their* hands, for God's sake? Did you tell them anything?"

Glaring, Tim turned his back once more. "Oh, for Christ's sake!" he all but wailed, throwing up his arms.

"I'm sorry, Tim, but it happens to be the truth. We haven't the time to beat it out of Lin, and perhaps not even the time to persuade him it's where his best course lies."

"Does it?"

"To most it would. Money, safety, secrecy. He seems weary of something, but I'm not sure whether it's a manifestation of fear or of something much more intractable . . ." Aubrey rubbed his chin.

Tim glowered. "I don't want a solution next week or next month, I have to know what their plan is *today!*"

"Tim, this is not some registry office affair because the girl is pregnant—this is a cathedral espousal. Choir, flowers, organ, the complete works! What *he* knows—" He pointed toward the shuttered window of the smaller hut. "—can't be solved by your handful of brave men." He lowered his voice. "Please understand that, Tim."

The silence between them seemed enveloping, close; increasing the temperature of the afternoon.

"Blackmail," Tim scoffed eventually.

"What other weapon do we have?" he retorted angrily.

"In which case you'd better get a bloody move on, Kenneth. Because they're really looking hard for us now—and they're close by!"

Aubrey compressed his lips, straightened his suddenly heavy frame, and nodded.

"Very well. I shall open another dialogue with Colonel Lin this moment."

As he entered the hut he smelled the remains of their food and dust and Lin's stale clothes—and forgot his fears for Tim, forgot Tim.

Lin looked up vaguely as the door opened. The light made him squint, then his eyes grew larger like those of a cat as the door closed. His body tensed only for a moment, then became all but supine once more, his back angled against the wall of the hut, his legs still crossed as if he had not moved once since Aubrey had left him. He had used the bucket in the corner, Aubrey noticed, wrinkling his nose. The noise of flies seemed louder, more urgent, and despite his control Aubrey could not prevent the clock begin in his head or fail to notice that the light from the shutter's slats had risen up the opposite wall like an incoming tide.

Aubrey placed himself on the chair, hands clasped on the head of his stick, feet apart. The man seemed soiled, grubby, withdrawn; Aubrey thought of Peter Lorre in any of a dozen films as he studied Lin's face. And yet he was much more than that. He was self-contained, calm. The first interrogation weighed on Aubrey's shoulders.

"Colonel, thus far you have admitted—at least, you have not denied—that Babbington bought your services in Malaya in 1958, after your capture by British troops." He paused, then continued smoothly: "You have been a double agent for the Soviet Union, like your *master*, for thirty years." He cleared his throat. Lin was staring at him with the incomprehension of a small dog. "Therefore, perhaps if I could convince you that I, too, am in a position to offer you money—a great deal of money—for changing sides once again . . . ?" He inspected his lapels and dusted them with small, neat, fastidious gestures. Then he looked up quickly. Lin's eyes gleamed in the shadows.

A hit, if not a palpable one.

"What do you say to that, Colonel? This time you can have fifty-pound notes, not old white fivers! Or Swiss francs, Dutch guilders, US dollars . . . oh, plus the usual anonymity, the large house, the big car, the false papers . . . though your places of exile might be rather limited, what with your appearance, old man."

Lin's body *was* tense, but the realization puzzled rather than excited Aubrey. His eyes glared and his jaw was tight, his lips compressed, cheeks sallow. Hands—hands hidden, so probably clenched. He might have been straining to evacuate his bowels or to suppress a cough. The forehead was creased as if with an effort of recollection.

Recollection?

Aubrey glanced at the table and he could not suppress the involuntary reaction of his hand as it reached out to pat the briefcase, lift its flap to check that the contents were undisturbed.

There was a photograph in shadow near Lin. He had been curious, had opened Aubrey's briefcase and found Scudamore's notebooks and the snapshots that were speckled with mold. Lin's eyes had followed the movement of his hand.

"Old times, Colonel, eh? Old times . . ." He sighed.

Lin's eyes were bright, fixed in their attention on Aubrey's briefcase, even after Aubrey had gently removed his hand. Something had thrown him back, thrown him out of kilter. Aubrey watched the man. He overlay himself now like a double-exposed negative of the same person. The subject had moved very slightly between the first click and the second and he was fuzzily outlined by himself, his face smeared with its own features.

Speak to him—

"A lot of water under the bridge since then, mm, Colonel?" he drawled, inspecting his clasped hands. "And for you, a great deal of tension, a doubly secret life. But, you've survived. Your hands can be absolutely filled with money just so long as—"

"No."

"I beg your pardon?"

"No. I do not want money." That double exposure again. The voice was quiet, apparently calm, but there seemed effort behind the detachment now.

"Then—name your price, Colonel," Aubrey said very deliberately. "Name your own price—cash or kind." But Lin was shaking his head as if amused, even contemptuous. Again, that impenetrable, infuriating detachment like a superiority of class or intellect, from the unshaven, sallow, ill-smelling Chinese squatting on the floor like a statue of the Buddha! Then Aubrey managed a controlled: "I see."

"You do not understand," Lin volunteered after a long silence. The slatted bars of sunlight coming through the shutter were further up the wall. He watched the light rather than Lin's face, measuring the minutes hurrying away from him.

"Don't I?"

"There is nothing you can offer me or do to me."

"That dangerous boy who kidnapped you seems to think the physical alternative might provide results."

Lin rubbed his lips. "I do not think so."

"Why do those old photographs still mean something to you, after thirty years?"

"Do they?"

"I think so." The topmost bar of sunlight had crept nearer a long, jagged, horizontal crack on the wall, close to the edge of a bright, complexly patterned rug that hung there. Lin sighed. Aubrey added: "I do know a great deal, you know."

"I understand. And yet you know very little."

"You know what I'm attempting?" Lin nodded. "Then why not help me and save yourself."

"Why? This will be just another small country where thousands die. You can find them in every part of the world."

Aubrey's knuckles tensed into a fist near the briefcase. "You don't care?"

"No."

The bars of light touched the dull, dented gleam of a copper kettle against the wall. Touched the horizontal crack, the sunlight clock ticking on against the wall behind Lin. Some light had spilled like water on his passive hands, but there was none on his features.

Passive, contemplative . . . what was it Tim had said? Where had they first picked up Lin, before they snatched him? Durbar Square.

The door opened, startling Aubrey. Tim's outlined shadow stood there.

"Kenneth—" he said urgently. "Please."

"Yes, of course. Excuse me, Colonel." As he closed the door behind him, Tim whispered: "They're in the village now and the helicopter's about." He pointed. A squat black spot in the sky, lower down the hills. Aubrey could just make out the wooden roofs of part of the village.

"What do we do?"

"Wait and see. This trail leads nowhere except here. They may miss it. I've got everyone under cover. Just sit tight?" He ended interrogatively, seeking approval. Aubrey nodded a moment later.

"Police or army?"

"Police. A handful. We're able to cope . . . even if response would blow our cover!"

But something else concerned Aubrey, something Tim knew: "Where did you pick him up—firstly?"

"Lin? I told you, Durbar Square."

"No, it wasn't that . . . what was he doing?" Aubrey clicked his fingers in self-impatience.

"Out for a stroll?"

"Something you told me—"

"The temple, you mean?"

"*Yes!*" Aubrey snapped his fingers, now in triumph. "A *Buddhist* temple . . . thank you, Tim. I must get back to him. Can we move quickly from here if need be?"

"Yes."

"Good." He opened the door after breathing deeply, calming himself. The sunlight clock had moved two bars onto the hanging rug. "Colonel Lin," he announced, sitting down lightly, "you asked me a few minutes ago whether I understood. Well, perhaps I can answer you now. All this, what? Passivity, shall we call it? Indicative, I feel, mm?" Lin was watching him intently yet unemotionally. "I understand your need but not your indifference. I would have thought that clashed with your beliefs?"

For the first time Lin's breathing was audible in the silence. "You *think* you understand."

"I understand the hole you have tried to fill—" Was that the helicopter's noise or just insects? His hand jumped on the plain, scarred table. Lin saw the movement—damn!—and his head cocked immediately, listening, his small frame tense. "—the hole you have tried to fill . . ." His voice was amplified just enough—it *was* the helicopter and Lin had heard it, too!

"Do not patronize me, Mister Aubrey." The man was listening intently. He was staring directly at Aubrey, eyes gleaming, his whole face alert, his body taut as wire.

Aubrey leaned forward, the noise much louder now. He adjusted his grip on his heavy stick, so that it might be used quickly. The helicopter was almost above them now, its drone seeming to use the light-leaking roof as a resonating board. Dust floated down on them, into the bars of sunlight higher up the wall. Lin's body was tense with expectancy, even the preliminary to flight, like an athlete. Aubrey moved the tip of his stick, demonstrating its weight, its ease of movement. The noise thudded.

Aubrey shouted: "*What* do they intend? What is Babbington's plan?"

"Does it matter?" Lin shouted back as if they were engaged in some naked, violent quarrel.

"When the killing begins, won't that conflict with your philosophy just a little?" Aubrey shouted. Dust swirled, the sunlight filtering into the room seemed to fly and whirl with the flickering shadow of the rotor blades above the roof. Lin glared at him, his body leaning slightly to one side, hand taking his weight like a runner rising from his blocks . . .

He struck Lin across the shoulder and arm with one violent, surprising blow of the stick. Lin clutched his arm, and slumped against the wall, as Aubrey heard the rotor noise retreating. The dust settled, the roof no longer quivered, he could hear his own harsh breathing, as the noise slipped away down the hills. Lin seemed defeated, hurt more by the retreat of the helicopter than by the blow.

Aubrey's breathing calmed. The helicopter was gone. Lin's face tilted into the sunlight that was invading half of the hanging rug now. Aubrey sat down.

"Doesn't your philosophy emphasize the sanctity of life above all else?" he asked, the early taunting tone once again in his voice.

"I shall not be killing anyone," Lin replied.

"Colonel—surely you realize that our mutual friend Andrew Babbington is all *karma?*" Lin's eyes widened and Aubrey smiled. "I see you do. Cause and effect. Bad *karma* I believe they would call it in Beverly Hills?" He chortled. "Hardly the path of *dharma,* eh? Getting mixed up with Babbington, I mean?"

Lin's face pictured failure, then immediately dismissive contempt. He had returned to the confines of the interrogation. Good.

"You know a few words," he scoffed.

"The dangerous boy outside—he is a Buddhist, too. Like you, a *bhikku*—or does that not mean student? I forget. I learned a little in order to debate with him. He, too, at the present time sees the advantage of suspension of belief—preferring the old, *favorite* faith of expediency, violence, action, ruthlessness. All the things you profess to have wearied of, learned to view with disgust!" He ended with a vigor of contempt in his tone and a flourish of dismissal with his hand. Lin's face was enraged.

Light suddenly splashed in, all but making Lin cower into the corner.

"OK, Kenneth!" Tim exclaimed. "The helicopter's dropped down to the lakeshore again, the police patrol's moved on, away north of here."

Aubrey studied Lin's face, saw that he understood, then

waved Tim out of the hut. "Thank you, Tim." He leaned forward on the stick, his features glowing with satisfaction. The sunlight clock reassured itself against the complex pattern of the rug. Dust motes drifted tiredly and settled. "Now, Colonel—where were we?"

Lin had retreated into a silence that was now stubborn, even defensive, as if he had already revealed too much. Aubrey weighed his approach. He had moved by instinct and guesswork like a blind man in an unfamiliar room. And he had discovered yet another secret life behind Lin's secret profession and his career as a double agent. He had no idea why Lin had *needed* to become a believer in something. Had he lost his appetite for the secret life? Unlike himself, Aubrey admitted, still watching Lin.

He stood up. Lin seemed surprised, his eyes on the heavy stick, as Aubrey murmured: "I'll leave you to reflect for a moment or two, Colonel."

The light of afternoon-becoming-evening made him blink as he closed the door behind him. There was a Gurkha guard with a gleaming, stubby rifle outside the hut once more. Tim had driven the Land-Rover out of the larger hut. Gurkhas milled purposefully around it, all of them armed, drawing up as Tim watched them form into a column of twos.

"Tim!" Aubrey called out. "What's happening?" Tim had already climbed into the driver's seat, even though he had seen Aubrey. It looked like a child's act of defiance.

"I can't hang around any longer, Kenneth!" he called back, watching as Aubrey scurried toward the vehicle. "I've got to do *something!*"

Aubrey clamped his hand over Tim's as it gripped the steering wheel. "What do you mean?"

"Look, Kenneth—you're getting nowhere. It's five-thirty or didn't you realize . . ." He bent closer to Aubrey. "You'll be safe here while you carry on trying to get him to talk. I'm leaving you three guards—"

"And you?"

"Look, it's coming to the boil, down there"—there was thicker, heavier smoke over Pokhara—"and in Kathmandu. I'm going to try to get through to Tamang, the Foreign Minister. Maybe *he'll* listen to me!" He shook off Aubrey's hand. "I'm not letting it all go to hell in a handcart, I'm at least going to *try* to do something about it!"

Angrily, Aubrey snapped: "You have no proof to show him!"

"You need *proof?* A *timetable?* They're setting fire to the whole fucking place and you want a timetable?"

"But what can you do?"

"I don't know—but *something!*"

The Gurkhas' faces were intent, patient, yet eager to be gone. Ten men, Ganesh the pilot, and Tim. What in God's name could they possibly *do?*

Then Tim smiled. "You do your job, Kenneth, and I'll find something to occupy *me!*"

"Then take care . . ."

"I will. If you need to move, these men I'm leaving know where to take you." He seemed to weigh Aubrey carefully, then added: "You couldn't get out, not along the hill trails, Kenneth—but you already knew that?" Aubrey nodded. "You'll be safe here, I should think. For the duration."

"But, if Lin talks, if I have proof?"

"Then call the bloody British Embassy with the good news!" Tim retorted stubbornly. "The corporal will take you down to Pokhara, or take any message. If the phone lines are still working, if Middleton's available, if, if, bloody-*if*—you'll get your proof out. And a fat lot of bloody use it'll be to anyone!"

Aubrey clamped Tim's arm and shook it gently. "Do take care."

Tim's glance darkened. "Yes." He added after a moment: "Right, we'll be off, then. To Kathmandu—and Tamang. If they haven't arrested him already!"

"Very well!" Brandis exclaimed with utter exasperation. "We wait until it gets dark!" He grimaced, and was further infuriated when Brigitte seemed to regard it as no more than the face-pulling of a schoolboy. "We should have checked out those huts, taken nothing for granted," he concluded, unable to disguise the lameness of his tone.

Brigitte sat holding a glass of Perrier water—he'd had to send someone to one of the hotels for it!—in front of the red-shaded map, watching it like some absorbing movie. Occasionally, she sipped like a dowdy, ancient bird at the very lip of the glass. Like some damned Buddha, all but lifeless!

She said: "The helicopter reported vehicle tracks. In the village, a child mentioned a Chinese, a white man also. *I* am certain, Gerd—so should you be."

"Then let's get them!"

"After dark. All of them."

There was very little activity up there now. The Puma couldn't be sent back, it was too noisy. Their surveillance told them there were less than a handful of Nepalis visible at any one time. It made sense, he had to admit. They were still there, trying to crack Lin open and find out about *Topi*. If they already knew, they'd have left altogether and tried to get Lin out, into India or even bloody China. They hadn't even slipped away before he could infiltrate surveillance back into the area after the bluff of moving on. Brigitte was right. They were there.

And they weren't going anywhere, not now. He watched the opaqueness of the windows dim and the air outside purple.

"Should I make another report to Babbington?" he asked, a clutch of unexpected guilt tightening his chest. Damn her, he thought. He was still frightened of her authority—and stung by her contempt, her knowledge and even amusement regarding his shift of loyalties.

"If you wish, Gerd." There wasn't the slightest hesitation in her voice. He resented the fact that Babbington had both bribed and frightened him and yet Brigitte Winterbach seemed unaffected by him! Babbington *was* the future, the old woman was on her way to oblivion . . . but he could no longer quite believe that. He rubbed his hand across his hair in exasperation.

"What shall I say? This time?"

"Tell him Kathmandu's burning very nicely. That should please him."

Her contempt for Babbington was unguarded, foolish, but it wasn't just the recklessness of age or approaching redundancy, it was—confidence. Sheer and utter assurance. Cleverness unmatched by anyone—except the old man she was now hunting down. He felt his old affection for her revive.

The Foreign Minister, Tamang, was about to be arrested, the Prime Minister had been briefed to make his appeal for Soviet intervention . . . all of that had passed her by. She remained intent upon Aubrey, Lin, and perhaps Gardiner. He shrugged behind her back, reminding himself that she was still his superior, that this was his old job and old place of work and the promise of new employment still lay in the future. Strangely, he hardly resented her renewed vigor, rather admired it.

"I'll go and make my report, then," he said.

"Yes, Gerd, you do that. What is the time?"

"Six forty-five." He saw her look at her own watch and then adjust it.

"Yes. Good," she said, then added: "Be ready to move at seven. I shall be coming with you"—there was a kind of girlish luxury in her voice—"to see for myself."

Aubrey glanced surreptitiously at his watch, its hands difficult to make out even though he had lit the single lamp. Seven-twenty. It was almost dark outside. Occasionally, he and Lin reacted like startled animals to the noises of the three Gurkhas Tim had left to guard them. Low chatter, the rattling of utensils, the rub and click of weapons, laughter.

Aubrey and Lin had reached an accommodation, if not an accord. The hut no longer completely contained them. He was increasingly concerned for Tim, his imagination attempting to trace the line of the main road from Pokhara to the capital and trying to avoid the paucity of numbers Tim had with him—while Lin seemed slumped in an invalid's sleep of retrospection. Effectively, the interrogation was over, even if incomplete, like a boxing match in which the two opponents showed a very real unwillingness to emerge from their corners long before the scheduled end of the bout.

Aubrey rubbed his hands across his eyes. There was no sense of defeat, only a recognition of events. Lin *would* eventually break, but it would take time and he knew that Tim was right. They had run out of available time. The situation in Nepal was showing the needle well into the dangerous red. Action was what was required.

Would an invasion happen tonight? Would they come? He stared at Lin, rubbing his rasping stubble as he did so. It seemed inevitable, some kind of takeover through the use of force. Yet, hadn't they *learned* from Afghanistan? Perhaps not . . . Nepal would seem an easy prize, and useful to have in one's international portfolio. China blocked, Gandhi propped up. And with a zealot like Babbington to peddle the idea, yes, the Russians could easily be persuaded. An appeal for help to restore order, a few hundred men, well armed, and . . .

Aubrey yawned, and the sound of the helicopter came out of the cavernous noise his tiredness provoked, just as a moth was finally achieving immolation in the flame of the lamp. The downdraft through the gaps in the roof blew the flame wildly but did not save the moth. The noise banged about them like a storm.

His hand was under Lin's elbow, dragging the man—who seemed as stunned and fearful as he did himself—to his feet, panicking him toward the door. There was no resistance. Lin's breath smelled of stale food and weariness as he turned to Aubrey, guessing his own future as certainly as that of his erstwhile captor.

"Quickly, quickly!" Aubrey shouted unnecessarily but to mask the thudding of his heart and the fears that eagerly crowded. He pulled open the door.

Searchlight, but splaying over the open ground. Moments still left. The Puma settled gently, its light swallowed by the dust it threw up, its cabin door open, soldiers poised to jump from it.

"This way!" He dragged Lin along the wall of the hut into deeper shadow. The Chinaman's mouth opened as if he still clung to old duplicities, then he hurried with Aubrey, intent only on escaping his rescuers. He knew he would not be believed.

Where were the Gurkhas? They'd been surprised, yes, but there was no firing, no shouts, no one—

He stumbled over one of them in the darkness, falling to his knees. His hand was suddenly wet, sticky. There was a second lump hunched on the ground a few yards away. Lin had stopped moving. Lights flashed out, coldly bathing them. Aubrey felt the stuff of an army pullover, saw the V-shape of a corporal's stripes on the limp sleeve. The wet stickiness. He squinted into the headlights of the vehicle . . .

. . . and slowly recognized the silhouette that awkwardly coalesced out of the glare as it moved toward them. An old, dumpy woman, the shadow of her head haloed by frizzy, unkempt hair. She was as short as he remembered her.

The figure halted a few yards away. "Lin," she said first, then: "Kenneth." As if they had met by accident in mutual distrust in one of the corridors of their place of work.

15

The Wildcats

She moved toward him, seeming to stir up behind her the quick stutter and bark of walkie-talkie messages like a cloud of insects. The harsh glow of the headlights outlined her and shadowed her face. She moved arthritically while he remained on his knees, a disturbed thief kneeling with his ear against a safe. His hand plucked at the sleeve of the lumped, pullovered corpse beside him, as if trying to awaken assistance. He blinked in the lights from the truck.

"Where is the boy—Christ, where is he?" That was Brandis shouting. Brigitte's hands were at her sides or making occasional darts toward her chest as if to calm the baffled old pump that controlled her breathing. Despite the other noises around them, he could hear the sound of each breath clearly as she halted only a few yards from him. An old cat coming out of the dark and somehow resenting the light and the confrontation, however much it had been anticipated. Lin knelt beside Aubrey, crouching like the Fool to his old man, once King. Brigitte watched both of them warily, almost disbelieving. "How the fuck did he slip away?" Brandis bellowed as if in pain. "With how many people?" Aubrey and Brigitte continued to stare at one another. "How many of them are still here? Just the three buggers you've accounted for and the old man? I don't fucking well *believe* it!" English shouted in a heavy German accent, ringing in the darkness. Brigitte was wound tight as a spring. There seemed no disappointment for her in their meager haul of corpses and prisoners.

"Brigitte," he said eventually while Brandis' people searched the huts once more. The helicopter's rotors had finally wound down into silence. It was still now, almost breathless. *"Such a long time,"* he managed to add with a modicum of ironic calm.

Momentarily, it broke whatever spell there had been between them. He dusted his hands. They were sticky with the dead corporal's blood. Slowly, awkwardly, he got to his feet, determined not to scrabble for his stick.

"Kenneth," she seemed obligated to reply. There was a sigh of what could have been triumph in her voice.

He realized how familiar she was, that he knew her better than any other intelligence officer, had for most of his life. Yet all that prior knowledge was worthless as he looked at her, their eyes almost level, the headlights of the truck haloing her frizzy, untidy hair. The same intense, staring little girl from the Venetian gondola and the train through Italy and France in the first winter of the war was still there. Clever, secretive, sensitive; loving, easily wounded. He had wounded her a second time, as she would see it. This time, unforgivably, perhaps. It was the little girl who wore an old-woman Halloween mask who truly unnerved him. It explained the energy that seemed to emanate from her.

Aubrey looked at Lin, who seemed apprehensive, then ignored him for the moment. Brandis' anger and orders flashed like a disturbing storm along their mutual horizon as he stared at Brigitte. There were perhaps two dozen men around them now. Then she moved quickly and struck him violently across the cheek with her open hand. He gripped his mouth until his partial dentures were settled. His cheek and jaw ached and he tasted blood on his tongue.

"Civility, Brigitte," he said thickly, "after all, you hold the winning hand!"

"I do, yes," she replied, watching intently as he wiped at the corner of his mouth where blood had dribbled. She turned to Lin. "Are you well, Lin Yu-Chiang?"

The Chinese got to his feet. Seven-thirty, Aubrey thought. Where *was* Tim? Brandis was not the only one who wished he knew.

"Yes, General," Lin replied with inexpressive formality. "I am well."

"What does he know?" she asked.

"A great deal—but nothing in the sense in which you mean the question."

"Good." She nodded, accepting Lin's word at once, then turned to Aubrey. "Answer Gerd's question, Kenneth. Where is the boy? The other Gurkhas? Where are they?"

Aubrey merely shrugged in reply to her questions. Then Brandis was beside her, eager as if straining on her leash. Brigitte smiled and removed her hand from Brandis' sleeve. The man bullied forward, his face close enough to Aubrey for his last meal to smell on his breath. Beer, too. Then Aubrey was aware of a sharp pain in his midriff and the ground thudding against his buttocks. He touched his glasses back onto his nose as Brandis hoisted him to his feet by his lapels. It had all happened with the surprised alarm of a playground fight.

"Where is the boy? Where is he?"

He tried to answer but there was no assisting breath. He gagged and choked, eventually swallowing air as if it had had to break through some tough membrane into his chest.

"Don't know!" he burst out. Then, after two more grateful breaths, he snapped: "Would I tell you if I knew? Would *he* have told me, expecting you might come?"

Brandis seemed surprised, as if the boy he sought was suddenly more elusive and dangerous.

"What the hell is he doing, then?" he demanded, shaking Aubrey with a terrier's rage.

"I do not *know!*"

"Gerd!"

Brandis' shoulders flinched as if her voice had been laid on his back like a whip. He continued to glower into Aubrey's face, his breath smelling of food and alcohol.

"What?" Brandis replied.

"Leave Sir Kenneth Aubrey alone—for the moment. The boy wouldn't have been stupid enough to tell him anything—and I don't think he's working to any scheme of yours, is he, Kenneth?" Aubrey stared beyond Brandis' shoulder. "No, I thought not."

Brandis stepped back as if to inspect his handiwork. Aubrey looked at the circle of people about himself and Lin. Soldiers, police, a microcosm of the situation in the country. They owned police and army already; soon, they would own Nepal. His anger surprised him, as if he were reading something from Tim's script, not his own part in this play.

Someone turned out the truck's headlights and the pale moonlight seeped back over the scene.

"Let me rip that village apart," Brandis was saying, but Brigitte was waving her hands decisively.

"It would be wasting time."

"Then what do we do about the boy?"

"Is he important?"

"What is he *doing?*"

"Does it matter—now? Send the signal, Gerd. As soon as we return to Kathmandu, send the signal."

Brandis shrugged. "Very well." He moved toward Aubrey once more, who could not prevent his frame from flinching. His heavy hand gripped Aubrey's shoulder. "Let's go, old man."

Lin moved ahead of them and Brigitte, too, turned toward the helicopter.

"If that Chink bastard gave your boy any clue, I'll kill him," Brandis murmured. "The faintest idea and he's dead, old man— as dead as you."

Aubrey watched Brigitte's back, shrouded in her cardigan, her arthritic walk, her flat, old-fashioned shoes. She represented a physical fear as no one else had ever done, a directness of threat that weighed like a stone on him.

"But, *Minister*—" It was increasingly difficult to hold his temper on a leash as he confronted Tamang. "—you simply can't sit there and *ignore* what's happening!" It was as if he battled against huge, repetitive waves, even though he displayed all the energy in the scene and Tamang remained unruffled . . . run to fat and ease, almost boneless in his deep leather chair behind the broad mahogany desk; any minister anywhere. His contempt grew, crowding a new sense of defeat and failure to the back of his mind. "You can't! Don't you realize what's happening?"

Tamang's eyes did, he was certain of that. They flickered before returning to their heavy lidded impassivity, glancing toward the broad windows of his vast office in the Foreign Ministry. There was, Tim realized, a sense of tidiness about the desk; of imminent departure.

"You're getting out!" he blurted, banging his fist on the desk, sounding like a disappointed child, even to himself. Tamang smiled as if he at last comprehended his opponent, and seemed to relax more expansively into his chair.

"Captain Gardiner," he murmured, "your story simply isn't credible. I don't believe the Russians intend to invade my country." He made it sound ridiculous, even managed to sound convinced. His eyes slid as if in oil toward the windows once more, where the whole town seemed to glow orange and there were distant noises like a fitful wind. "Why should they?" he continued. "How could they? Nepal is recognized internationally as a Zone of Peace—by the Russians, also." He spread his hands, now confident of his control of the boy opposite him, and smiled, his eyes regarding Ganesh, who stood behind Tim's chair like an unreliable, secretive interpreter—except that he had remained silent.

"I *know* that!" Tim protested, hunched forward on his chair. The size of the great room on the second floor of the Singha Durbar oppressed him. The glow at the windows was emphasized as the fires of the city were reflected by the huge ornamental pool in front of the palace. Images of rioting, of bodies like discarded rubbish in the streets, flickered in his thoughts. "But what do you think all that out there—" He waved his arm abruptly at the windows. "—is leading to? Can't you understand, Minister? Someone is going to come in with the promise of restoring order here—and they're going to be Russian *spetsnaz* troops. That Antonov landing was no accident, it was a dry run, a practice!"

Tamang was already shaking his head regretfully. It had taken Ganesh and him an hour to be admitted to Tamang's office after they had driven from Pokhara. The ten Gurkhas with them had remained near the truck and the Land-Rover, outside. It had been a waste of time, a silly, half-formed idea that had caused him to rush with a child's enthusiasm into this brick wall of indifference. Or self-preservation.

"Captain Gardiner—there is unrest—" Tim sneered. "Unrest—things will be back to normal very soon. Once the King broadcasts, calms the people . . ." Involuntarily, Tim glanced toward the television set in its ornate cabinet, at the radio, the row of telephones near his hand. Props for a stage set, none of them real.

And there was Tamang's distrust of him because he was English, a former Queen's Gurkha Officer . . . the very fact that had gained him admittance here. All three of them were former QGOs, but two of them were Nepali. Tim sighed and got up, walking toward the windows with his hands above his head as if surrendering. Fires shone in the dark water of the Rani Pokhri ornamental lake on Kanti Path near some of the tall, new hotels beyond it. A small explosion lit part of the Exhibition Ground like a flare. Fires were reflected in the distant, sacred strip of darkness that was the river. He rubbed his face, hard. His stomach was hollow. It seemed the whole bloody place was catching alight, burning up. He turned to face Tamang.

"It's because you can't do anything, is that it? Is that why you won't try? Where's the bloody army and the police if order's that easy to restore? Who the hell is the army loyal to at the moment—*you?* That telephone hasn't rung once since we arrived. No one's reported to you—why?" He hesitated, realizing the import of his accusations. "You're out of touch. You've got an army unit guarding the ministry and what else? Nothing!" Tamang's features were mobile with anger, discomfort. He was leaning forward on his desk as if his breathing was difficult. Tim approached the desk, the room shrinking to the pools of lamplight as if he drew a curtain across the rest of it as he moved. "You're just sitting here, waiting. For what, Tamang? The bloody cavalry?"

"You—will leave. This meeting is at an end."

"What are you waiting for?"

The telephone blurted, surprising them all. Tamang's hand snatched it away from its rest.

"Yes?" An agitated voice. Tim leaned closer and Tamang tried to shield the voice by turning away, his face chalky. Airport? *Airport!* "I see—yes, *yes!*" Tamang put down the telephone, his breathing loud, his eyes fleeting over the office, over their faces, toward the windows.

"Well?" Tim demanded.

Tamang shrugged and muttered: "The—airport has been closed. By units of the army. Closed."

Tim banged the desk, triumphant despite the icy chill he felt in his back. "And your escape route's gone down the pan, Tamang!" The glitter of the Foreign Minister's eyes was a guilty admission. "You *shit!* No wonder you didn't want to listen, you were getting on a plane tonight!"

His head rushed with half-thoughts. They'd begun it, closing the airport was the first step, had to be. No flights in or out, except—

He hurried to the television. A bad picture, rolling and flashing with interference. Damage to the transmitter? He turned up the sound. Nepali music from an instrumental ensemble, a *damai baja* dressed folksily, squatting on the studio floor. A ludicrous image of the normal . . . trumpets, two snakelike shawms, kettledrums and cymbals. Ridiculous and somehow ominous.

"What is it?" Ganesh asked urgently. The picture settled.

"What are you doing, Captain Gardiner?"

Tim ignored Tamang. "I think there's going to be some kind of—appeal or something . . ." The music continued, even behind the formal studio card that suddenly replaced the musicians, announcing the Prime Minister, who addressed the nation with an urgent fatherliness.

" . . . nest of traitors to the nation—right-wing agitators—rioting—arrests have begun . . ." Tamang flinched as he heard his own name. His eyes sought the doors, the windows, avoiding the two people in the room with him until finally lighting on them in utter blame. " . . . taken into custody and charged . . . desperate times, the fate of the whole nation—rioting under control and those responsible . . . speaking in the name of His Majesty, with full authority . . ." Tamang was white, bereft. " . . . therefore make a solemn appeal to our friendly ally, the Soviet Union, to come to our rescue, to help us restore order and rebuild our nation . . ."

The plea was repeated in three, perhaps four different, unmistakable expressions. " . . . supporters of freedom and national integrity . . . join with the forces of patriotism and freedom . . . restore the sovereignty of . . . help eradicate those forces of reaction and corruption which have . . ."

Then only the studio card, instructing viewers to await further bulletins. And the national anthem, muted and solemn. Slowly, Tim turned from the screen, possessing as little volition as Tamang in his chair.

"What do we do now?" Ganesh asked, wiping his lips.

"Now?" Tim's head ached dully. What *should* they do now?

"That—*bastard!*" Tamang spat out, clenching his fists on his desk, his face twisted like a child's on the verge of a tantrum. "That bastard . . ."

Why couldn't he think? He was the fucking *prophet* of all this so why couldn't he *think?* There must be something. Ganesh was almost on tiptoe with angry, frustrated energy . . . what the hell could they *do?*

"You must leave at once," Tamang announced.

"Inform the King!" Tim snapped. "The army won't defy him—inform the *King!*"

"Rubbish! Do you think he would listen? He's in that bastard's pocket." There was a galvanic bustle about Tamang now. "You must leave—I must leave at once."

"Go to the King, tell him!"

"Out of my way!" When Tim did not move, Tamang pressed a button on his desk. Two armed soldiers responded immediately, standing on either side of the open door. "They're leaving," Tamang snapped. Then a captain was standing between the soldiers.

"Did you hear the—" he began.

"These people are leaving. Have my car brought to the door—and an escort. Quickly, Captain!"

The captain saluted and turned away. His footsteps hurried. Tamang glanced at them, then ignored them both. He scurried between the soldiers and disappeared, becoming more hurrying footsteps on a marble floor.

Tim's mouth opened and closed like that of a goldfish. Ganesh was staring at him as if he were the cause of the Nepali's anger. Creaks and a violent, wrenching squeaking from outside, louder than the fitful wind of the rioting. Tim moved like an automaton to the windows. Headlights moving slowly along the wide boulevard of the Prithwi Path, already past the Bhadra Kali temple. Perhaps as little as four hundred yards away. Ganesh was at his side.

"What is it?" The strange noises were clear and ominous, as if amplified electronically to frighten and unnerve.

"Two of those bloody French light tanks the army's got! They're coming for Tamang and serve the bastard right!"

"Coming for him and they'll find us!" Ganesh turned toward the door. "Come on—" Then he halted.

Tim saw the doorway empty. The two soldiers had vanished. Two light tanks, Land-Rovers, trucks filled with troops. There could be three, four, a dozen ministers and senior officials in the complex of the Singha Durbar palace. All to go straight into the bag—

—with them! The corridor outside the room echoed with footsteps, dozens of them. There were distant noises of car engines starting or accelerating. Doubtless, Tamang was already gone—bastard! He was sweating with anxiety now, his thoughts tangled like briar around any capacity to reason. He and Ganesh clattered down a marble staircase, past Buddhas and ornately erotic gods and goddesses, past photographs of the late King draped in black and new, stylized portraits of his malleable successor. Men and women hurried through long corridors and scrambled down staircases into huge foyers and lobbies. The car engines chorused the promise of escape from open doors. The smell of petrol was rank. The confused scene hurried and blurred like something captured by a news camera rushed through dangerous streets.

The captain to whom Tamang had given the order for his car was near the main doors, his eyes coming to rest when he saw them. His approach suggested urgency, even arrest.

"What do you—Captain Gardiner, I remember you . . . the Minister has gone—" It was as if he had forgotten poorly rehearsed lines. He gripped Gardiner's arm. "Seven of my men have remained, they are here . . ." He seemed to be pleading with Ganesh more than Tim. The noise of a tracked vehicle on the sloping approach to the building. "The others have vanished—" Again, he was at a loss.

"Come with us—bring your men!" Gardiner surprised himself with the order. "Gan—no, Captain, show us the back way out!"

The captain nodded, ushering him with his hand still gripping his arm. The captain's free hand waving, conjuring up the NCO and the soldiers who suddenly seemed to hem them, then hurry them down corridors without ornament or decoration, which smelled of dust and moldering paper. Fans turned slowly against cracked and stained ceilings. Frosted-glass doors and the sudden cool of the evening air, becoming humid and warm almost at once, causing sweat to break out.

The Gurkhas sprang from tense idleness into aggression as they saw Tim and Ganesh surrounded by soldiers.

"No, no! It's OK!" he soothed in a yell, arms waving. The engines of the small truck—vegetable litter from the village still on its floor—and the old Land-Rover were running, their drivers aboard; expectant faces awaiting orders, a course of action.

Shooting. A few sporadic rounds from a weapon on automatic. Screams, then the almost-silence of a herd corralled and restive. There were a few fleeing figures in the darkness at the rear of the palace, some in uniform, but no one with any purpose other than panicky flight. Twenty of them, including himself.

Two old vehicles, a scattering of light weapons. To do what? The crump of another explosion in the city, apparent even above his harsh breathing. Small, dark figures and an English officer— pathetic!

"What do we do now?" Ganesh demanded.

The crunch and creak of tank tracks, the noises of arrest. A single shot, a distorted voice through a megaphone. A startled car squealed its tires in making a break for it, and there was a long burst of gunfire and an impact. The orange light of flames seemed to bathe them and illuminate the corner of the palace, then die down. The noises pressed for action, just like the excited, frightened faces that crowded around him.

"How long before the Russians land?" Ganesh demanded.

"Uh—depends where they . . . they'll have been waiting for the invitation—if it's from an Afghan air base, maybe as little as two hours! From Alma-Ata or somewhere north, maybe four hours, maximum—Christ . . . ."

"Won't anybody do anything?" Ganesh asked, tugging his mustache violently.

"What do you think?"

"Then what do *we* do?"

It was the pitiful collection of weapons that freed his thoughts—that and the increased urgency and volume of the voice through the loudspeaker. They were rounding people up now, identifying them.

"We need weapons!"

The captain was nodding vigorously, prompting more of the ridiculously obvious.

"I know where we can lay our hands on anything we want!" Tim announced.

"Where?" Ganesh asked suspiciously.

"Let's get out of here, quickly! Come on, before they find us!" He raised his voice. "Into the truck! Hurry! The Kot," he added to Gan in a quiet, intense voice. "In the Kot armory!"

"There!" Brandis announced, his sigh of excited relief audible to Aubrey on the far side of the airport manager's office. Even the shoulders of the armed guard at the door seemed to twitch in response to the Prime Minister's broadcast appeal.

Brigitte's eyes gleamed, seeming ill-focused and shortsighted at the same moment. Lin remained abstracted, a machine without an engine. Not Brigitte, though. She was the pedant marking her way toward the end of a student's paper.

"Well, Kenneth," she said, "*Topi* is running, it's under way."

"So I gather," he replied as dryly as he could. "That, I take it, was the signal to your forces of—liberation." She nodded, while Brandis studied them both, involved and yet excluded. "The signal for them to take off?" Again, Brigitte nodded carelessly. "How long?"

She made a theatrical business of studying her watch, upstaging Brandis, who wished to reply, then she said: "Four hours."

Aubrey considered her reply, then asked: "Alma-Ata is their point of departure, I presume?" Brandis' eyes widened.

"Yes," Brigitte answered.

"How many aircraft?"

"Four large Antonovs—filled to overflowing with *spetsnaz* troops. More than enough—they say."

"It will be," Brandis growled.

"I dare say . . ."

Brandis looked at Brigitte, who nodded. Then he switched on the radio transmitter and placed a headphone against his left cheek. He was at once caught up by the excitement of the operation. "Tower—report, please. What? All four confirmed in the air? Good. Yes, I'll be across at once. Out."

He put down the headphone. Aubrey saw the shoulders of two uniformed guards edging around each side of the open door. Beyond them was the deserted VIP lounge, small, glass-walled, silent. Beyond that, he could only imagine the silence of the airport rather than sense it. Were he to open the slats of the Venetian blind behind him, he would doubtless be able to see the fires in the city, just as he had when the Puma had wobbled in half an hour earlier, before he had been hurried between two soldiers through the almost deserted main concourse of the passenger terminal up to this place. But he preferred not to see the fires or hear the muted whisper of the rioting or the occasional crump of small explosions.

They'd secured the tower against—who, what? There was no opposition. Only the four transports and their troops mattered now, and their flight's timescale of four hours. Once they landed, unopposed, the rioting would die down, and the broadcasting media, the ministries and the Royal Palace would all be as secure as the airport was now. Frustration welled up; his knowledge of what they intended was irrelevant now, far too late. He left all sadness to Tim. For himself, he was angry at a personal defeat by Babbington . . .

. . . and frightened for his life.

Brandis was using the radio again, headphone pressed against the side of his face like a cooling compress. "Arresting groups, report in . . . yes, yes—where is he, then? Find him . . . both dead? Yes, very well—and they're secure? Good. Durbar Square is quiet now—good. Yes, get the army units to keep moving the riot areas north, away from the center. Keep me informed. Out."

The young man Brigitte called Pieter—from Penang—stood in the doorway, grinning, one hand brushing hair from his forehead.

"Yes?"

"The airport staff are accounted for. We've got them in the cafeteria, under guard, along with a total of twenty-three stranded passengers—mostly Nepalis, a few Indians, two English . . . that's all, General."

"Good," she acknowledged quietly.

"Good," Brandis reiterated, "that brings us up to date. It's time, General, to report to Moscow . . . I think."

"You make the report, Gerd. I'm sure he'd rather hear it all from you."

"Yes, General. Shall I make my report from the tower?"

"As you please, Gerd." She waved him languidly away. "I already know what you have to report. Yes, do it from the tower."

She had not bothered to turn to look at him as she spoke. Brandis glared at her back, then, seeing Aubrey watching him, smiled and drew his finger across his throat. A moment later he was gone.

"You're certain of success, then?" Aubrey asked.

"What? Oh, why not?" She really was confident to the point of indifference. "Are *you* going to be able to stop it?"

Aubrey shook his head. "I meant, afterwards. How do the Russians expect to hold on here? I accept the world would care little at present, even if it knew, but as the weeks and months go by . . . What will the Chinese think, for example?"

"Oh, Kenneth," she replied with something like amusement, "you really are so out-of-date. We will be *asked* to stay here by the King, by the government. To help them prevent Nepal being occupied by unfriendly powers. Hadn't you thought it through? Babbington has."

"I see." All very plausible. "Yes, perhaps so."

"Good. You see now." The subject evidently bored her. Then her eyes glittered. "Why did you take away my son?" she all but hissed, her lumpy old body leaning forward in her chair, hands knotted together in her lap.

"I didn't. One might well say you drove him away."

"*I?*"

"Possibly. Kurt was—" He swallowed and continued. There would be no reprieve for him, any more than for Nepal. He might as well speak. "—a greedy, lazy, rather stupid young man. But, hadn't you thought it through?" he mocked. Her face narrowed. "He wanted all the cheap baubles he thought the other side of your Wall would give him." Then, more softly, he said: "I did not wish it to happen. He—attempted to escape. You *frightened* him into wanting to come back, there was no other reason for his death!"

She hesitated, taut and quivering in the chair, her face flushed at the cheekbones, her lips mobile. Her struggle for control of herself was evident on her lined, tired face, so much so that, unexpectedly, sympathy plucked at him momentarily, before fear of her returned. She said with recovered calm: "Nor for yours . . ."

"What is it you want? Revenge for your son's death? Or is it that you just want to *win* against me?"

She smiled almost at once.

"Either way, your future appears a little tarnished—and brief." With Brandis' departure, she had begun to indulge the personal life again, now more vigorously than before. The four aircraft were in the air. The operation's successful conclusion was, to her, inevitable. "Very brief," she added unnecessarily.

"Then you'll be doing just what Babbington wants." Brigitte shook her head. "What I want." She smiled, opening her hands in a showing, proving gesture. "You can watch them land, Kenneth. I will allow you that long." She looked at her watch, ostentatiously so. "Three hours and fifty minutes."

She settled back in her chair. Despite the fear tightening his throat and his thoughts, he could almost imagine her, in that matronly, certain calm, pulling unfinished knitting from her handbag.

Durbar Square was unreal in the moonlight, filled with pale patchwork light and vast shadows, and the litter of a riot that must have passed like a tornado. The occasional, white-wrapped lump of a dead body, glass pricking out the moonlight, a burned-out car that still smelled of scorched rubber, an overturned bus, paper and leaflets, cloth, bottles, trodden vegetables.

They left the Land-Rover and the truck, guarded by three Gurkhas, near the silence of the Kumari Temple, and flitted through shadows beneath the wooden, crudely painted faces of Shiva and Parvati looking down from the upper balcony of their temple house. Tim glanced upward. They seemed like statues of a roué and his mistress as he hurried past. A gap of moonlight and the shadow of a police vehicle heading sedately for the rear of police headquarters. Tim pressed back into shadow and felt his heart and flesh thudding against the wooden door at his back.

Then the oversized relief of the Black Bhairev, Shiva in his most terrifying form, confronted him from no more than yards away, as the Gurkhas hurried on, faces averted. A garland of skulls, protruding eyes and fangs, three pairs of arms all bearing swords, severed heads, shields. The feet of the relief stamped upon a corpse. He shivered, only partly from the danger and the sense of time escaping him. All around him, between one breath and the next, he was aware of the forest of temples, the dull gleam of gold, the solidity of wood and stone. The protruding eyes of the god glared at him. Then Gan's urgent whisper broke the moment and he hurried through another stream of pale moonlight into deeper shadow. The façade of the Police HQ was flanked with parked vehicles and gleamed with lights. In the shadows near him were Gan, the captain—somehow still confused at any moment he was not obeying a direct order—and fourteen Gurkhas and soldiers from the detachment guarding the Foreign Ministry. He forced aside the ludicrous, pitifully small figure and the sense of the police building and the number of its lights, its vehicles, the shadows passing across curtains and closed blinds.

Guns. A mortar. Any weapons.

He looked at his watch, holding its dial toward the gleam from the building opposite. There was a smell of spilled petrol, the sigh of smoke from a fire that had been extinguished. 10:30. His fist clenched involuntarily. *The plan is crazy, crazy—*

That was Gan. With the captain's support. Argument, discussion, persuasion, all absorbing time like sponges, mopping clean nearly two hours. Together with the hiding, the enforced concealments, the long, slow route that skirted the riots and the army patrols and the police sweeps. *It's the only way to stop them landing,* he had pressed, over and over, wearing them down, the tense, anticipatory presence of the Gurkhas doing much of his work for him. Eventually, they had reached a kind of agreement; reached Durbar Square.

A pathetic little collection of small arms and Indian rifles, a handful of two-way radios, two grenades . . . They'd finally agreed because they needed more and better weapons even to defend themselves. The Gurkha ahead of them waved his arm, clear in the moonlight, and Gardiner pushed himself away from the wall as lights sprang out from the police building and men emerged hurriedly. It seemed less than seconds before engines grumbled and caught, brakes rasped off, headlights shone out. He crouched in a temple's small doorway, his face averted, his hands squeezed beneath his armpits, utterly aware of the whiteness of his skin. Noise filled the square, booming off the silent palaces and temples, while the glare of headlights and the squeal of tires seemed to accuse. Above all, drumming most insistently, was his renewed sense of time. 10:30. At best, *they* were halfway to Kathmandu already.

Amid the noise, the walkie-talkie in his breast pocket began reporting. He flicked it to Transmit without removing it from his pocket, his mouth close to it already in his concealment.

"Yes?" he snapped in a hoarse whisper.

He strained to hear Harka, reporting from opposite the Kot. Even the thought of the place brought the stench of blood to his nostrils. The glare of headlights dimmed, bouncing off ornamental façades, illuminating Shiva's glare, the Buddha's compassion.

"A few guards on duty. Much of the place is in darkness, Captain Sahib."

It fitted with the almost deliberate quiet of the square, this sudden activity from the police. They and the army were moving rioters and themselves north and east, away from the center of Kathmandu and the airport. Durbar Square fell into silence again, the noise of the police patrols lost in narrow, twisting streets. Their HQ now suggested emptiness.

Gan's fierce whisper startled him into a narrowed, calculating awareness. He felt a sense of calm and purpose fill him, assisted by renewed urgency. He glanced at his watch. 10:33. The past two hours became of no account. He slipped into another narrow doorway, alongside Gan, whose eyes gleamed in the moonlight. He pressed the walkie-talkie to his lips.

"Move up, everybody—stay out of the light!" he ordered. At once, shadows flitted silently up toward the courtyard of the Kot and its surrounding walls.

The gate was open. From the shadows beside it, he studied the two-story building that adjoined the sacrificial courtyard. And the armory, lightless and lumpy in the night. He waved his arm twice, vigorously. Harka and his companion slipped along the shadow of the wall. Tim could smell the old, dried blood. Dasain had begun this, it had been the day of sacrifice in the Kot when he had seen and been seen by Brandis.

There were two guards outside the entrance to the barracks. The noise of a radio from somewhere, the smell of cooking, the occasional punctuation of laughter or argument. A sense of somnolence; tired units off-duty or reserves held against some emergency. Harka and his companion were lost in deeper shadow. The backup was in place. Tim turned to the captain, hesitant beside him.

"You know what to do, Captain?" He leaned close, studying the man's face. The uniformed soldiers from the Singha Durbar lined up in a loose double column and his Gurkhas slipped between them, at once smaller, defeated; shoulders hunched, faces hanging. The rattle and clink of weapons being adjusted. "Captain?" he insisted.

The captain nodded. It had become an order, and he was able to envisage his next moments clearly. Tim stooped to the ground and rubbed earth onto his hands, then his face, smearing the dry, crumbling dust as well as he could, spitting onto it to make it adhere to his skin. Gan was grinning. He, too, seemed to embrace his situation now that its crisis was imminent, and ignore what lay beyond this preliminary raid on the armory.

"Harka—we're coming in now," he whispered, knowing the Gurkha would be listening to his radio through the thickness of his pullover, pressing it against his ear as he hunched into a corner.

He waved his arm, once. Gan fell in behind him as he slipped into the middle of the ragged column of prisoners being brought back, on orders, to the Kot barracks. It did not matter who they were, what they had done . . . there *had* to be prisoners. There was always an enemy, people to be rounded up.

The guards became wakeful, tense, then comforted by familiar

uniforms and defeated shoulders. Tim watched them with a joggling camera's eyes, beginning to feel edgy as the distance short-
ened. Their pace seemed slow-and-quick at once. The tension
of the Gurkhas around him, without even their *kukris,* was like
the close heat of a sauna. The smell of the blood was persistent,
alarming. His stomach churned with tension and revulsion.
Then, just as his head was thudding with the need to give the
man an order, the captain raised his hand and ordered prisoners
and escort to halt directly in front of the two guards.

The Nepali was quick, incisive, not open to question. The
Gurkhas seemed to shuffle, stamp like nervous grazing animals.
*Terrorists . . . disaffected groups . . . these were caught looting—
Gurkhas once . . .* The captain spat at that point, simply to in-
crease his authority. Then the moments stretched, thinned,
threatened to snap.

"I will see to it personally that they are locked up. And make
my report—" The captain was extemporizing, luxuriating in his
pivotal role. He mounted the two low steps, motioning his men
to follow.

Tim held his breath, then the guards moved almost deco-
rously aside.

"Quickly!" he snapped at his men, "I haven't all night to
waste on these people!"

Tim bowed his head and Gan pressed concealingly close. He
stumbled slightly on the first step and then they were past the
guards and inside the empty, echoing hallway of the barracks.
Corridors led off, green-painted, drab. A smell of damp. The
captain, the moment he looked at Gardiner, seemed to mentally
stumble until Tim said:

"Good. Now, quickly!"

The rattles and catching noises as weapons were handed or
thrown back, the quick, explosive breaths, the sheathing of
kukris; again, the nervous stamping of boots and bare feet as
of anxious, excited animals. Racehorses now, he thought. He
pointed silently, watching the doors through which they had
come. Outside, Harka and his companion were disposing of the
guards. He fancied he heard the gasp of a choked, violent breath,
the fall of a body. They'd change into the uniforms, please God
they hadn't bloodied, and take the guards' places on the steps.
Their emergency way out.

The building closed in for a moment, trapping him and the
others, then he pointed down a long, ill-lit corridor that might

have been in some dilapidated hospital, and they moved off, slowly at first. Gurkhas and soldiers fell away from them like leaves at the junction of each corridor. He could not quite suppress the sense of struggling deeper and deeper into some unretraceable complex of mole-tunnels and his breathing became difficult, was done by swallowing. They were halfway to the armory, then three-quarters, almost there, it was the next turning and the place was still empty on the ground floor, *this* turning—

They stumbled upon an officer coming out of a lavatory door, watched his surprise like spectators, a small, sweating, herded group of men he did not recognize and some of whom were in remnants of Gurkha uniform. Gan shot him and the noise banged back behind them down the last corridor and into the next, dying away with distance. Tim grabbed the rifle's hot barrel angrily, but Gan merely glared at him and stepped over the dead officer.

An office, a glass wall behind which were surprised faces, and the guards outside the doors who were little more than bulky, wavering shadows against frosted glass. There was the sweet smell of lubricating oil and coffee before the firing began. Ganesh's Ishapur rifle had been switched to automatic. The glass crazed and fell inward. The men in the office fell away gently but the guards, struggling to bring their own weapons to bear, were flung against the frosted glass—one of them through it so that his body hung suspended, as if on barbed wire. It was over in less time than it took the echoes of the firing to drain away. There remained the stench of firing until the spilled, holed coffeepot reasserted its aroma. The smoke cleared.

"The keys—in the office!" Gardiner snapped, surprisingly unmoved by the bodies. He felt nothing—nothing, he assured himself.

Gan entered the office through its smashed door, his boots crunching on a litter of glass fragments. A box had been knocked over, presumably by one of the two men who had died in the room. The stubby shapes of silencers rolled under Gan's feet with a painful, unnerving irony. They had had to make the noise, knew they would have to, but the sense of blind mole-tunnels returned and he shivered before hurrying into the office. Gan waved a bunch of keys in the air that he had removed from a labeled board. Beyond the office's wreckage, the bodies of the two guards, their rifles appropriated, were being bundled aside.

Gardiner fumbled with the keys, found the two for the locks, and he and Gan opened the doors by heaving against them.

"Watch the corridor!" he called over his shoulder. The smell of oil again. The scent of weapons. He fumbled his hand along, up and down the wall for the light switch. In the moment before he found it, he remembered the blood on one wall, drops as big as petals. The misshapen, unmoving bodies were near his feet as the light gleamed a dusty pale white down the steel-shelved corridors of the armory. "You two with Major Gan, quickly! Remember, ammunition, right caliber and plenty of it—Bren guns, a mortar, two . . . don't play toyshops, anyone, we haven't got time!"

The Gurkhas scattered, tugging rifles off their racks, hefting boxes of labeled ammunition that would fit the Ishapurs they already had, the Sterling submachine guns, the pistols . . . 7.62, 9 millimeter—36M grenades, British OML 81 millimeter mortars or RPG-7 antitank weapons and explosives. *He* had to find the explosives. His sense of an altered *karma* was with him for the first hurried steps into the armory, the Gurkhas and the captain's soldiers spreading out ahead of him like people admitted to the opening day of a store's January sale. His new *karma* was waiting for him somewhere ahead—

—but not as urgently as the need for these weapons. Someone cried out they had a mortar, rattling and grunting and banging echoed throughout the armory. He glanced at his watch. Explosives, explosives . . . even Gan didn't know what he needed them for, because Gan would have ridiculed the idea. Forty-five seconds since he had switched on the lights, a minute and more since the shooting had echoed away down the corridors. The keys were warm in his clutching hand, his forehead sprang perspiration, his shirt was beginning to stick to his back.

"One box 7.62, Captain Sahib!" Something was being dragged along the concrete floor with a grinding sound that set his teeth on edge.

"One box 9 millimeter, Captain Sahib!" yelled another, excited, high voice.

The chorus continued. "*Two* mortars, Captain Sahib!"

"L-15-A cartridges, Captain Sahib!"

"Fuses, Captain Sahib—number 162!"

Explosives, fucking explosives! He looked at his watch. Their voices were like those of kids playing some game! The two on the door, Harka and the other Gurkha were about to go out of the main gate to the courtyard—*now!* Engine start for the Land-Rover and the old truck . . . *now! The fucking explosives!* He ran haltingly past rifles, ammunition, rifles, pistols—he snatched up a 9mm Browning HP slick with oil, fumbled some clips from an unlocked box—sloppy that!—but there were no explosives. He was near the end of the shelf-lined corridor.

"Explosives!" he yelled at the top of his voice. First two guards falling back down the ground floor corridor now!

"No, Captain Sahib . . ." No, no, no, the chorus responded, exerted voices full of effortful breathing. No explosives!

"Mines, Captain?"

He pressed away confusion, contradiction. There was a moment of standing apart from himself and observing these soldierly routines, this conditioned, planned activity, then the ill-focused image of himself became clear.

Mines, mines . . . ?

"Yes! Where are you?"

"Here, Captain Sahib!"

"Third set of shelves from you!" Gan's voice, the only one seemingly without excitement.

He careered around the end of his corridor, saw them twenty yards away from him, reached them, panting. A box had been broken open. Cyrillic lettering. The mines had come via the Indian Army. He rubbed his face. The radio in his pocket chirruped. The Land-Rover and the truck had begun moving through Durbar Square. He looked at his watch, at the box of mines, the stacks of boxes all similarly, mysteriously labeled . . . which bloody mine? He needed to know! Yes, they were the best second option, but mines matched fuses and fuses had to be used for hand laying! The Gurkhas in the corridors beyond the armory were falling back into the final corridor where the officer's body lay—*now!*

He recognized the mine. "TM-46!" he shouted as excited as the men around him, his body bathed in sweat, his cheeks hot. "Find MV-5 somewhere!" His hand traced across boxes, he shuffled along the shelves like a panicky clerk. Cyrillic letters—M—V . . . 5, 5 . . . M was M, even in Cyrillic!

White-stenciled letters and a number, in English! MV-5.

"These! As many mines as you can—you and you, yes, Corporal—leave the second mortar, bring the mines!"

"No—" Gan began to interrupt, but Gardiner merely glared at him, and snapped:

"Yes!"

He glanced along the corridor of shelves and racks. He could hear hurrying bootsteps. No alarm, not yet, but they're running fast—

Alarm and firing in the same moment. The first Gurkha appeared, weaponless, arm hanging limply, then the second Gurkha held him, began pushing him.

"The loading bay!" he shouted. "Give us cover!" He was aware of the keys in his hand once more. Gan's face was dark with fear, but he felt only a wild, almost irrational exhilaration. He grinned vividly at Gan, waving the Gurkhas past him toward the doors to the armory's loading bay. The Land-Rover and the truck should be pulling into it in another minute. Wood scraped and splintered along the concrete floor as the shooting began immediately outside the armory door—or just inside it. A loudspeaker bellowed orders to cease firing, warning of the danger. His Gurkhas fired back. There was one kneeling in the hard dusty light near the doors, clutching his stomach, abandoned and dying. Another Gurkha's face was pale as he passed Gardiner.

Why was that alarm so *long* in sounding? He had almost ignored its absence, but it had been late. Delayed? As if in answer, the walkie-talkie chirped again and it was Harka's voice.

"Captain Sahib!" A note of panic. The small, vulnerable group was waiting near the loading bay's steel roller door like agitated yet successful looters. "A tank, Captain Sahib! Near the main gates, coming towards the courtyard. Two trucks, but the tank, Captain—"

They hadn't sounded the alarm because they'd wanted to set the trap first. The tank was moving into position. He looked at the keys in his hand. He didn't even have the time to discover which one unlocked the steel door. They were trapped and their vehicles, waiting outside, were bottled up, too.

The alarm seemed frantic, even exultant. There were troops moving cautiously into the armory now.

"The tank is at the gates!" he heard Harka cry.

He felt a weariness that was beyond fear and the prospect of his death. Even so, his damnable brain continued to function like that of someone half-asleep, and he could not stop himself analyzing, collating—*thinking*, for Heaven's sake! Without turning to face her, he announced: "You killed Mrs. Carteret, Brigitte—you can't be forgiven for that."

An hour and twenty minutes remained before the four transports reached Kathmandu. The radio behind him had been silent for forty minutes now. The aircraft were passing through the bony radar shield of the Karakoram range, in Indian airspace and maintaining a strict radio silence. Gandhi may have secretly allowed their flight, for all he knew. It did not matter. They were coming.

And still Brigitte fascinated him. She remained the only problem unanswered in his near half-century in intelligence. Resolution lay in her hands now. The girl in the gondola, her face dim in the foggy lamplight, the girl on the train, the growing young woman in America, the face dislocated by shock and pain at the barrier to the Russian Sector in Berlin . . . the woman growing older, seen only in photographs or read of in intelligence reports. The woman climbing to the peak in East Berlin . . . The images flitted and troubled like moths, distracting him whether he willed it or no from the prospect of death.

He looked out through his own reflection in the lounge window across the unlit, silent airport. There seemed to be fewer fires in the city now, but the tension out there thrummed against the glass as if it were some sensitive membrane. He touched the window, almost expecting a small electric shock. It was cool. Straining eyesight, he could make out the undefined lumps that were light tanks, trucks, Land-Rovers, an armored car. He discerned the occasional flitting of shadows, sometimes the glow of torches and the lighting of cigarettes.

He turned toward Brigitte. Her face was puzzled, but her eyes were clear and bright.

"You killed my son," she announced quite calmly. Certain and untroubled.

He shivered as he replied.

"I did not. I did not cause his death. He was not innocent. I would forgive you the danger you posed to me, even to Tim—but I will not forgive you the innocent *bystanders!* The civilians . . . and don't answer me with some glib assertion that there are no civilians anymore. You are not a *terrorist*—not yet."

An anger was welling up in him that had nothing to do with his personal danger. The words forced themselves out. "Kurt was involved, he was playing the Great Game, Brigitte. But, for all your cleverness, your detachment from the personal life, you

had to use a bomb in London and you killed a dotty old lady—
rather loud-voiced, bigoted . . . but *innocent.* I presume someone
is feeding her cats . . ." He broke off, strangely affected by that
irrelevant idea. His voice was rougher as he continued. "I'm
tired of it, Brigitte, and so should you be. This place—the
slaughter, the putting down of opposition, the occupation . . .
that damnable pattern which is all you people seem to have to
offer the world!"

Immediately, she snapped back: "Kenneth, you always were
a moralizing old bore!" Her lips moved slowly, unfamiliarly into
a smile. "You're looking for something to salvage here . . . oh,
yes, don't forget how well we know each other. You want to
feel good." She sighed. "I suppose I should not complain. It is
all you have left."

"What do you intend doing with Lin?" he asked of the silent
airport, the runway lights the only illumination as they retreated
away to almost meet in a distant point.

"Why should you be concerned?"

"I'm not." And yet he was. Concerned even with Lin, his
mind nagging over that bone along with all the others that filled
his thoughts. "I'm not," he repeated softly, stroking his chin.
His mood suggested that he and she were equals, debating the
fate of others. "But can't you see that *he's* tired, Brigitte? All
he wants to do is to walk out of this imprisoning palace, like
the Lord Siddhartha did, cut off his hair—symbolically, of
course—and renounce his life up to this moment . . . Can't you
understand that, Brigitte?" And he shivered because he realized
he was no longer speaking of Lin at all.

He glanced at his watch. Fifteen more minutes in Indian airspace, then the aircraft would contact the Kathmandu tower,
an hour away from touchdown. By daylight, the Russians would
be in possession of the capital, their people would form the new,
pro-Soviet government, and the world would then be forced to
stand by and simply watch or else be accused of—

He smiled bitterly. Defeat rankled like an ague. Any move
against Nepal after tomorrow, whether by the West or the Chinese, would appear an act of war. And Babbington would be
halfway up the ladder and climbing like a monkey towards . . .
what? The Chairmanship of the KGB?

The brute reality of his situation barged against him; he could postpone and disguise fear no longer. In less than two hours, he would simply cease to exist.

His whole body felt hollow.

"Which key—which damned key?" His forehead and cheeks were hot, his whole body quivering. There were shouted orders behind them, the cautious, dodging advance of the first soldiers. The Gurkhas and the captain's men twitched and shuffled. "Which *key?*" He glanced up into Ganesh's face and saw that the trap had already closed for the Nepali. There was nothing but panic in his eyes and around his mouth.

He thrust another of the keys into the first lock, and it slid home. He turned it, heard the click. The walkie-talkie spilled words like the ticks of a clock. *Through the gate, Captain . . . men getting down from the trucks, spreading out . . . dozen, twenty . . .* Harka was up on the low eaves of a temple's roof, spotting for them, watching the net tighten. The voice of Dhanraj from the Land-Rover punctuated the excitement of Harka's commentary. *They have not seen us, not yet . . . hurry, hurry, Captain Timothy Sahib, hurry . . .* a wild, tormenting undercurrent to the troop dispositions being taken up in the shadows of the Kot. Second key, second—

It turned, the click was lost in his own sigh of relief and Gan's explosive breathing.

"Up with the door!"

The steel door rolled upward, noises of effort drowned by its rattle. The air outside the armory seemed cooler. The door clanged into stillness, the sound of wood again as the boxes were dragged across the loading bay toward the Land-Rover and the truck. He looked behind him, even as he pointed his orders with his hands and fingers. He could see them approaching in cautious, half-concealing little spurts. Now, they would move more quickly, there would be lines of fire in moments. He listened but could not hear the tank, not yet.

Boxes thudded into the rear of the truck, a panic of men surrounding its open tailgate. Shouts of effort. "Yes, there! Pick that box up! Get aboard—yes, you! Leave that! In, in, *in!*" He scrambled into the passenger seat of the Land-Rover. The driver grinned shakily at him. Gan's features were a grim mask.

The tank slid and swerved around a corner and was ahead of them. Its 105mm cannon dipped like the long proboscis of some huge insect. The machine gun mounted close to it flicked and came to bear more quickly. The tank paused, becoming a gun platform, no longer a vehicle. The cannon steadied . . . he was mesmerized. The Land-Rover's engine idled, the truck's caught and roared, but neither vehicle moved. The tank appraised them, almost leisurely. Moonlight shone on its flanks. The noise of its rumbling engine and the noise of their vehicles filled the space below the overhanging corrugated roof of the loading bay.

Gardiner dragged his eyes away from the tank and glanced wildly behind him. The first soldier peered around the edge of the door, his rifle upright, pressed against his cheek. Someone fired two rounds from the truck and the face ducked away out of sight. Gardiner seemed awakened by the noise, the finger-click of the hypnotist.

The tank stared at them, its machine gun pointing and still silent—

—bluff! *It was a bluff!*

"Fucking hell, fucking hell . . ." Gan was repeating in his now-absurd Sandhurst accent.

Bluff! The tank was being dangled in front of their eyes, freezing them to the spot, while the soldiers behind them reached the loading bay and surrounded—

It couldn't fucking well risk opening fire down here, with all that bloody ammunition in the armory! For Christ's sake move, then!

He raised his hand to signal the truck, yelling at Dhanraj, the driver of the Land-Rover: "Go, go, *go!*" A hesitation, then he bellowed, almost standing up in his seat: "Go *round* the fucking tank! Go *round* it! They won't *fire!*"

He fell into his seat as Dhanraj let out the clutch and the Land-Rover squealed toward the tank like a rabbit rushing into a car's headlights. They'll open fire as soon as we're in—

—moonlight slid over them as they came out from beneath the roof. He flinched even before the first shots, at once aware that there was live ammunition all around him like a bomb awaiting a detonator. Something thudded into the door at his side, another bullet nipped past his head. There was a pain, and his ear stained his hand as he held it, then inspected his palm. The driver's side of the vehicle crunched against something soft, then against the brick of the courtyard wall as Dhanraj fought it through the gates, which two soldiers were trying to close before they panicked and ran aside from the Land-Rover. Then the truck tore at the wood of the half-shut gate before it, too, was outside the Kot, back in Durbar Square.

Figures were running toward them, Harka and his companion both grinning, clambering aboard the truck as it barely slowed for them. The noise of tires and engines boomed back off temples and sounded hollowly into courtyards. His wild exhilaration filled his chest and throat. Pointless firing behind them as they careered toward Basantapur Square. He looked back. Running soldiers and the tank emerging from the Kot as slowly as a huge snail.

He'd done it . . .

. . . and only just begun.

16

The Empire Strikes Back

Babbington watched Kapustin leaning heavily over the intercom, ordering his limousine to be brought for them. It was not merely his imagination that painted the older man as hesitant, unsure of his mental footing; aware, perhaps for the first time in years, of the distances between offices inside the Kremlin, of the necessity that the heavy doors be opened for him. In contrast, the idea of the car, of *any* movement now was like the thrill of an electric current through Babbington's body.

The Antonov transports with the cargoes of *spetsnaz* troops and equipment were fifty-four minutes from Kathmandu, seven minutes into Nepali airspace and back in satellite radio contact with the *Topi* Planning Group. He breathed calmly, satisfyingly, like someone who had just undergone a searching but satisfactory medical.

Kapustin flicked off the intercom and looked up at him from beneath his thick, black eyebrows, his square features suspicious. Babbington smiled generously. Kapustin grimaced in response.

"All going very nicely!" he observed. It was an exact repetition of what he had said before ordering his Chaika. Babbington would ride in the black limousine like a man being taken for a test drive in a car he was thinking of purchasing.

"I think so," he murmured, plucking his beard.

"All turning out *very* well for *you!*" Babbington held his breath. "The Chinks have another plateful of trouble in their

Politburo, playing musical chairs again, the Americans are about to vote for their new President and don't give a damn about the rest of the world, the UN has its dark glasses on as usual and the British are indifferent, as is their way . . . I congratulate you, Andrew!" There was a sense of ingratiation about the observations, stronger than their resentment.

Babbington shrugged irritatingly. "Ah, my friend," he drawled. "I prefer to think of it as good intelligence assisting good, thorough planning . . . shall we go?" He ostentatiously looked at the clock, then at his watch.

"Very well . . ." Kapustin hesitated, then said bluntly: "You'll do very well out of this, Andrew. Just *wait* until I retire." He sighed. "It won't be long."

"I think I can do that," he replied. Kapustin nodded mockingly.

"After all," he observed, "one old man tonight should satisfy you."

"Perhaps . . ." There was a niggling little resentment that he had thrown Aubrey to the old German woman rather than savoring his destruction by personal direction, but it did not alloy his satisfaction. It was gratifying to think of himself above that kind of petty personal vengeance. *Topi* was more important than Aubrey's life and death. That boy Gardiner was out of it now, vanished somewhere into Kathmandu with a pathetic bodyguard of ex-Gurkhas. Lin would have to go, of course. He was effectively blown and no longer *sound*. He himself was the runner with no more hurdles to clear, the other competitors behind him, and only the tape ahead. His chest expanded, as if straining for the imagined tape. "Yes," he added.

He caught the noise of snow tires crunching beyond the window. Sleet blew across the dark gap between the long curtains and the red stars on the Kremlin towers twinkled like lights on a Christmas tree.

"I think our transport has arrived."

He glanced at the clock one last time as Kapustin struggled into his heavy greatcoat and cast about for his gloves and fur hat. Fifty minutes to touchdown, and the tower in Brandis' safe hands—Brigitte's successor—as *he* was undoubtedly Kapustin's. He looked proprietarially around the vast office. Much of the furniture was not to his taste, but soon he could loot the Kremlin for anything he wanted.

He picked up his coat and fur hat. And smiled. He could envisage, with startling clarity, that final moment of surprise-becoming-pain on Aubrey's face as the old woman disposed of him with a bullet.

"Shall we go?" he asked, blithely.

There were a few scattered lights against which the high perimeter fence of the airport seemed intermittent, in disrepair. The runway lights, a glow from windows in the terminal building, a spillage of light from near the cargo terminal, the empty shadows of a handful of parked aircraft. It was like a decaying, barely inhabited suburb surrounded by wasteland. The silence pressed around them when the engines of the Land-Rover and the old truck were switched off.

Gardiner bent low, trying to make a backcloth out of the rows of runway lights. The lumpy shadows of aircraft like huge cattle in a darkened field, fuel tankers, a tug and a little train of baggage trolleys . . . the crash and fire tenders and ambulances all tidied to one side of the terminal like household items cleared on the expectation of visitors. And the dim glow from behind green glass of the lights in the control tower.

Then Ganesh was crouching beside him and he remembered the Land-Rover careering through Durbar Square. Time had clicked away in his head, yet they had had to crisscross the old city, throwing off all pursuit . . . and they'd had to check dispositions as best they could. He had had to know locations, distances, response times—how long he could hold the tower after taking it . . . if they could take it. The Nepali army units were well to the north and northeast of the city center and the rioting had died into sporadic outbursts of fire, violence and looting. The whole city seemed to be paused between one violent breath and the next. His exhilaration was diminished by two dead and three wounded.

Then he stood up, waving his hands above his head. "Gather round!" he called in a loud, hoarse whisper. "To me, everyone, to me!" The crunch of dust and gravel under their boots, the rustle of footsteps, the grins and nerves electric in the darkness. Gardiner unfolded a sketch of the airport and flicked on the pencil beam of a slim flashlight from the Land-Rover's dashboard compartment. The heat of their bodies stifled in the warm night, he could smell their bodies, their mouths. His nerves jumped and flickered like a neon striplight that would not come fully on. "Here," he said, indicating their position outside the fence.

"Tower—here . . . Terminal, here . . . there must be an army unit over there—" He waved toward the cargo terminal. "—they may have been clearing mustering points. It looks as if the passenger terminal's been cleared, for the most part . . ." He paused, his attention straying toward the dark, star-filled sky and the pale halo of the new moon. Silence, still nothing more than silence. Perhaps he had an hour, perhaps half an hour, perhaps no more than a few minutes. Once they began their final approach, it would be too late to stop them. Within ten minutes of first catching the noise of their huge engines or glimpsing their navigation lights floating through the stars, hundreds of armed men would be debouched from the big Antonovs.

He spoke quickly, breathlessly. "Aitasing, yours is the diversion. Take the Brens and clear out the cargo terminal. At *least* keep them pinned down there—"

"Captain Sahib," the NCO acknowledged gravely.

"Grenades, the mortar, anything you need . . . but wait for my signal. Harka?"

"Yes, Captain Sahib!"

"Crossfire around the main gates . . . you take the RPG-7s and a handful of mines. *Nothing* comes through those main gates, not even one of those tanks—understand?" There was an instant's fragility, as if his frame was buffeted by illness—the tiny, inadequate group of men around him, the spreading acres of the airport, the numbers that could be massed against any action of theirs—and then he said firmly: "Gan—your job is the mines . . . use the touchdown-zone markings as your starting point and the runway centerline lights as your guide and spread them out in this loose pattern . . ." He pointed at his sketch. "Be *accurate* about distances, especially the point where you begin laying . . . OK?" He looked up at Ganesh, who bit his top lip and merely nodded, curtly and quickly.

Gardiner's ear ached, the pad and plaster on it making it feel heavy, emphasizing its steady throb. The shoulder of his shirt had dried.

"OK, Dhanraj—wire cutters. Let's get on with it!" There was a collective sigh like the noise of a small breeze and he felt that if he touched any of them, sparks of static would fly. "You two men—on guard here." Was there something else? Yes. "And look after our three wounded . . ."

"Captain Sahib."

The latticed wire of the fence snapped in small detonations

then creaked as it was pulled back. Gardiner looked across at the tower, then at the Nepali army captain and the two men who remained closest to the Land-Rover: a uniformed soldier with a corporal's stripes on his sleeve and Harka's brother, Lal-bahadur.

"Ready, Captain Nima?" he asked, his breath catching in the words as if snagging on the cut fence.

The captain managed a weak smile. "Yes, Captain Timothy."

He watched Aitasing's group slip through the wire and flit away into the moonlit darkness, then Harka's party, made strange in outline by the lumps and pipes of the weapons they carried. He turned to Ganesh and the two Gurkhas with him. Pitiful numbers—

He rid himself of the thought.

"Gan?" he inquired, hesitantly offering his hand. There was a flash of Ganesh's habitual skepticism in the gleam of his eyes, then he took Gardiner's fingers, touching them lightly. "OK," he said.

"I'll keep in contact if I can. I don't know how much time we have. Give me—fifteen minutes, no more, before you begin. If I haven't got an accurate timing by then, you get started . . . or start the moment you hear engine noise, however faint!" He took the two pairs of night glasses from the Land-Rover—courtesy of Gan's quick collection of souvenirs the day he was dismissed from the Brigade—and handed one to Ganesh. "Keep us in sight."

He turned to the fence. Raised and focused the glasses and the world went gray and ghostly. Shadows flitted, the whole scene was like a moving photographic negative. Aitasing's group hurrying toward the explosion of gray light that was the cargo terminal, Harka's group running semicrouched alongside the runway's edge, weighted by weapons, the two RPG rocket launchers sticking up like breathing tubes. Movement near the tower, stranded like a lighthouse in the middle of the darkness. A man coming from the terminal building, smoking. A soldier in shadow greeting him.

He watched for a few moments, then said: "OK, we're on our way."

The night glasses, as soon as he lowered them, reminded him that others may be similarly equipped and they might already have been spotted, selected as targets. Then, swallowing fear and feeling excitement well up in its place, he ducked through the hole cut in the perimeter fence, waited until Nima and the others joined him, then they set off on a ragged, crouching run across the grass toward the runway.

Concrete and the smell of old rubber and oil and the dotted white line and the centerlights as if he had strayed onto a suburban road. He paused, looking along the runway's length toward the threshold lights and the rows of receding approach lights, then the terminal. A few mines like cow pats, what good would they be! He *had* to get the lights turned off, the whole place plunged into darkness!

"Captain?" Lalbahadur prompted.

"What? Oh, yes, Lal—move on, quick as you can." They scuttled across the runway, its reflected heat hotter than the air coming up off the grass. The tower loomed now, the green-glass globe at its top larger, like a flower opening in the night. Subdued, filtered light, and human shadows moving across the glass. The light from a ground floor doorway, from occasional windows.

He motioned them to drop and heard his own breath thumped out as he fell. An horizon of intermittent, glowing light showed him the guard beside the doorway before he brought the night glasses to his eyes and the man sprang out of grayness, almost white with proximity. The repeated glow of a cigarette, his head tossing as if in conversation. Then he saw the second guard, lying on the grass, also smoking. Two rifles. He looked at his watch, then refined the focus of the glasses, trying to penetrate the subaqueous glass at the top of the control tower. Shadows whitened but did not take on substance as they moved with an air of unhurried calm.

He rolled onto his back and sat half-upright, focusing on the cargo terminal—he could see no one except a loose group of soldiers around a truck—then past the terminal. Nothing in that farthest darkness, only whitened, negative shadows. He scanned the terminal's entrances, then its few illuminated windows. Lounges, the bar, a restaurant . . . He orientated himself. A parked armored car—damn!

He flicked on the walkie-talkie. "Harka, are you receiving me? Over."

"Yes, Captain."

"The armored car—you saw it?"

"Yes, Captain—we will take it out, sir, when you give the

order. There is one of the tanks near the main gates, sir. The crew are drinking coffee. We can take that out, too."

"Good. Wait for my order. Out."

He swept the glasses once across the row of lit windows on the terminal's upper floor. Then slowly back . . . slowly, stop . . . The shadow of a small man at the window, the light coming from behind him, his features hardly distinguishable, his face and figure the white of a negative. Shoulders hunched, hands obviously behind his back, his whole manner brooding and defeated. He swallowed the dryness in his mouth and throat, sucking his cheeks. He knew, with all but certainty, that he was looking at Aubrey. Then the figure brushed his hand across a bald head with a swift, dismissive gesture and the identification was indisputable. They'd got Aubrey, put him in the bag and brought him here.

He lay on his back for a moment, oblivious of the clock in his head, and Nima and the others near him. He sighed and gritted his teeth. Aubrey could be killed at any time, he was in danger . . . but they wouldn't until the planes came in, that's why he's here . . .

He rolled over and got to his knees, crouched like an animal. Two guards . . . only two.

"Lal—and you . . . around and behind the tower. Wait for my signal!" he whispered. He waved them forward and they moved off. Nima's breathing was quick beside him. He flicked the glasses across the scene again and again, gradually forgetting the figure of the old man at the window. The two soldiers remained unaroused, unsuspicious. Lalbahadur and the Nepali soldier disappeared, sinking into the grass on the other side of the tower. Waiting with the patience of sheepdogs.

He looked at his watch. Six minutes gone. He had nine minutes to discover the exact timetable before he was forced to take the tower anyway and set the clock of counteractivity in motion. Would the guards know? Was it worth the risk of taking them out, leaving one alive to question? He shook his head. Not yet . . . eight and a half . . . there'd been that bugger strolling between the terminal and the tower even as he watched through the night glasses! Now, no one. But would the guards *know?*

His head ticking as loudly as the old grandfather clock in his parents' hall . . . his watch losing time like a dripping tap . . . eight, seven and a half . . . seven . . . he was getting hot, his forehead stung with sweat, his palms were greasy. The old man at

e their own controllers—" Almost without deci-
er began to tighten his armlock on the man's wind-
merely a reaction, a gathering of tension, from what
rned. The man had answered his questions; he had
of killing the Nepali, no intention . . . He squeezed.
writhed a little, the breath tried to come, then the man
in his arms. Gardiner, dreamlike, simply dropped the
gardless of the appalled look on Nima's face. Then the
fell to his knees, his head against the man's chest, his
Gardiner was indifferent, his head whirling, his body hot
e attempt to cope with what he had learned. His planning
into the air like scraps from a bonfire. *Fifteen minutes* . . .
or seven they'd *hear* the fucking planes! He looked down
dly.

ima said: "He's still breathing—just!"

Fifteen minutes!" Gardiner growled at him as if Nima were
ridiculous. He snatched the walkie-talkie from his pocket,
g the stitching. He whispered into it, angrily: "Gan—start
those mines now, quick as you can. You've got fifteen
utes before touchdown. Don't *argue* with me, get bloody on
it! No, just do as I told you!" He was breathing like an ex-
sted runner. "Harka—give me two of your people now, ren-
zvous the tower—not tomorrow, now! Fifteen minutes is what
e have! Lal—take out those guards immediately! Don't wait
for us, do it!" It was calming and it fended off the encroachment
of failure which was creeping over his skin like a disease, like
leeches from one of those Borneo swamps—

"Aitasing—be ready to open fire the moment I give the
word . . ." He paused for a moment, then murmured—"Good
luck, all of you," sounding pompous even to himself. The unconscious man at his feet insisted he would fail. He breathed deeply,
then listened to the silence. The moment he gave the order, it
would tear, break. He would begin the slaughter of his handful
of Gurkhas and most probably kill himself. He could not move,
as if the man on the ground had firm hold of his ankles, restrain-
ing him.

Then he heard Lal's voice, down by his thigh, from the
walkie-talkie he loosely held.

"They are dead, Captain Sahib—come quickly, sir!"

Irrevocable. The two guards at the foot of the tower were
dead, Gan was already laying the first mine—

the window was his responsibility and came back to him like
a plea . . . six. Gan would be getting tense, checking and recheck-
ing the fuses, their placement in the mines, the sketch, the runway lights . . . Don't turn around to look, he told himself, nor
at the terminal windows or the perimeter fence . . . five and a
half—

—voices. *Namaste, namaste* from the guards, and a response
from a shadow in the doorway, a new shadow and the leap of
a cigarette lighter's flame, then the saunter across the concrete
toward the terminal and the Nepali for *Not long now* echoing
in the night.

He nudged Nima, who was shiveringly alert, and began crawling forward across the cropped, tussocky grass toward the path
to the main terminal building that the Nepali had taken. Gardiner watched him as he passed in front of a light, his cigarette
smoke hanging white in its glow, big insects gleaming within it.
He thrust forward with his toes, his knees, his elbows, wriggling
across the ground, hearing—too loudly—Nima's efforts behind
him. He glanced continually toward the two guards in the shadows of the tower. Hearing their boots scrape as if impatiently
on the gravel, he bent his lips to the radio clipped to his breast
pocket.

"Watch those two, Lal, they're restless. If they spot us, you
must take them out immediately. Over."

There was a muffled acknowledgment and then he was moving again, the muscles in his arms cracking and protesting, his
heart thudding. The Nepali was outdistancing him easily,
though he no more than sauntered. He felt a pluck of desperation. The shadow of a parked baggage cart fell across the grass
and he rose shakily to his feet, his whole frame quivering with
exertion. The Nepali no more than thirty yards ahead had
turned the bend in the path and was beginning to move along
the blind ground-floor façade of the terminal. Nima rose beside
him, breathing stertorously. The smell of diesel fuel. Gardiner
pointed.

"You try to outflank him—stop him going through that door,
whatever! I'll try to overtake him the quiet way." Nima nodded.
"OK—go."

Gardiner stepped onto the concrete path, his heart still beating heavily, his thoughts racing as he measured distances and
did not seem to be overtaking the Nepali . . . who even paused,
then ground out his cigarette butt before moving on. Gardiner

strode out without concealment, suggesting the normality of his being there. His footsteps echoed back out of an alleyway between the terminal and another building as he passed through a stream of light from a lamp and averted his face.

A light glowed on the blind wall, jutting out from it. *Staff Only* it announced in Nepali. It was perhaps twelve or fifteen paces ahead of the man, he was about twenty-five paces behind him. He looked for Nima but could not see him. The apron in front of the terminal was littered with vehicles, including the rank of ambulances and fire trucks, all of which seemed deserted. The quiet was unnerving, the distance defeating between himself and the Nepali.

He ran—and called out.

The Nepali turned, surprised—light face, his own language, an order from the tower . . . the chasing responses joggled and became uncertain as Gardiner closed on him. There was the hesitant, obsequious smile but that was gone in a moment to be replaced by fear of giving displeasure, then the realization that the man coming toward him was moving too quickly to be anything other than a danger. The Nepali turned half-away, flinging up a protecting hand before remembering he was armed and reaching behind his back for the gun that came out, waggled, tried to draw level—

—it clattered against the wall as Gardiner gripped the man's wrist and banged his hand against the brick. The man howled with pain and dropped the pistol, which tinkled like breaking glass but did not fire. Nima came running at once as Gardiner turned the man, squeezing his plump body against him with an obscene tightness, his hand clamped over his nose and mouth. The illuminated sign was almost directly above them, the closed door beside them. The Nepali struggled until Nima picked up the gun and immediately jabbed it hard into the man's padded ribs. There was a damp expulsion of breath and terror against Gardiner's clamped palm. He noticed other signs now. *Authorised Personnel, Staff, Passengers, Arrivals* . . .

At any moment, through any door—

The man's heels scraped on the concrete. "Watch those guards!" Gardiner snapped in a loud whisper. The man struggled now that the gun and the attention of the man holding it were withdrawn. Gardiner crooked his arm across his throat and dragged him, backward, the Nepali's arms banging feebly against him, like those of a drowning man.

The alley. Nima scuttled [ ] from side to side. When he w[ ] ioned Nepali and jabbed the [ ] again and again as if to locate so[ ] Below the man's waistband—th[ ] Gardiner, the mouth trying to bit[ ]

Gardiner leaned his head against t[ ] fiercely: "How long before they get [ ] doing in the tower! Tell me how long [ ] was no interrogative tone, only the inc[ ] pistol jabbed on and on as if wielded by a[ ] flabby body of the Nepali twisted and buc[ ] to wriggle away from the fear Gardiner's v[ ] me how long! Tell me or he kills you! How lon[ ] Tell me, *tell me!*" The necessity to whisper was[ ] pali's body stopped moving, just shivered.

Gardiner glared and nodded at Nima, tossing hi[ ]ead to[ ] cate movement. Nima was puzzled, then understood, placi[ ] barrel of the pistol against the Nepali's temple. Gardiner fe[ ] body pressed against his shoulder in an analogy of climax[ ]

"How long before they land? How many men with gun[ ] the tower? Why are you not at your post? How long before t[ ] land?" He recited the same questions, in an identical, unvary[ ] whisper into the man's ear. He felt his shirt soaked with th[ ] man's sweat, smelled his body as he removed his hand from the Nepali's mouth. "How long before they land? How many men with guns?"

Then he paused and heard the chorus of their breathing, the noise of a tannoy or radio somewhere, the buzz of insects around a light. The thud of the man's heart, the chatter of his teeth. Eventually, he asked in an almost polite, conversational tone: "How long before they land?"

Nima moved the pistol slightly against the man's head, creating sensation where numbness must have grown.

"Fif—fifteen minutes!" the Nepali blurted and the pistol fell away from his temple as Nima's mouth opened. Then his eyes became self-deludingly suspicious. Gardiner forced himself to keep his hold on the man unrelaxed. It was his own heart he could hear now, his own quick breaths.

"How many men with guns?"

"Six, seven maybe."

"Why aren't you there now?"

"—those white lines *there!*" he heard the panicky voice shouting tinnily. Excitement, nerves, fear. Twelve minutes—

"Come on, Nima," he whispered gruffly, grabbing the man's sleeve, dragging him down the alleyway. "Come on! Twelve fucking *minutes!*"

Lin had been turned on like some rusted tap that was now difficult to turn off. Aubrey, staring out of the window, listened because the voice's unexpected smoothness distanced his fears for his own life. Lin talked in what might have been the debating manner of an academic.

The shadows Aubrey had thought he had seen flitting in the darkness down there must have been illusions, created by his slowly, inexorably mounting panic. His heart knocked like someone at a door. There was a sickness in his stomach, a queasiness that rose occasionally like a tide to the back of his throat. And he was weary, too, of the rancorous sense of his defeat and their complete victory. He was waiting for the navigation lights of the first transport to appear against the darkness.

Perhaps Lin talked to avoid staring at his own death? Babbington would not want him now. He was blown.

" . . . riot as a political weapon . . . I have seen it before, Brigitte . . ." Aubrey could see him reflected in the window, rubbing his arms with his hands as if cold. His face was impassive, his eyes deeply sunk, hollowed. Like some skull at the banquet. " . . . burned down a Buddhist shrine!" There was something prim, self-righteous about his anger.

Brigitte tossed her head and blew smoke at the ceiling. Aubrey realized she was watching him, looking into the window's reflection as if into another room.

"I want to stop," he said quietly. "Don't *you* want to stop, Brigitte?"

Aubrey turned to face her, his voice suddenly angry and contemptuous as he said: "Can't you see how sick of it all he is, Brigitte?" She seemed about to answer him as he pressed on. "You blame me for your son's death . . . you blame me for your father's death forty years ago! My God, Brigitte, has your whole life been so damned disappointing and empty that you still cling to *him?* Your father was a traitor, he was taking American atomic secrets to the Russians. He was shot while trying to cross into the Russian Sector of Berlin. I followed you halfway across England, then to Berlin. I caught up with you at the crossing point into the Russian Sector. And the moment you saw me, both of you tried to make a run for it. Your father was shot after the British officer with me had called on him to halt. Three times." He cleared his suddenly tight throat. "Those are the facts of the case." Lin was attentive, Brigitte somehow frozen in her chair, her face white. The images had returned more clearly than newsreel pictures. He plowed on. "I gave no order for his death. He himself provoked the soldier's response by attempting to escape arrest. You reached the other side of the checkpoint and he did not. A simple and rather unedifying tale—but not a religion. Not something to sustain the human spirit for forty years and more!" Her face appeared bruised by his words, then she recaptured certainty with insight.

"What is it, Kenneth? Are you becoming desperate? The truth shall make you free, is that it?" She laughed hoarsely, coughing, shaking her head in denial and amusement.

He postured his contempt, half-turning from her rage. He looked into the darkness outside and toward the spill of light from the cargo terminal where they were preparing for the landing, deplaning and regrouping of the Russian troops. Most of the army must be keeping the city battened down tight. There was no need for more than a few detachments at the airport . . . who else but the Russians were coming to this party? Damn it —*damn* it!

As he dismissively raised his hand to stifle a deliberate yawn, he glanced at his watch. Brandis had cut the relay of contact between the tower and the Antonovs . . . Ten minutes, perhaps a dozen, before they landed.

She was standing now. He watched her turn away and walk out of the room, pausing in the doorway to light another cigarette. As she disappeared, a noise seemed to come to Aubrey from more than forty years before, something banging and scratching at the darkness outside, a plucking noise like a cat's claws pulling silk to pieces. A Bren gun.

He whirled around and stared through the window. Tracer rounds arching slightly before flowing into the lights coming from the open doors of the cargo hangars. Two arcs of red, silkworm light and the noise of two Brens. His mouth opened. The toy sparks of smaller weapons raggedly returning fire. Lin was beside him in a moment, his hand on Aubrey's shoulder, his grip tense. The tracer rounds wriggled through the dark, hundreds of them. The firing was continuous.

"What is it?" Lin asked.

Confusion—he didn't care who or what. It didn't matter. Confusion and distraction. He must get past the guard. He turned.

Brigitte was in the doorway, her eyes glaring and shocked, and the Nepali's rifle had come to bear instinctively at the sound of gunfire. The guard in the corridor beyond the glass wall of the VIP lounge was also alert, waving his rifle menacingly. Too late, too damned late!

Brigitte crossed the lounge to the radio set. As if divining Aubrey's thoughts, she snapped at the guard in English: "Keep your rifle on them—both of them. Shoot if they make any attempt to leave this room. Understand?" The man nodded.

Clenching his hands in his pockets, Aubrey turned to the window, Lin still beside him, and watched the pattern of tracer and the sporadic, intermittent flashes of returned fire. Then a grenade or something helped to lift a truck into the air, ignited its fuel tank so that the light blazed against the window. Instinctively, he turned his gaze to the tower. Tim?

The truck slid smoothly, slowly out of shadow, its engine noise only then apparent. He pressed back into the alleyway, his hand clamped against Nima's chest. An open truck, four soldiers perched on the rear, two men including the driver in the cab, making for the tower where now Lal and his companion waited, two bodies at their feet.

"Christ . . ." he whispered. There was nothing he could do, he had no rifle, no silencer, nothing but the Browning handgun which could not be accurate at that distance, in darkness. He raged inwardly.

A splash of light against the tower. He could make out Lal, the soldier, the two lumps like untidy blankets on the ground beside them. The truck, the soldiers' faces, were vivid. Then the noise of firing. The truck stopped. Faces stared, the soldiers on their feet in the back of the truck. The crump of an explosion, then a second rumble, like thunder. The truck hesitated, then reversed, turned, and began to accelerate away from the tower, bouncing across the grass toward the cargo terminal.

"One truck coming, Aitasing!" he shouted into the walkie-talkie. The noise of firing was amplified yet made less real. He switched off and nodded at Nima.

"Quickly!"

They ran carelessly along the concrete path. His excitement began to itch across his skin once more; raise his temperature and his recklessness. Lal grinned shakily. Gardiner did not look at the bodies, only at his watch. Eleven minutes. The darkness was hot around them, close and stifling. The tower soared over them, making the four of them seem puny, inadequate—

—six of them as two of Harka's Gurkhas came jogging toward them. Almost equal odds, he reminded himself. Almost equal. He waited, impatience now uppermost, the watch on his wrist and the clock in his head both racing. The watch's digital display changed the minute. He twitched at the noise of another explosion away behind them. The constant chatter of the Brens and the steadily strengthening noises of returned fire pricked at his hearing and his nerves. They'd be staring out of their green glass now, anxious, undecided, perhaps only now coming out of delaying shock. Then they'd be in radio or walkie-talkie contact with the cargo terminal, would be trying to establish who, how many, where—

He thrust open the doors into the tower. A corridor of closed doors, a row of offices from any building anywhere. A set of lift doors, a flight of stairs.

"Lift!" he snapped, pressing the button. "Watch the doors and those stairs!" Come on, come on, his thoughts began at once as the light above the door indicated that the lift was near the top of the tower—

—would they *hear* it moving?

The row of lights illuminated one by one. The ground floor. There was a basement below them. The doors opened. He hesitated, then waved them into the lift. He pressed the two-way radio against his cheek. "Aitasing—report, please." The lift hummed slowly upward. He could smell the bodies surrounding him, his own body, in the cramped steel box. His free hand waved urgently. A clicking of mechanisms, eyes inspecting rifles, handguns.

" . . . pinned down, Captain Sahib—cut off the truck you warned us about . . ."

The lift sighed to a stop on the floor below the control tower's operations room. Packing cases, an equipment store, the smell of machine oil and dry air. Nima held the doors open. Tension crackled like static around him.

"Harka—come in. Report."

"No activity at the main gates, Captain Sahib. Soldiers have headed from the terminal towards the cargo area, sir."

Ten minutes—

"Gan?"

"—no bloody time!" he heard. "Yes, there—no, the width of the undercarriage is—" Gan's voice was high, on the edge of panic.

"Any activity?"

"No!"

"Out. Nima—ready? All of you?" A clicking of rounds into chambers, the tap of a rifle barrel on the steel wall of the lift. He breathed in deeply. "Don't worry about damage," he insisted. "OK!"

The doors closed and the lift jerked upward. Tension gripped him, viselike. There was no fear, just an exhilaration. The doors were opening—

Subdued lighting, banks of screens, the sweep of radar, the dim flare of burning and another explosion from beyond the windows. Brandis! —looking up from a radio set, microphone in one hand, shock on his face, reaction beginning to replace it almost at once. His men pushed him out into the room. The squeak of a chair on the floor. Headphones and glowing screens, the place quiet—for an instant—

"Don't move—any of you, stay where you are!" he bellowed. "No, don't *move!*"

One of the screens, four white blips on it, shattered as he fired past the head of a blond young man about to rise from his seat. A voice speaking English, repeating numbers, distances, altitude issued from somewhere. A smell of electrical burning, the snap and fizzle of something fusing. Lal and the others spread out in a loose semicircle, weapons bearing on the operators and soldiers. He turned to face Brandis. And grinned.

"Colonel," he announced, "I'm relieving you of your post." Brandis glared at him. Lal removed the rifle from a soldier's hands, shunted the man against the glass.

"How the fuck did you—" Brandis began, his eyes filled with calculation.

"Easily," Gardiner replied, his excitement one of triumph. He had the tower, and Brandis.

"They're your people out there? *Who,* for Christ's sake?"

"Gurkhas. You shouldn't have ignored them, Brandis. It's their country."

"For the moment." Brandis perched himself, seemingly at his ease, on the edge of the table, next to the radio. The casual movements, the apparent indifference of his mood, altered the atmosphere of the room. Brandis had somehow taken control of the situation, just by sitting down, appearing undefeated. "How long can you hold the tower?"

"Long enough."

"And out there? Just a hiccup. Once those Antonovs get down in . . ." Exaggeratedly, almost gloatingly, he looked at his watch. " . . . oh, four minutes . . ."

"Four?" he could not avoid blurting out.

Brandis nodded, then bent his head to look through the slanting, tinted glass. "Probably less . . . if you look carefully, you can see the navigation lights and the strobe of the first one . . . there, see it? Parallel to the runway, just turning now crosswind, to begin its final approach." Brandis smiled.

"Watch him!" Gardiner barked out, hurrying to the windows. Big, dim stars, the sickle of the moon. A flickering white star and red navigation lights, turning, coming head-on now toward the runway. He stared, but could make out only faint shadows on the runway. The first Antonov was probably little more than five miles away, less than a thousand feet up—

"Gan! Gan!" he yelled into the walkie-talkie. "Can you see the lights of the first one? It's on final approach, for Christ's sake!"

"What?" Gan muttered something unintelligible, then Gardiner heard: "There's no more than half a dozen fused, Tim! It's no fucking *good!*"

"Shit—" Then he said: "Get out of there, Gan, get off the runway now!"

The radio failed to answer him. He could not see Gan or the others down there. Nothing except the lights stretching away into the darkness, almost meeting at a point where the first big transport would sag onto the concrete and begin its rollout.

He turned to Brandis, his mind frozen. Brandis was grinning at him! He raised the Browning, arm extended, directing it at Brandis' face—which ceased smiling but still did not lose its confidence. The moment of blind, unthinking rage passed and he lowered the pistol. Brandis' smile reappeared at once.

The Gurkhas and Nima and his men were staring at him. He was the focus of the entire room. There was silence now, except for insistent, muffled demands from a discarded headset. Undoubtedly the pilot of the first Antonov. He turned away from Brandis and watched the navigation lights coming toward him. Saw the aircraft's landing lights spring out, staring downward toward the nearing runway. It was as if the lights were trained on him; he flinched. Brandis chuckled audibly, a chair scraped in the suddenly hotter room, a pencil scratched, then rolled across a desk and fell to the floor with a tiny clatter. Cigarette smoke and the smell of the short circuit he had caused with the one shot that had been fired. He'd won, for Christ's sake—and lost! He'd changed nothing. Six mines, just six, out there on the bloody runway, the tower in his hands but he might as well still be outside the bloody door!

Lights. The landing lights walked nearer, dropped lower. Lights.

"Nima!" he shouted in a high, choked voice. "Cut the runway lights! Find the panel and switch off the runway lights! That big bastard can't get down if he can't see the bloody runway!"

The navigation and landing lights dropped further. He could be only hundreds of feet up, hundreds of yards beyond the runway threshold now. One, two, three . . . He glanced wildly along the banks of screens and control panels, looked out at the lights stretching along the runway's thousands of feet. The landing lights of the Antonov were now suspended from a big, visible shadow.

And there were other lights, a couple of thousand feet up in the darkness, a shadow slipping across the thin moon—

The runway vanished. His heart banged in his chest.

The room no longer stifled him. He turned to Brandis. Shock, but defeat had already been replaced by that same easy confidence. Christ, he'd won *now*, couldn't the bastard see that?

As if in answer to his silent anger, Brandis announced: "Too late, Captain . . . it's too late. He's on autoland, using the ILS. He has no need to touch the controls until he's on the runway."

"What?"

"He won't pull out just because you've switched the lights out, sonny. He knows exactly where he is and where the runway is. He must be over the middle marker by now, half a mile out. Fifteen seconds to touchdown—and there's not a damned thing you can do to stop it!"

The runway lights disappeared. The radio was silent, but it seemed Aubrey could hear the tense breathing of the tower's oc-

¬upants. just as he had heard the voices, the exchanges between Brandis and Tim. Now his exhilaration, brimming only a moment earlier, drained from him despite the illusion of safety the darkened runway aroused.

He heard Brandis' voice calmly announce: " . . . not a damned thing you can do to stop it!" He knew it was true. Brigitte seemed doubtful as he turned back to face her, but he was not. The ILS beams, onto which the Antonov's autopilot had locked, would bring the big transport and its cargo of two hundred men and their equipment down the glide path, would raise the aircraft's nose, and drop its undercarriage gently onto the concrete. There was nothing Tim could do. Nothing.

"Is it all right?" Brigitte asked him.

"It seems so."

" . . . bastard!" he heard Tim growl. "Where are the ILS controls? How do I switch the ILS off? Tell me" —his voice was louder, nearer— "before I blow your fucking brains out!"

"They're not here . . . somewhere else in the building. Too far away—"

"This bloody radio's open!" Tim shouted, then the channel went dead. He must have switched it off. Just like Tim, Aubrey had no idea where the controls for the airport's ILS system were located.

A cargo shed erupted. He saw the bulky shadow of a slow-moving tank. Its cannon fired a second time and the corner of a building collapsed. Shadows ran or limped or lay still. One burned brightly for a moment, rolling on the ground, then it, too, was still. There were flashes of firing near the airport's main gates. He'd seen that just before the lights had gone out on the runway. A great many flashes from beyond the gates, little response from inside the airport. Tim's group was outnumbered, had lost the initial advantage of surprise, was falling back or being eliminated.

Aubrey looked across at the tower, but his attention was drawn to the plane's landing lights and the bulky dark shape above them. Like a huge truck rushing out of the night, the Antonov was dropping the last hundred feet or so to the runway threshold. The tower's glasshouse filled with dim lighting like a fishbowl, the fiercer lights of burning and violence near the cargo sheds and gates. The tank fired once more. There was no tracer directed toward the cargo area now, only firing from it, out into the burning, shadowy darkness.

Strangely, time elongated rather than hurried. The lights were hypnotic, like those of a car to a rabbit in the middle of the road. He felt his shoulders slump. He twitched at a further detonation near the cargo sheds, the lapping of fire at the corner of eyesight. The sewing-machine noises of small arms were intermittent now and lessening. Perhaps the transport aircraft was no more than fifty feet up. He could see the landing lights splashing down and spreading like spilled water. Shadows enlarged, became mis-shapen, seemed to be fleeing—men? Surely not men?

Then he sensed rather than saw the moment the wheels touched and the Antonov began rushing along the runway to-ward them alongside the terminal, its belly bathed with reflected white light like the underbelly of a huge, hunting fish. Shadows enlarging then shrinking as if flung aside or shriveled by heat. Lin was beside him, his knuckles white on the polished wood of the handhold that ran the length of the windows.

Fire. The Antonov staggered like a wounded animal, and then a water spray seemed to envelop it for an instant before its fuse-lage was utterly obscured by orange flame and streaming, billow-ing smoke that was luridly lit from within. His mouth opened slowly. Fire. Like some vast enlargement of that fleeing then rolling figure he had seen on fire near the cargo sheds, the An-tonov slewed to one side, its port wing dipped, scraped, ex-ploded. The fuselage went on, leaving a snail-trail of burning fuel and debris behind it, and gouged its way for twenty, thirty, forty yards across the grass before it opened like a pod and threw up new flame. Then, almost at once it seemed, it became the ru-ined crater of a volcano after eruption, smoking, burning, its vio-lence lessening.

He turned to Brigitte, his eyes filled with the scene outside, black and haloed spots on his retinae. So that at first it was diffi-cult to make out her expression and what she held in her hand. Only after he had blinked and rubbed his eyes could he distin-guish with any clarity the surprise on her face and register the shape of the small pistol she held.

Even then, he could not prevent a fierce triumph appearing around his mouth. It acted on her like a cattle prod. He flinched against her determination, and raised his hands in front of him as if to ward her off. He sensed Lin slip from his side.

Then she fired. He felt a tearing, hot pain and a buffeting im-pact that flung him violently off his feet. His body shuddered uncontrollably. There was a black, burning pain down one side of his body, through his arm, in his head. Vaguely, through dazed, wet eyes, he saw her walking slowly toward him, the small pistol raised.

He was dazzled by the explosion. All he was able to see was the tiny, fleeing figure caught in the landing lights as the Antonov touched down. The figure enlarged into a huge, misshapen shadow, then diminished to almost insect proportions as it was struck by the clump of wheels of the port undercarriage. Gardiner shuddered, gripping the desk on which he leaned his whole weight. He knew it was Ganesh. His lips were wet, his body quivered with weakness. The burning mass of the Antonov ran on slowly then careered off the runway onto the grass, plowing a wide gouge. As many as two hundred men . . . there were smoldering scraps, burning little torches, staggering away from the blazing crater of the plane. One by one, they subsided, became still.

Gan—

The Antonov lurched to a standstill and became a smoking crater after the third explosion. He could make nothing out within the torn-open fuselage scorched blacker than the moonlit grass and runway. Nausea heaved itself up into the back of his throat and he swallowed desperately, again and again, choking. A cold sweat soaked his brow and shirt.

Then Brandis was beside him at the window. Gardiner glanced fuzzily at his face and saw a moment of furious, defeated anger replaced by some kind of reassurance. There was even a thin, humorless smile of satisfaction which Gardiner could not understand.

The walkie-talkie in his pocket clucked and chittered to him. " . . . falling back . . . casualties, Captain Sahib . . . reinforcements . . . just two of us, Captain . . ." The reports buzzed like flies, like conscience. He could not stop feeling sick. It was as if the detonations out there continued to resonate against the window, against *him*.

"Re–regroup at the tower . . ." he muttered. "Regroup on the control tower, fall back at once!"

He continued to stare at the smoldering mass grave. The fuel from a ruptured wing tank had flowed in the slipstream over the entire fuselage, then exploded. The aircraft had shriveled and split like skin. It was awful, horrible. He could not begin to feel the success it demonstrated.

Why wasn't Brandis appalled? He'd *won!* Brandis had to feel defeated, had to acknowledge, otherwise, all those—those *things* out there . . . He waved his hand weakly toward the window as if he had been speaking aloud and were trying to emphasize his words. He glared into Brandis' blunt, unmoved features.

"What—is it?"

"You don't know—you haven't noticed . . . ?" Brandis was pale beneath his tan, something of the horror out there had reached him. But he wasn't beaten! "Look," he said, pointing straight-armed. "There's three more of them. There's the first one now." His voice became a growl. "I don't know how you did it, but it won't happen again. And you haven't even blocked the fucking *runway,* have you?" He grinned savagely. "Three minutes—maximum. Got any good ideas?"

He turned and walked away, arms folded.

"Where's the ILS?" Gardiner yelled, hurrying to him, dragging him around by the shoulder.

Brandis laughed. "The thing is—I don't know! Somewhere in the bloody building, I expect! But I don't *know!* Go and play hunt-the-slipper—you've got three minutes, after all!"

Gardiner struck him with his fist but the blow hardly caused Brandis to flinch. He rubbed his cheek as if a fly had landed there, surprising him. Gardiner turned on his heel dizzily, taking in the faces in the control room. They knew! One of them, all of them . . . He raised the Browning to shoulder height. *For Christ's sake, make them tell you!* he bellowed at himself. Young, frightened, wary faces, most of them Germans. He aimed at one of the staring, pale faces, seated half-turned to him from a screen on which three bloated white dots hung against a smeared green background.

"Less than three now," Brandis said, his voice warning his people, encouraging them. "He's turned onto his crosswind leg already. Two and a half, I'd say . . ." The chuckle was forced and theatrical, but it relaxed the faces, made their bodies tense with determination rather than terror. "Hunt-the-slipper, Englishman," Brandis whispered.

The walkie-talkie began to fade out. He reached to switch it off as Harka reported in. "Two more trucks outside the gates as we left, Captain Sahib, and an armored car . . ."

Harka! He lowered the gun.

"Harka—where are you?"

"Near the tower, Captain Sahib!" The voice was almost affronted.

The RPG-7 . . .

"How many rockets do you have—how *many?*"

Brandis' face was alert to possibilities. Gardiner stared out through the tinted windows toward the navigation lights of the second Antonov. Another two hundred men. His stomach lurched and then the impossibility of the few scattered mines working a second time and the smallness of an RPG-7 rocket launcher made the nausea subside.

"Four, Captain—"

"Wait for me, I'm coming down!"

Brandis' mouth was slackly open. Disbelief, of course. It couldn't work . . . but he *was* worried. It had happened once.

He had to block the runway, it was the only way to stop them. He had to go through it all again, all of it.

"You won't stop an Antonov with anything you've got!" Brandis taunted, but his voice lacked certainty.

"I'm going to fucking well *try,* Brandis!"

"Two bloody minutes!"

"I'm going to try!" he shouted back, as if he believed winning the argument would be sufficient. "Watch him—all of them! You two, with me!" he ordered, making for the lift doors. They sprang open as he pressed the button, to the accompaniment of the muffled, sudden noises of a struggle, the rasp of metal against something.

He whirled around in an anguish of delay. Brandis had wrested the rifle away from Lal and thrust him aside. The gun was coming up, the click of the bolt stop being opened and the movement of a cartridge—

He shot Brandis through the face almost without taking aim and hardly paused to watch the effect of the bullet or the collapse of the body as he stepped into the lift with the two Gurkhas. The doors closed behind him and the lift began to sigh down to the ground floor. He gripped the pistol with both hands—to prevent them shaking. As the doors opened, Harka was standing in the corridor and he sprang to attention at once, only his eyes those of a troubled civilian. Gardiner took in the RPG-7 over Harka's shoulder and the clutch of projectiles.

Two minutes. In a few seconds, the Antonov's landing lights would come on, it would be a minute and a half away and only

hundreds of feet up. Locked onto the ILS he had no idea where
to find and destroy.

"Come on!" He roughly clutched at Harka's shoulder, turning him and pushing him ahead. Five of them altogether. Aitasing, who was wounded in the side, his shirt darkly stained and
his hand pressed against the wound, holding a reddened pad,
and Harka from the main gates . . . none of those who had been
with Gan, none . . .

Eight missing. Oh, Christ . . .

"Quick!" he shouted. "This way!" His retinae still seemed to
retain the image of the smoking crater that had contained two
hundred men. It was the smell, he realized. Clogging his nostrils.
He was revolted at breathing air so vile, so sickening. Two hundred incinerated men. It was everywhere. He rubbed at his face,
even his arms and clothes, as if it clung to him like an invisible
soot.

Landing lights. He staggered to a halt near the end of the runway. The Antonov's navigation lights were almost lost in the
glare of the landing lights streaming down whitely from its wing-
roots. It was a visible bulk against the moon. Coming in.

"Where are the *others?*" Gardiner wailed, though the question
was irrelevant now.

"The aircraft—caught them, Captain Sahib," Aitasing replied. "I saw them—burning . . ."

The Antonov enlarged, the landing lights spread. He could
hear its engines now. The lights would be their target—Harka's
target. The smell of burning fat and flesh was all around them.
He retched once and swallowed the bitter taste. His stomach
heaved. There was a muffled, lost screaming from somewhere.
Patches of smoke rising from small lumps scattered over the
grass and the runway and billowing up blackly from the wreckage of the burned-out transport. He'd killed them all just to
strand the wreckage uselessly, fifty yards from the runway!

A minute now. *That bloodyfucking smell, for Christ's sake!*
Are you going to do it, going to try? The Antonov's engine noise
loudened, its bulk increased against the big, soft stars. The
mountains were huge, pale shadows beyond the aircraft.

"Harka," he said, then cleared his throat. "Harka, load."

"Yes, Captain." Harka spoke as if he were shivering.

"Is there a nightsight on it?"

"Yes, Captain Sahib."

Harka screwed the cardboard cylinder containing the propellant to the missile. Gardiner watched intently, narrowing his concentration and awareness. The Gurkha inserted the grenade into the muzzle. The safety pin on the fuse dangled, tinkled. Harka removed it and cocked the hammer. There was nothing else to watch, to concentrate on. He turned back to the Antonov, lower now, larger, louder.

Range for a moving target, no more than three hundred yards and a bit . . . landing run for the Antonov once its wheels touched, much more than that . . . they would have to wait, let it rush toward them.

Harka knelt down, the RPG-7 on his shoulder, Aitasing and the others looking like survivors of the wreckage of the first transport, dazed, numb, dislocated. Gardiner rubbed his face. Half a minute.

"When I give the order, Harka . . ." He meant to pat the man's shoulder reassuringly but touched only the launcher's cool barrel. "Fire and reload as many times as you can. Aim for the center of the aircraft, above and inside the landing lights."

"Yes, Captain Sahib." Harka had recovered some kind of trained detachment, like himself. *Target, it's a target, they must be stopped, it's the only way* . . . The back of his mind repeated the rosary of excuses over and over again, in an attempt to keep his forebrain detached. *Target, target, only a target* . . . If only there wasn't the *smell!*

A small, fitful breeze raised the hair on his arms. The smoke from the Antonov bent sideways like a tree in a storm. He smelt coolness, something akin to freshness.

Distance. It was splashing its landing lights just beyond the runway. Moments from touchdown, less than a hundred feet in the air. How would they tell the distance? His hand gripped the barrel of the RPG-7 again, convulsively. Three hundred yards away, no more than that or they'd waste the first grenade and its HEAT charge.

He bent swiftly. On the darkened runway, they'd never see the moment of touchdown!

"Nima!" he shouted into the walkie-talkie. "Switch on the runway lights! Switch them on *now!*"

The huge aircraft dropped sacklike, nose up, its lights reflecting back from the runway's concrete and whitening its belly, its noise becoming deafening, its speed terrifying. Lights sprang on around them, away from them like tracer rounds aimed at the incoming Antonov—

Touchdown! He could make out the bunch of lights beneath it marking the touchdown zone, then the huge, dark bulk was over and past the lights, obscuring them. He had no idea how long the runway was, but he knew the Antonov required all of it . . . halfway along the runway, halfway, halfway—

"—halfway, halfway—steady, steady, *halfway!*" He was yelling now, staring into the onrushing transport's lights, its bulk like that of some gigantic monster rushing at him. "*Now!*" he screamed.

The noise of the RPG-7 deafened him. The grenade ignited ten meters ahead of them and thrust toward the rushing transport. Its small flame disappeared in the glare of the landing lights. As his hearing returned, he could hear Harka loading another grenade and it already seemed too late. There was a tiny detonation on the fuselage and nothing more. The transport was a couple of hundred yards from them, it hardly seemed to be slowing. A spit of flame, the hurrying trajectory, the grenade lost to sight—explosion. The landing light on the starboard wing-root wobbled like a leg giving way, the whole huge machine seemed stunned, then its nose erupted, there was the spray of unignited fuel, then the starboard inner engine blew up, glaring orange.

"Get out, get out!" he screamed. It was seventy yards away and coming on.

Harka fired again. The grenade was swallowed by the Antonov's huge bulk almost immediately. The aircraft staggered, glowed, parts of the fuselage were thrown up into the night, and the spilled fuel ignited as the aircraft sank on its damaged undercarriage and began to slide terrifyingly toward them. Gardiner threw himself on the ground, his hands over his head, deafened and petrified. He lay there feeling the shock waves of successive explosions, the ground beneath him heaving nauseously.

When he looked up, it was into the heart of a single huge bonfire in the middle of the runway. Blocking it. He pushed himself to his knees. That smell was back, stronger than ever. He vomited until he was empty, until his stomach heaved without result and his throat was raw. He looked up finally through wet eyes, his body shaking.

Aitasing helped him to his feet. He managed to indicate the Gurkha's walkie-talkie.

"Tell them—tell them!" he shouted above the noise of the burning. "Abandon the tower—get out . . ."

"Where should they go, Captain Sahib?"

"Anywhere!" he yelled venomously. "Just get the hell out before they get killed!"

He staggered away from the Gurkhas, awkward and weak on his feet, wiping at his eyes, his running nose, his wet mouth. Everywhere, even if he closed his eyes, he could still see the reflected glare of the bonfire . . . the two bonfires. He could hear screams and he put his hands over his ears. He could not close his nostrils to the smell.

He fell to his knees again, vomiting dryly. Overhead, he heard the noise of retreating aircraft engines. Get out now, he told himself, go away from here, a long way away. It was not a question of survival, just need. He was alive, he wasn't burning. Get away from the sight of it, the smell . . .

Gan was out here somewhere, at least his broken remains were . . .

He realized he was crying, helplessly. Christ, Christ . . . what had he *done?* He hugged his arms across his stomach as if mourning.

"I have ordered them to leave, Captain Sahib," he heard Aitasing say from somewhere above him. He looked up. The man's face gleamed in the firelight. His shirt and khaki shorts were stained and torn. He stood to attention and it seemed like a kind of rebuke, with the bloodstained pad still pressed against his side.

"Yes, yes . . ." he muttered. "Yes."

He had no idea what would happen now. He had blocked the runway. Nothing else could land until it was cleared. He had killed perhaps four *hundred* people to block one single runway . . .

"What is to be done now, Captain Sahib?"

"What? *More . . . ?*"

He glanced wildly toward the passenger terminal. Aubrey! He'd seen Aubrey at the window! He staggered to his feet, clinging to Aitasing's shirt, holding two large handfuls of its material. Making the wounded corporal wince with pain. Aubrey—

"You, Corporal! Harka, come with me! You two, get away from here, out of sight! Go to ground—back to Pokhara if you can!" Harka joined him and Aitasing. "The passenger terminal—there's someone we must get out of there. Understand?" They nodded. There was a residue of eagerness jutting through their tiredness. "We'll skirt the tower, make off that way, come around . . ." They nodded again.

The smell was strong in his nostrils and it evoked the smell of blood in the Kot during Dasain, the slaughter of hundreds of animals as sacrifices to Shiva's *shakti* in her most awesome manifestation. Shiva, destroyer of both good and evil. Goats, chickens, buffalos, men—all sacrificed.

He turned away from them and began jogging, stumbling at first with a drunken weariness, then forcing himself to concentrate. They fell in behind him. The fires near the cargo sheds were dying down, he could make out army vehicles, a tank near the tower, an armored car slowing to a halt. There was an atmosphere of aftermath, of force and passion spent. Shiva seeking sleep, his *shakti* satiated.

It takes only a single white man to slaughter on the grand scale . . .

He dropped to the ground, scanning the outline of the terminal. There was no one at the windows, a few scattered lights still burning, no army vehicles, a handful of soldiers moving listlessly without orders or purpose. It was as if they, too, knew it was over for the present.

Thank God.

"OK," he announced, standing up. "We march in. Understand? Try to look like soldiers." Harka grinned. The remark had been nothing but reflex. They moved forward as if returning from some inspection of the wreckage out on the runway and with someone to report to, someone impatient and senior. His face was smeared with *soot* . . . soot and earth. A temporary Nepali.

The doors slid back with a sigh. They were unguarded. He heard the noise of a car moving away, a car rather than a truck, but it was of no importance. Those windows? The second-floor lounge at a guess.

Huddled civilians, the occasional soldier. But he and the others were inside now and therefore not out of place. He went up the escalator, looking back at the main concourse. Empty check-in desks, empty seats, the listlessness of every airport everywhere. No need for guns or even for caution. Everything had slowed, as if exhausted.

Someone turned up a radio. He stepped off the escalator, listening. The voice sounded distorted, very young.

" . . . therefore loyal commanders have . . ." he caught. "My loyal Ministers assure me . . ." The King's voice. Tamang must have gone to him! " . . . appeal to my people in this hour of— struggle . . . return to your homes . . . army units will patrol, a curfew . . . Foreign Minister Tamang—" He had, then. " . . . arrest of the Prime Minister . . . interference by *any* foreign power in the internal affairs of the nation will be . . ." He turned away. Aubrey—

He ran along the gallery above the main concourse until he reached the glass wall of the VIP lounge. Someone was lying awkwardly on the floor near the windows, unmoving and alone. He burst through the door. Apart from the still form on the floor, an ashen version of Aubrey, the lounge and the adjoining office were both empty.

Aubrey wasn't moving, wasn't moving at all.

He knelt by the old man, touching him gingerly. The crumpled, strangely young suit was blotched red down the left arm and across the waist. Aubrey's face was blank.

"Kenneth . . ." he whispered, lifting the old man into a half-sitting position. "Kenneth . . ." He stroked Aubrey's cheek and the old man's eyelids fluttered. "Kenneth!"

Aubrey opened his eyes. His body was exhausted by the impact of the bullet and the moments following the shot when she had stood over him, the small pistol clutched in her liver-spotted hand. He winced with pain as he moved. It hurt everywhere! He looked at his jacket, and groaned. The dark, dirty-faced young man was bending over him . . . only gradually did he realize that it was Tim. He gasped, clutching Tim's hand, his wrist.

"Are you all right?" Aubrey nodded, but the room revolved slowly as if on a giant axis, then he whispered an affirmative, lying back against Tim's supporting arm. "What happened? Who shot you?"

"Brigitte . . ." Tim looked puzzled. "It doesn't matter. Lin was here."

"Where are they?"

"Gone. When—when the aircraft exploded. Lin dragged her away with him . . ."

He closed his eyes, afraid of the vivacity with which her image had returned, as if he had conjured her up. She had meant to fire again. Lin had held her arm, wrestling the pistol upward until it pointed at the ceiling. Perhaps he no longer cared? She had snarled at him like a cat, sworn, argued, struggled. Aubrey shivered. The wound in his side—or arm, was it?—hurt like the devil. The bullet had clubbed him to the floor, its impact jolting through him as if he had been battered.

"Why didn't they kill you?" Tim asked. Aubrey blinked. Tim's eyes were glazed, his interest, now that he had found Aubrey alive, lessening. He was retreating from something . . . the slaughter outside?

"I—don't know . . . help me up." He was lifted to his feet, and leaned heavily against Tim, breathing very loudly. "Lin was like someone not really here—most of the time. At others he talked like a tap running . . ." Aubrey looked at Tim. "I think you were right . . . he'd got religion—*your* religion!" He tried to smile, but his mouth was lopsided, as uncontrollable as if after a stroke. He dribbled onto his chin and closed his eyes. His weakness was appalling. There were two men in the doorway of the lounge. Gurkhas, he supposed. Tim's Gurkhas? Yes, he recognized one of them.

When he opened his eyes, Tim was staring over his shoulder, out into the night. His face was set, his eyes bleak. His nostrils quivered as at some offensive smell. "Anyway, he stopped her," he sighed, leaning on the handrail across the windows. "I—you've stopped them?"

"Yes . . ."

"Well done—" Tim looked appalled. "I—should talk to someone. London, of course, and your Foreign Minister chap . . ."

Tim said bluntly: "The King's thrown his weight against the Soviet faction."

"I see . . ." Good God, how his wound *hurt!* "Help me," he said, "get me to the Embassy. I must talk to London."

"You need a hospital."

Aubrey shook his head gingerly. "No, they can patch me up at the Embassy. Get me to—to Middleton, and I'll brief him on what to tell London."

Tim had moved away from him. "Aitasing and Harka can take you there. There's no danger. It's obvious the army's back under the control of people loyal to the King. They'll take you." He sounded vague, detached.

"Why not you?"

"I have to go away for a while. Get away from this place." He was looking beyond Aubrey, out toward the two wrecks, the cargo sheds, the litter of bodies and the few survivors wandering dazed and hurt. "You won't understand it," he announced with absolute conviction, "but I have to . . ." He turned away. "Take care of him," he instructed the corporal. "Do as he wishes."

"Take care!" Aubrey blurted out, dismayed.

Tim did not stop, but simply passed along the corridor beyond the glass wall like an indifferent stranger. In a matter of moments, his head had disappeared as he went down the escalator. He had not once looked back.

Aubrey began to turn clumsily, painfully, on his heel, in order to look out of the lounge windows. It was not, he was certain, his harsh breathing or the pain of his wound or the wreckage of the two Antonovs which made him keep his face averted.

"The British Embassy," he announced eventually to Corporal Aitasing and Harka, both late of the Brigade of Gurkhas.